MY

"What do you w[...]heart pounding.

Wind Cloud didn't answer, but reached out until his hand touched her cheek. He brushed his fingers gently over her face, pausing to trace the contours of her lips, then slipped his hand under her chin to raise it until she was forced to look into his eyes. "Mine," he murmured, then took her in his arms and murmured again, against her lips, "Mine."

He stroked her cheeks with his thumbs and she tried to turn her head away, but he wouldn't let her. "My heart is yours," he whispered, and he kissed her. His hands warmed her, caressed her, making her moan as waves of pleasure washed over her. His kiss deepened.

And then, like an arrow, she felt herself fly high into the sky, higher, higher, until she reached the heart of the sun and was consumed. She opened her eyes and looked deeply into his, but she could not speak for the beating of her heart.

"Your heart is mine," he whispered, his breath warm against her lips.

And it was true. His kiss had changed her, forever, and her heart would never again be her own . . .

JEWELS OF THE HEART

JANE TOOMBS

PINNACLE BOOKS
WINDSOR PUBLISHING CORP.

PINNACLE BOOKS

are published by

Windsor Publishing Corp.
475 Park Avenue South
New York, NY 10016

First Printing: February, 1993

Printed in the United States of America

Chapter 1

Standing at the rail of the barkentine *Prince,* Octavia Livingstone shifted to keep her balance as the ship plowed through the choppy waves of Lake Ontario. A fine, navigable lake, her father called it, with no rockbound shores for ships to fear. In truth, the forest-rimmed lake seemed as large to her as the Atlantic Ocean.

The rising sun glinted on the water, promising a clear day. Though the April wind blew chill, her beaver-lined, hooded cape of scarlet wool shielded her. Without her consciously willing it, her right hand crept inside the cape and sought the familiar, comforting shape of the heart-shaped locket she wore on a gold chain.

Grandmother Ballantine's gold locket, set with five gems—a sapphire, an emerald, a ruby, a topaz, and a diamond—had been hers since her mother's death four years before.

"The gemstones in this locket lend strength and courage to its wearer," Penelope Livingstone had said as she lay dying in England. "Wear the locket, my dearest girl, and you'll always be protected by your own courage."

But two days ago, in York, the capital of Upper

Canada, it had been Octavia's father who had saved them both. She glanced at him, standing next to her at the rail, tall and stalwart, wearing black, as he'd done ever since her mother's death—black boots, black trousers, black cape—his once auburn hair now gray under his beaver hat.

He'd often told her that she resembled her mother, but the truth was that she'd inherited his coloring and height. Her blue eyes were the only feature she and her mother had shared.

"There it is," Horatio Livingstone said, gesturing toward a smudge barely visible to the north, the only land in view. "Kingston, on the St. Lawrence, at the mouth of the Rideau River. We've long since outdistanced the Yankees; we should make port without difficulty. My number three fur post is no more than five miles up the Rideau from the town, and my factor at the post will collect trustworthy men to see us on to Montreal." He draped his arm around Octavia's shoulders. "We're safe enough for the time being, child."

Even as Octavia smiled at him, she wished he wouldn't call her "child," since at nineteen she was hardly a little girl. Still, she suspected he'd go on calling her "child" no matter how old she became. "I wasn't worried, Papa," she said.

His arm dropped away and he gripped the rail with both hands. "*I* certainly was! Not for myself, but for you. I never thought when we set off from London that we'd be sailing straight into another war with the colonies. If I'd had any idea, I'd never have listened to your pleas and brought you along."

"America is no longer our colony, Papa. At least, the United States isn't."

"Or so they'd have us believe," Horatio said. "After we trounce Napoleon once and for all, we'll be free to

6

turn our attention *and* His Majesty's Army and Navy toward teaching these recalcitrant Yankees a lesson they've long deserved. But war is no place for a lady. How I wish you were home safe in England."

"You hurried us away from York so fast last evening that I didn't hear so much as a single shot fired," she reminded him.

"You were perilously close to worse than hearing shots." Horatio's voice was grim. "What with Yankee ships heading for York's harbor and the raffish rabble they call soldiers reported to be only miles from the town, I fear for those unfortunates who remain in York."

"I think it's all rather exciting."

"No, child. Though a necessary evil, war is always a nasty business, a very nasty business, indeed. I'll breathe somewhat easier once we reach Montreal, but I won't rest comfortably until I have you safely back in Devon."

"Will there be Indians at the post, Papa?"

He eyed her. "You and your Indians! Haven't you seen enough of those savages?"

Octavia shrugged, knowing it would be impossible to describe to her father just what she meant. Yes, she'd seen scores of Indians on the way to and in York. But they'd been what she thought of as tame Indians, ones friendly with the English and French of Upper Canada. Not once had she even been close to a wild Indian, one who lived in a woodland village far from the haunts of white men.

Perhaps there'd be little difference, but she longed to see for herself.

"Lord Randolph won't thank me for bringing you into danger," her father said. "He opposed this trip from the beginning."

"I'm not yet married to Alexander." Octavia spoke

7

tartly, but her tone was meant more for her absent fiancé than for her father. Alexander Simmons, Lord Randolph, was a bit too authoritarian for her taste. Not that she regretted their engagement—or at least, not exactly. Hadn't Alexander been the top-of-the-trees catch of the season—handsome, polished, wealthy, everything a young lady could desire?

Once they were wed, though, she foresaw herself relegated to Monmouth Hall, the Randolph estate, while Alexander traveled to interesting places alone. He believed women of all sorts, from scullery maids to ladies, belonged at home. But then, such was the belief of most men of her acquaintance. She'd thought of this trip to Canada with her father as her last bit of freedom.

"Alexander certainly wouldn't approve of your interest in Indians," Horatio said. "Nor do I. Dirty, unpredictable savages, one and all, including this Tecumseh fellow they make such a fuss over."

Octavia stared at him. "But aren't they our allies? You said yourself it's fortunate the Indians chose to fight on the side of the British rather than with the Americans."

"Though war does make for strange bedfellows, one doesn't necessarily have to approve of one's allies."

"War or not, Indians or not, this is the most fascinating journey I've ever taken," she said, impulsively hugging him. "I'll never forget it as long as I live."

He patted her shoulder. "I admit you've been good company. I've not often been able to deny you once you made up your mind you wanted something. I fear you inherited the Livingstone stubbornness. Alexander had best beware."

The sun was halfway down the afternoon sky by the time the *Prince* anchored among the cluster of islands near the entrance to the St. Lawrence River, and a

8

batteau, a large transport canoe, pulled alongside the ship to bring passengers and goods ashore. Once the other passengers disembarked at Kingston, Horatio successfully bargained with the batteau's owner and he, Octavia, and their baggage continued up the Rideau River to the fur post.

Octavia noticed the men paddling the boat were French Canadians, *voyageurs*—or, perhaps, a mixture of French and Indian. Her father had told her the French, unlike the English, often married Indian women. She disliked the derogatory term—"half-breeds"—used to describe children of these unions.

"Guy Johnson, my factor at the post, will put us up for the night and we'll be on our way to Montreal at dawn," Horatio said. "I fear you'll find the accommodations rather primitive, but this is the best I could arrange on short notice."

"I don't mind, Papa. It's a splendid adventure, far more exciting than those tedious parties and balls where I must keep smiling no matter what. During my come-out season in London I swear I came close to forgetting how to scowl."

"My mother warned me I'd regret raising you much as I would a son, but I have not," he said. "Perhaps you will regret it someday, but—"

"Never!" She spoke with all her heart. Papa had taught her many skills usually reserved for boys. Among other things, she could ride astride, swim, fire a pistol, and handily manage the reins of spirited horses, and she had received an excellent education.

No other young lady of her acquaintance in England had had the freedom she'd known. Even in Canada, colony that it was, a lady's role in life was restricted—as hers would be, once she became Lady Randolph. No doubt her father was correct in believing she and Alexander would often be at sixes-and-sevens.

9

A small weathered pier thrust into the water, breaking the line of trees along the river. As the paddlers slowed, maneuvering the batteau alongside the pier, Octavia eyed the log cabin set back from the bank. Letters burnt into a slab of wood above the door read, "Fur Trader." A crow on the cabin's roof peak cawed and flew to join two others in a nearby pine.

While the batteau was being tied to the mooring post, the cabin door opened and three Indian braves walked onto the porch, followed by a white man in buckskins. Octavia's attention focused on the tallest of the Indians, a man dressed in fringed buckskin leggings and moccasins, with a bright blue blanket wrapped around him in such a fashion as to leave his right arm and part of his chest bare.

His head had been shaved, except for a roach of hair running from above his brow to the nape of his neck, and it was decorated with eagle feathers and bands of silver. Yet it wasn't his colorful garb that fascinated her most, it was the man himself. He stood on the top step of the porch, the others behind him, in a regal stance that suggested he owned not only all he surveyed but the entire world.

She lost sight of him as her father assisted her onto the rough wooden pier, but when she looked again he hadn't moved, forcing the white man to skirt around him in order to descend the stairs and approach the dock.

"Octavia, this is Mr. Johnson," her father said as the man reached them. "Guy, my daughter."

"Delighted, Miss Livingstone," the factor said, bowing slightly.

She smiled and inclined her head. As soon as he gave his attention to her father, she glanced once more toward the Indian who'd captured her imagination, found his dark eyes staring boldly at her, and felt her

10

heart begin to pound.

"Friendly Indians?" her father asked, nodding toward the cabin.

"They're Seneca who came in for supplies," Mr. Johnson said. "Neutrals, like all the Iroquois tribes. Neither for us nor against us."

Horatio's eyes narrowed. "Never trust a neutral, is my advice. Nor an Indian."

The Indian men were standing out of earshot, or so she hoped. "Are those Seneca wild Indians?" she asked the factor.

Mr. Johnson looked puzzled. "Pretty much any Indian's wild, when it comes right down to it."

"The one in front has the bearing of a chief," she said. "Do you know if he is?"

Mr. Johnson glanced back at the braves. "His name's Wind Cloud; I don't know much else about him."

At that moment Wind Cloud made a slight gesture to the other two Seneca and all three left the porch and strode off toward the woods.

"Good riddance," Horatio muttered. "One never knows what those savages are thinking. To get down to business, Guy, the bloody Yanks have marched on York, forcing us to leave in a hurry. Here's my plan—"

While her father spoke to the factor, Octavia watched the Seneca braves reach the woods. Even at a distance she recognized which was Wind Cloud. Was she mistaken, or did he glance over his shoulder just before disappearing between the trees? She flushed, realizing that if he had, he'd almost certainly seen her gawking after him. He must think her most discourteous.

That is, if Indian men thought like Englishmen. Perhaps they didn't; her father seemed to believe not.

11

She had no idea and wished she knew more about them.

"I haven't heard any rumors of a Yankee raid hereabouts," Mr. Johnson said. "It's true we're just across the end of the lake from Sackets Harbor, where the Yanks have their naval dockyard. No doubt they'd like to put our shipyards at Kingston out of commission, but with our new Fort Henry guarding the town, they're not likely to bother us."

Her father shook his head. "I hope you're right. The government officials in York put their faith in the fort there, but the Yankees attacked anyway."

"Good strategy on their part. York's the capital of Upper Canada; capturing it is a coup for the Yanks. But I think we're safe enough here. Come along into the post, sir, if you will. I'm happy to share what I have with you and the young lady."

Octavia trailed after the two men, pausing before climbing the stairs, the image of the tall and handsome Wind Cloud still occupying her mind. His skin wasn't coppery, as some said, nor yet the color of bronze, as others described it. His face was actually no darker than that of English sailors who spent much of their time in the sun.

"Pardon, mademoiselle," one of the boatmen said from behind her, making her realize she was blocking the stairs. She stepped aside so he could carry their baggage into the cabin.

Moments later, he trotted back down the stairs, flashed her an impudent grin, called, *"Au revoir,"* and went on to the dock and untied the mooring rope. All the men in the batteau waved to her as they cast off, something she doubted they'd have done if her father had been by her side. Smiling, she waved back.

"You do not wave to me," a man's voice said in a low tone.

12

Startled, she whirled to stare at the speaker. Wind Cloud stood at the corner of the cabin, his dark, hypnotic gaze causing her breath to fail.

"You speak English!" she exclaimed.

He smiled, a brief flash of white teeth. "I feel here—" he struck his chest with his fist "—Octavia and Wind Cloud meet again. Like *voyageur,* I say, *Au revoir.*"

He vanished around the corner of the cabin, leaving her bewildered and breathless.

"Octavia," her father called from inside.

"I'm coming," she told him.

As she walked slowly up the steps she reviewed every word Wind Cloud had said. Obviously he'd overheard the conversation on the dock or he wouldn't know her name. Which meant he'd also overheard her questions about him as well as her father's condemnation of all Indians.

Her father would be outraged if she told him Wind Cloud had returned and spoken to her. Best to keep quiet. Confess it, Wind Cloud's unexpected reappearance had left her more thrilled than fearful, it was an event to be remembered, a memory not to be shared with another. Her cherished secret.

Au revoir, he'd said, so apparently he also spoke French. Wasn't that unusual for an Indian? Her name on his tongue had sounded so strange, almost as though it didn't belong to her but to another, more primitive Octavia, one who wasn't a prim and proper lady, an Octavia who couldn't possibly become the wife of Lord Randolph.

I'd like to meet Wind Cloud again, she thought. I'd like to talk to him, to learn more about him.

But, of course, it was extremely unlikely she'd ever see either the French *voyageur* or Wind Cloud again. Not that she cared in the case of the Frenchman, but as for the Seneca . . . Octavia sighed, knowing she'd never

13

forget him.

That night, on the narrow cot provided for her, with a suspended blanket separating her from where the men slept, she carried Wind Cloud's image into her dreams.

In the morning, her father prepared for their departure down the St. Lawrence to Montreal. He planned to take the trading post batteau, a boat equipped with a sail, which would be manned by the four men Mr. Johnson had recruited to travel with them. Horatio questioned the selection of one of the men, claiming he mistrusted those of mixed blood, but the factor convinced him this *metis,* the French word for half-breed, was reliable and, in fact, someone he often used as his assistant.

In Octavia's opinion the black-beared young *metis,* called Louis by Mr. Johnson, looked very little different from the *voyageurs* who'd transported them up the Rideau the day before.

The overcast sky and the damp, chill breeze promised rain, but Horatio was convinced the sooner they reached Montreal, the better, and so they set off shortly before noon in the boat down the Rideau toward Kingston and the St. Lawrence.

And sailed into hell.

The first warning was the crack of a musket. Though the shot might well have come from a hunter hidden by the trees lining the riverbanks, the men glanced uneasily at one another and began scanning the woods to either side.

"Get down in the boat, Octavia," her father ordered as he picked up his gun. "Now!"

Accustomed to obeying him, she immediately slid from the seat onto the bottom of the canoe, grateful that hardly any water had seeped in so far. She was attempting to find a comfortable position when a bloodcurdling shriek froze her. She'd never heard such a sound before but she knew right away it was the dreaded Indian war-cry.

"Too late to retreat, they've spotted us," Louis warned in French, his words punctuated by musket fire from the riverbank.

"Bloody bastards," her father muttered, ramming a ball into his gun. "Never trust an Indian."

"They ain't redskins," the man in the bow said. "They's Yanks trying to scare us with their damn war-whoops. Learned 'em from the Iroquois, they did."

"Our only chance is to run past 'em," another put in.

Octavia tried her best to make herself as small as possible in the batteau's bottom so as to keep out of the way.

Suddenly the man in the batteau's bow screamed. Shifting to look at him, the horrified Octavia saw him clutching at his groin, blood spurting through his fingers to redden the wood of the batteau. The roar of her father's gun all but deafened her, the stink of powder stung her nostrils. She huddled under her cape, one hand clutching her locket, too terrified to pray. Amid the gunfire she heard the ungodly shrieks of the attackers and the thunk of bullets hitting the wood of the boat.

After a time she realized those aboard the boat were no longer returning the fire. Or cursing. Or making any noise. Fearfully, Octavia pushed her hood aside and craned her neck to look at her father.

His head hung over the edge of a seat, blood dripping from the wound in his temple and pooling on the bottom of the batteau. His glazed eyes stared blankly at her.

"No," she whimpered, "oh, no."

Papa couldn't be dead. It wasn't possible.

15

"Help him," she begged, starting to rise. "Please help Papa."

"Don't move," a voice warned—Louis's, she thought, though she couldn't see him—"or they'll kill you, too."

Through her haze of grief and terror, she realized he was right. She was alive now only because Papa had made her lie flat in the boat.

"Where—where are you?" she whispered.

"I'm hanging onto the far side of the boat." Louis's voice was markedly weaker. "The others are dead, and I can't hold on much longer."

Octavia swallowed. "Can you swim to shore?"

When he didn't answer, a new frisson of fear shook her. "Louis?" she called. "Louis?"

There was no reply. She was alone in a boat filled with dead men. "Papa," she whimpered, closing her eyes. "Dear God, please, no."

She didn't know how long it was before she realized the firing from shore had stopped. Mustering her sluggish thoughts, she finally understood that the boat must have drifted past the Yankee attackers.

Was she safe even now? She feared to sit up and take stock of her surroundings, but she made herself crawl to her father. Lying next to him, holding one of his flaccid hands between hers, she wept, oblivious to all else.

Suddenly something struck the boat with a loud thump. At the same time a man shouted, "Hooked her, by God!"

Octavia's tears dried abruptly as she swung her head around. She found herself staring at an iron grappling hook embedded in the boat's stern and then felt the batteau move backward.

By "her," the man—a Yank, by the sound of him—had meant he'd hooked the boat. But once he'd hauled the batteau to shore, she'd be discovered.

With grim determination, she grabbed a musket from the bottom and began to search for the powder and balls. To her dismay, she found none. If she stood up to look, she'd be seen and have no chance whatsoever. Her attention focused on the sheathed knife at the waist of one of the dead men. Steeling herself, she reached for the bone handle, then paused. If she meant to conceal the knife, she'd need the sheath.

Bile rose in her throat as she forced herself to unfasten the dead man's belt and slide off the sheath. She hoisted her skirts, jammed the sheathed knife into the top of one of her low boots, then rearranged her skirts to conceal what she'd done, and waited for the boat to reach shore.

In her mind echoed the last words she'd heard from her father. Bloody bastards!

The batteau jolted when it rammed the bank. Octavia stood up, meeting the astonished gaze of a blond-bearded man in buckskins. She wrapped her cape closely about herself and glared at him.

"Hey, lookee here what I landed," he called.

A ragtag group of seven men trotted up, each carrying a musket; any one of them could have shot Papa.

"You killed my father," she said accusingly, sweeping them all with a defiant gaze.

For a moment no one spoke.

"She be an English maid, sure enough," a grizzled older man announced finally. "Ye can tell by her talk. So it stands to reason her pa was an Englishman."

"These be war times, miss," Blond Beard told her. "Enemies be enemies. But we mean you no harm, you being a lady and all."

"Best to get her and us out of here," the grizzled man said. "I tell ye again—I smell Injuns, and we all know there ain't no Injuns on our side." He nodded at

Octavia. "The boys and me'll see ye safe to Kingston, that we will."

Octavia found she didn't fear the Yankees as much as she'd thought she would. Since they'd been polite enough so far, she decided to be as civil as she could, under the circumstances.

"I can't forgive you," she said, "but I appreciate your courtesy in assisting me. My father—" Her voice broke, but she swallowed and went on. "I must see my father receives a proper burial."

There was another silence. "That ain't going to be easy, miss," Blond Beard said at last. "Best we can do is dig him a grave here and now."

The grizzled man scowled at him, but Blond Beard stood his ground. "Won't take but a few minutes, and *I* don't smell no redskins."

Octavia started to argue in favor of bringing her father's body with them to Kingston to be buried but caught herself, afraid if she protested too vehemently they'd be annoyed enough to leave his body where it lay or, perhaps, cast him into the river. "I'm grateful for whatever you're able to do," she said carefully.

A half-hour later she stood beside the heap of stones the men had gathered to place atop the earth concealing her father's body—"keeps the varmints from digging him up," one of them had informed her, making her shudder. No tears came; she had none left.

The grizzled man, Eb by name, came to her and offered, "I can say a few words if ye like, miss. Me pa was a preacher so I know 'em pretty well."

She hesitated, then decided it was better than nothing. "Please."

Eb bowed his head and began. She recognized much of what he said as the same burial service she'd heard at English funerals. She hadn't expected to be comforted by his words, but she was.

18

When he finished, she stepped forward and placed the single white stone she'd found on the riverbank at the top of the cairn. "Goodbye, Papa," she whispered. "May you rest in peace."

She turned away, swallowing hard as she forced herself to thank Eb. For all she knew, he might be her father's murderer, but she owed him the courtesy of recognizing that he'd tried to make amends.

Not that she'd ever be able to forgive any of them.

"'Tis high time we got us to Kingston," Eb told her. "No offense meant, miss, but the delay's put us all in danger, besides holding us back from our bounden duty."

Fighting, she thought angrily. Fighting the Canadians and her people. And the Indians as well. Killing those who weren't even soldiers. A horrid, distorted duty. Difficult as it was to keep quiet, she said nothing, as eager as he to be on his way.

A gun roared. Octavia stared uncomprehendingly as Blond Beard clutched at his chest. Blood oozed over his fingers. He staggered a few steps and dropped on his face.

"Take cover, boys," Eb shouted.

The Yankees scattered.

Were the Canadians attacking? Before Octavia could move, strong arms wrapped around her from behind and swept her off her feet. She was flung over a naked shoulder. An Indian! She tried to scream, but the breath was jolted from her body as he ran with her.

Along with three other Indians, he raced through the woods and down the riverbank and flung her into a large birch-bark canoe. He and the others jumped into the boat, shoved away from the bank with their paddles, and rowed rapidly downstream. All the Indians had painted faces; three red stripes covered her captor's left cheek.

Red Stripes set aside his paddle long enough to bind her wrists behind her back with a leather thong, then pushed her into the bottom of the boat. Resting one moccasined foot on her, he took up the paddle again.

Octavia strained against the binding thong to no avail. She was helpless, unable to so much as reach the knife in her boot, much less use it.

"English!" she cried. "I'm English! English are friends!"

Red Stripes' only reply was to kick her in the ribs.

Either he hadn't understood, or he didn't care. Or worse—he was from a tribe that hadn't allied with her countrymen. She recalled her father saying neutrals couldn't be trusted.

"English," she said once more, desperately. "Me. English."

Another kick convinced her it was no use, and she gave up. First her hands grew numb and, after a time, the numbness seemed to seep into her head and body, suspending movement and thought. She hardly noticed when it began to rain.

She was jarred into awareness when her captors beached the canoe and Red Stripes hauled her up from the bottom, lifted her onto solid ground, and forced her to walk ahead of him into the woods. When she stumbled, he jerked her erect and shoved her on. She was staggering with fatigue when she smelled woodsmoke and saw, among the trees, the glow of a small fire.

Moments later she found herself in the midst of an Indian camp. Gathering her wits, she looked about in the gathering gloom, staring at Indian warriors much like those who'd captured her. She counted fifteen in all as they encircled her. Exhausted as she was, terror gripped her when she understood she was the only woman present.

Red Stripes freed her hands, forced her back against the trunk of a sapling, and tied her wrists again with tree trunk in between, making her truly a prisoner.

He pointed to her, then to himself as he spoke to the gathered warriors. When he finished, an argument ensued, some of the men shaking their fists in his face. The desperately frightened Octavia couldn't understand their speech, but their gestures made it clear the disagreement was over who she belonged to. No matter how it might be resolved, she feared what would happen to her.

How hideous they were, these painted, half-naked savages! Whatever had given her the strange notion she'd like to know more about them? She'd rather a bullet had killed her in the batteau than to be their helpless captive. At least she'd have died immediately. Perhaps they'd kill her eventually, but she had no doubt that before death's release she must endure the vileness of despoilment and the misery of torture.

One of the men held a birch-bark box over his head, shaking it. As the others noticed, the hubbub died down until she could hear something rattling around inside the box.

They rapidly reached an agreement and crouched in a circle around a blanket spread on the ground. The man with the box reached in and flung the contents—round white stones, dotted with red and black—onto the blanket. Though she'd never seen such stones before, they reminded her of a gambling game favored by gentlemen of the *ton* in London.

Her Indian captors were dicing. But not for money. For her.

Chapter 2

Octavia slumped against the tree she was tied to, fear battling with fatigue. She was dimly aware the rain had ceased. The click of the stones being tossed by her captors mingled with night noises—the hoots of an owl, the distant caterwaul of a hunting lynx. When the faintly sweet aroma of rum reached her, she realized what the Indians were drinking from the tin cup they passed from one to the other, occasionally replenishing the contents from a wooden keg set well back from the fire.

She shuddered. How many times since her arrival in Canada had she heard men say there was nothing more dangerous than a drunken Indian? Horrors she'd been told of Indian tortures slithered into her mind—fingernails pulled out, strips of skin torn from living bodies, tongues ripped from screaming mouths, hair set afire. She closed her eyes and tried to pray but was too distraught to find the words.

The sudden thwack of metal splitting wood startled her. Before she could determine where the sound had come from, sizzling flames leaped from the rum keg, snaking across the ground toward the Indians as the spilled rum burned. They leaped to their feet, shouting.

"Gaiwiio!" A voice, loud and commanding, rose above their cries.

All the men froze, heads turned toward the darkness between the trees. It seemed to the confused Octavia that they were suddenly as terror-stricken as she.

The voice spoke again in the same commanding tone, alien words she didn't understand, though she sensed the scorn and condemnation they carried.

Her captors listened as though entranced.

"Skaniadaiyo," the one nearest her whispered as though to himself. He reached for his knife and turned toward her. She sucked in her breath.

Knife raised, he approached her tree, glancing fearfully from side to side. Did he mean to kill her outright? Octavia swallowed, reaching deep within herself to find the determination to confront whatever was to come as bravely as she could. With great effort, she forced herself to meet the man's gaze, but instead of facing her, he circled behind her.

As she bit her tongue to keep from whimpering in terror, she felt the thongs binding her wrists loosen and fall away, freeing her. Expecting him to drag her to the others, she stumbled in bewilderment when instead he shoved her toward the darkness that hid the voice, then scuttled back to his freinds. She staggered on, not understanding why they were turning her loose, as afraid of what awaited her among the trees as she had been of her captors.

She stepped into the shadows. Strong arms grabbed her. Too terrified to scream, she felt herself slung once again over a man's shoulder and borne rapidly away through the night woods. Though she'd always taken pride in being a woman who didn't swoon, inner darkness overcame her. For the first time in her life, Octavia fainted.

When she came to again and opened her eyes, she

was completely disoriented. In pitch blackness she lay on her back on a hard surface that swayed beneath her. She heard the faint splash of a paddle hitting water. She must be in a boat. Reaching out with tentative, shaking hands, she felt rough wood to either side. Not a rowboat, then, but a dugout canoe.

An Indian canoe. The identification brought back all that had befallen her, and she stifled a moan.

"No fear, Octavia." The man's voice, deep and low, came from above her, a voice she recognized.

Wind Cloud! Without thinking, she sat up abruptly, rocking the canoe and making her head swim.

"No one follows," he assured her.

Still dizzy and confused, she clutched the sides of the dugout with both hands. "Is it really you, Wind Cloud?" she quavered.

"You are safe with Wind Cloud."

Was she really? Octavia strained to see him in the moonless dark but could make out no more than a vague outline.

"You rescued me," she said slowly. "Were those— those terrible warriors—your people?"

"They Onondaga, me Nundawaga—you say Seneca. All one—Onondaga, Mohawk, Oneida, Cayuga, Seneca, Tuscarora."

"Iroquois," she said, recalling the name for the six united Indian tribes of the Lake Ontario region.

"Iroquois is enemy word. We are *Ongwanosionni,* People of Long-House."

Whatever he called himself, he was an Indian and she mistrusted him. "Will you take me to my people?" she asked.

"You child of Great White Father across big salt water."

She knew he meant King George but his words reminded her of her father's death, and grief closed her

24

throat, bringing tears to her eyes. "My father's dead," she sobbed. "Dead and buried."

His hand touched her hair briefly and was gone before she thought to flinch away. "We go to my village," he said.

His words frightened her, drying her tears. "No! You must take me to—" She paused. Where could she go? They couldn't be too far from Kingston, but for all she knew, the town was in the hands of the Yankees by now. York might be occupied by the Americans as well, and besides, it was days away.

"I wish to go to Montreal," she finished finally, realizing her only real choice was to return to England as soon as possible. Return home . . . how impossibly far away it seemed.

"Montreal is many sleeps north. My village is two sleeps south. We go there." He spoke with finality.

Overcoming her rising dread, she said with as much emphasis as she could manage, "I don't belong in your village with your people. I want to find my own people. In Montreal."

"I have spoken."

Argue though she did, he said no more. Octavia fell silent, huddling into her cape, as chilled by her renewed fears as by the damp night breeze. His village was two sleeps south. That meant they'd soon stop and camp for what remained of the night before going on. What would he do to her then? And if she survived the night, what about the next night? And what unspeakable terrors awaited her when they reached his village?

As he paddled on in the darkness, she fell into a half-doze, starting awake she knew not how much later when the canoe jarred as it scraped the bottom.

"What—where are we?" she asked.

"We cross the lake, go upstream."

She decided he meant they'd come across Lake

25

Ontario from the Onondaga camp and were now paddling up a river on the eastern shore of the lake, the American shore. She slumped in her seat, over-whelmed by the hopelessness of her situation.

"Camp here," he said some time later, and helped her from the canoe.

By the time flames rose from his tiny fire, she was stiff with apprehension. She watched nervously as he piled the cedar boughs he'd cut into a rough pallet, shaking her head when he gestured for her to lie on them. He waited a moment, then picked her up and deposited her onto the boughs, her feet toward the fire.

"Sleep," he advised.

Turning away, he wrapped himself in a blanket and lay on the ground on the opposite side of the fire. She stared through the flickering flames at his unmoving form for a long time before, using her fur-lined cape as her blanket, she stretched out at last on her aromatic cedar bed.

She lay tensely, wondering if he was waiting until she fell asleep before attempting to ravish her. Despite the care he'd taken to try to make her comfortable, she couldn't believe he meant her no harm. But, exhausted as she was, she felt sleep eventually sweep her into its dark embrace.

A bluejay, scolding from the bough of a pine, woke her at dawn. She sat up quickly, clutching her cape around her in the cold April morning. The fire had burned to ashes and Wind Cloud was nowhere in sight. Had he deserted her? A new kind of fear clutched her. If he'd left her alone in the wilderness, ignorant as she was of how to survive in the woods, surely she'd perish before she found her way to any settlement.

Lord Randolph had been right—this trip she'd undertaken with her father so lightheartedly had been ill advised. If only the two of them had remained in

Devon, Papa would still be alive and she'd be safe at home with him. Perhaps at this very moment they'd be planning her wedding to Lord Randolph. But, alas, they'd sailed to America, and now her poor, dear father lay in a wilderness grave far from his own land while she was at the mercy of a savage redskin.

Octavia rose from the pallet and searched the surrounding trees, endeavoring to pierce the shadowed depths between them. Where *was* Wind Cloud? Overhead, wild geese called mournfully, making her glance up at their vee winging northward.

"Eat." Wind Cloud spoke from behind her; she stifled a startled cry as she whirled to face him.

He removed a strip of dried meat from a deerskin pouch and offered it to her. Her heart still thudding from her fright, she accepted the food. Hunger guiding her, she gnawed off a piece of the jerky, chewing it with relish. Without comprehension, she watched him gather the cedar boughs and carry them off, then return and carefully scatter the ashes of the fire.

"Why?" she asked, gesturing so he'd understand what she meant.

"Enemies read sign," he told her. "Know we camp here."

She frowned. Enemies? Hadn't he told her the warriors he'd rescued her from were his allies?

"Huron warriors fight beside your people," he said. "Enemies."

"The English aren't your enemies," she said. "You traded at my father's fur station and he's—he was English." She blinked back tears at the mention of her father. Now was not the time to cry.

"Huron warriors, King's warriors, kill Ongwanosi-onni, burn villages. Enemies. We go now." He turned and strode away and she stumbled after him, fearing she'd be left behind.

27

There was no cup, so to relieve her thirst, she used her hands to drink from the stream. Wind Cloud pulled the dugout from concealing bushes, slid the canoe into the water, and gestured for her to get in. Moments later he was paddling upstream.

"After we camp tonight, when will we reach your village?" she asked some time later, resigned to their destination because she had no choice.

"When sun halfway down sky."

Before evening tomorrow. She found it somewhat reassuring to know she wouldn't be entering an alien, inimical place in the dark. But she still had tonight to suffer through.

Trying not to stare at Wind Cloud, naked to the waist as he skillfully wielded the paddle, she couldn't help but notice his superbly muscled chest and shoulders, and the sight unsettled her. Though he was no menace at the moment, she was not accustomed to unclothed men. And certainly not to a half-naked man close enough for her to reach out and touch . . . not that she would!

He was a savage, no different from the others who'd captured her, equally ferocious and dangerous. Yet somehow, even though she feared him, he fascinated her.

"I didn't believe you when you said we'd meet again," she told him after a while.

He glanced at her and smiled. "Wind Cloud follow you."

She stared. "You . . . you followed me?"

"Wind Cloud paddle ahead, pull canoe ashore where river meet lake. Watch for you. Hear guns. See you with Onondaga. Follow in canoe to island." He scowled. "*Ohnaya* no good. Teharonhiawagon, Master of Life, say *ohnaya* bad medicine of white man; not meant for Ongwanosionni, bring trouble. Wind Cloud

28

see Onondaga brothers drink *ohnaya.*"

"The rum, you mean. They were drinking rum."

"Set fire to *ohnaya;* warn brothers of evil. Tell them free you."

"They thought you were someone else, someone they feared." She did her best to repeat the name she'd heard them mutter.

"Skaniadaiyo," he said.

She nodded. "Who is he?"

"Seneca man of great medicine. Ongwanosionni all listen, all obey him."

"They did free me, thank God."

"You not belong to Onondaga brothers."

Perhaps he understood more than she gave him credit for. Savage he might be, but he did speak English and, she recalled, French, so he must have learned something of white ways.

Giving him a tentative smile, she said, "Thank you for rescuing me. I was terrified."

"Wind Cloud no hurt Octavia."

So far he hadn't, but she didn't dare trust him. "Why won't you take me to Montreal?" she asked.

"Washington Father's ships fight King's ships on lake. Block way to big river. Montreal on river."

Octavia bit her lip. If he was telling the truth it might well be impossible at this time to reach Montreal by going down the St. Lawrence River, and traveling by water was the only reasonable choice in this wild country.

"Will you help me go to Montreal when the fighting is over?" she asked, worriedly wondering what might happen to her in the interim.

"King fight Washington Father in my father's time. Fight now. Fight in my son's time. In his son's time."

"The war won't last forever!"

He shrugged. "War bad for Ongwanosionni. Many

winters ago my father fight Washington Father's warriors. Soldiers kill many people, burn many villages. We make peace. Peace no last. War come. Some Seneca fight for Washington Father, some fight for King. Some fight for no white man. King's soldiers, Washington Father's soldiers, kill people, burn villages. Very bad. Master of Life says live at peace. No can."

She thought over what he'd said. It suggested a reason why the Onondaga warriors who'd captured her had ambushed the Yankee soldiers who'd killed her father and then proceeded to ignore her claim to being an Englishwoman. Perhaps they were allied with neither side but out to avenge themselves on all white men.

Wind Cloud seemed equally bitter. Under the circumstances, she decided it was useless to plead with him about journeying to Montreal. She'd best drop the subject for the moment and await another, more favorable chance to bring it up again if such a chance ever came.

Brooding over her possible fate in the Seneca village, she recalled what he'd said about fathers and sons. Did he have a son?

"Are you married?" she asked after an interval of silence.

"No wife. You wife to white man?"

"No." His pleased expression alarmed her, making her add hastily, "But I have a man waiting to marry me."

"Man in Montreal?"

"He's across the ocean. In England." How she wished she were there with Lord Randolph!

"Wind Cloud here. You here. We marry."

She gaped at him in horror. Good heavens, what was he suggesting?

"No!" she blurted. "Oh, no, I couldn't possibly marry you!"

He stopped paddling to gaze at her. "Why? Wind Cloud strong hunter." He tapped his chest. "Good heart."

"Yes, of course. I mean, I'm sure you're an excellent hunter and a kind man and would make some Seneca woman a fine husband." She realized she was babbling, but couldn't stop herself. "It's not that I don't like you. I'm extremely grateful to you for helping me, and I wouldn't want you to take my refusal as a sign I find you an undesirable person. I don't, no, not at all. But you must remember, we come from different people and neither of us would be happy with such an arrangement. You must understand it's clearly impossible."

He grasped her hand and put her palm flat against his bare chest, over his heart. "Wind Cloud see you at fur post. Feel you here."

A frisson shivered along her spine at his words and at the feel of his heart throbbing underneath her hand. Excitement rather than revulsion bubbled in her veins. This man was unlike any she'd ever met or even imagined. She feared him, yet from the moment she'd first set eyes on him, she'd been inexplicably drawn to him. She could almost imagine that she felt him in her heart as he was insisting he felt her in his.

A moment later she pulled her hand free. God help her, what was she thinking? She was a civilized Englishwoman and he was a savage. Furthermore, she was betrothed to another. But his dark gaze trapped hers and, to her dismay, she thought she saw a distinct glint of satisfaction in his eyes. And something more, an undefinable glow that made her skin prickle in half-frightened, half-eager anticipation.

Her Devon home and even Montreal seemed

31

impossibly distant and dreamlike, while the woods surrounding her, the rapid stream, the canoe, and the rise and fall of Wind Cloud's paddle were vivid and real. No longer pretending not to watch him, she admired the powerful sweep of his arms and the natural grace of his every movement. His tan skin was unblemished, except for a long scar on his left shoulder that extended onto his upper arm. Without stopping to think about what she was doing, Octavia leaned toward him and touched the scar with her forefinger.

"What happened?" she asked.

"Panther."

Octavia drew in her breath. Though she'd never seen one, she knew that panthers, larger and more dangerous than the lynx, roamed the northern woodlands of America. "Did you kill it?" she asked.

"Panther nursing kits. If Wind Cloud kill mother, kits die. No can kill."

"But how did you get away?"

"Jump in lake. Swim fast."

"Panthers can't swim, then?"

"Can swim. Panther no like swim, no follow."

Octavia marveled at his reasoning, wondering how many men of her acquaintance would have refused to kill an attacking animal because it was nursing its young. Not even her beloved father would have hesitated to shoot the beast dead.

Reminded once more of what had happened to her father, she bowed her head.

"Master of Life make sun live, moon live. Sun, moon no die," Wind Cloud said. "Master of Life make my people die. Make your people die. Wind Cloud no can change. Octavia no can change."

She realized he sensed her grief and that, in his way, he was trying to comfort her. His understanding undermined the dam she'd constructed to hold back

32

her tears. No longer able to control herself, she began to cry, great, wrenching sobs that hurt her throat as they tore from her.

She was hardly aware when the canoe headed in to the riverbank and Wind Cloud gathered her in his arms. As she wept against his chest, he held her close, crooning words she didn't understand but knew were meant to soothe the hurt. She clung to him, tears, streaming down her face as she mourned the loss of her father.

As the spasm of grief began to ease, she grew more aware of where she was, yet she hesitated to pull away. Not since she was a child and her father held her had she felt so safe and protected as she did now in Wind Cloud's arms.

At last, with a sigh, she freed herself. Using both hands, Wind Cloud brushed the wetness from her cheeks with his palms and the unusual gesture warmed her, making her believe that a man who could be so tender might keep his promise not to harm her.

When he saw she'd recovered, he eased the dugout back into the center of the stream and paddled on. Octavia, though still apprehensive about what awaited her in his village, found herself more at ease. Wind Cloud, she thought, would be beside her to protect her.

As he paddled, Wind Cloud watched the fire-haired woman who shared his canoe. He understood her grief for her father, but he also knew her father's death had removed the major obstacle separating Octavia and him.

From the moment he first saw her at the fur post, he'd known she was meant to be his. He didn't like or trust whites, but where she was concerned, his heart told him it made no difference.

He realized she didn't yet understand he was her man, but her hand had trembled against his chest when he'd laid it there and there'd been surprised wonder in her sky-colored eyes as they'd gazed into his. She hadn't experienced the hot rush of passion that swept through him at her touch, but neither had she been indifferent to him.

To try to rush her into marriage would spoil the sweet unfolding of her trust and the slow blossoming of her love, so he must be patient. In time she'd know the truth, know that he'd settled as deeply into her heart as she had into his, and she'd welcome him into her arms. Wondering how long he must wait, he sighed.

How his mother would laugh when he told her, for she well knew he'd never been a patient man. At the same time, she'd be happy not to lose him. When he married, a Seneca husband went to live with his wife's people. Octavia had no people among the Seneca, and so when they married, they both would live with his mother's clan.

While there must always be trust between a man and his wife, Octavia was not yet his, and he was free to bend the truth to suit his purposes. He'd do whatever it took to keep her in his village until she became his wife. She would never marry the other man, the one who waited across the big salt water. Such a man was a fool for letting her go on a journey without him, and a fool didn't deserve a woman like Octavia.

No one had ever accused him of being a fool.

Much as he wanted her, it wouldn't be easy to sleep across this night's fire from her. But she didn't yet understand her own heart, and he'd take no woman against her will.

The night camp went well and, as he'd predicted, they reached his village on the Genesee River when the sun was halfway down the sky. As he beached the canoe, he thought about how difficult this must be for Octavia, a woman used to white man's ways and dwellings. What was ordinary and right to him would be new and strange to her.

When the children came to stare at her and the dogs circled to sniff the stranger, Octavia edged close to him. She didn't protest when he took her hand to lead her up the hill to the stockaded village.

Since the war with the whites of the Thirteen Fires, most Seneca villages had been rebuilt. They were smaller than before because the people were fewer. His had ten long-houses behind the palisaded walls. As best he could in their climb up the path through the young but thriving apple and pear orchards, he tried to prepare Octavia for how people lived inside the long-houses, one family to each fire. He could tell she didn't understand and so would have to see for herself . . . see and accept. For this would be their home.

He smelled the savory scent of venison and corn mingling with the smoke and he smiled, happy that hunting had been good in his absence. Running Bear and Sun-in-Cloud had returned ahead of him with the trade goods the three had purchased with beaver skins—little enough this time. Like the Seneca, the beavers grew fewer with every winter, no longer building their homes in nearby streams.

Skaniadaiyo counseled a return to the old ways of the people and Wind Cloud had no quarrel with the prophet's advice. Much that came from the white man, such as *ohnaya,* was not made for the Seneca and caused nothing but evil. Still, he knew his mother and the other Seneca women would never give up the brass kettles they had received after the war as peace offerings from the Washington Father. The white man's metal kettles cooked well and lasted long—they were far superior to those the Seneca had used in the

35

old days. And he himself preferred guns to bows.

The white man's coming had changed the world, and Wind Cloud doubted the Six Nations could reverse the changes. Difficult as it might be, perhaps it would be better to abandon their home country and travel west, beyond the reach of the whites. He'd asked his mother to bring up the question in the Women's Council, for women's opinions were powerful and affected the deliberations of the Great Council of the Confederacy that represented and made decisions for the Six Nations.

Octavia spoke and he ceased his speculating to listen.

"Your village looks like a fort," she said.

"Guard against enemies," he told her, not adding that the stockades had proved of little use against the cannon of the whites. The best protection for the Seneca was to hope their villages would not be found by white soldiers.

"Where—where will I stay in your village?"

"In Wolf Clan long-house; Wind Cloud's mother and sisters welcome you," he assured her.

She stared at him wide-eyed, reminding him of a frightened fawn.

He longed to take her into his arms as he had when she'd wept for her father, to hold her close and soothe her, but he knew that even if she were to accept his comfort, it would be wrong for him to embrace her in full view of his people.

"You safe with Wind Cloud," he said.

Octavia drew a deep breath and tried not to shudder. Safe *with* him, possibly—but would she be safe *from* him? From what she could glean from his comments, the long-houses were warrens where the Seneca denned, entire families together, male and female, willy-nilly. Obviously there'd be no chance for privacy.

He'd mentioned his mother and sisters. Surely he

had a father, too, and, for all she knew, brothers as well. She pictured his family crowding around her, gaping at the stranger as the Indian children were still doing. Would she be expected to sleep between them, around a fire. Or worse, would there be some sort of huge communal bed where everyone not only slept, but—? She bit her lip so hard she tasted blood.

If she had any place to run to, she'd flee. But she did not. She was helpless as a trapped beaver.

Chapter 3

With one hand in Wind Cloud's and the other clutching her locket as though to gain strength from its familiar contours, Octavia passed through the open gates of the Seneca stockade and into the village. Her gaze flicked over long bark-covered dwellings which seemed to have deerskin doors at both ends. Wind Cloud approached one that had a wood carving of a snarling wolf face above the open door. A dark-haired older woman wearing a cloth skirt and a beaded blue tunic stood there watching them.

She opened her arms and Wind Cloud released Octavia's hand to embrace her. As they conversed in their own tongue, the woman shifted her gaze to Octavia, examining her from head to toe before nodding slightly. She drew herself up and said something Octavia could not understand.

"My mother welcomes you," Wind Cloud told her.

"Thank you," Octavia said, impressed despite herself by his mother's bearing, every bit as regal as that of an English dowager. As she spoke she caught sight of two young women peering at her from in back of his mother. She blinked, certain she must be imagining that one had light hair and skin as fair as her own.

The older woman gestured her into the dwelling and

the two girls retreated to allow her to enter. With her eyes accustomed to the bright sunlight outdoors, Octavia couldn't see well in the dim interior, although she received an impression of a long hallway running from one end of the lodge to the other, where several small fires burned at regularly spaced intervals.

As her vision improved, she noted partitions on both sides of the hallway. Within each partition were two platforms, one over the other, reminding her of the bunk beds aboard ship. A blanket was suspended and looped back from the frame of the upper platform, leading her to believe that, if necessary, it could be dropped to shield the lower bunk. The upper platforms seemed to be used for storage.

Various vegetables and herbs hung from poles suspended along the lodge's supporting timbers, and the dirt floor was covered, inside the partitions, with reed mats. The smoke from the fires rose to exit through holes in the roof, rendering the interior slightly smoky, though no worse than the air inside some of the Canadian cabins she'd visited. After the miserable warren she'd expected, the tidiness of the dwelling surprised her.

Octavia glanced at Wind Cloud's mother, who, as she stirred the brass kettle hanging over the fire, gave orders to the older of the two young women. There was no sign of the younger, light-skinned girl.

"Everything is so neat," Octavia murmured.

"Room for all we need in lodge." Wind Cloud gestured to the left of the hall. "Here sleep my mother, younger sister." He gestured to the right. "Here sleep older sister, husband."

Where would she sleep? Octavia avoided asking, afraid of what he might tell her. "You don't mention your father."

"Soldiers kill father ten winters ago."

Killed, as her father had been. Before she could say

39

she was sorry, Octavia noticed his mother gesturing to her and walked to the fire. To her great astonishment, the older woman spoke to her in broken French.

"You fine, strong body, Fire Hair. Make good wife."

Wind Cloud stared at his mother. "You speak French," he said in that language.

"Your father teach you, I listen, I learn."

"You never told me."

She smiled at him. "I do not tell many things."

Octavia decided she must challenge what his mother had said to her. Carefully putting the French words together, she said, "I am not Wind Cloud's wife."

"You learn Seneca ways first," his mother said. "I teach."

Octavia, realizing it was useless to protest, took what comfort she could in the reprieve she believed such instruction would bring her. Gathering her courage, she asked, "Where do I sleep?"

It turned out to be to the left, in the second partitioned cubicle. Octavia learned that all four cubicles belonged to Wind Cloud's mother. When Wind Cloud dumped a pouch he'd carried from the canoe onto the lower platform across the hallway from hers, she understood that that was his bed. She could only hope he'd remain in it at night and not cross over to where she slept.

Her first lesson was immediate. She was to call his mother *"Mère"* and his sister *"Soeur,"* the French words for "mother" and "sister." "Now French," the older woman explained. "Later I teach you our tongue."

While she was talking, Wind Cloud's younger sister came into the lodge with a kettle of water and Octavia stared at her light brown hair, fair skin, and hazel eyes. Surely she was white!

Though Octavia hesitated to ask, she glanced questioningly at Wind Cloud.

40

"My little sister Blue Water," he said.

"She looks white." Octavia spoke English, keeping her voice low, not wishing to offend his mother.

"My mother adopt Blue Water," he said. "Seneca custom."

Octavia, aware the girl was glancing curiously at her, longed to ask more but did not. She'd wait and find a chance to speak to Blue Water privately.

Soeur's husband did not appear for the evening meal of what tasted to Octavia like corn and venison stew served in wooden bowls with wooden spoons. After two days of eating nothing but the dried meat Wind Cloud had carried with him, she was starved and found the stew delicious. Mère seemed pleased to see her eating heartily, making Octavia reflect that no doubt the older woman believed a good appetite betokened a healthy wife for her son.

Octavia sighed. However was she to persuade Wind Cloud that she couldn't possibly marry him and that he must return her to her people?

So far the Seneca didn't fit her image of bloodthirsty savages, but the fact that they seemed to live very much like white settlers in the wilderness didn't make her any more resigned to becoming Wind Cloud's wife.

As she ate, she watched him across the fire—already she'd learned that the men were served first and on the opposite side of the fire from the women—the silver ornaments on his black hair gleaming in the flickering light. The other women obviously didn't find it unnerving that he was naked to the waist; no doubt it was Seneca custom.

His gaze met hers and held. The glow deep in his dark eyes warmed her against her will, making her remember the moments she'd spent in his arms. The strange feeling that had coursed through her when he'd pressed her palm to his heart returned to puzzle her again.

In his own way he was a handsome man, with high

cheekbones, an aquiline nose, expressive, dark eyes, and beautifully curved lips. Did Indians kiss? Realizing what had brought that question to mind, she flushed and looked away.

At that moment someone called from outside the lodge door. Wind Cloud sprang to his feet, strode to the door, and stepped into the gathering dusk, the door closing behind him.

Soeur asked her mother something in the Seneca tongue and, after Mère answered, appeared stricken and huddled into herself.

"She fears for husband," Mère explained in French. "My son goes to find him." She regarded Octavia thoughtfully. "Fire Hair journey far to come here. In my lodge you are safe. Sleep now."

Tired as she was, Octavia didn't argue. She found a red trader's blanket along with her fur-lined cape on the platform bed she'd been told was hers. Removing only her boots, she climbed onto the bed, pulling the deerskin covering across the opening before she settled herself under cape and blanket. Trusting in Mère's words about being safe, lulled by the murmur of unfamiliar words as Wind Cloud's mother and sisters talked to one another, she fell asleep almost immediately.

Octavia woke to darkness. For a long panic-stricken moment she couldn't imagine where she was and started to call to her father. Then she remembered: Papa was forever beyond hearing her. Tears welled in her eyes. She would never forget how he'd been killed; she'd never get over his death.

She attempted to calm herself with prayer, but the terrible events since she'd left the fur lodge on the Rideau River circled endlessly in her mind, coming out always the same—Papa dead and she a captive of the Seneca.

Sobs rose in her throat and she tried in vain to choke

42

them back, surrendering at last to her grief and a keen fear of what was to befall her. The grubby handkerchief she found in her pocket was soon soaked through with her tears. She was too miserable to pay attention to the slight noise when a hand eased aside the deerskin, but she did notice when the darkness was no longer absolute. Her weeping stopped abruptly.

Sitting up, she stared apprehensively at the corner where the deerskin had been pulled aside, certain Wind Cloud had returned to ravish her.

"No cry." The soft voice was hesitant and, she realized belatedly, spoke English. Yet it wasn't a man's voice; it couldn't be Wind Cloud.

Octavia brushed tears from her face with the back of her hand. "Blue Water?" she whispered, for who else could it be?

A slim figure slipped under the deerskin and perched on the foot of the platform. "No one hurt you here." The English words were spoken haltingly, as though the speaker had to search for them.

Though she couldn't make out any features in the darkness, Octavia was sure it was Blue Water. She thought the girl must be about fifteen. "How long have you lived with the Seneca?" she asked.

Blue Water was silent for some moments. "Eight," she murmured at last.

"Eight years?"

"Yes, years. Forget how to say."

Eager to learn how the girl had come to be here, Octavia felt her own troubles slipping from her mind. "Do you remember being captured by the Seneca?"

"Man shout, 'Indian raid!' Guns shoot. Belinda scared."

Octavia fastened on the name. "You're Belinda?"

"Belinda then. Blue Water now. Uncle bring me here."

Taken aback, Octavia finally realized the girl must

43

be referring to the warrior who'd taken her captive and given her to Wind Cloud's family. Perhaps he was Mère's brother.

"My mother good," Blue Water said. "Kind. Good sister, good brother. You no cry, you be happy here. I go now."

Blue Water slipped from the bed and disappeared before Octavia could stop her. As she eased under the blanket again, the momentary distraction of Blue Water's visit dissipated and was gone. An impressionable seven-year-old girl might be able to transfer her affection from her natural mother to her adoptive one and might easily accept the ways of the Seneca as her own. But Octavia was no longer a child, she was a grown woman. How could she adapt herself to an alien people? Accept one of them as her husband?

Anxious and fearful, she tossed and turned on the hard platform for what seemed hours. Her last grim thought before she finally slid into sleep's welcoming arms was whether she wanted to or not, whether she could or not, it seemed certain she'd be forced to try to change her ways to suit the Seneca.

It was two days before Wind Cloud returned. By then, Octavia, now called Fire Hair by all the village, had been taught how to hoe and to plant—corn, beans, squash, pumpkin, melons, and sunflowers—as she worked with the women in a communal garden. The small trees in the orchards surrounding the village, she learned, would yield a harvest in the fall of apples, pears, plums, and peaches.

"In old village big trees, many fruits," Mère told her. "Soldiers burn village, cut down trees. We start from beginning here. Much work."

Octavia nodded, regarding her blistered, dirty hands ruefully. She didn't find the work demeaning, but since she was unaccustomed to physical labor, she did find it hard. Mère had given her a dark blue broadcloth skirt

44

with a red flannel underskirt and an overdress of light blue flannel to wear instead of her rather bedraggled wool traveling gown and more delicate undergarments. Her boots had been replaced with deerskin moccasins decorated with porcupine quills.

On the fourth day of Octavia's stay with the Seneca, she was in the garden with the women when Soeur cried out, dropped her hoe, and ran toward the stream. One by one the other women followed until Octavia was left alone. Blue Water rushed back to her and took her hand.

"My brother, he comes," she said. "You come see."

Refusing would be churlish, so Octavia allowed herself to be pulled along in Blue Water's wake. She hadn't missed Wind Cloud's presence, she told herself, denying the speeded-up beat of her heart when she caught sight of him aboard the overloaded dugout, pulling into the shallows.

Blue Water sucked in her breath, putting a hand to her mouth in dismay as Wind Cloud, after leaping from the canoe and assisting in dragging it onto the pebbled beach, reached into the dugout and, with another's help, carefully lifted out an obviously injured man.

"Who is he?" Octavia asked Blue Water.

"My sister's husband." After a moment she added somewhat hesitantly, "Twisted Tree," and Octavia realized she'd translated the man's name into English.

Work was abandoned for the day as the entire village gathered inside the stockade to listen to the tale of the two men who'd accompanied Twisted Tree on the hunt. Blue Water translated for Octavia as best she could.

"Sun go down. Then is good time to shoot deer who come to drink at stream. Twisted Tree stay by fire to cook fish they catch. Then bear cub smell fish and come to eat. Twisted Tree see him, see mama bear follow. She fear he hurt her cub, and try to kill him. He grab

45

gun and shoot quick, but not kill her. Then he fight her with knife. She claw, bite. Men hear Twisted Tree shoot. They come running and shoot mama bear dead. Kill cub, too, because cub no can live with mama dead. Much meat for village. But Twisted Tree bad hurt, he no can walk. One man run long way to our village, get help."

The injured hunter had been taken inside the medicine lodge, and no one except the medicine man was allowed to be with him, not even his wife. Soeur drooped mournfully outside the door until Mère took her by the arm and led her home, where she placed half-finished moccasins in her hands.

Watching Soeur repeatedly wipe her tears away as she tried to sew, Octavia felt her heart go out to her. "Will her husband live?" she asked Mère out of Soeur's hearing.

"Master of Life says who will live, who will die."

Wind Cloud had used the same words—Master of Life—in discussing her father's death. Perhaps it was the Seneca name for God.

She didn't see Wind Cloud until late afternoon. Octavia was sitting on a reed mat outside the lodge, sewing with his mother and sisters. With her it was more a case of *trying* to sew, for though she'd learned as a child to wield a needle to embroider and do other fancy-work, she certainly had never made her own clothes.

He stopped beside her, saying, "Come with me."

Octavia glanced at Mère, who nodded. She set her partly finished green tunic aside and rose. Without speaking, he led her from the village, through the orchards and along the stream into a stand of pines. Noticing how the westering sun scarcely penetrated the thick branches, leaving them in gloom, Octavia halted in alarm.

"No fear Wind Cloud," he said.

46

"What—what do you want of me?" she asked, her heart pounding.

He didn't answer but reached out until his hand touched her cheek. He brushed his fingers gently over her face, pausing to trace the contours of her lips, then his hand slipped under her chin to raise it until she was forced to look into his eyes.

Slowly he leaned toward her, closer and closer. She couldn't move, couldn't breathe. As his lips touched hers, a fire was kindled deep inside her and, involuntarily, her lips parted to taste him and draw his intoxicating, alien flavor into her mouth.

When he pulled her into his arms, she clung to him, helpless to withstand her own yearning to press herself against him as heat rose from her inner fire until it threatened to consume her.

The skin of his back was smooth under her fingers, his muscles hard and firm underneath. She'd never dreamed touching a man could be so exciting. He smelled of the woods, of tobacco, and of himself, too, a male scent that sent frissons of anticipation along her spine.

"Mine," he murmured against her lips as his hand sought the curve of her breast, thrilling her anew.

A moment later he held her away from him, gazing into her eyes while she forced back a moan of disappointment, wanting to be held, craving his kiss.

"Wait," he said hoarsely. "First bathe." He untied the laces of her tunic, easing it over her head and dropping it on the ground.

She trembled, apprehension cooling the flames leaping within her. He was undressing her! Crossing her arms over her breasts, covered only by her thin batiste shift, she inched away from him.

"We bathe in a stream," he said. "No clothes."

"I—I don't want to."

"Seneca way."

47

"I'm not Seneca."

He grasped her shoulders and pulled her to him, bringing his lips down hard on hers. She tried to resist but the insidious warmth creeping through her made her respond to his kiss instead.

Wind Cloud had meant to be patient, to wait for her to adjust to the village and to him. But the sight of his sister's husband, mauled by the bear, had brought back his own wounding by the panther. He'd faced death then and lived. Yet no man was truly safe. Danger lurked behind every tree, and what man knew when and where he'd meet his death?

His mother had named her Fire Hair, a good name, one that fit. Not only his body but his spirit needed Fire Hair. If he waited, who knew what might happen? To him. To her. He refused to wait any longer. He knew she wanted him, so he'd tried to prove it to her and gloried in her eager response.

But he wouldn't take her without marriage, and marriage meant a man and woman coming together clean in body and spirit.

He had smoked and offered tobacco to the Master of Life, cleansing his spirit. Fire Hair was pure in spirit, she needed no cleansing. All that was left was to clean their bodies, but he could tell she must have a taboo about taking off her clothes. Other people's taboos were not easy to understand or to alter and should be respected, but his passion, none too securely banked, drove him to kiss her again, hard and demandingly.

Stiff at first, she soon melted into his arms. Tempted by her parted lips, he eased his tongue into her mouth to taste her essence and she moaned, pressing closer to him. His hands, as though acting apart from his will, unfastened her skirt and her underskirt, allowing the garments to fall onto the pine needles. He found her thin white undergarment would have to come off over her head and decided that could wait until they were in the shallows of the stream.

Still holding her, with one hand he removed all he wore. Naked, he lifted her into his arms and carried her into the stream. Though it was only a moon away from summer, the water bore the chill of winter as it lapped around his calves. In one swift movement, he stood Fire Hair on her feet, jerked the last bit of cloth from her body and pulled her down with him into the icy, flowing water until it covered their naked bodies.

He emerged gasping and shivering, still holding the sputtering Fire Hair.

"What are you doing?" she cried.

As he carried her from the stream, he tried to explain how the Master of Life required a man and woman who intended to marry to come to one another completely cleansed of the past.

"I'm freezing," she muttered, her teeth chattering.

Accustomed to bathing in cold streams, he didn't feel the chill as keenly as she. Swooping, he gathered up the white garment he'd thrown onto the bank and dried her dripping body before kneeling on the pine needles and laying her on top of their discarded clothes. He covered her chilled body with his own, making no attempt to enter her, for the moment intending only to warm her.

Octavia tried to squirm from under Wind Cloud, but the weight of his body pinned her fast. Even though the heat from his skin felt good against hers, she was determined not to submit meekly to whatever indignity he meant to subject her to.

He stroked her cheeks with his thumbs and she tried to turn her head away, but he wouldn't let her.

"My heart is yours," he murmured, and kissed her.

Despite her intention to fight him off, his words and his lips took the edge off her anger and soothed her fear. She'd been too shocked to really heed his explanation but apparently her forced dip into that ice-cold stream had something to do with his Master of

Life and wasn't meant to harm her.

When he stopped kissing her, instead of lashing him with angry words, she'd calmly persuade him to free her and allow her to dress. If he ever did stop kissing her. And if she could remember what it was she meant to do when it was so much easier to forget everything but the warmth within his embrace.

His lips traveled to her throat, then to her breast. She'd thought the fire inside her had been quenched by her chill immersion, but when he took her nipple into his mouth, flames flared through her, making her arch against him in sudden need, no longer able to think, only to feel.

The silken caress of skin against skin sent quivering thrills along her spine. His hands touched her in secret places, making her moan as hot waves of pleasure washed over her. Then he was hardness against her softness, a probing hardness she welcomed, desperately wanting what he offered. She moved against him, with him, seeking.

And then, like an arrow, she felt herself fly high into the sky, higher, higher, until she reached the heart of the sun and was consumed.

When she could think again, she found herself with Wind Cloud's arm around her. He was on his back, she was cuddled against him. He turned and placed his palm between her breasts. "Your heart is mine," he murmured.

She couldn't deny the truth of his words. What had happened between them had changed her forever, and her heart would never again be her own.

Chapter 4

Now married in the Seneca way, Fire Hair and Wind Cloud returned to the village as man and wife. Usually a Seneca husband moved in with his wife's relatives, but since Fire Hair had none, they continued to live with his mother. As Wind Cloud's wife, Fire Hair was accepted as one of the People, just as Blue Water had been after her adoption.

The People's ancient custom of adopting enemy men, women, and children into their tribe was, the Seneca believed, *orenda,* the spirit of good, as opposed to *otgout,* the spirit of evil. The *orenda* of adoption strengthened them against the draining *otgout* of war.

As one moon waned and the next grew fat only to dwindle in its turn, the corn grew tall, the hunters found ample game, illness didn't visit, and no enemies disturbed village life. Many believed the good fortune might be due to Fire Hair's coming, and Mère was congratulated on her son's far-sighted choice of a mate with *orenda*.

"It makes me uneasy to be thought of as a lucky talisman," Fire Hair told her husband as they walked hand-in-hand by the river on a warm evening near the end of the Moon of Ripening Corn.

"It is the way of the People. They believed the same of my father. Like Blue Water, he was adopted. He told me that after his adoption the village had the best harvest in years and all were certain his *orenda* caused the good yield." Wind Cloud mixed three languages as he spoke—French, English, and Seneca—for she was learning his tongue as he improved his knowledge of hers.

"Your father was adopted?" she asked. "Do you mean he was a white man?"

"No, not white. An enemy of the People, a Chippewa. He'd seen thirteen winters when he was captured by our warriors during a raid on a Chippewa camp far to the northwest. A turtle clan woman claimed him as her son after he braved the gauntlet."

Fire Hair tried not to shudder as she recalled the Canadians' horror stories of captured white men being forced to run between a double line of Iroquois men and women armed with clubs, all intent on maiming or killing the captive. Few survived the gauntlet.

These people she lived with had very different customs from hers. Still, despite their sometimes violent ways, she no longer viewed them as evil torturers or wild savages. Though she might not approve of some of his customs, the husband she'd come to love more than herself was as good and kind a man as she'd ever known.

"Then you're half Seneca and half Chippewa," she said.

"No, I'm all Seneca. My father's Chippewa blood was changed by the adoption."

She accepted the correction without comment. Wind Cloud did not and never would think like a white man, nor did she expect him to. He didn't lecture her about her beliefs; she extended the same courtesy to him.

"He was handsome and brave, my father," Wind

Cloud said. "My mother chose him for her husband when first she saw him."

"She must have been a mere child at the time."

Wind Cloud smiled. "She was. But she knew, just as I knew you would be my wife when I saw you step from the batteau at the fur post." He drew her closer and then stopped to kiss her.

Heat blossomed within her, his embrace creating a fierce craving only he could satisfy. She marveled anew at the passion his touch evoked. No other man could ever make her feel as Wind Cloud could. Certainly not a man like her former fiancé, Lord Randolph. Her engagement to him seemed no more than a long-ago dream, as did everything about her life before coming with Wind Cloud to his village.

No matter how difficult adapting to Seneca ways was for her at times, she didn't complain, wouldn't complain because her learning those ways pleased him. He gave her so much joy that sometimes a frisson of fear shivered through her. How could such happiness last? As a girl she'd studied the Greek tragedies and learned how grievously the gods punished those who were too happy . . .

She clung to Wind Cloud, willing every thought from her mind. The ancient Greeks and their gods were far in the past, and their beliefs posed no threat to her. The English-educated Octavia was no more. Octavia herself was no more. Nothing existed but the present and the magic between Wind Cloud and Fire Hair.

He led her into the pines to their own special place. With the warm night wind of summer soughing through the boughs above them, they made love with one another as eagerly as if for the first time and as intensely as if it might be the last. She couldn't imagine living without Wind Cloud.

Afterward she told him how she felt.

"I will never leave you," he murmured, holding her close. A trace of amusement crept into his voice. "How can I, when you have my heart?"

She lay with her head on his chest, warm and content, listening to the strong and steady throb within. "How is it I hear a heart beating then?" she teased.

"I put yours inside me for safekeeping." He caressed her bare shoulder and the outer curve of her breast, his touch gentle and loving. "We are two halves come together to make one. Never can we be torn from each other."

Much later, as they walked toward the village, Fire Hair's thoughts returned to her husband's adopted father. "I know Blue Water came to your mother when she was very young and so has no memory of her birth parents," she said, "but your father was thirteen when he became one of the People. Did he ever mention his Chippewa family?"

"Once only he spoke to me of his birth mother," Wind Cloud said. "His memory of her was of a young and pretty maiden. At no other time did he talk of her or of his life before he became a Seneca—until the moon before he was killed, when he had a dream."

She waited, hoping he'd go on. She'd learned that the Seneca took dreams very seriously, being careful to remember those they could not understand. During the nine-day Festival of Harvest, before winter set in, they related these perplexing dreams to the dream guessers for interpretation.

"My father told my mother and me how the dream vision showed him that he would soon walk the Star Path," Wind Cloud continued. "In the dream he saw himself leaving behind the names of his Chippewa ancestors for his son, even though he'd exchanged their blood for the blood of the People."

Wind Cloud looked up at the night sky and she knew he was gazing at the white haze among the stars that the Seneca called the Star Path. As a child she'd known it as the Milky Way.

"A dream must not be ignored," Wind Cloud went on. "That same sun my father drew a map on bark with charcoal and sealed the drawing with pitch. The map shows how to journey to the land where he was born, and he explained its meaning to me over and over until I understood each marking.

"Drawings alongside the map give the Chippewa names and clans of his once-ancestors and he taught me how to say the words. Since my father's death, my mother keeps the map safe for me."

Warm as the night was, a chill shivered through Fire Hair as she listened, but she didn't understand why. The disquiet remained, keeping her awake as she lay next to her sleeping husband in their compartment in the long house. She pressed close to him until, comforted by the warmth of his presence, she allowed herself to accept sleep's dark embrace . . .

A young girl, carrying a map, followed a faint path beside a river. At first Fire Hair believed she was the child, but then she realized that, though she felt the girl's confusion and fear, she was only a watcher. It was as though she'd grown eagle wings that enabled her to hover over the child as, wearied and footsore, the girl journeyed far from everything familiar into an alien land.

Winding snakes of rivers passed beneath her wings, the shining waters of giant lakes and the trees of many forests. West she traveled with the child, north and west. She watched, hurting with the girl's pain, frantic to help her, but unable to.

Danger threatened from all sides with certain death behind and the terror of the unknown ahead. The girl, and Fire Hair with her, despaired of ever reaching her goal. Even if she did, would she be safe there? Only the Master of Life held the answer, and she greatly feared she was leaving him behind with the remnants of her people . . .

She woke weeping, with Wind Cloud holding her. "A dream," she whispered when she could speak.

Try as she might, she couldn't truly comprehend the meaning of her dream. It seemed to have nothing to do with her experiences. Though she'd traveled from England to America, she hadn't in those times been a child or alone. True, she'd unexpectedly come to live in an alien land with an unfamiliar people, but she no longer felt strange with them, and she'd found safety and security as well as joy in her husband's arms. Her travels led to happiness.

Because Wind Cloud urged her to, she saved the dream for the Festival of Harvest and, in her halting Seneca, aided by his interpretation, related it to a dream guesser, an ancient, wrinkled woman who looked to Fire Hair as though she'd seen at least ninety winters.

After Fire Hair finished describing her dream and the dream guesser sent Wind Cloud away, a long silence settled over the two of them. Finally the old woman rubbed dry leaves between her fingers and tossed the remnants into the flames of the tiny fire burning in the center of the ceremonial lodge. A pungent aroma swirled from the smoke. The dream guesser gazed into the flames for a time. Then, without looking at Fire Hair, she began to speak.

"You have seen your child," she intoned. "Your daughter."

Gooseflesh prickled along Fire Hair's arms. Though she hoped to bear Wind Cloud's babies, there was yet no sign she was with child.

56

"Your daughter travels to the land of her father's father," the dream guesser went on. "She travels alone to the place of her ancestors."

Anguish stabbed Fire Hair's heart as the image of the lonely, frightened girl in the dream filled her mind. "No," she whispered.

"I speak truly; it is what I see," the dream guesser said with finality.

As she left the lodge, Fire Hair found her husband waiting and told him what the old woman had said.

"The dream guesser's words disturbed me," she finished. "I don't want to remember that dream or speak of it ever again."

"I hear you; we will not."

She banished it from her mind but she was never able to completely forget the dream.

As one moon succeeded another, her love for Wind Cloud grew stronger and deeper. By the time she'd passed her first winter in the village, she not only spoke his tongue fluently but found herself beginning to think as his people thought. She didn't mind, for she believed it would bring her even closer to him.

Her biggest regret was not yet being with child. Soeur had given her husband a strong and healthy son, Little Bow, whose gurgles and chuckles brightened the lodge. Playing with the baby both warmed Fire Hair's heart and saddened her, even though Wind Cloud didn't seem to care that she showed no sign of accomplishing what his sister had done.

After her second winter in the village, word came that the fighting between the white men had ended, leaving the boundaries of both Canada and the United States, from what Fire Hair could make out, about the same as they'd been before the war had begun, in 1812.

"Now that they've made peace, we won't have to worry about soldiers attacking the village," she said to

Wind Cloud as they walked through the blossoming apple orchard early in the spring.

"Soldiers, no," he agreed. "Others, yes."

She gazed at him in surprise. "Other tribes? Which ones? The Huron are no more, and the Chippewa lodges are too far to the northwest for them to be a danger. What other enemies are there?"

"He may not attack with soldiers and guns, but I fear the Washington Father wants our land. Our brothers the Mohawks and the Oneidas have been forced to sign treaties that gave him their land in exchange for nothing of value."

Fire Hair struggled to understand. Though the Seneca would defend their village fiercely against any invaders, she'd learned enough about them to know they didn't believe they or any man owned the land itself. They, the land, the animals and vegetation, the moon, sun, and stars—all were parts of a whole and could therefore be owned by no one.

Alien as this way of thinking was to what she'd been taught as a child about man as master of the world and, specifically, of all he could acquire, she'd managed to put aside her early training and accept Seneca beliefs. In their eyes, to become rich at another man's expense was evil; one shared good fortune with the less fortunate—not merely the crumbs from a lavish repast, but equal portions.

"If you don't own the land, you can't sign a treaty giving it away," she said.

She followed Wind Cloud's gaze to the white and pink blossoms of the apple trees. Some of the petals floated free in the cool morning breeze. One drifted onto her hair and he reached for it, smoothing the petal between his fingers as he spoke.

"What you say is true. But in the Great Council of the Six Nations we were warned that, if we refused to sign, the Washington Father's people would hunt us with guns and take what they want by force."

As she breathed in the delicate sweetness of the apple blossoms in the peaceful morning, Fire Hair thought that trouble and strife seemed worlds away. Yet she didn't doubt her husband's words.

"Have the people of our village been asked to sign such a treaty?" she asked.

"Not yet."

She smiled, relieved there was still time to enjoy the freshness of spring, time to be happy. "Maybe it won't happen for many moons. Maybe not for many, many winters. When and if it does, we'll face it together."

He held the petal to her cheek. "This is the color of your skin," he murmured. He released the petal and it fluttered to the ground as he caressed her cheek with his fingertips. "The petal is soft, but not so soft as your skin."

Her breath caught as she looked into his dark eyes, warm with love. He traced the curve of her lips with his finger, then touched the gold chain she wore around her neck.

"If I could, I would be the ornament on this chain, warmed by your skin, always close to you," he said.

"You're closer to me than the locket," she told him, "for you are and always will be a part of me."

As he reached for her the village dogs began to bark, warning of strangers. Wind Cloud whirled around, his gaze searching the surroundings, his head cocked, listening.

She tensed, realizing their danger if enemies approached. The orchard was not only outside the stockaded walls, but some distance from the village.

"A canoe," he said. "One man only."

Fire Hair relaxed—one man presented no peril—

and focused her attention on the river landing below the village.

"A Mohawk brother," Wind Cloud murmured as a dugout paddled by a man with roached hair eased into the bank. "He brings news." He caught her hand, hurrying her along with him toward the village.

Or maybe a warning? she wondered uneasily. A Mohawk was an uncommon visitor. After the American rebellion against England, most Mohawks had fled north to Canada to live, preferring the King-Across-the-Water to the Washington Father.

There would be a council called, she knew, to listen to the Mohawk brother. Though she wouldn't be invited to attend, both Wind Cloud and Mère would be. Among the Seneca, women often served as village council members. Though they were not seated at the Great Councils, the women of the Six Nations were responsible for choosing the men who did attend. No man could become a leader unless the women decided he was capable.

In the long house Fire Hair found no one but Blue Water, who was tending Little Bow.

"Soeur is in the women's house," Blue Water said, watching the toddling baby, who approached the fire, but stopped before reaching it, already aware that the dancing yellow flames bit hard.

In the way of the Seneca, he'd been allowed to discover for himself that fire hurt. The result was a burned hand that had healed in a day or two and Little Bow's lifelong knowledge that fire was better left untouched.

Clutching his tiny play bow, he sat down on the mat and concentrated on fitting a blunt-ended arrow into it.

"Soeur and her husband believe he'll be a great hunter," Blue Water said, smiling fondly at the boy.

Fire Hair told her about the Mohawk.

Blue Water seemed incurious about why he'd come. "Was he young?" she asked. "Handsome?"

"I didn't see him clearly," Fire Hair said.

Blue Water sighed. "Only the old men who no longer have wives court me. I want to marry, but I don't care for any of them."

"You're young yet."

"Mère believes I've seen seventeen winters. I'm strong and healthy and a good worker."

Distracted from her worry over the reason for the Mohawk's visit, Fire Hair smiled at Blue Water. "You're pretty as well. Surely some of the younger men must have noticed."

"I don't think so, because they don't come to court me. Just the old ones." Blue Water grimaced.

"Is there any particular young man who interests you?"

"No. They're all dull. That's why I asked about the Mohawk." She bit her lip. "My sister, you married the best man in the village. No one measures up to Wind Cloud."

Blue Water spoke the truth. In Fire Hair's eyes, no man could ever measure up to Wind Cloud.

She watched Little Bow play at hunting as she listened to Blue Water discuss the shortcomings of her suitors until Mère returned to the long house.

The older woman gazed long at her daughter-in-law. "A man who comes from across the water searches for a woman with hair the color of fire," she said at last. "He offers a ransom. The Mohawk messenger is a friend of the wolf clan. When he learned from one of his people who attended the Great Council that we harbored a fire-haired woman in our village, he journeyed from Canada to warn us of the searcher."

Shocked, Fire Hair stared at Mère. "Someone searches for me?"

61

"I believe it is you, for never before have I seen a woman with hair like yours."

About to argue that there was no one left who'd search for her and ready to point out there *were* other redheaded women in the world, Fire Hair held back, a frightening possibility occurring to her.

Lord Randolph!

His name echoing in her mind, she shook her head. Surely he hadn't sailed all the way from England on the off chance he might find her. Why, more than two years had gone by since she last saw him!

Still, Alexander Simmons, Third Earl of Randolph, was a stubborn man, one who didn't easily give up anything that belonged to him, and they *had* been officially engaged. Since he would feel that made her a possession, he might well have decided to endure the inconvenience of traveling to America for the purpose of recovering her—recovering his possession. But she didn't belong to him; she never had and never would.

"This man, this searcher who offers a ransom," she told Mère, "is no relative and has no claim on me."

"No one in this village will betray you, nor would we willingly give you up. I cannot speak for those people of the Six Nations who live outside our village. Be careful, Fire Hair. Tread warily."

For many suns Fire Hair didn't venture outside the palisaded walls unless Wind Cloud was with her. But soon she chafed at sitting alone in front of the long house sewing while the other women tended to the plantings in the gardens. Sewing was her least favorite occupation, and she missed the company of the women. Even Little Bow deserted her to play with the other toddlers, the group watched over by a wolf clan girl of ten winters.

Wasn't it possible she was wrong in believing Lord Randolph searched for her? With the many available

62

English beauties, some with far wealthier fathers than hers, why would he trouble himself over her whereabouts? For all he knew, she might be dead like poor, dear Papa, making the tedious ocean trip to America doomed to failure.

The more she thought about it, the more convinced she became that Alexander was still in England and had nothing to do with any search for a red-haired woman. She was certainly not the only one with such hair.

In the middle of the Moon of Strawberries, Fire Hair could bear her confinement no longer. The year before she'd found a large bed of wild berries on the side of a hill after the village women thought they'd picked every strawberry in the surrounding area. She should have shared her discovery with the others, but she hadn't yet grown accustomed to thinking like a Seneca, and so she'd kept the location a secret.

As far as she knew, it was still her secret. Soeur and Blue Water had brought home a meager gathering of strawberries and she knew how Wind Cloud relished them. She pictured him enjoying her freshly picked berries; she could almost taste them herself, their sweetness tempered by the tang of wildness. What danger could there be in venturing outside the palisades to her secret hillside? Especially since she'd decided the Atlantic Ocean still separated her from Lord Randolph.

Making up her mind, Fire Hair rose and entered the long-house. She put her sewing aside and took down a large bark container from the storage ledge above their sleeping compartment. Smiling at the picture in her mind of her husband's surprise and delight when she offered him the berries, she left the lodge.

On her way to the open gate, she passed only children playing. The adults seemed to be busy

63

elsewhere—the women in the gardens, the men hunting or fishing. A village dog, white and black, with a curly tail, followed her.

She talked to him as she skirted the orchards and, keeping to the opposite side of the hill from the gardens, hurried into the woods. Though she didn't think any of the women would try to stop her, she wasn't sure and didn't want to cause any commotion. Tonight she'd explain to Mère and to Wind Cloud why she'd decided she was in no danger.

"Why would Alexander bother when in truth he didn't care a fig for me?" she asked the dog. "Or for my feelings. Perhaps he desired me, but now that I've discovered what love is, I realize he didn't love me, not at all. And I never, ever loved him."

The dog wagged his tail, then, nose to the ground, ran ahead of her, disappearing into the gloom between the tall oak and beech trees that were coming into full leaf.

The woods smelled of leaf mold and of new growth, a heady June scent that lightened her heart. Being outside the village walls at last made her feel so carefree she was tempted to skip between the trees like a child. She glided along the deer trail through the woods, turning left when the path turned right toward the river. Some forty paces away, if she recalled correctly, and she was sure she did, would be the tiny clearing where wild strawberries grew profusely on her secret hillside.

As she emerged from the trees into the forest glade, the dog reappeared, bounded to her and ahead, stopping short of the hill. He faced west, the hair along his back bristling.

No doubt it was an animal, Fire Hair told herself as she halted, warily watching him. "What is it?" she whispered, hoping it wasn't a strawberry-loving bear.

If so, her human scent coupled with the dog's should convince the bear to look elsewhere for his berries.

Wind Cloud would assure her this was true. But the possibility of confronting a bear made her nervous all the same.

The dog began to growl, convincing her that whatever he heard and smelled was still present. What should she do? She hated to flee without picking a single berry, but a careful retreat might be the prudent course. She could always persuade Blue Water and Soeur to come here with her tomorrow.

Yes, that's what she'd do. And she wouldn't retrace her steps now; she'd take a roundabout way back to the village, one that wouldn't bring her anywhere near whatever lurked among the trees.

"Come on, dog," she said in a low tone, "let's go."

He burst into frenzied barking, turning tail and running past her, skirting the hill to head for the opposite side of the glade. Exactly where she meant to go. She turned to follow him, casting an apprehensive glance over her shoulder.

She gasped as a man burst from the trees, racing toward her. A scream stuck in her throat as she began to run from him.

"Octavia!" he shouted. "Octavia, wait! I've come to rescue you."

As she recognized his voice, shock robbed her of movement and she stumbled to a halt.

Alexander!

Chapter 5

Wind Cloud stood among the trees, bow in hand, looking down at the terrified fawn that sprawled on the forest duff at his feet. Tracks leading away from the fawn showed how its mother and a small sister or brother had fled at his approach.

This fawn couldn't flee. Its hind leg was broken from stepping into a groundhog hole, and it would never walk again. For a deer a broken leg meant death.

Wind Cloud knelt beside the fawn. "Little brother," he said softly, "the only help I can offer is to bring you a quick death instead of a slow and painful one. Already Brother Raven waits at the top of a cedar, watching until you weaken so he can steal your eyes. I take your life to spare you pain. Know, little brother, that my people will be grateful for your skin and meat."

Drawing his knife, he drew the blade swiftly and deeply across the fawn's throat. Blood spurted; the tiny deer convulsed once and then moved no more. Wind Cloud gutted the animal, leaving the entrails for the patient raven. Then, hoisting the fawn's body onto his shoulders, he turned toward home.

He'd been hunting southeast of the village but hadn't traveled far before hearing the frightened bleat of the fawn when its leg bones snapped. As a hunter he spared young animals, but with the injured fawn he'd had no choice.

Once cured, the hide would make a soft, warm robe for his sister's son. Little Bow brightened the lodge with his presence. The time would come, he knew, when he and Fire Hair would have a child of their own. Hadn't the dream guesser foreseen a daughter? He smiled, picturing a tiny girl as lovely as her mother.

As he came nearer to the village, the excited yapping of a dog caught his ear. The barking came, he thought, from the oak woods to the west. When he came to the verge of the woods to the east and stepped free of the trees, he saw a black and white dog racing across the grassy meadow toward the village. A moment later he spied Blue Water running through the grass away from the village. He called her name.

She turned, saw him, and changed course to intercept him.

"Brother!" Blue Water cried as she came closer, her breath short from running. "Fire Hair has left the village."

Wind Cloud stopped and flung down the fawn's carcass. "When?" he demanded.

Blue Water halted beside him. "I came away from the gardens to the lodge to talk to Fire Hair because I knew she was lonely. She wasn't there. A child saw her go through the gates carrying a berry basket. A dog followed."

The black and white one he'd seen?

"Bring the deer to the village," he ordered, aware other women approached. "I will find my wife."

Wind Cloud set off at a trot, heading west toward the oak woods where he'd heard the dog earlier. Now that he knew about Fire Hair the barking took on a more ominous meaning. What danger had the dog warned

67

of? What had made it flee? He set his jaw, increasing his pace, bow clenched in his fist.

Why had she disobeyed him?

Fire Hair faced Lord Randolph in the glade, staring in disbelief at the blond, blue-eyed man she'd once thought to marry. When he was about to embrace her, she held up her hand.

"Don't touch me, Alexander. I am no longer your fiancée."

"Good Lord, Octavia, you can't think I'd blame you for what happened. How you must have suffered!" Again he moved as though to take her in his arms.

She stepped back a pace. "You don't understand."

"There's no need to be ashamed, my dear, no need at all. I'm only thankful you survived."

She shook her head, amazed he could be so obtuse.

"Believe me," he went on, "my marriage offer stands despite—"

"I'm not ashamed!" she cried, cutting him off. "And I'm not in need of rescuing."

"You don't know what you're saying." He grasped her shoulders. "No wonder, after such a terrible ordeal. But soon all will be well, my dear. Once we're back in England, this will seem no more than a fading nightmare."

She tried to free herself, but he refused to let her go.

"Come," he urged, "my men are waiting. We've been fortunate so far; let's be off before we're beset by those howling savages who've kept you prisoner."

"I'm not going with you!"

He blinked, annoyance clouding the blue of his eyes. "You're clearly out of your head, Octavia. Of course you're coming with me." One hand slid down to tighten on her arm. He began pulling her toward the trees.

68

"Let me go!" she cried, fighting him.

With a yell of rage and challenge, Wind Cloud leaped into the glade some twenty paces away, an arrow nocked in his bow.

Lord Randolph pulled her in front of him, yanked a pistol from his pocket, took aim, and fired.

The gun roared. Wind Cloud staggered forward, blood welling from his chest, and collapsed.

"No, no, no!" she screamed, struggling in vain to reach him, barely aware of the five rifle-carrying white men who slipped into the glade, surrounding her and Lord Randolph.

"There's another of them bloody redskins coming," a man's voice said. "I'll pick him off."

"Wait," Lord Randolph said. "It looks like a woman."

"My brother!" a woman's voice cried in the Seneca tongue.

Through the haze of anguish dimming her senses, Fire Hair recognized Blue Water's voice.

"Don't kill her," she begged, fearing for Blue Water's life. "She's not an Indian."

"Another white captive?" Lord Randolph said. "We'll bring her along."

Helpless and despairing, Fire Hair could only watch as one of Lord Randolph's men dragged Blue Water away from Wind Cloud's body and forced her to go with them. No tears came to ease her pain and grief as she was pulled, stumbling, toward Lord Randolph's batteaus, concealed by brush.

Numb, feeling the greater part of her had died with Wind Cloud, she no longer cared what might happen. But as they traveled upriver, she finally became aware of Blue Water sobbing beside her. It took all the strength she had to raise her arm and put it around the younger girl.

69

With Blue Water huddled against her, Fire Hair began to realize that, whether she wanted to or not, she had to pull herself together in order to protect her far-more-helpless sister. She took a deep, shuddering breath. First of all, she could no longer be called Fire Hair. The name had died with her beloved. She was once again Octavia Livingstone . . .

By the middle of July—Octavia had made herself stop thinking in terms of moons—she and Belinda, formerly Blue Water, were living in Canada, in the Kingston house Lord Randolph had rented as his headquarters during his search for her. Mrs. Campion, the stiff and proper widow of a British major killed in battle, moved in with them to help dispel any gossip as to the propriety of two unmarried young women living alone in the same house as Lord Randolph.

Kingston had grown to a town of some four hundred people, but the streets were still dirt and there were few places of business. Fort Henry, on the bluff above the town, remained as a reminder of the recent war.

After Octavia discovered Belinda hadn't seen who'd shot her brother but had only seen him fall, she decided not to tell the girl Lord Randolph was responsible. It was difficult enough for poor Belinda as it was . . .

As soon as they'd settled in, Octavia, who'd been unable to bring herself to speak to her husband's murderer on the journey, forced herself to confront Lord Randolph about returning to her father's house in York.

"I've been to York," he told her behind the closed door of the library. "There's nothing left of your father's house or any of his possessions—they were looted and the house was burned by the Yankees during the war."

Octavia bit her lip, not wishing to accept anything from her former fiancé, not even hospitality. Unfortunately, she had Belinda's welfare to consider, and to support the two of them would take money she didn't have.

"What about my father's fur station up the River Rideau?" she asked.

"That's another matter. The factor managed to save the place and he's doing quite well."

"Then I will have an income?"

"Of sorts, yes." He seemed reluctant to admit it. "But, of course, this is a legal matter and it will take time for me to sort things out. Why do you ask? Haven't I made you comfortable here?"

She drew herself up, still feeling uneasy dressed once more in English clothes. "I didn't ask to be brought here; I came against my will."

Lord Randolph—she now refused to use his first name even in thinking about him—rolled his eyes. "Still going on about that, are you? Good Lord, you're an Englishwoman, not an Indian squaw. The sooner you remember that fact, the better. My patience has about run out."

"I prefer not to live in your house any longer than necessary."

He studied her for a long moment, his blue eyes calculating. "Then perhaps we'd do well to marry now, before we return to England. As my wife you can hardly complain about living with me."

Her seething rage against him burst from her control. "You killed my husband. I'll *never* marry you!"

He laughed, but there was no humor in the sound. "Don't be ridiculous, Octavia. Sooner or later we'll wed, exactly as we agreed some years ago. As you know, I'm not a man given to changing his mind or his plans."

71

She hugged herself, chilled by his words, suddenly afraid she'd never be free of him no matter what she did or said. No matter how bitterly she hated him.

"In any case, there's nowhere else in Kingston for you to live," he went on. "But we shan't remain here long. As soon as I have your father's affairs in decent order, we'll leave this miserable wilderness behind for our own civilized country. And now, my dear, if you'll excuse me, I have some business matters connected with your father to take care of."

Without waiting for her to agree, he strode from the small side room that he called the library, leaving her staring after him with angry apprehension. She hadn't missed the threat in his words. If she persisted in defying him, she feared he'd find a way to force her to marry him before they sailed for England—perhaps by refusing to take care of Belinda.

She closed her eyes, shuddering at the thought of lying in a bed with him. No, she could not—never. But she had no one here to whom she might turn for help. In Devon, there were friends of her father who could protect her from Lord Randolph, but in Kingston she was alone. If she wanted to keep Belinda safe now and eventually reach England unmarried, there was nothing for it but to bury her rage, stop protesting, and treat him with cool politeness.

Belinda peered around the half-open door. "Is he gone?" she whispered in Seneca.

Since she'd heard the front door open and close, Octavia nodded. Looking at Belinda, she sighed. No matter how they practiced improving the girl's English, she continued to lapse into the Seneca tongue.

Evidently reading the disapproval in Octavia's eyes, Belinda put her hand to her mouth. "I forgot," she said in English as she slipped into the room.

"It's for your own good. You said yourself you wish

72

to marry. We live here among Canadians who are white. Any man who might become interested in you wouldn't want a wife who spoke Seneca."

"I know. But English words come slow."

Since Belinda couldn't recall her family name, it was impossible to discover where she might have been living when the Seneca warriors had captured her. From the girl's scanty memory of the raid, Octavia thought it likely her family had been wiped out, so she'd given Belinda her own name of Livingstone.

"Mrs. Campion says we all are—" Belinda paused, searching for the right word—"invited to a dance. Do white men and ladies dance like the People do?"

Octavia shook her head. "But you'll learn the steps quickly and enjoy the English dances." *She* wouldn't enjoy going, but she knew she must attend for Belinda's sake. The girl would be afraid to go without her, and it was important that she learn to fit into the community.

Belinda fingered the soft cotton of her rose-pink gown. "White clothes are pretty. Will I wear this to the dance?"

"No." Octavia's tone grew brisk as she summoned false enthusiasm for the girl's sake. "What we both need are new gowns, appropriate for evening. I'll speak to Mrs. Campion about a dressmaker."

As they left the library, Belinda tucked her arm into Octavia's. "I miss Mère," she said haltingly. "I miss the village."

Octavia saw tears glinting in the girl's eyes. Grimly, she forced back her own tears. It would do no good to have them both sobbing over what they'd lost. She didn't dare allow herself to dwell on Wind Cloud's death or she'd be incapacitated by grief—unable to help Belinda and likely to become Lord Randolph's unwilling bride.

The girl should never have been taken from the

73

People. Yet it had happened, and Octavia knew Belinda had to learn Canadian customs as quickly as possible for her own safety, as well as to have any chance for happiness. Octavia knew it was up to her to see this quickly accomplished.

She'd considered bringing Belinda with her to England but had feared the girl would never adjust to conditions there. Here, in this still raw country, she had a better chance. If only she could find Belinda a husband before she sailed away, a good man who would appreciate the girl's many fine qualities and capabilities. Maybe at the dance . . .

"What color would you like your new gown to be?" Octavia asked, forcing a smile. "Green, to match your eyes?"

In the end, with a limited choice from the draper's meager stock, they both chose green. Belinda's gown was the shade of new birch leaves, a soft, pale color, while Octavia's held the deep richness of a pine forest. The waists were high, as was still the fashion, with the lace-trimmed bodices cut low.

Mrs. Campion, not yet out of mourning, wore a new black dress.

Lord Randolph, their escort for the evening, duly admired their attire—the widow's perfunctorily, Belinda's more genuinely, and Octavia's with lingering interest.

"I see you're wearing your great-grandmother's locket," he said, his gaze on her décolletage. "A rather charming albeit old-fashioned bauble, no doubt quite adequate for this colony town. At home, of course, you'll be wearing the Randolph emeralds with your ballgowns. That precise shade of green is most becoming to you, my dear. You do, though, appear a trifle peaked. I've noticed your appetite isn't all it should be."

74

Octavia shrugged. She knew she'd lost weight. What did she care? Without Wind Cloud, it didn't matter how she looked, didn't matter if she slept or ate. Nothing mattered.

The dance, arranged by the town council, was actually a party celebrating the anniversary of some minor victory of the Canadian Navy during the recent war and was held in the community hall. Festoons of flowers and garlands of leaves did their best to turn the hall into a colorful, perfumed bower. As they entered, Octavia was aware they commanded unusual attention. Belinda, unaccustomed to being stared at, shrank against her.

"Stand up straight," Octavia ordered in a low tone, "and smile."

Belinda obeyed, but Octavia knew she was trembling. Lord Randolph led them to where the town officials were holding court with their wives and presented them.

"I believe you gentlemen and ladies know the estimable Mrs. Campion," he said. "I also have the honor of escorting Miss Belinda Livingstone and Miss Octavia Livingstone."

Octavia had drilled Belinda in making proper responses and the girl, except for speaking so softly she was all but whispering, didn't fail her. Almost immediately they were surrounded by young men, including some in uniform from Fort Henry, all seeking an introduction so they might request a dance.

"I'm afraid Miss Octavia Livingstone has reserved her time for me," Lord Randolph announced. "You will have to be content with soliciting dances from Miss Belinda Livingstone."

Belinda proffered her dance card shyly. Octavia had been trying to teach her to read and write but had barely begun. Though she was almost certain Belinda couldn't read a single one of the names that rapidly filled her card, it didn't matter.

"Belinda's the belle of the ball," she remarked, pleased, speaking as much to herself as to Lord Randolph.

"Only because I removed you from the running," he told her.

She glanced sharply at him. "Nonsense. Belinda's a real beauty."

"Oh, the chit's attractive enough, now that you've dressed her up and taught her some manners. I don't doubt the local swains will compete for a smile from her. But the woman they really desire—and can't have—is you." He smiled. "You're mine, my dear. You always will be. I made that clear to one and all."

She flushed with annoyance, tempted to set him straight, to inform him she never, ever would be his. She managed to hold her tongue with great difficulty.

"How lovely you are when you blush," he murmured, infuriating her further.

Since she could find no way to avoid it, she was forced to dance with him, but she found the touch of his hand repugnant. After their second turn about the floor—a waltz—she pleaded fatigue and returned to Mrs. Campion only to discover he intended to sit out the remaining dances with her and the widow. Seeing it would prove impossible to rid herself of his company, she gave up trying and focused her attention on Belinda.

Octavia soon noticed that the girl was bestowing most of her smiles on one of the uniformed men, a handsome captain with a luxuriant dark mustache. Pointing him out, she asked Mrs. Campion if she knew the captain's name.

"Patrick Morrissey." There was a hint of disapproval in the older woman's voice. "'A man who knows his way around the ladies,' my late husband used to say. Not that he faulted him as a soldier, you understand."

"Irish, obviously, and a bounder on top of it, I suspect," Lord Randolph remarked with distaste.

"I believe Captain Morrissey's company will soon be returning to England," Mrs. Campion said.

The sooner the better, Octavia thought, watching Captain Morrissey. For once she agreed with Lord Randolph. Though she had no quarrel with the captain's being Irish, he was far too smooth a ladies' man for Belinda. He wouldn't do for the girl, not at all—even if he offered for her, which Octavia doubted was his intention. She'd take care to warn Belinda.

She did so the next afternoon, telling Belinda she'd best not see the captain again. To Octavia's dismay, the girl didn't agree.

"He told me I was the most beautiful girl in the world," Belinda said dreamily. "He said he wanted to be with me forever."

"Coming from a man like the captain," Octavia said, "such words don't mean he intends to marry you."

Belinda gazed at her, frowning. "How do you know?"

"I've met others of his type. And Mrs. Campion says . . ."

Belinda put her hands over her ears. "I don't care what anyone says. If I want to see Patrick again, I will."

Patrick? Good heavens, the girl was already calling him by his given name. Octavia launched into a lecture, reminding Belinda of the proper use of names, but she had a dismal feeling her words were in vain as far as Patrick Morrissey was concerned. She determined to keep as close a watch over the girl as she could.

"Why do you fret about that chit?" Lord Randolph asked her some days later, after she'd found Belinda unaccountably absent from the house. "You can't expect a girl raised by savages to have any notion of propriety, no matter what you try to teach her. No doubt she's accustomed to freely indulging her passions and will continue to do so."

"Belinda's an innocent!"

He raised a disbelieving eyebrow. "I believe I've had more experience in such matters than you, my dear. Short of locking up the chit, you haven't a *chance* of preventing her from taking up with Morrissey. I daresay this isn't the first time she's gone to him behind your back."

If it wasn't the first time, it certainly proved not to be the last. Neither Octavia's pleas, nor Mrs. Campion's shocked disapproval, nor Lord Randolph's displeasure, influenced Belinda in the slightest. Despite everything, she kept sneaking away to meet the captain.

Octavia was at her wit's end by the last week of August when, without warning, Captain Morrissey's company marched into Kingston from Fort Henry, boarded boats, and sailed down the St. Lawrence on the first stage of their journey home to England.

At first Belinda wouldn't believe he was gone, and when she finally had to face the truth, she couldn't be comforted. "How could Patrick leave without telling me?" she sobbed.

Octavia refrained from stating the obvious—that everyone but Belinda knew the captain was a rotter. "I know you're hurt, but it's best this way," she murmured consolingly. "He never would have married you."

"But we *were* married!" Belinda cried. "I told him how the People become man and wife and he—we—" She couldn't go on.

It was even worse than she'd feared. Octavia closed her eyes, gathering strength. "The captain is a white man," she began, knowing her words would hurt, but also aware they must be said. "I've told you over and over that white people neither understand nor believe in Seneca ways. Captain Morrissey has only contempt for the People's marriage custom, but it suited his purpose and so he misled you. In his eyes you are not and never have been his wife."

Belinda's sobs wracked her body. Despite all Octavia could do, the girl cried unconsolably for several hours, then fell into an exhausted sleep. When she woke, pale and drawn, she would speak only Seneca and refused to answer any of Octavia's questions unless she, too, used the Seneca tongue. She put on her Seneca clothes, spurning her white gowns.

"I want to go home," she said repeatedly. "Please take me home."

Octavia could do nothing with Belinda—or Blue Water, as she once again insisted on being called. In the midst of all this, fortunately, Lord Randolph had to travel to Montreal on a matter connected with her father's business. Otherwise, Octavia feared, he'd have done as he'd threatened—summarily married Belinda off to any man he could bribe, to rid himself of the problem.

Knowing she must find a more reasonable solution for Belinda before he returned, Octavia came to the reluctant conclusion that the girl would be better off with the Seneca than she was here in Kingston. But how to get her back? Who would know how to travel to that remote village? The only possibility that occurred to Octavia was the fur-post factor.

On the first of September, against the advice of a disapproving Mrs. Campion, she and Belinda set off in a batteau up the Rideau River. As the *voyageurs* paddled the boat swiftly and skillfully, painful memories of her last time on the river came to haunt Octavia. She thought of the boatmen who'd died then, last of all poor Louis, clinging to the side of the batteau until he was swept away by the current.

She blinked back tears, remembering her father's death and rude burial. Then there'd been the Indian attack and her rescue by Wind Cloud. Wind Cloud, who'd become her dearly beloved husband . . .

Unable to prevent her grief from overflowing, she dropped her head into her hands and wept. The touch of a hand on her shoulder brought her back to the present.

"I'm sorry to trouble you," Blue Water whispered. "Forgive me."

Octavia wiped her eyes with a lace-edged handkerchief. "It's not your fault. My thoughts were of Wind Cloud."

Blue Water sighed. "Sister, you have lost far more than I, for you lost a true husband, an honorable man. The man I foolishly chose was a false husband. His heart was black. It's just as well he's gone back across the water."

Octavia blinked in surprise. This was the first Blue Water had admitted that Captain Morrissey had been anything but wonderful.

After a long silence, Blue Water said, "Lord Randolph will be angry with you for traveling to the fur post without his permission."

Words she'd heard her father use came to Octavia's mind. *To hell with him.* She smiled, her heart unaccountably lightened. "It's of no importance," she told Blue Water.

At the fur post, Mr. Johnson seemed pleased to see her. "I regard your survival as a miracle, Miss Livingstone," he said. "Your father was less fortunate." He shook his head. "We can be thankful the war has finally ended. I pray there won't be another."

"I came to you for help, Mr. Johnson," she told him. "My friend"—she paused, ashamed she was not being

80

honest and corrected herself—"my sister wishes to return to her mother, who lives in a Seneca village in the United States. I hoped you might have some idea of how she might get there."

His gaze shifted to Blue Water, then back to her. "Indian villages are usually on a river. Any idea which river this might be?"

"I think the village was on the Genesee," Octavia said. "When I was here with my father several years ago, there were three Seneca men just leaving the post." She took a deep breath and eased it out. "One was named Wind Cloud. It is—was—his village."

Mr. Johnson's brow furrowed. "Wind Cloud? Yes, I do remember trading with him. As for his village—" He paused, obviously thinking. "Yes, the Genesee," he said at last. "That's the river. The Genesee. As for getting your sister there—" He paused again, strode to the open door and bellowed, "Louis!"

Octavia started, then chided herself. Louis was a common enough name. Nevertheless, she held her breath as she waited for someone to appear.

She gasped when he walked in the door. "Louis!" she cried. "It *is* you! I thought you were dead."

He grinned, his teeth white against his black beard. "It's good to see you again, *mademoiselle*. Like you, I live. The river, she bring me to shore and I find I am not hurt so bad. We *métis* have nine lives, like cats—we're hard to kill."

While he spoke to her, his interested gaze drifted to Blue Water more than once.

"Louis is my assistant," Mr. Johnson said. "He knows the rivers and lakes of this Ontario country better than any man around," Mr. Johnson said. "He can guide your sister to the Genesee, Miss Livingstone. I have no doubt he can find the village as well."

"Yes, certainly, I can do it," Louis said. "Wherever

81

you wish to go, Louis can take you."

Octavia glanced at Blue Water to find her looking up at Louis as though he was the sun. Lord help us, she thought, not again.

"I wish you would come with me, my sister," Blue Water said, switching her attention back to Octavia.

Octavia opened her mouth to list the reasons why she couldn't return to the Seneca village, but no words came. From deep inside her a desperate longing welled up, dazing her with its intensity.

"Come home, Fire Hair," Blue Water whispered.

Listening, Octavia suddenly realized what she longed for. More than anything else on earth, that's what she wanted to do. Go home.

Chapter 6

Their first night's camp was across the lake from Kingston, in the United States. With Louis's dugout pulled onto the shore and the small fire he'd made, Octavia was reminded of the night camp during her journey with Wind Cloud after he'd rescued her from the Onondaga. How frightened she'd been! For no reason, but she'd had no way to understand that until she came to know Wind Cloud better . . .

After the three of them had eaten, Octavia sat under a pine, apart from Louis and Blue Water. Intent as they were on one another, she doubted if they even remembered she was with them. They spoke softly in the Seneca tongue, their words not quite audible.

She wasn't envious of their preoccupation with each other. After she'd discovered Louis had no wife, she'd decided he might prove to be a very good choice for Blue Water. Apparently the abrupt departure of Captain Morrissey had not damaged the girl's heart as much as she'd believed at the time. Which was good.

As she pondered Blue Water's future, Octavia grew aware their voices had stopped. She glanced over to find them both staring at her.

"Mademoiselle," Louis said, hesitantly, "Blue Water

and me, we make the agreement. Maybe you think it too quick, eh?"

"Pray, tell me what the agreement is, Louis."

He shrugged, as if that were obvious. "We marry. Her people's way first, then by a Blackrobe."

"I have told him everything," Blue Water put in. "He understands." She smiled at Louis.

"It is well for him *le capitan* is gone," he said, scowling as he drew a finger suggestively across his throat. "Dog of a betrayer!" He pressed Blue Water's hand between his, gazing fondly at her. "Me, Louis, I will protect you. Always!"

"Louis is like Wind Cloud," Blue Water told Octavia. "He is brave and strong, and his heart is good."

An arrow of grief pierced Octavia's breast. No one could ever measure up to Wind Cloud.

"I've made you sad, my sister," Blue Water said.

Octavia tried to smile and failed. "I'm glad you and Louis have found each other." She focused her gaze on Louis. "As you say, your agreement to marry comes very soon after your first meeting. I don't argue against the marriage, and I freely give you my blessing. But be warned! If my sister ever comes to grief through you, I will pray you rot in hell throughout eternity."

Louis, obviously taken aback, protested that his only object in life would be Blue Water's happiness.

Octavia didn't doubt he meant what he said. Now. She could only hope as moons and winters passed, he'd continue to cherish Blue Water. Still, she'd learned happiness was never certain. At least these two would be happy for a time, as she had been.

"Does this change the plans for our journey?" she asked.

"*Non, mademoiselle.* We travel to the Seneca village. Blue Water wishes me to meet her people, and we'll marry there. Me, Louis, I'll be welcome. My mother, she is Oneida; they are brothers to the Seneca. You still wish to travel to the village, eh?"

Octavia was beginning to regret her impulsive decision to go back to the People with Blue Water, to go to what she thought of as home. On reflection, she realized her return to the Seneca might bring trouble to the village.

Once she'd thought the matter over, she knew beyond a shadow of a doubt that Lord Randolph meant exactly what he'd said about possessing her. Sooner or later he'd realize where she'd fled and hunt her down.

The last thing she wanted was to harm the People. Perhaps Mère might help her find refuge in another Seneca village where Lord Randolph couldn't locate her.

Octavia sighed. She'd never be safe. Even if she sailed back to England and sought help from her father's Devon friends, she feared Lord Randolph would find a way to make her his. He was a stubborn man. As he'd warned her, he was a man who refused to change his mind or his plans. No matter how long it took him, he'd keep searching. She could continue running from one place to another, but it would be useless.

What was the point in going on? Since she'd never be free of Lord Randolph, why not give up here and now? She ought to tell Louis to take her back to the fur post and leave her there before continuing on to the Genesee with Blue Water.

Octavia bit her lip, remembering how proudly her father had quoted the Livingstone motto: *Never cede.* Since she was a Livingstone, the motto was hers. Was she to cede to her husband's murderer? Her fingers crept up to touch the locket and, as she caressed its familiar outline, she knew the answer was no. She refused to give up, refused to become Lord Randolph's possession without fighting him—until the day she died, if necessary.

"I still wish to visit the People," she told Louis, choosing her words carefully, for she realized she couldn't remain long in the Seneca village. What she'd do after she left she wasn't yet certain. Mère was a wise woman and she'd consult with her.

"We go on at daybreak," he said.

The next day Louis paddled the dugout along the eastern shore of Lake Ontario until early afternoon, when an approaching late summer storm roiled the waters, forcing them to pull into the mouth of a river.

"We travel by river now," Louis said. "It's true the boat goes slowly upstream and we must make portages. On the lake she is faster, but on the lake she is dangerous."

Impatient as Octavia was to reach the village, she knew the delay couldn't be helped.

"The rain begins soon," Louis went on. "We cannot travel far or we will get very wet. Better to stop. I make the shelter."

They spent late afternoon and all night in a brush leanto. By morning the rain had stopped; but Louis didn't return to the lake, but continued to travel by stream. Two night camps later, he announced they would reach the Genesee the next day.

He was preparing to put the boat into the river the following morning when another dugout appeared, heading downstream. Octavia tensed, fearing trouble. But Blue Water ran to the riverbank, calling to the two men in the canoe.

"Turtle clan brothers! Do you not know me?"

When they pulled into the bank, Octavia recognized them as men from the village and came forward to greet them.

"We travel home," they told Blue Water.

"I, too, go home," she said. "Fire Hair is with me, as you see. This is Louis, Oneida brother and the man I will marry."

The men smiled. "It is good. We paddle ahead and bring the news."

Octavia watched them until their dugout rounded a bend in the river and vanished from her sight. Was it good, her coming? Was it *orenda?* Or would she bring with her only *otgout?*

"This river feeds the Genesee," Louis said as he launched the dugout. "I will get you to the village before dark."

Unfortunately, when the sun was halfway up the sky, the dugout rammed a submerged rock while Louis was negotiating the rapids. Water poured into the canoe, forcing Blue Water and Octavia to swim to shore. Louis worked the damaged dugout free of the rock and managed to paddle the sinking boat to the bank.

Standing on the bank, looking at the canoe, they all agreed it was impossible to repair.

"We must walk," Louis said. "Maybe they will send someone to look for us."

Octavia thought it quite possible, though perhaps not before tomorrow. The day was warm and sunny, and their wet clothes soon dried as they hiked along the riverbank after Louis cached some of his possessions near where they'd left the dugout, carrying only what he considered necessary.

As they traveled on, Octavia grew more and more tired; her failure to eat and sleep normally after Wind Cloud's shooting had sapped her strength. Finally, just as they reached the Genesee, they found a clearing where a patch of bushes laden with sweet, luscious blackberries grew, and she gave in to her need to rest. Sinking down onto the bank of the Genesee with a handful of berries, she watched Louis and Blue Water eat as fast as they could pick berries from the bushes.

Suddenly Louis raised his head. "I hear paddles," he said in a low tone. "One large boat, maybe batteau, coming from downstream."

The village was downstream from where they were, Octavia knew. But the People used only dugouts, none of them large.

"Who do you think it is?" she asked Louis.

He shrugged. "We must hide and watch." He grasped Blue Water's hand and pulled her with him away from the bank and across the clearing toward the trees.

Octavia made haste to rise and follow, but her foot slipped on damp grass and she lost her balance, sliding down the low bank to the river's edge.

She sprang up the bank as fast as she could, catching a glimpse of a masted batteau rounding a bend in the river as she fled toward the trees. Who was in the boat? Had its occupants seen her? Reaching the trees, she plunged between them and, gasping for breath, flung herself behind a trunk and leaned against it.

"*Bigre!*" Louis muttered. "They pull into the bank."

Blue Water, standing next to him, clutched Octavia's arm. "It's him, it's Lord Randolph," she whispered.

"And three men with rifles," Louis added.

Octavia peered around the trunk, shivering when she saw the four men disembarking. "I didn't expect him so soon," she whispered as much to herself as to the others.

"The batteau, she has mast," Louis said. "They travel faster than us, they sail up the lake to the Genesee."

With a sinking heart, Octavia watched Lord Randolph gesture toward the trees where they hid. They could flee, but she was near exhaustion and wouldn't get far.

"Louis," she said urgently, "take Blue Water and run. Hide deep in the woods where they can't find you. Chances are once Lord Randolph captures me he won't look for anyone else."

"Me, Louis, I will not run!" He pulled his pistol from his waistband and began to prime it.

"They have three rifles," Octavia pointed out. "And Lord Randolph has the pistol he used to kill my husband. If he kills you, too, what will happen to Blue Water?"

Louis blinked, considering her words. Before he came to a decision, Blue Water gasped and pointed.

"Three canoes!" she cried. "The People come to rescue us!"

Lord Randolph saw the canoes, too. Octavia watched him order the men to crouch along the bank with rifles aimed toward the river. The men in the canoes stopped paddling, allowing their boats to drift back downstream.

"Ah," Louis said, nodding. "The Seneca, they are clever warriors. They will come ashore below us and use the woods for cover."

Apparently Lord Randolph had no difficulty anticipating this maneuver for, leaving one man to guard the batteau, he and the other two ran downstream along the bank until they disappeared into the trees at the edge of the clearing, to the right of Octavia's hiding place.

"I don't know what he's ordered the other two to do," she said, "but Lord Randolph will be searching for me. If he saw me fleeing, he knows exactly where to look. We'd best move deeper into the woods."

Louis shook his head. "I say we steal the boat. Follow us, *mademoiselle.*" He grasped Blue Water's hand and headed upstream, keeping within the cover of the trees.

Octavia hesitated only a moment before hurrying after them, trailing behind Louis as he circled toward the riverbank. What Louis expected to be able to do against a guard armed with a rifle she didn't know. If he shot the man with his pistol, the sound would alert the others. Though Louis might gain the boat and launch it, on the river the three of them would be sitting ducks for the armed men on the bank. Still, anything was better than aimlessly running.

She hoped the three Seneca warriors she'd seen in the canoes would prove more than a match for Lord Randolph's men, but she doubted the Seneca were carrying rifles. Bows and arrows were more likely.

Had the warriors come after the batteau because they'd noticed armed white men? Or were they merely paddling upriver to escort Louis's boat to the village? The Seneca would have no way to know the boat had been damaged, leaving the three of them afoot.

She caught up with Louis and Blue Water, who'd stopped near the riverbank where the trees ended and the clearing began.

"You wait here," Louis said. "I will crawl through the briars to the guard, surprise him, and slit his throat."

Thinking of the many sharp thorns on the blackberry vines, Octavia shook her head. "You'll never get through."

"I will follow rabbit tunnels in that patch. You will see, I will get through. After he is dead, I will make noise like a crow. You run to the boat; we will escape."

Octavia thought it a dubious plan, but she had no better one. Blue Water, her eyes shining with mixed admiration and apprehension, nodded, and Louis slipped away.

"Can you see where he is?" Blue Water whispered after a few minutes had passed.

90

"No, the blackberry vines are too thick."

"If I climb into this beech tree I might be able to spot him from above."

"Don't climb too high," Octavia advised. "If his plan works, we'll need to get to the boat fast."

Blue Water pointed upward. "Just to that limb—I can climb down quickly from there."

Octavia helped boost her onto the lowest of the thick branches and watched her climb onto the next, all but losing sight of her in the thick foliage. She leaned against the trunk, waiting. Some time passed and she began to wonder why Blue Water hadn't called down to her. Perhaps the girl was afraid she'd be heard.

Octavia stepped away from the trunk to peer out at the blackberry vines. She saw no sign of Louis nor any movement except the tremble of the leaves in the warm breeze.

A jay flew past her, his raucous call making her start. He perched on a branch of an oak beside the beech tree, still squawking. The hair rose on her nape—jays warned of intruders.

Before she could turn to look behind her, an arm snaked around her neck, cutting off her scream before it began and stopping her breath as well. Choking, with darkness threatening to overwhelm her, she became dimly aware she was being dragged away from the beech tree before she was swallowed by blackness.

She came to herself flat on her back in the forest duff with the crack of rifle fire in her ears. A large handkerchief smelling of snuff gagged her so she couldn't speak. When she tried to move, she found her wrists were bound together.

"I have little taste for the present dance of war," Lord Randolph said from behind her, "so I'm sitting this one out with you, my dear." He pulled her up until she stood facing him.

She was helpless to do anything but glare at him.

He shrugged. "If you persist in running off, you must accept the unpleasant consequences."

Grasping the ends of the leather thong tied around her wrists, he led her deeper into the woods.

"If you believe your Indian friends will track us down," he told her, "you're quite wrong. Arrows are no defense against musket balls. Those three braves lie as dead as the one I shot two months ago. As for the half-breed and the chit, my men will see to them as well."

Octavia prayed Louis had somehow managed to carry out his plan, launch the batteau, and bring Blue Water safely through the gauntlet of rifle fire; but she feared he'd failed. She'd come to love Blue Water as she would a blood sister and couldn't bear to think the girl might be dead.

How she hated this man who held her captive, hated him with all her heart and soul. She'd never expected to feel the impulse to kill, but she did now. Lord Randolph didn't deserve to live.

Shaken by her own bitter emotions, at first she paid little attention to where he was taking her, but finally she realized he seemed to be looking for something. But what? Judging by the sun, which sent its slanting afternoon light through the branches of the oaks and beeches, they were traveling away from the Genesee.

Octavia was stumbling with fatigue by the time he exclaimed "Ah!" and halted near giant slabs of gray rock thrusting up from the forest floor.

She followed his gaze, scanning the rocks, noting many nooks and crevices and one good-sized hollow high up.

"I do believe we've found a temporary hidey-hole," he said.

He forced her to climb up the rocks ahead of him until she reached and entered the cavelike hollow. He

92

pulled himself in after her. A quick look around the gloomy cave showed her it was about seven paces deep and five wide, and not quite high enough to permit her to stand. Lord Randolph was forced to hunch over to avoid the low ceiling. Though it was dry and clean inside, a chill shivered through her.

Otgout, she thought. A place of bad spirit.

Lord Randolph noticed her shudder and said, "You don't care for your bridal chamber, my dear? I'll admit the place is a trifle lacking in the amenities, but I would have thought you'd grown used to such a lack during your stay with the savages. You were certainly eager enough to rejoin them, despite the demise of your so-called husband."

Bridal chamber? Fear of what he must mean held her motionless.

"Since you eschewed a churchman's blessing with your redskin mate, I assume you won't mind forgoing such blessing a second time." With his face shadowed in the cave's dimness, his smile took on the sinister cast of Mephistopheles bargaining for a human soul.

He untied the cloth gagging her but didn't remove the cord binding her wrists. "Do you understand me, my dear?"

"Whatever you do, I'll never belong to you," she told him, her words tinged with revulsion and anger.

"You're quite wrong but I shan't take the time to argue. Suffice it to say you seem to have forgotten man is always the master of woman. I am your master and you will do my bidding."

"Never!"

A quick downward jerk of the thong brought her to her knees in front of him. "I do believe I prefer you as a supplicant," he said, "but I must warn you that your pleas will be in vain. I've decided we'll wed here and now Indian-style, since that appears to be your preference, and as you know, once my mind's made up I don't change it."

She gazed at him in consternation. "I don't wish to marry you in any style or fashion."

"My dear, you lost any say in the matter when you left Kingston, fleeing from me."

"Stop calling me your dear!" she cried. "I'm not and never will be. I despise you."

"That will change once I possess you. I must say, I find your protests most tedious. No more words; our time is limited." He twisted the thong, pulling her sideways, tumbling her onto her back on the cave's floor, where he straddled her.

His weight pinned her to the floor. With her wrists bound and him holding the thong, she found herself all but helpless. She could do nothing to prevent him pulling up her skirts with his free hand.

"No!" she cried, desperately trying to writhe free of him and failing. "Let me go!"

He ignored her and moments later her skirts were up so high she felt the cold hardness of the rock against her bare skin.

This isn't happening, she thought dazedly. She'd feared her Onondaga captors had meant to rape her, but she'd never believed a gentleman such as Lord Randolph would ever force a lady. How treacherous he'd proved to be! Wind Cloud had saved her from the Onondaga, but there was no one to rescue her this time.

He spread her legs, the touch of his hands on her bare flesh revolting her, making her taste bile. She screamed in protest as she felt his hardness against her.

With her scream echoing in her ears, she heard a soft, familiar swishing sound she couldn't quite place. Lord Randolph gave a grunt of pain and suddenly she was free of his weight. Finding he no longer held the thong, she lost no time in rolling away and pulling her skirts down as she struggled to her feet.

To her right, Lord Randolph fought to rise. To her amazement, an arrow protruded from his left shoulder. A man stood at the mouth of the cave, bow in hand, blocking what little light entered so she couldn't see his face clearly; but she knew he must be one of the Seneca warriors. For an instant her relief prevented her from thinking. Then she remembered Lord Randolph was still a threat.

"Watch out, he has a pistol!" she cried in Seneca.

Paying no heed, the Seneca leaped toward Lord Randolph, the bow and the arrow he'd held clattering to the cave floor. She stooped, groping awkwardly on the rock until she found both, her gaze fixed on the two men.

She gasped. Though Lord Randolph hadn't been able to prime his pistol, he held a knife with a wicked curved blade in his right hand. The Seneca's back was to her, but she saw he had a knife, too. The men circled one another, blades slashing. Blood showed dark on the Seneca's arm as, despite the arrow in his shoulder, Lord Randolph pressed him back, using his long knife almost as though it were a sword. The Seneca gave ground, stumbling, alarming Octavia. He was clearly in a weakened condition. Had he been wounded by Lord Randolph's men before reaching the cave?

"I've dueled better men," Lord Randolph taunted the Seneca. "Unlike you, I'll live to duel again."

"No," she muttered, dropping the bow. "You won't murder any more of the People. I won't let you." With her bound hands holding the arrow like a short spear, she advanced warily toward the fighting men, awaiting her chance.

When at last she maneuvered behind Lord Randolph, she raised the arrow and lunged forward, striking between his shoulders as hard as she could. She felt the arrow point pierce his flesh, felt it grate as though on bone. He cried out, jerking away, and she lost her grip on the arrow shaft.

With a triumphant yell, the Seneca sprang forward and plunged his knife into Lord Randolph's chest. For an instant the Englishman didn't move. Then, with a sickening, bubbling cough, he listed sideways and, like a rag doll, crumpled to the cave floor.

The Seneca dropped to one knee beside his body. "And who's the better man now?" he asked, staring into Lord Randolph's face.

Only after a second or two did Octavia realize the Seneca had asked the question in English.

To her astonishment, the Seneca grasped the dying man's hand, shoving the palm against his bare chest. "Know who I am, King's man," he demanded. "Did you think to kill me twice? The Master of Life wills otherwise. I live and you die."

That voice, she knew that voice. But it couldn't be, it was impossible . . .

Stretching her bound hands toward the kneeling man, she whispered, "Wind Cloud."

Chapter 7

"I knew you would return to me, my Fire Hair," Wind Cloud said as she knelt beside him.

With Lord Randolph's discarded knife he slit the buckskin thongs binding her wrists, then took her in his arms. She clung to him, tears in her eyes.

"I thought you were dead," she whispered.

"It was not my day to die," he said, releasing her. "Come, we must climb down from this cave of *otgout* so we can reach the river before dark."

When they reached the cave mouth, she glanced back at Lord Randolph's motionless body.

"He's gone to join his ancestors; he'll never trouble us again," Wind Cloud assured her.

"But his men are dangerous—they have rifles," she said as they climbed down the rocks in the fading light of late afternoon.

He didn't reply. Once they reached the ground, he puckered his lips and whistled four times, imitating the trilling call of the cardinal. After a moment she heard a faint cardinal's call in return, repeated four times.

"All is safe," he said.

Staring at him, she scarcely heard his words. She hadn't been able to see him clearly in the cave's dim light, but now she could. How gaunt he looked! With trembling fingers she traced the angry red scar high on his chest, marking the healing wound made by Lord Randolph's bullet two moons ago.

He caught her hand in his and brought it to his lips. Then, holding hands, they set off for the Genesee. Noting that Wind Cloud's once rapid stride was slow and hesitant, she realized he hadn't yet regained his strength. It explained why Lord Randolph had come so close to besting him in the cave.

They hadn't gone far when Twisted Tree came trotting toward them.

"Brother, sister," he said in Seneca, "we have gained three fine rifles for the village."

Then she knew Lord Randolph's men were dead. "Blue Water?" she asked. "Louis?"

"Our sister is unharmed," Twisted Tree replied. "The Oneida brother bears only scratches from blackberry thorns. He has a brave heart; Blue Water has chosen well." He smiled at her. "It's good to see you, Fire Hair."

Tears filled her eyes as she reached to hug him. "It's good to be home," she said.

Twisted Tree walked beside Wind Cloud. "Don't be ashamed to lean on me," he told him. "I don't forget how I once had to lean on you."

Wind Cloud sighed and accepted Twisted Tree's help, making her realize how weak he really was. Obviously he was still a long way from recovering from the bullet wound.

"He is dead, the evil one?" Twisted Tree asked.

"With the help of my wife, I killed him," Wind Cloud said. "I wasn't strong enough to best him alone. Together we overcame evil; now we will always be together."

She pressed close to his side, vowing they would

never again be parted.

Later, traveling to the village in one of the dugouts, she realized if she returned to Kingston and tried to claim any part of her father's estate, she was certain to be asked questions about Lord Randolph. Quite possibly she'd plunge herself and the Seneca into trouble.

I don't need my father's money, she told herself. I have Wind Cloud; I need nothing else.

And so, before Blue Water and Louis left the village to return to the fur post, she made them promise to tell everyone Octavia Livingstone was dead. It was the truth—she was now and always would be Fire Hair. As for Lord Randolph—if asked, they would claim to know nothing.

By the Moon of Falling Leaves it seemed to Fire Hair that she had never been away from the Seneca village. Wind Cloud rapidly regained strength even though the bullet remained lodged somewhere inside him.

"I was lucky you had my heart," he teased her, "so it wasn't there for the bullet to find."

"He lost much blood," Mère told her in private. "The medicine man thought he wouldn't live. But Wind Cloud refused to die and leave you a captive. And so he lived to rescue you."

By living, Wind Cloud had brought her back to life. As one moon succeeded another, they agreed that they'd never been so happy.

The winter passed. In the Moon of Ripening Corn, Blue Water and Louis came to visit, bringing with them their newborn son. Admiring the baby, Fire Hair tried not to feel a pang of envy. But later, alone with Wind Cloud, she admitted to her disappointment.

"The moons pass and still I have not borne you a son," she said sadly.

"Someday we will have a daughter," he assured her. "Don't you remember?"

"That was just a dream."

"It was a true dream; the dream guesser said so. When I was shot and lay near death, I knew I wouldn't die because you were not yet carrying our daughter. Since this was so, I had to live so she could be born."

Fire Hair realized he truly believed in this dream daughter, even if she did not. As the winters came and went and she remained barren, it seemed less and less likely to her that she would ever have a child.

Though she became a Seneca in thought, word, and deed, Fire Hair still noted the passing of the years in the white way as well. The treaty Wind Cloud feared, granting land to the United States, had been signed by Seneca leaders before 1820, but the village was so remote that it wasn't until 1823 that whites settled close enough to trouble the People.

In that same year, Fire Hair discovered she was at last with child.

Silver Grass was born during the waxing of the Moon of Strawberries in the white man's year of 1824.

"She is as I always knew she'd be—as beautiful as her mother," Wind Cloud said.

Gazing at her newborn daughter, Fire Hair felt so full of love and happiness that the old Greek myths of jealous gods began to trouble her again. She did her best to brush her uneasiness aside and enjoy the baby.

Silver Grass had hair as dark as her father's, but it curled like her mother's, and her eyes were a tawny brown. Her skin was neither as pale as her mother's nor as dark as her father's. When she'd seen five winters, the People packed their belongings and moved from

100

the village, tired of enduring the depredations of the encroaching settlers.

"To fight the white man is to court death for us all," the wise women of the village advised, and most knew the words for the truth. The young men grumbled, wishing to show their courage by defying the whites who made trouble, but they reluctantly abided by the rule of the council. As Mère pointed out, the Seneca were few and the whites many. Besides, hadn't the Master of Life himself told the People they must live in peace?

The site for the new village was carefully chosen to be as far from white settlement as possible, but it was not as desirable a location, for the soil was less rich. The hunting, though, was fair, and the fishing good. Five springs and summers of hard work established fledgling orchards and flourishing gardens. Two autumns later, as they picked their first apple and pear harvest of any size, one of the men brought news that a white family was building a cabin no more than a mile away.

At the end of the Moon of Falling Leaves, Fire Hair found Wind Cloud by the river, showing Silver Grass the bark map his father had made and explaining to the child what it meant. Her heart grew chill as she watched and listened, for the dream she'd had many years ago had never completely faded from her memory.

Silver Grass solemnly repeated her father's words when he prompted her, showing she'd paid careful attention.

"It is good," he told her. "Now carry water to your grandmother."

Fire Hair waited until Silver Grass had filled the containers from the river and started back to the village before speaking to Wind Cloud.

"Why do you make her learn the map?" she demanded.

"The time will come," he said, "when this village, too, must move. Where will we go? White men choose the best land, claiming it as theirs. We can't live near them because they will not keep the peace. If we don't keep the peace, they'll destroy us. Where can we move? Are we to live in swamps? Are we to live on land too poor to grow corn and beans? What will happen to Silver Grass when I can no longer protect her and she has no place to go?"

Dread rose in Fire Hair as she stared at him. "Surely it won't come to that."

"I hope not. But I rest easier knowing my daughter can reach her grandfather's people if she needs to."

Fire Hair bit her lip. "She's but a child; she couldn't possibly make such a long journey alone. Why, from what you've told me, she'd have to travel hundreds of miles!"

"Many moons will pass, and winters, too, before such a journey might be necessary. Perhaps it never will be. But Silver Grass must be prepared. It would be well if you speak only English to her when she helps you in the garden or the house."

"I've already taught her English. And French, too, for that matter."

"If she doesn't speak the words, she'll forget them. Who knows when she may need them?" He put his arms around Fire Hair. "It hurts my heart to see you look so sad. I only do what is best for our daughter."

"I know, but it frightens me."

He held her close, making her forget her fears in the warmth of his embrace. He led her deeper into the woods, finding a secluded spot where they wouldn't be disturbed and they made love with one another, the slow, sweet love of husband and wife.

Four winters later, Fire Hair, to her great surprise and joy, found herself with child once again. "We'll

102

have a son this time," she told Wind Cloud happily.

But when she'd carried the baby inside her for five moons she began to bleed. Mère's remedies, as well as those of the medicine man, proved ineffective, and she continued to bleed, so much blood that by the third day Mère despaired.

"Your wife will soon walk the Star Path," she told Wind Cloud.

Because she felt cold, Fire Hair had been moved to a pallet near the fire. Wind Cloud eased down beside her and lifted her into his arms, holding her. She opened her eyes.

"Take the chain with the locket from my neck and give it to Silver Grass," she said, finding the words an effort. She'd never felt so tired and weak. "Tell her to wear it always."

"I will," he said.

The tears she saw in his eyes confirmed what she already knew in her heart—she was dying. "I love you," she told him and closed her eyes again, too tired to keep them open.

She felt him brush her lips with his and smiled. "I have always loved you, my Fire Hair," he whispered.

Near sunset, held in Wind Cloud's arms and surrounded by her family, Fire Hair breathed her last.

With great care, Wind Cloud unfastened the thick gold chain and put it around Silver Grass's neck. "One day you will give this locket to your daughter," he said. "You will tell her of your mother, whose heart was strong and good."

He then left the long-house, for he could bear no more.

It was as though with the passing of Fire Hair the village had lost its *orenda*. A Seneca woman was

103

attacked by white men from the growing community downriver, and when two men of the People tried to rescue her, they were shot and killed. The village orchards and gardens were repeatedly raided until little remained to harvest.

It was time to move—again.

The council, hoping there to find safety in numbers, decided to journey north to the Great Falls of Niagara and on into Canada, where other Seneca lived. They also hoped the King-Across-the-Water would prove more sympathetic than the Washington Father.

Once Wind Cloud's family had settled into a wolf clan long-house in Canada, he walked through the village, noting the worn clothing and meager supplies of its inhabitants. He'd already seen that the nearest white community was far too close to suit him.

This isn't good, he told himself, his hand rubbing his chest where, it seemed, pain had lodged permanently—*otgout* from the white man's bullet, he believed.

He returned to the long-house, took down the bark map, and summoned Silver Grass. "We will walk to the lake," he said.

Though obviously curious, she asked no questions as they made their way through the sparse growth on this other side of the People's lake. Wind Cloud tried not to think of the tall trees they'd left behind, never to return to. When they at last came to the great water, Silver Grass, like the child she still was, pulled off her moccasins and waded into the lake.

He watched her for a moment, appreciating her supple grace as she splashed in the water. She would one day be as lovely as her mother. His gaze shifted beyond her to the lake itself. How beautiful it was with the sun glittering on the blue water, and how hard to leave behind.

Ontario, the whites called the lake. Already their

sailing boats far outnumbered the canoes of the People. He must remain firm in his resolve.

"There's no time for play," he warned his daughter. "We go on a long journey, you and I."

She hurried to his side, glancing at the map he carried. "To the land of your father's people?"

"It is so. On the way I will teach you all my father taught me of the Chippewa tongue and customs."

They left early in the Seneca Moon of Strawberries and had reached the great lake the Chippewa called Kitchigami and the English called Superior by the time the Chippewa Moon of Raspberries began to wax.

As they rose from their night camp with the dawn, Wind Cloud consulted the bark map with Silver Grass. "We are here," he said, showing her. "There is a Chippewa village one sleep to the north, but it is not my father's. His lies—" He stopped abruptly, clutching his chest as the pain pressed his heart as though it was a kernel of corn being ground between two stones.

Silver Grass eyed him in alarm, but he was unable to reassure her because the pain was too severe. When it finally eased enough so he could speak, he knew what was happening.

"My daughter, it is my time to die," he said with effort. "You must follow the map alone."

The pain returned, crushing him. His last thought was that he'd soon walk the Star Path to where Fire Hair waited for his coming . . .

Silver Grass knelt weeping beside her father's body. When her first spasm of grief passed, she began to recall what he'd told her at the start of the journey:

"If anything happens to me on the way, take the map, the bow and arrows, the knife, the flint, and any food we might have. If there are stones, cover me with them and then go on."

Carefully she eased the map from his hand, retrieved

the bow, arrows, knife, flint, and deerskin sack of provisions, then curled him onto his side, facing east. Seeking stones, she found many along the beach. The sun was halfway up the sky before she had him covered.

Blinking back tears, she left the cairn and, standing on the lake shore, stared at the bark map. Each line and symbol on the bark was as familiar to her as her own name. She could follow it alone. But ahead lay Chippewa strangers while behind were her beloved Seneca family. Though it would take longer to return to Niagara than to go on to her grandfather's village, she had no doubt she knew the way. She was tempted to go back.

Her hand came up to clutch her mother's locket. What should she do?

A feather drifted down onto the sand at her feet. She knew immediately it was an eagle's feather. A treasure! Scooping it up, she craned her neck to look for the bird it had come from and drew in her breath.

Sun shining on his white head, the eagle brother perched on the tip of a dead pine at the edge of the woods. As she watched, he launched himself into the air, soaring up, up, circling high above her.

And then she remembered her mother's dream and her heavy heart lightened. She was not alone.

Thrusting the eagle feather into her braided hair, Silver Grass began walking north and west, toward the strangers who shared her blood . . .

Chapter 8

A vast forest of pines swept down from the eastern flank of the Porcupine Mountains to meet Kitchigami, the big lake. Under the gloom of the pines lay the last few scattered, stubborn patches of snow, not yet melted though the Moon of Flowers waxed and the sun was warm. Carrying her cakes of maple sugar in a sling made of blue trade cloth, Silver Grass slipped along a deer trail beneath the towering pines toward the mining town at Iron River's mouth.

She wore a buckskin skirt and tunic decorated in beaded designs of flowers, sewn lovingly by her great-grandmother. Her dark hair, as always, fought against the restraint of braids, stray strands working their way loose to curl about her face. She smiled at a chickadee chirping to her from a branch—the little snow bird was one of her favorites.

Her great-grandmother had told her that in prosperous times, before white men had come to dig the copper from the land, the Chippewa village had been located at the mouth of the river, near Kitchigami, exactly where the white man's town was.

But now this village, where Silver Grass lived with her great-grandmother, Broken Reed—in the Chippewa way she called her grandmother—was a long paddle and a longer walk up the river. She'd been there three winters and each winter she'd sadly watched Broken Reed grow more frail.

There was no man in the wigwam to hunt for them, so they depended on the charity of village hunters and on the money Silver Grass earned in the spring selling her maple sugar cakes to the whites.

Silver Grass tried to grow beans and corn as the Seneca did but the summers beside Kitchigami were much shorter than summers near Lake Ontario and her yield was meager. Some of her apple seedlings had survived behind Broken Reed's lodge, but it would be many winters before they bore fruit. The pear seedlings hadn't lived through the first bone-chilling winter.

Life among the Chippewa was no easier than with the Seneca. In some ways it was harder. Though she missed her father very much, Silver Grass couldn't help but be thankful he'd been spared disappointment. At least he—

She stopped abruptly, her thoughts scattering like doves from the hawk as a white man stepped from between the trees into her path.

"Olav don't hurt you," he said, speaking heavily accented English. He held out four fresh-killed, gutted rabbits. "I bring to grandmother."

Silver Grass nodded. She knew Olav Johansen; he'd been leaving game at their lodge for many suns, beginning when the Moon of Boiling had faded into a ghost. He'd startled her by this sudden appearance, but she wasn't really afraid of him, giant though he was, because he'd never tried to harm her. Somehow she didn't believe he ever would.

He was taller and broader across the shoulders than any man she'd ever met, white or of the People. His hair and beard were the color of the sand along the lakeshore and his eyes were the deep gray of stormclouds. Loath as she was to admit it, for she despised white men, he fascinated her.

"My grandmother will be grateful," she told him.

"I bring for you, too," he said, smiling.

Against her will, her lips curved into an answering smile. "Thank you," she told him.

"Beautiful. Your smile. You." Olav flushed, his fair skin reddening as he spoke.

He'd never said anything about how she looked before. Pleased but suddenly unsure of herself, Silver Grass shifted her gaze from his, staring at the toes of her beaded and quilled moccasins. Olav wore heavy black boots, miner's boots, very large boots. He had big hands and big feet. It would take her many suns to fashion moccasins large enough for him.

When she realized what she was thinking, it was her turn to blush. Unmarried women didn't make moccasins for men not related to them, and she certainly didn't intend to marry a white man. Never!

"I hang rabbits in tree," he said. "Get on way back."

She glanced up at him, frowning as she tried to decipher his meaning. Did he intend to go with her into town, wait while she sold the maple sugar, and then walk back to the village with her?

"I don't let men bother you," he added.

The few women in town were no problem, but Silver Grass couldn't deny some of the miners *were* troublesome. She disliked their crude teasing, their insulting remarks, and the way they tried to touch her. If she and Broken Reed weren't in desperate need of the money to pay for the supplies it bought, she wouldn't go near the town.

He'd be protection against the insults. One look at Olav and any man would think twice before crossing him. Yet she didn't want him to think of her as his

109

woman. She was nobody's woman but her own.

"I can't stop you from walking with me," she said.

He looked so downcast she immediately felt sorry for the harshness of her words. Still, it was best he didn't assume too much. Deciding to say nothing more, she started to edge around him. He moved off the path to allow her passage, laid the rabbits high in the crotch of a tree, then fell into step beside her. Though she was taller than many white men, her head came but to his shoulder.

"You speak English good," he said after a time. "Me, not good."

She'd already made up her mind he was neither English nor American nor French. Yet he was white. "What do your people call themselves?" she asked, her curiosity getting the better of her.

"I am Swede, come from Sweden. Land across the ocean. Sweden like this, ya." He gestured at the pines, then toward the lake. "Hard times there. Good here."

He meant the copper, she supposed. He must work in the mines; almost all the white men did.

The Chippewa, she'd learned, had taken copper from the earth since long ago ancestor times, but only what they needed, only enough to fashion ornaments and tools. The white men dug deep into Mother Earth, carrying away great loads of copper, more than they could ever use. It was wrong to treat the land so cruelly, but the *wabishkize,* the whites, didn't care.

"Did you dig copper in Sweden?" she asked, pronouncing the strange new word carefully.

"I am blacksmith there. I learn to be ore driller here."

"What is blacksmith? What is ore driller?"

"Blacksmith works iron, makes horseshoes, makes kettles."

Silver Grass nodded. "Iron kettles are good for cooking."

110

"Ore is rock. Drill is tool. Use drill to break copper ore from rock."

"Blacksmith is better," she said.

He grinned, his teeth white against his sandy beard. "Ya, is better. But ore driller make more money."

White men, she knew, liked money.

"Grandmother is only family?" he asked.

"Yes." It was true enough. Her Seneca relatives were so far away she'd never see them again. The thought made her sigh. She loved Broken Reed, her father's grandmother, but Broken Reed was very old and would soon travel the Star Path. Then she'd have no one.

"My mother, father, old grandmother in Sweden," he said. "I am alone here."

She felt a bond linking them. He, too, knew the ache of being parted forever from beloved relatives. If he were one of the People she could easily grow fond of him. But he was not. He was white, and white men, even those from Sweden, were not to be trusted.

"I bring grandmother new iron kettle," he said.

Silver Grass could hardly refuse. The old one they'd been using had sprung a leak, and they'd gone back to the ancestors' way of cooking in birchbark vessels using heated stones.

"Your gift will make my grandmother's heart light," she told him.

"She good woman. I like her; she like me."

Silver Grass stared at him. "She doesn't speak English and you don't speak French or Chippewa. How do you know she likes you?"

"We sign talk."

Since she had no idea her grandmother had ever even met Olav, Silver Grass was taken aback to discover they'd been conversing in sign language. Why had Broken Reed never mentioned it?

"Grandmother say I come eat from new kettle," Olav went on. "Ya?"

Flustered by the thought of Olav in their wigwam, Silver Grass groped for words. "If my grandmother invited you, you're welcome in our lodge," she said reluctantly.

"Good. I come with kettle. I bring meat."

What had Broken Reed gotten them into? Silver Grass wondered. She didn't begrudge Olav a meal in exchange for his generous gifts, but inviting a white man into their lodge was unwise.

Soon the pines thinned and then ended as she and Olav approached the twenty or so frame buildings of the mining settlement on the Iron River. The buds of birch and maple saplings between the buildings had burst into the pale green of new leaves. *Shawshaw,* the swallow, returned with his tribe from the south, swooped, and circled over the river in his hunt for gnats.

When Silver Grass headed for the small house on the riverbank set apart from the others, Olav laid a hand on her lower arm, halting her.

"Bad place," he said, shaking his head.

His hand felt surprisingly warm and good on her bare skin so she didn't shake it off as soon as she should have. Her feeling about his touch confused her so that she didn't immediately understand what he'd said. She saw nothing bad about the house.

"The women buy my maple sugar," she told him.

"Bad women." He flushed, obviously embarrassed.

Then she realized what he meant. She knew men went to visit the women in that house and she knew why. In a village of the People, there was sometimes an unmarried woman who would share any man's blanket. In this town of the white man there was a house with four such women.

She couldn't understand why Olav called the four women bad. To her, bad meant evil-wishing or bringing harm to others. Among the People, women like these might be scorned, but they weren't considered bad. Whites must feel differently.

Silver Grass shrugged. The People and the whites rarely saw things alike. "I sell to those who buy," she said, and continued on.

Olav hesitated before following her.

Silver Grass stopped in front of the door. The custom of her people was to announce their presence outside a lodge to let those inside know someone was there. "I'm here to sell maple sugar," she called.

After a time the dark-haired woman named Mimi opened the door, purse in hand. "If it's one dollar a cake, like before, we'll take two," she said, holding out two silver coins.

As Silver Grass was handing her the two cakes of maple sugar, a man appeared behind Mimi, who was standing in the open door. Silver Grass recognized him as one she'd had trouble with before.

"Well, if it isn't that pretty little curly-haired squaw," he said, staring at Silver Grass in a way that made her skin crawl. "Come on in, honey, this is the perfect place for you and me to get better acquainted."

Before she could do anything, Olav, who'd been standing off to one side, stepped up next to her, fists clenched, and glared at the man in the doorway.

The man, almost as tall as Olav, scowled back, his pale eyes darkening with anger.

Mimi tucked her maple cakes into a pocket and laid a hand on the blue-eyed man's arm. "You can see she's the Swede's woman, Alex. What d'ya want to fight over a squaw for, anyhow?"

Alex shrugged Mimi off. "You know who I am, Swede?" he demanded.

113

"Ya." Olav clipped the word short.

"Then you know you'd better not cross me."

Olav clamped a hand on Silver Grass's arm. "You don't bother her, I don't bother you." He wheeled away from Alex and marched off, his grip on her arm forcing Silver Grass to walk fast to keep up with him.

"His papa, he run the mine, good boss," Olav muttered. "Son good for nothing."

Though she disliked the man named Alex, Silver Grass was silent. Mimi's words about her being the Swede's woman lingered in her ears. She wasn't, not in any way. Still, as long as Olav didn't start believing they were true, the words might help protect her against white men like Alex.

When she finished selling her sugar, she was quiet on the walk back to the Chippewa village, scarcely saying a word in her determination not to encourage Olav. She believed she'd gotten her message across because once he'd seen her safely to the wigwam, he didn't linger. Broken Reed, happy with the rabbits, removed the fur before adding them to the stew she was cooking.

Silver Grass took the rabbit hides outside to cleanse them in preparation for stretching them on wooden frames for curing. While she was at her work, one of the village men approached. She greeted Lame Wolf with a smile, only to receive a scowl in return.

"I saw you with that white man," he said, speaking Chippewa.

She held her temper even though Lame Wolf had no claim on her, no right to be angry because she'd walked with a white man.

"He brings food to our wigwam," she said mildly.

"If you'd marry me, there'd be no need for white men to bring food," he said. "I'd be the hunter for you and your grandmother."

Silver Grass put down the knife she was using to

114

scrape the hide and looked up at him. "I've told you I won't marry any man who drinks the white man's firewater."

Lame Wolf's scowl grew darker. "It's true I have in the past. If we were married I would not."

Silver Grass narrowed her eyes. "I have heard that when your wife was alive you drank firewater and then beat her. And that you lay sick from drink in her lodge instead of hunting with the other men. How can I believe you'd be any different if I became your wife?"

"I will prove it to you!"

"By not drinking firewater for twelve moons?"

He sighed. "That is long."

Silver Grass shrugged and went back to her scraping, certain Lame Wolf couldn't last even one moon without succumbing to his thirst for firewater. When he was himself he was reasonable enough, but when he'd been drinking it was as though an evil spirit possessed him. Because of the drink, no woman could depend on Lame Wolf to keep the wigwam in meat or to treat her kindly. But that wasn't the only reason she didn't wish to marry him—she could never bring herself to share Lame Wolf's blanket even if he became more trustworthy.

"I don't like white men in the village," he said after a time. "They bring trouble."

"Olav won't bring trouble. Only meat. And a new iron kettle for Grandmother. You know Broken Reed is not fond of the whites—but she likes him."

"And you—do you like him, this Olav?"

She didn't answer directly. "I know white men can't be trusted, but I believe his heart is good."

Lame Wolf turned his head from her and spat.

"If you hate them so much," she said, "why do you drink their firewater?"

She thought her words might annoy him, might

115

make him leave. Instead, he crouched down beside her. "I remember when I brought you to our village," he said. "A girl not quite grown with an eagle feather in her hair-that-curls. A grieving, frightened girl who'd traveled far to reach her grandfather's people."

Silver Grass sighed. Lame Wolf had been the one who'd found her wandering forlornly along the lake shore three summers before and had taken her in his canoe to Iron River, up the river to this village, and into Broken Reed's lodge. She'd be forever grateful to him for helping her find her grandfather's mother.

"My heart holds a place for you," she told him.

"As my heart does for you. That's why I want you for my wife."

"Twelve moons," she said firmly. "My ears will not hear your offer until then."

"I have always heard Broken Reed had a stubborn heart," he said, rising. "You are her true great-granddaughter."

Later, eating the rabbit stew with Broken Reed, Silver Grass told her about her conversation with Lame Wolf.

The old woman smiled, a faraway look in her eyes. "My father is the one who accused me of having a stubborn heart. He grew angry because I wouldn't choose any of the young warriors who courted me. I secretly languished for an older man, the medicine man of our village. He hadn't sought to marry me—I believed he'd never noticed me and that my love was in vain.

"My mother suspected. Since she was a woman who struck straight to the core of things, she went to this man and told him if he didn't want me he'd best tell me so, otherwise I might die of love for him."

"What happened?" Silver Grass asked, fascinated at the thought of Broken Reed ever being young enough

116

to be courted.

"He'd been watching me for two winters without anyone being aware of his interest, but didn't believe I'd ever given him a thought. He'd been sure I'd never consider him for my husband because I was so young and pretty. After we were married, I asked him why he hadn't slipped a love potion into my food if he wanted me so much." Broken Reed laughed. "He, the respected medicine man, much admired for his skills, admitted he didn't believe in love potions."

"You were happy with him?"

"My granddaughter, a woman is always happy when she marries the man she loves. As you will one day discover."

Silver Grass sighed. "That man isn't Lame Wolf. Even if he never drank another drop of firewater, he's not the one I'd give my heart to."

"Who is the man?"

Silver Grass hesitated. "Perhaps I haven't met him."

Broken Reed smiled. "That means you have but you fear to admit the truth to yourself."

Much as she disliked contradicting her grandmother, Silver Grass shook her head. "I don't think so."

"Olav Johansen walked with you this sun."

"But he is white!"

"What does it matter to the heart?"

Silver Grass felt her own heart leap in her chest at her grandmother's words, but refused to accept them. "I could never trust a white man."

"It's true trust should walk hand-in-hand with love, but this doesn't always happen. I tell you, my granddaughter, that I've lived many winters and learned much. I know men. Lame Wolf tries to be good, but there's something twisted in him that makes him fail—as you've noticed. Olav is white, but he is not twisted inside. He is a good man."

"I believe what you say. I feel in my heart that Olav is good. But I won't marry a white man."

"I hear your words."

That didn't mean Broken Reed believed them, Silver Grass knew. In time, though, her grandmother would come to realize the truth.

Three suns passed before Olav arrived at the wigwam with the promised kettle and a haunch of venison. Since it had been over a moon since there'd been any deer meat in Broken Reed's lodge, it was cause for celebration. Silver Grass was glad her grandmother had invited him to eat with them—it was only proper that they share such good meat with the provider. She told him so.

"I give venison to friends from copper mine, too," he said. "Grandmother is only person ask me to eat. But is all right." He thumped his fist against his chest. "Heart say here is best place for me."

Silver Grass, pleased despite herself, blushed, thankful her grandmother couldn't understand English.

But the old woman's sly glance told Silver Grass that Broken Reed had understood the meaning of Olav's gesture.

"While you fetch water from the river," her grandmother told her, "Olav and I will talk."

Certain their sign language would be about her and not happy about it, Silver Grass hurried to fill the skin pouches with river water. When she returned, she looked from Broken Reed to Olav, unnerved to find identical self-satisfied expressions on both their faces.

"Is there something I should know?" she asked her grandmother in Chippewa.

"I was trying to tell Olav about the tricks Mana-

118

bozho plays on the unwary, but it was too difficult in signs. While the meat cooks we will sit here and you will tell him a Manabozho story, one the snakes don't care about. Then he will understand what I meant."

Some Chippewa stories were sacred, Silver Grass knew, and could be told only during the cold moons when the snakes were asleep, lest they overheard and came to punish the teller. Most of the Manabozho stories were not sacred and could be enjoyed anytime.

She had learned of Manabozho only since coming to live with her grandmother. The Seneca had no spirit quite like this Chippewa shape-changer. Though powerful, he was a mischief-maker and constantly getting into trouble with his magic.

"My grandmother wishes me to tell you a story about Manabozho," she told Olav.

"He brings trouble?" Olav asked.

"Yes. But to himself as frequently as to others." If he knew about the trouble-making, she thought, maybe she'd been wrong in suspecting that he and her grandmother had discussed her while she was getting water. It must have been Manabozho instead.

"Chippewa stories are best told in our tongue," she said, thinking about which story would be the easiest to translate into English and what to leave in and what to take out to make it intelligible to a white man.

"There was a time," she began, "when Manabozho grew hungry. Though the animals were his brothers, he, like us, must eat to live. But instead of telling them he was sorry for what he must do and killing them outright, he decided to end their lives by trickery because trickery was in his nature.

"'We will dance in my lodge,' he told them. 'I will beat the drum and you must all dance past me with your eyes closed—first the feathered ones, then the furred ones.' The animals agreed, and the dance began.

119

"One by one, as they came close to him, Manabozho grabbed each bird and wrung its neck between drumbeats, piling the bodies beside him to be cooked and eaten later. Finally, of the birds, only Mong, the loon, and his cousin Skabewis, the diver, were left. Mong, noticing how quiet it had grown, suspected something was wrong and opened one eye.

"He was just in time to see Manabozho seize a fat swan and wring her neck. 'Skabewis!,' Mong cried. 'Fellow animals! Manabozho is killing the swan; he will kill all of us!'

"The animals opened their eyes, saw it was true, and fled in all directions. Manabozho, angry at being caught out, pursued Mong, determined on revenge. But the loon reached the water's edge and was leaping into the waves when Manabozho caught up with him. The wrathful Manabozho kicked him, a mighty kick that pushed Mong's legs far back on his body, robbed him of his tail, and turned his eyes red. Since that day Mong trusts no one and takes care to stay far away from people."

After a few moments of silence, Olav said, "Tell grandmother I understand now."

Silver Grass did as he'd asked, wondering exactly what he'd meant.

"Swan die in Manabozho story," Olav said. "In Sweden we have different story about Swan Maiden. I tell, ya?"

"I'd enjoy hearing your story," she said.

How well Olav remembered his grandmother telling him about the Swan Maiden when he was a boy. Though he hadn't understood it completely, he'd been caught up in the romance of the tale. In his teens he'd decided the story was for children, but as he grew older he began to appreciate the Swan Maiden story all over again. Still, it was only now that he realized how the

120

anguish of a lost love might affect a man all his days.

He searched for the right English words, sorry that he couldn't tell the tale in Swedish, fearing he wouldn't be able to do it justice in his limited English.

"Much better told in Swedish," he said, "but I try. Here is what happen: One night young man see swan, watch her take off feather cape and become beautiful girl. She bathe in lake. He watch her put on feather cape and fly away. He fall in love. Want only Swan Maiden. No other woman.

"His mother tell him what to do. He wait. Next time he see swan take off feather cape, he steal cape and hide it. She can't change to swan; she don't remember she is swan. He marry her. They are happy.

"Mother warn him never to tell wife she is swan. Man forget. One night he show wife feather cape. She take it from him, put it on, change to swan, forget she is his wife, and fly away. He never see her again. He die of grief."

Silver Grass sighed. "My heart is heavy for the forsaken man. And for the Swan Maiden, too, who'll forever be a swan and never remember the happiness she found as a woman."

Olav took a deep breath, his gaze fixed on Silver Grass. "You like Swan Maiden to me."

He could only hope she understood what he meant.

Chapter 9

By the time the Moon of Strawberries began to wane, no snow remained even in the deepest woods, and the berries ripened. Wild strawberries grow only in the sun, and since the forest covered so much of the land, they were hard to find.

Broken Reed was too feeble to wander far from the wigwam in search of the sweet red berries, but she told Silver Grass of the secret places she knew where windfalls and lightning strikes had toppled or burned pines, leaving an opening among the trees so Father Sun could send his warm light to Mother Earth.

In the warmth just after midday, Silver Grass, carrying a *makuk,* or birchbark box, to put the berries in, reached one of the clearings near a stream the People called *Amik,* Beaver Creek. Broken Reed had insisted she must come to this particular place today, saying the berries here were the biggest and the sweetest.

Four winters had passed since the fire caused by a lightning strike had destroyed many pines in this spot. Now maple saplings had taken root, thriving in the sun as the strawberries did. Soon the little trees would grow tall and the glade would once more become a woodland with trees that shed their leaves nestled among the evergreens.

After many winters, the maples would be big enough to tap and then, in early spring, the People would fill the grove with their sugar lodges and boiling kettles as they made syrup from the sweet sap. Silver Grass enjoyed Boiling Month; it reminded her of her happy childhood with the Seneca, for the sugar maple grew near Lake Ontario as well.

Red among the green ground growth showed her she walked among berries. She was about to drop to her knees and begin picking them when a sharp crack from the stream off to her left froze her. She recognized the noise—a beaver slapping the water with his tail, warning his kin of danger. She was too far from the creek to alarm the beaver, so something else had frightened Brother *Amik*.

She waited, every sense alert, her attention fixed on the stream, relaxing slightly only when she heard the faint splash made by an oar. A canoe of the People. Someone else from the village knew of this clearing. She didn't mind; there were many strawberries, plenty to share.

Listening, she knew when the boat pulled into the bank and was dragged onto the sand by the paddler. A rustling among the willow thicket by the bank told her the person was coming into the clearing. Coming toward her.

The willow branches parted. Silver Grass gasped. She'd been mistaken. Olav Johansen strode across the clearing, a small metal pail in his hand.

"Good berries here, ya?" he said, grinning.

Silver Grass clutched the *makuk* to her, trying to tell herself the pounding of her heart was from having been

123

startled. She knew better. She might be surprised to see him, but the drumbeats of her heart were not for that reason.

Why had he chosen this particular clearing? It was a far row upstream from the mining settlement, and supposedly secret.

Olav's grin disappeared. "You are not happy to see me."

She found her voice. "There are more than enough berries for us both."

He remained silent, watching her.

Unnerved by the warm glow in his gray eyes, she dropped to her knees and began picking. To her consternation, he knelt beside her.

"Wild strawberries, ya?" he said.

"Yes. Do they grow in Sweden?"

He nodded, popped a berry in his mouth, and chewed thoughtfully, his gaze holding hers. "Berries sweeter here, ya."

He held a strawberry to her mouth and she took it from him, tingling from the brush of his fingers against her lips. The berry, tart and sweet at the same time, melted on her tongue as she fought in vain to look away.

His hands cupped her face, strong but gentle, as he leaned to her until his lips touched hers. The kiss, tentative and brief, made her long for more.

"Girls sweeter here, too, ya," Olav murmured.

Flustered, unable to think of any response, she resumed her picking.

"You think I come for berries?" he asked.

"You carry a pail."

"I come to see you. Court you."

"Court me?" she echoed, unsure of the meaning.

She watched him struggle to find the right words to explain. "Grandma say you like me," he said finally.

124

"You know I like you." He shook his head. "Not right word. Love. I love you. Girl like man, he love her, he court her. Bring flowers." He plucked a yellow bloom from the grass and tucked it into her braid.

"He bring gifts." Olav reached into a packet and brought out a small packet, offering it to her.

Bemused, she took the packet and found herself looking at seven metal needles.

"Grandmother say your needles grow old. I bring new."

She smiled, touched by his effort to please her. But she was still wary. "You have a good heart," she said. "If you wish to make me happy, you'll help me fill my *makuk* as well as your pail with berries."

"Man does what she say," he told her, nodding. "We pick berries."

As, side by side, they filled their containers, Silver Grass kept wondering how else a man courted a girl, until at last her curiosity got the better of her.

"I have your flower and your gift, and you've obeyed me," she said. "Is there more to this courting?"

Olav kept on picking. "I show you. Wait." He ate a handful of berries, smiling to himself, leaving Silver Grass more curious than ever.

She thought over everything he'd said. When had her grandmother told Olav that Silver Grass liked him? Though he'd left fresh-killed game for them, he hadn't been inside the wigwam since he'd eaten venison with them. Broken Reed and Olav had been alone then, when she'd gone out to bring water from the river, so it must have been while she was gone. No wonder the two of them had looked so pleased with themselves.

And that was how he'd known where to find her today. Her grandmother had sent her here deliberately after telling Olav where this place was and when Silver Grass would be picking berries.

125

Her spurt of annoyance at what they'd arranged behind her back slowly changed to amusement. What a strange pair of plotters they made—her ancient grandmother and the giant Olav. It was hard to imagine how they'd planned so well when they understood one another only through signs.

She began to chuckle.

Olav looked at her, his eyebrows raised.

"I'm laughing at you and grandmother," she said.

He smiled. "Grandmother wise. Here you are. Here I am." He gestured at the containers. "My pail full. Your *makuk* full." He rose, pulled her to her feet, and held her loosely in his arms. "Now I show you other way man court girl."

Then his lips took full possession of hers, warm and demanding. She felt the urgency of the kiss in the very marrow of her bones, and her blood grew heated with the message of wanting, of need, of desire that it carried. Her heart opened to him, whether she willed it or not, letting her know this was a man she could love, if she would.

She'd never realized how good a man tasted. Olav's mouth held the tang of strawberries mixed with something darker and wilder. She opened her lips to savor the taste with the tip of her tongue. He groaned and pulled her tight against him.

She gloried in his strength; he was more than a match for any man she'd ever met. In contrast to the hardness of his body, his beard was soft, caressing her face.

Though she was yet a maiden, she'd been kissed before—but never like this. Never had a man made her insides melt with longing. She was helpless in his embrace, as though the berry he'd fed her had been a medicine man's love potion.

When he finally released her, she could scarcely stand.

126

"Stop now or we go past courting," he said hoarsely. "You I want very much."

The fire he'd lit within her told her she wanted him, too. She laid the palm of her hand against his chest, over his heart, feeling the rapid beat through the cloth of his shirt. He sighed and closed his eyes for a moment, his hand covering hers. Before he let her go, she felt something pass between them, an unspoken pledge.

"I take you down river in canoe," he said.

She remembered that when he'd arrived, because of the canoe, she'd thought he was one of the People. He wasn't; he was white. How could she have forgotten? How could she have allowed a white man to embrace her? She stepped back.

"I will walk," she told him, crossing her arms over her breasts.

"Get to village faster in canoe."

"I'll walk," she repeated, picking up her *makuk*. She turned and stalked across the clearing toward the trees, not looking back.

When she reached the village, she passed a glowering Lame Wolf on her way to Broken Reed's wigwam. He said nothing, but his expression let her know he'd seen Olav—either on his way up- or downstream. Or perhaps Olav had stopped in the village. Was he still here?

She entered the lodge with trepidation, finding Olav's pailful of strawberries sitting just inside the open flap. She glanced quickly around, but only Broken Reed was there.

It was time she spoke strongly to the old woman. Setting down her *makuk* next to the pail, Silver Grass crossed to where Broken Reed stirred the contents of the new iron kettle over the fire.

"Grandmother," she said, "please let me choose my own man."

127

"You've already chosen; why not admit it?" Broken Reed asked.

"I will not have a white man for a husband!"

"Why not? Your own mother was a white woman."

"Who told you that? She was Seneca!"

"You told me yourself when you repeated your father's stories about her. You also showed me a curl of her hair inside the metal heart you wear around your neck. No one but whites have hair the color of fire. If Fire Hair was Seneca, she was adopted into the tribe just as my son, your grandfather, was."

Silver Grass found no words to refute Broken Reed's arguments. She hadn't forgotten her mother's skin had been paler than that of any other of the People. Her eyes had been pale, too, and her hair fire-red. But her mother had always dressed and behaved like any other Seneca woman, so she'd never thought of her as being white.

Her hand went up to finger the locket around her neck. It came, she remembered, from her mother's people. She could almost hear her mother's words telling her how those ancestors had lived across the Great Salt Sea in England. Silver Grass tried to push the memories away, unwilling to be reminded.

"If your father, my grandson, preferred a white woman for his wife," Broken Reed said, "why do you argue against marrying a white man?"

"Olav hasn't asked me to marry him!"

"He will if you let him."

Would he? Silver Grass wondered.

"In the old days," Broken Reed said, "you would easily have found a brave warrior of the people for your husband. But those days blow away like dry leaves in an autumn wind, leaving barren ground. Can you name the brave warriors of our village?"

Silver Grass pondered. There were few young men in

128

their village, none unmarried. Lame Wolf was more than ten winters older than she was and there were several boys not yet fully grown.

Broken Reed shrugged. "It is as I said, even in Buoy's Ontonagon village, the only one close to us. Maybe in some of the farther villages you might find a man of the people worthy of you. Maybe not. Anyone with eyes can see you yearn for Olav—I think you're afraid of your own desire for him."

Silver Grass reddened, upset that her grandmother could see so clearly into her heart.

Broken Reed smiled. "Trust your heart, it speaks truth."

"I—I'll try," Silver Grass mumbled.

"It is good. Because Olav visits our lodge three suns from now."

An image of Lame Wolf's scowling face flashed into Silver Grass's mind for a moment, then vanished, replaced by Olav's, his eyes warm and glowing. No matter how much she might protest his coming to Broken Reed, she knew she could hardly wait to see Olav again.

In his nearly finished log cabin, every inch built by his own hands, Olav Johansen frowned at the letter lying on the pine table. Since it was from the Reverend Sven Mattson, his former pastor, he'd expected the letter to come from Sweden; but it had been mailed in Ohio, one of the United States. And the fact that his pastor was now in Ohio was not the only surprise the letter contained. To save his life, Olav couldn't recall saying the words Pastor Mattson claimed he had.

"My small congregation and I are newly arrived in Ohio," the pastor had written. "You'll be pleased to hear that your fiancée, Freda Lindstrom, is one of us.

You may write to her in care of me to let her know when you'll be joining us."

Fiancée? He'd never formally asked for Freda's hand in marriage. Because they'd been friends since childhood, others had always assumed they'd one day marry. Perhaps they would have if he'd never left Sweden. Still, to the best of his knowledge, he hadn't asked Freda to be his wife.

And now that he'd met Silver Grass, he never would. Freda was a cheerful, attractive young woman, a good housekeeper, and honest and intelligent as well. But for him she lacked the mystery and magic that made Silver Grass his Swan Maiden.

The minister rather than Freda must have made the mistake. He'd have to write and tell Pastor Mattson he had no intention of marrying Freda and that he planned to remain where he was rather than joining them in Ohio. It wasn't a letter he looked forward to composing because he knew whatever words he used, he'd upset the minister and hurt Freda.

But, damn it, he'd never offered to marry her in the first place. The pastor was well meaning, but he should have minded his own business.

The letter could wait until he'd seen Silver Grass again. He fell asleep each night reliving how she'd felt in his arms and rejoicing in how passionately she'd responded to his kiss. He counted the hours until he could hold her once more. How lucky he was that the old grandmother liked him.

He wondered if the Chippewa man who'd glared at him so darkly when he'd left the pail of strawberries with Broken Reed was a suitor rejected by Silver Grass. She was too beautiful not to have had suitors, but he thought he was her only one at present. God grant that he be successful; he couldn't live without her.

The scowling Chippewa didn't bother him any more

than Alex Fortrain's warning not to cross him. He didn't start fights, but he had faith in his ability to handle any man who threatened him or someone he loved.

He left the letter where it lay and reached for his boots. Time to go to work. The job paid very well, and he wished he didn't dislike drilling for copper. Then, again, it really wasn't the drilling he hated—hadn't he already made several improvements on the drills they used at the Boston Mine, making them easier to handle and more effective to use? He'd always been good with tools. What bothered him was having to work underground; he was no troll that he should enjoy grubbing in the rock tunnels of the mine. He was a man, and the open air better suited Olav Johansen, if he had a choice.

When the day came to visit Broken Reed's lodge, Olav scrubbed himself in the stream that ran by his cabin—he'd moved out of the boardinghouse and into the cabin as soon as he'd finished the roof. For privacy he'd deliberately chosen a location on the opposite side of the Iron River from the mining settlement and some ways from the town.

Once he was clean, he put on freshly washed clothes, and, carrying his fishing pole, walked down to where his canoe was pulled onto the bank of the stream. He'd bought the canoe cheaply from an ancient Chippewa who lived in the Ontonagon village, paying the old man more to teach him to patch the birchbark than he had for the canoe itself. Olav considered it a bargain. He'd never handled a more responsive boat.

He removed his boots before climbing in, laying them carefully in the bottom, afraid of damaging the birchbark. He paddled upstream in his stocking feet to where water cascaded into a small pool, beached the canoe, and fished until he had seven fat trout on a string. He portaged around the small rapids and continued to paddle upstream until he was near the Chippewa village. Since this stream didn't join Iron River, he had to walk. Leaving his canoe hidden by brush as the old man from Ontonagon had advised him always to do, Olav struck out for the village with his string of fish.

The village dogs, barking and snarling, came to meet him, staying carefully out of kicking range. Tiny naked children of both sexes joined the dogs, escorting him into the village. As soon as he saw Silver Grass, seated on a mat outside the wigwam sewing, his heart began to thunder in his chest. Broken Reed appeared in the opening of the lodge, smiling as he handed her the fish. She spoke, but his attention remained fixed on Silver Grass.

She rose gracefully. "You are welcome in my grandmother's lodge," she said with downcast eyes. "She says you are good-hearted to bring us a gift of trout."

He willed her to look at him, but she would not. The morning was warm; it was too lovely a day to sit inside the wigwam, but he didn't enjoy being goggled at and listened to by every child in the village while he tried to talk to Silver Grass.

"We take walk," he said firmly, hoping she'd agree.

She hesitated before nodding slightly.

He decided to bring her to the canoe. They could drift downstream to the falls, where he'd try to persuade her to wade in the pool—among other things. He was all but trembling with his eagerness to take her in his arms.

He had no trouble convincing her to climb into the canoe. She smiled as she watched him remove his boots.

"You need moccasins when you paddle a boat of the People," she said.

"No one to make me moccasins," he said.

She flushed and looked away, saying nothing until they'd traveled downstream for a time and a blue-gray bird with a jaunty crest swooped from the bank to their right and hovered above the stream. "Kingfisher," she murmured.

After the canoe was well past, the kingfisher dived into the water, rising almost immediately with a fish struggling in his long black bill.

"Brother Kingfisher nests in the banks," she said. "Kingfisher's a favorite of Manabozho. Maybe Manabozho lurks nearby, watching."

He saw her slight smile and smiled himself. She was teasing him. "He won't trick me."

"With Manabozho, who knows?"

"Woodpecker with red head live in dead pine by cabin I build," he said. "Make more noise than my hammer."

"That's Brother *Mama*. He is noisy."

He'd hoped she'd ask about the cabin and was disappointed because she hadn't. I'm building it for you, he wanted to say. For you and me. For us to live in. As he tried to think of another way to mention the cabin in casual conversation, he heard the sound of fast water ahead and knew they neared the rapids.

"Rapids come," he said. "We beach canoe, wade in pool below."

"I'd like that."

His heart lifted. He was aching to touch her. First he'd take her hand as they waded together. Then— He paused, considering. Be patient, he warned himself. She's shy, don't alarm her.

He left his boots in the canoe and climbed down the bank alongside the waterfall in his stocking feet, sitting on a rock at the bottom to remove the socks and roll up his pants legs. Silver Grass bent to take off her moccasins, then gathered up folds of her long blue tradecloth skirt with one hand, revealing shapely calves. He tried not to stare as he reached for her free hand to draw her into the pool.

Silver Grass was not a tiny woman, and he knew she was strong and healthy, but when his hand closed over hers, he marveled at how small and fragile it felt within his grasp. I'll look after you and keep you safe always, he wanted to tell her. By God, he *would* tell her!

As Olav opened his mouth to speak, Silver Grass screamed and jerked at his hand, pulling him off balance. As he fell, before he hit the water, pain pierced his left shoulder. He heard a man shout above the roar of the rapids, heard Silver Grass cry out again, and then water washed over him.

Her firm grasp helped him struggle to his feet. Almost immediately she let go of him and his freed right hand sought the source of the pain in his left shoulder. The point of the arrowhead thrusting through his skin scratched his palm.

He'd been shot! Casting a quick glance around him, he saw nothing threatening. "Silver Grass!" he cried in panic, noticing her bending over at the far side of the pool. Had she been wounded, too? He splashed to her side.

"Help me," she ordered.

He reached for her despite the blinding pain in his shoulder, but she shrugged him off.

"Help me pull him out before he drowns," she cried.

Then he saw the man whose head she'd raised above the water and he crouched to lift him, dragging the limp body onto the bank. When he knelt beside the man he realized he'd seen him before—the scowling Chippewa from the village who now lay motionless with blood trickling from multiple cuts on his face and head. The man stunk of whiskey.

"Drunk," Olav muttered.

"Lame Wolf shot you from the top—" Silver Grass pointed up at the rapids—"and then he fell over the edge. He could have been killed."

The man moaned and opened his eyes, struggled to rise, and then fell back and lay still. Olav saw that he breathed without effort. Not dead but dead drunk.

"Thanks to us he'll live," Silver Grass said. "He'd have drowned if we hadn't pulled him to shore. I mean to tell him so." She shook the man's shoulder, spoke angry words in Chippewa, then rose to her feet.

"Come," she ordered Olav. "You lose blood. The arrow must be cut out. I'll paddle you back to the village and—"

"Not village. Go to my cabin. Closer. Easier downstream." He started to rise and staggered, lightheaded. Blood trickled down his arm and dripped from his fingers.

"Sit," she commanded. "I'll fetch the canoe."

Olav fought to hang on to consciousness as she paddled in silence downstream. He knew he had to walk from the canoe to the cabin because he was far too heavy for her to manage otherwise. As it was, he had to lean heavily on her the last few feet. She got him to his cot, where he collapsed, blacking out for a time.

When he came to, she was kneeling beside him. His left arm hung over the edge of the bed because of the arrow. On a stool pulled up beside her she'd placed a pan of water and some leaves he didn't recognize. Silver Grass grasped the arrowhead in one hand, a knife in the other. The knife was his, honed, as he well knew, razor sharp.

He braced himself, waiting, choosing to watch her face rather than what she was doing. Eyes intent, she raised the knife, her hand. To his surprise she didn't dig into his flesh. A moment later, when she dropped the arrowhead on the bed, he saw she'd cut through the wooden shaft of the arrow just behind the joining of the arrowhead. Before he quite understood her next move, she grasped the shaft extending behind his shoulder and yanked. He clamped his lips shut on his yelp, but the pain didn't last long. Without the arrowhead, the shaft pulled out easily.

I should have realized she'd know the right way, he thought groggily, drifting in and out of consciousness. He was vaguely aware of feeling cool wetness on his shoulder and hearing her soft voice telling him what she did.

"Water cleanses, a clean wound heals," she said. "The leaves stop the bleeding. I'll take good care of you, Olav."

The sound of his name on her tongue made him smile, dazed and weak as he was. He slipped into sleep without fighting against it.

When he woke, the cabin was dark except for a small blaze, in the fireplace which he was proud he'd built. Confused, he couldn't recall lighting the fire. Then she moved and he saw her, saw Silver Grass sitting on a stool stirring a pot over his fire, just as he'd dreamed she would one day. He decided he must still be dreaming until a twinge of pain in his shoulder reminded him of what had happened to bring her here.

"Silver Grass," he whispered.

She turned toward him. "The cornmeal is cooked," she said. "I will feed you."

He didn't feel as weak as before and he thought he could manage by himself but decided not to say so and miss the intimate delight of having her spoon the food into his mouth.

He ate two bowls of cornmeal mush sweetened with crumbs from his brown sugar loaf, feeding himself the second helping. He would have eaten more, but he knew Chippewa custom prevented her from taking any food until the man had had his fill. He lay watching her eat, his head propped on the pillow he'd made by stuffing an empty flour sack with cedar fronds.

After she finished, she returned to sit on the stool beside his bed. "I saw Lame Wolf with his bow at the top of the falls," she said, "but my warning came too late."

"Not too late," he said. "You pulled me down. Saved my life."

"He was drinking firewater, otherwise he wouldn't have tried to kill you."

Olav wasn't so sure. "He is jealous."

She sighed. "Lame Wolf is an old friend. He helped me find Grandmother."

"Find Grandmother?" Olav echoed, not understanding.

He listened in amazement as she told how she and her father had set out on the long journey from the shores of Lake Ontario to Lake Superior and how her father had died on the way, leaving her to travel alone.

"Lame Wolf found me and brought me to the Chippewa village," she finished. "I'll always be grateful to him. But—" She paused and shook her head.

Being grateful to Lame Wolf wasn't the same as loving the man, Olav told himself. He wondered how she felt about him but feared to ask.

"You have much courage," he told her instead.

"Your strength comes back," she said. "You don't need my help."

"You stay here tonight," he said in alarm. "Not good to travel in dark."

She nodded. "I'll leave in the morning."

"Only one bed."

"I'll sleep on a blanket by the fire." She started to rise from the stool.

137

He knew the bed was too small for the two of them and, even if it hadn't been, he wouldn't have expected her to agree to share it with him. Yet his unsatisfied need to hold her gnawed at him.

"Kiss me, my Swan Maiden," he said softly.

She leaned over him and hesitantly touched her mouth to his. His right hand rose to her nape, pressing her closer so the kiss deepened. He'd intended no more, but the sweetness of her lips kindled his desire. Before either of them realized what he meant to do, he pulled her down on top of him, then eased her to his right side, tucked between him and the wall.

"Oh, God, how I love you," he said hoarsely. "I will never let you go."

Chapter 10

Silver Grass, nestled next to Olav, had no urge to fight free of him. Though she'd tried to deny her need to have him hold her, she'd wanted him to touch her from the moment she'd seen him outside her grandmother's wigwam. But she worried about his injury.

"Your shoulder?" she murmured.

"You heal me," he said, covering her lips with his.

She melted into his warmth, yielding like the snow to the heat of the sun. How was it a kiss could be so powerful? No, not *a* kiss, *his* kiss. Drumbeats of need thrummed through her, desires she'd never known until this man had taken her into his arms.

His lips left hers to travel along her throat in a tingling passage. "My beautiful swan," he murmured into her ear.

For him she would willingly be *Monahbezee,* the swan; she would gladly remove her cloak of feathers and lie naked beside him. And she would never fly away from him.

He shifted, reaching for her with both arms, and she felt him flinch. Hearing his muffled gasp of pain, she understood he'd forgotten about his injury until he'd tried to move his left arm. He muttered words she didn't understand.

You damn fool, Johansen, Olav told himself. Wait! With that arrow hole in your shoulder you don't dare to go on loving her tonight. The first time for any woman should be perfect, should be beautiful. And she is not merely any woman, she's your Swan Maiden, the loveliest woman in the world. How can you make the right kind of love with her when you can use only one arm?

Ah, but it was difficult to stop when every inch of him yearned for more. She wanted more, too, he sensed, making it all the harder.

"We sleep now," he whispered into her ear.

He echoed her sigh. Since she was yet a maiden and he was not fluent in English, there was no easy way for him to gloss over or adequately explain why they must stop.

"Stay with me," he said, when he felt her move as though to get up. He was reluctant to relinquish the feel of her soft curves against him.

When she relaxed he took a deep breath of relief, inhaling her scent with pleasure. She smelled not only of the leaves she'd used to poultice his shoulder, but of the fire she'd made and of herself, an earthy female odor that was more provocative than any French perfume. He cursed Lame Wolf. If it hadn't been for that jealous Chippewa, Silver Grass would now be completely his.

He fell asleep with her cuddled next to him.

Silver Grass woke, coming immediately alert, aware something was wrong. She listened but there was no sound foretelling danger. The coals in the fireplace winked redly at her, giving enough illumination for her to see that no threat lurked within the cabin. What was it she sensed?

She felt very warm—too warm. Beside her, Olav

radiated heat like Father Sun himself. Silver Grass bit her lip. Fever. A bad sign. As she'd feared, the arrow wound was not healing cleanly.

She eased away from him and crept as quietly as possible over the bottom of the bed to the floor. As soon as dawn grayed the sky she would seek the bark of the willow to brew into a bitter drink to help his fever. There was nothing to be done for the wound itself, other than to wash it often with water. He'd need meat broth for strength, so she must set rabbit snares, the way her father had taught her.

Olav's boots had leather thongs, she'd use them. And she'd noticed a small clearing near the creek where blackberry bushes grew—there'd be a rabbit run nearby. Alder saplings sprouted close by the bushes. It would be easy to bend one across the run and set it into a notch cut into another sapling with Olav's sharp knife. She'd make a loop in a thong and suspend the thong from the tip of the bent sapling so that part of the loop rested on the ground. A rabbit hopping into the loop would release the bent sapling from the notch and the tree would spring upright with the rabbit caught in the tightened loop.

Later, she managed to coax Olav to drink the willow medicine she'd brewed and he was able to stagger outside to relieve himself. She washed his wound, noting the red puffiness with dismay. By the time the long shadows of evening crept close, he was tossing on his bed, muttering and sometimes shouting in his own tongue. He didn't seem to know her and she couldn't get him to swallow any of her rabbit broth.

Using a blanket for a pallet, she lay beside his bed that night. Sometime in the darkness he sat up, shouting his strange words. When she tried to quiet him, he struck at her and she knew the fever had taken him to that strange and fearful nightmare land where everyone is an enemy. Realizing she couldn't coax him

141

to swallow the willow brew while he remained in the fever country, she sat on the blanket and began singing soft and low a medicine song in the tongue of the People, weaving her healing words through his hoarse shouts:

Umbu, sa	Come, behold
Bebamamoyan	I am gathering
Migwun	The feather of
Geminwunac	The rain bird
Dedabicac	Birds fly low over earth
Bebamamoyan . . .	I am gathering . . .

Over and over she sang the soothing words until at last his ranting stopped and she knew her song had reached him. Now she must bring him back. She began another, first in her tongue, then in English:

Na	Listen
Kiblin	I have been waiting for you
Mewicu	A long time
Ninimuce	My love
Na . . .	Listen . . .

After repeating the words four times, she paused.
"Silver Grass?" he whispered.
She rose and persuaded him to drink the bitter fever medicine.
In the morning Olav was weak, but himself. Yellow matter drained from the wound when Silver Grass washed it, and she nodded with satisfaction.
"Now you will begin to heal," she told him as she fed him rabbit broth.
He slept most of the day.

*   *   *

142

Olav woke to find the cabin shadowed by early evening. He had a confused memory of unpleasant dreams of creeping through fetid underground tunnels with the fiery breath of dragons singeing him from behind while from both sides and ahead dark and deadly bowmen shot flaming arrows at him. Struggle though he might, he found no way out.

Then a soft and gentle rain began to fall, a rain that changed to a shower of swan feathers, white and cool. A woman's voice beckoned him. "Come," she sang. "Listen. My love," she called to him.

And the sound of her voice led him from the darkness into the light.

As he remembered, his gaze fixed on the open cabin door. There she sat, the woman of his dreams. "Silver Grass," he called.

She rose and glided toward him, her movements as graceful as a dancer's. Olav eased himself up onto his pillows, inwardly cursing his painful left shoulder, wishing he didn't stink of sickness and fever.

"You're stronger," she told him, smiling. "When the sun rises again you'll no longer need me to care for you."

He didn't want her to leave his cabin . . . ever. Yet he hesitated to ask her to stay because he'd recovered enough to manage for himself while alone in her wigwam the old grandmother waited. She needed Silver Grass's help to survive.

"Stay tonight," he said. "Don't leave in darkness."

She nodded. "I don't wish to travel at night. None of the People like to. Evil spirits come with darkness and lay traps for the unwary."

The white paper on the desk caught his eye. The letter from Pastor Mattson. He kept forgetting that, wonderful as she was, Silver Grass wasn't a Christian. Her Kitchi Manitou might be the same as his God, but

143

her beliefs were otherwise very different from his. The minister would be appalled, but as for him, he didn't care.

"I'll bring you a bowl of stew," she said.

He caught her hand, urging her down onto the bed. "Sit by me. I want to look at you."

She blushed, glancing away from him. He ran his forefinger along her cheek to her throat, encountering a gold chain.

"What is this?" he asked.

She hesitated, then reached under her tunic and brought forth a golden heart set with gems. "My mother's locket," she told him. "It was her grandmother's." She pressed a catch and the locket opened, revealing a lock of hair. "My mother's."

He stared in surprise at the hair. "Red," he muttered as much to himself as to her.

Silver Grass smiled. "My father's people called her Fire Hair. She was very beautiful."

Olav couldn't help but wonder if the woman with red hair who'd owned this locket might not have been a white captive. It would explain how Silver Grass spoke such good English.

"Fire Hair," he repeated. "She had another name?"

Frowning, Silver Grass rose. "You must eat." She crossed to where the kettle sat on its crossbar over the fire.

As he spooned up the best rabbit stew he'd ever tasted, Olav continued to wonder about her mother, but he asked no more questions.

Silver Grass refused to share his bed and also refused his offer to let her have the bed alone, insisting she preferred her blanket pallet by the fire.

"In my grandmother's lodge we have no beds such as yours," she told him. "You will sleep better in the bed. Sleep brings back strength."

He couldn't wait to regain his. Though he felt feverish in the night, he rested well enough. When he woke to the hammering of the woodpecker outside the cabin, the sun was up and Silver Grass was gone. Though he'd known she would be, still he felt bereft.

"Lame Wolf has left our village," Broken Reed told Silver Grass on her return. "He visits relatives among the Pillagers."

The Pillagers were a Chippewa clan living three sleeps to the west. Silver Grass hoped Lame Wolf would decide to remain there.

"How is Olav?" her grandmother asked. "Since you are back so soon, I know his wound can't be a bad one."

She was unsurprised that Broken Reed knew what had happened. Word spread quickly among the People. "He is healing," she said.

"It is good that he'll be able to hunt again soon. We have little food."

No money remained, Silver Grass knew. She'd spent every penny on badly needed supplies and had no more maple sugar cakes to sell.

As if reading her mind, Broken Reed said, "I've been weaving baskets. You will help me and then you can offer them to the whites."

Silver Grass nodded. Secretly, she dreaded returning to the miners' town, but she knew there was little choice. Soon blueberries and raspberries and plums would ripen. And when the time came to pick the corn and beans she'd planted, the wild rice would also be ready to harvest; but in the meantime they'd need food.

As she sat on a mat outside the wigwam sewing beaded leaf and flower designs onto her grandmother's baskets, her thoughts were of Olav. Her cheeks flushed as she recalled how she'd felt when he'd held her next to

145

him in his bed. What would happen when she saw him again?

Olav reported to the mine office four days after being shot by Lame Wolf's arrow.

"You can't handle a drill with a goddamn hole in your left shoulder," the shaft boss told him.

"I can drill with one hand," Olav said, flexing his right arm.

The boss eyed his massive muscles, finally shrugging. "You want to give it a try, go ahead. Old Fortrain don't care how in hell we get the ore out as long as it gets out."

By the end of the following week, Olav was able, without too much pain, to use his left hand to steady the drill. He was glad the exertion didn't seem to slow the healing because drilling paid better than most of the mine jobs and he was in a hurry to earn enough money to finish the cabin properly for his bride.

He knew he hadn't quite regained his strength because he dropped into bed at night so tired he was asleep almost before his head hit the pillow. He did nothing but work, eat, and sleep ... and dream of Silver Grass. God, how he longed to see her. By next Saturday he'd have made up the time he missed and then, ah, then ...

Early Friday morning he left the cabin, whistling as he walked to the mine. The sun was just rising when he reached the town, there joining other men heading for work.

"Ya hear about Mimi?" a short and stocky ore loader named Bill asked one of the other miners. "Got beat up pretty bad last night."

"That bastard's meaner'n skunk shit," the other man muttered, glancing around. "I mean, she's only a whore'n all, but it wouldn't surprise me none if he

146

treated his own ma just as rotten."

"Who beat Mimi?" Olav asked Bill, though he thought he already knew.

"Hell, ya don't need t'ask," Bill said. "We only got one bugger up here that bad."

"He's the nastiest bit o' work I ever seen in me life," the other man said. "Ya can't claim he takes after his pa, neither. His old man's a tough son-of-a-bitch, all right, but he ain't low-down dirty mean."

Olav nodded. Alex Fortrain, sure as shooting. The mine superintendent's son. In Sweden men sometimes beat their wives, but Olav had been raised to believe a man should never hit a woman and, by God, he never would.

When he reached the shaft, Olav paused, as he always did, bracing himself. He didn't like being underground, and he had to force himself to walk down the slanting tunnel into darkness lit only by the men's lanterns. Once he reached his work area and started drilling it wasn't so bad, but he couldn't help thinking of what he did as troll's work, not man's work.

He wasn't certain how long he'd been drilling when he heard someone shout, "She's flooding!"

At the same moment, water swirled around his boots and he knew one of the drillers had broken through rock into a spring or underground stream, one of the dreaded nightmares of miners. As the water poured in, he grabbed his lantern, holding it high, and slogged through the darkness as fast as he could toward the entrance shaft.

In his fever, he'd had a dream of being trapped underground and menaced by fire, not water. But the water, now above his thighs and rising, was no dream.

"Is that you, Swede?" a man called.

"Ya." In vain he searched the darkness for a light. The feeble rays of his lantern revealed no one. "Where are you?" he demanded.

"Up the left tunnel. Fell. Dropped my lantern. Hurt my leg." Desperation tinged the voice he recognized as Bill's. "For the love of God, help me, Swede."

He'd passed the left tunnel. And the water had reached his waist. Olav hesitated. He could make it out. If he tried to find Bill, maybe not. Shaking his head, he turned back and plunged into the left tunnel.

He found the short and stocky Bill clinging to a rock, the water almost to his neck. "Hang onto me," Olav ordered as he fought his way out of the left tunnel.

Struggling against the flow of the water to return to the entrance shaft, he lost his grip on the lantern. It slipped into the water, leaving them in darkness.

"We're goners," Bill mumbled.

"No!" Olav was determined not to die, drowned like a rat in this troll's cavern. Feeling along the wall of the tunnel, he found his way back into the entrance shaft, Bill floating along behind, gripping Olav's neck and half-strangling him.

Just as the water reached Olav's armpits, he saw light ahead but stumbled and fell before reaching the entrance. The water caught him in its wet embrace, tearing Bill loose and tumbling him head over heels in its furious race to escape. Choking, he tried to hold his breath as he fought to reach the surface.

Something grabbed him. He tried to struggle loose but could not. Then he was dragged up like a hooked fish. His feet found rock; he staggered erect and discovered he was in the open air. Two of the miners had pulled him from the water surging and foaming from the mine's adit. Bill crouched on his knees a few feet away, gasping and coughing.

As soon as he regained his breath, Olav looked around, counting the water-soaked men clustered near the mouth of the mine. Ten. Not all of them had made it to safety. He waited with the survivors hoping the others, by some miracle, might be washed out alive.

After the first of the bodies was fished from the water, Bill limped over and clapped him on the back. "Wasn't for Swede here, you'd be hauling me out drownded dead like that," he announced. "Came back for me, Swede did."

Embarrassed, Olav shrugged. When it became obvious there were no more survivors, he slipped away, intending to return to his cabin. As he passed through town, he was stopped at the river by two of the women from the whorehouse. Though he'd never been a customer, he knew their names. Hallie was the redhead, and they called the tough-looking blonde Tabaccy because she chewed tobacco like a man.

"Trouble up at the mine, hey?" Tabaccy said.

"Mine flooded," he said.

"Yeah, you look kinda wet. Many get drownded?"

"Some." He didn't want to talk about it.

"Too bad that piss-poor excuse for a man wasn't inside when it happened," Hallie said. "Alex, I mean."

Tabaccy spat a brown stream into the river. "He don't deserve to live, but drownding's too good for him." She eyed Olav, looking him up and down until he shifted uneasily from one foot to the other. Finally she nodded. "Mixing in other folks' business gets a gal in trouble, so I don't. As a rule. Gonna break that rule. That squaw of yourn was in town today."

"Selling baskets," Hallie put in. "I bought one with beads and—"

Tabaccy flashed her a look that shut Hallie up abruptly.

Olav tensed. "Silver Grass was in town?"

"What I said, ain't it? When she left, she went that way." Tabaccy jerked her thumb toward the river. "Thought she was going to that cabin of yourn to meet you. Didn't know you was down in the mine, so I figured you'd take care of things. Hope it's not too late."

"Too late?" Olav echoed, apprehension spearing through him.

"*He* followed her," Hallie said. "Alex." She reached up, extracted a slim, wicked-looking dagger from her ornate coils of hair, and offered it to Olav. "Take this; that pig-sticker he carries ain't for show."

Olav scarcely heard her for the blood thundering in his head. Ignoring the dagger, he raced for the wooden bridge spanning the river, pounded across, and ran toward his cabin.

When she saw Olav wasn't at home, Silver Grass laid the pair of moccasins she'd made for him at the bottom of his bed and slipped from the cabin, happily anticipating his surprise when he came in from the mine and found them. Rather than crossing back over the bridge, she decided to avoid the town, take the trail along the east bank of the river, and use the stepping stones near the village to get across to her grandmother's lodge.

She hadn't walked far when she heard noises behind her that warned something was coming. Someone. A white man, for one of the People would move silently. Thinking of Olav's massive boots made her smile. When he walked along a trail, every living thing within earshot heard him. Perhaps wearing her moccasins would help him to be quieter, but probably not by much.

Was it Olav? Had he returned to the cabin, found her gift, and come in search of her? She paused, frowning. Wouldn't he be more likely to take the canoe to her village? She'd seen where he'd hidden it in the brush by the stream that ran past the cabin.

Uncertain, Silver Grass stepped off the trail, concealed herself in a willow thicket beside the river, and waited. If Olav appeared, she'd leap out and startle him as a joke. If the noisy walker wasn't Olav, then she'd remain hidden.

A snuffling grunt from the riverbank tensed her. She peered cautiously through the willow leaves and stiffened. Little more than four paces away, a mother bear and her cub splashed in the shallows. Already the mother's head was lifted, sniffing for scent. Aware the wind was not in her favor, Silver Grass eased from the thicket, moving away from the river toward the trail, glancing back to make certain the bear wasn't following. Whoever walked along the trail couldn't be as dangerous as a *mukwah* protecting her cub.

When she turned her head, she found herself face-to-face with the man called Alex. Taken by surprise, she hesitated, rather than immediately fleeing. She was sure she could outrun him, but it was too late to find out. Before she could move, he grabbed her arm and shoved it behind her back, twisting it up painfully as he yanked her off the trail, shoving her ahead of him away from the river and into a stand of pine. He flung her onto the brown needles. Grasping the copper-studded hilt of a knife, he pulled it from the sheath at his belt and knelt beside her.

"Don't think I won't use it if I have to," he told her, his thin smile chilling.

Silver Grass stared up at the knife's long blade, a blade for killing, sharpened on both edges.

"And now we'll have a bit of fun," Alex said. "Let's see how quick you can get your clothes off without sitting up."

Terrified as she was, she scowled at him rather than obeying.

He tipped the knife so the blade was poised over her

throat. "No Indian squaw defies me. Snap to it or I'll cut your damn clothes off."

The thought of him slashing at her with that blade made her shudder. He wouldn't care if he cut her along with her clothes. The malicious gleam in his eyes told her he might even do it deliberately. What were her chances for escape? They were now too far away from the river to annoy the bear—no hope of *mukwah* charging in to frighten him. No hope of any rescue. Silver Grass swallowed and began unlacing her tunic.

"That's better," he said, watching her avidly.

She undressed as slowly as she dared, the lust glazing his eyes sickening her. When she was naked, he reached over and pinched her nipple hard and painfully, his gaze fixed on her face, waiting for her to cry out. She did not, would not. She glared her hate at him.

He shoved her legs apart and knelt between them. Keeping a careful grip on the knife hilt with his right hand, he fumbled at his white man's trousers with his left, opening the front. Sickened by the thought of what he meant to do to her, she jerked away from him.

Alex touched the tip of the knife to her thigh and she felt the sting of a shallow cut, felt the trickle of blood.

"Fight me and there'll be more of the same," he warned.

I'd rather die than lie with him, she told herself.

Yet she feared if she struggled he wouldn't kill her but would use the knife only to mutilate and wound. A voice deep within warned her that he wanted an excuse to slash open her flesh and gloat as she bled.

"Now, you little bitch," he said hoarsely.

Helplessly, she watched him poise himself above her, her heart hammering in terror. Holding herself rigid, she closed her eyes, biting her lip to keep from making any sound.

He made a strange noise, like a man being choked.

When nothing else happened, her eyes popped open in time to see Alex yanked up and away from her.

"I kill you!" Olav shouted.

Silver Grass scrambled to her feet, grabbed her tunic, and backed away from the two men wrestling on the ground in front of her. Olav gripped Alex's wrist so he couldn't use the knife, but he held onto it while he hammered at Olav with his other fist. She slid the tunic over her head and looked around for a weapon. There wasn't a rock in sight. Nothing she saw was of use. And, with the two men rolling back and forth as they pounded at one another, she'd have trouble trying to stun Alex if she did find a sharp and heavy rock.

She gasped in horror when Alex broke free and leaped to his feet. Olav was up in an instant and they circled each other, Alex thrusting with the knife, Olav avoiding the slashes and trying to grab Alex's wrist. In their maneuvering, they worked their way free of the pine grove and onto the trail.

As she followed, she noticed a small black animal come out of the willows on the river side of the trail. The cub! She caught her breath in dismay. The mother wouldn't be far from her baby.

"Mukwah!" she shouted. "Bear!"

Neither man paid the slightest heed. Each was intent only on his opponent.

Chapter 11

"*Mukwah!*" Silver Grass shouted to the oblivious Olav and Alex as they continued to circle each other.

As if summoned by her name, the mother bear charged from the willows toward the men. Silver Grass cringed against a pine trunk as *mukwah* rushed, roaring in rage. She stopped when she reached them, rising to her hind feet behind Alex. Olav, facing the bear, flung himself backward, scrambling away. *Mukwah* reached for Alex, wrapping her front paws around him in a bonecrushing hug.

He screamed, struggling to slash at her with his knife. Her sharp talons dug into his flesh. Blood spurted as her yellow fangs bit into his neck.

Olav rushed to Silver Grass. He grabbed her hand and together they raced for the nearest safe place—his cabin. Once inside with the door barred, he took down his rifle and turned to go out again.

Silver Grass stepped in front of the door. "No," she said. "He can't be saved; *Mukwah* has surely killed him by now. My heart isn't troubled because he's a man who deserved to die. But the bear is still angry, fearful for her cub's safety. If she sees you she'll go after you and you'll kill her to save yourself. Why should she die

154

for trying to protect her baby? Wait. *Mukwah*'s anger will fade and she'll lead her cub away. Then we will go after the dead and return his body to his people."

Olav thought it over, nodded, and set down the gun. The bear had deprived him of the satisfaction of killing Alex Fortrain with his own hands, but he didn't wish to kill her. He put an arm around Silver Grass and drew her to him.

"Did he hurt you?"

"Only a scratch from his knife. You came before he—" She paused.

Rage against Alex rose anew in Olav when he noticed the bloody cut on her leg, inadequately concealed by her tunic, the only garment she wore. Its laces .hung loose, partially revealing her rounded breasts. The sight stirred another emotion in Olav, one more powerful than rage.

Another man had tried to take her from him, had tried to force from her what should only be freely given. That man was dead and he rejoiced.

But his own near brush with death had dissolved his patience. He couldn't wait to possess Silver Grass; he wanted her desperately, he wanted her now. Would she give herself to him?

"Your clothes are wet," she said, easing away to look at him.

"I take off," he said eagerly, releasing her. He untied and kicked off his boots, flung away his shirt, then hesitated before removing his sodden trousers, gazing into her eyes with a wordless appeal.

Silver Grass interpreted his look with no difficulty. Will you have me? his gray eyes asked. Will you take me as your lover?

How different from the ruthless Alex, she thought, a man whose heart was filled with hate. Alex enjoyed giving pain rather than love. What if *mukwah* had not

155

appeared? What if Alex had killed Olav with his knife? Then it would have been forever too late to let Olav know he already had her heart.

But it was not too late. He lived and she could show him how much she loved him. Keeping her gaze locked with his, Silver Grass slipped out of her tunic and stood before him in silent offering.

"You are beautiful," he whispered. Then his trousers were gone and he stood as naked as she.

How strong he was, how good to look at. Unlike many white men, he had little hair on his chest, merely a few soft swirls. His skin was very pale where the sun didn't reach, and its whiteness reminded her of her mother's skin under her tunic.

Not that she found him womanish—how could she when his desire for her was so obvious? Though of a different people, he was a brave and fearless warrior . . . her warrior. She held out her arms and he stepped into them, pulling her close, his lips covering hers in a kiss that made her forget everything else.

Her hands caressed his skin, smooth on his back and shoulders except for the puckered scar of the healing arrow wound. His hardness pressed against her, sending an urgent message of need that sparked an answer deep within her. A fierce wanting, hot and steamy as boiling syrup, seethed through her. Here at last was the man she'd waited for, the man she'd yearned for.

Her breath caught as he scooped her into his arms, carried her to his bed, and eased her gently onto the cover. Now, at last, he would make her his and he would become hers.

It was impossible to have lived years in a Seneca long-house, as she had, without learning what went on under the blanket between husband and wife. Olav, though, didn't attempt to pull her on top of him or to lie

156

over her. Instead, he rested on his side, holding her with one arm. His free hand caressed her breasts, sending tickles of delight through her. Then he put his mouth to her nipple and the strange and wonderful sensation forced whimpers of pleasure from her throat.

His hand dipped lower, his fingers finding the throbbing heat between her legs, caressing her there until she felt she would burst into flame like a *makuk* set too near the fire. She moaned his name.

He eased between her legs, his fingers replaced by his seeking manhood that probed at her softness, easing slowly inside her.

Too slowly. Wanting more, she raised her hips, eagerly seeking what she needed. His hoarse breathing changed to a groan as he lost control and plunged deep within her in a single violent thrust. She felt a flash of near-pain that vanished quickly, swept away by ripples of pleasure that grew more and more intense as they swayed together in a rhythm of love until, like Namid, the Bright Dancer, she reached the stars.

Much later, he murmured into her ear, "Tomorrow we marry."

She wanted no other for a husband. She would belong to him and to no one else for as long as she lived. But there was her grandmother to think of.

"Broken Reed can't live alone," she said.

"I take care of old grandmother. She live here."

Silver Grass sighed. "She won't leave her lodge."

"Then we move wigwam here, beside cabin."

Overcome by happiness, she hugged him close. One caress led to another until he eased her on top of him and they began their star-dance of love all over again.

Broken Reed died in the Moon of Snowshoes. Since the snow-covered ground was frozen deep, the body was wrapped in a deerskin robe and hoisted into a tree where it immediately froze and was also safe from animals. She would be buried in the spring.

For four nights Silver Grass burned a torch beside the tree, keeping a silent vigil for the time it took Broken Reed's spirit to make the journey to the Land of Shadows. She mourned her loss, regretting that her grandmother wouldn't be alive to hold her great-great-grandchild.

The baby, small yet, grew within Silver Grass. The child would, she thought, be born in the Moon of Flowers. It had been in that very moon last year when she'd first known she was attracted to Olav. Yet her grandmother had been far quicker than she to see through his pale skin to the great and generous heart within. Truly their child would have a good father.

Olav had never returned to the mine after the water had been pumped out of the shafts. "No more troll's work for me," he'd told her. Instead, he'd set up as a blacksmith and toolmaker in the town. Since he was the only smith for hundreds of miles, he did well. Silver Grass had never believed she could be so happy.

When the Boiling Moon waxed, the baby inside her had grown so big she could hardly fit into her loosest tunic and her winter bearskin coat. Even her fur-lined moccasins felt tight. Though it wasn't far, Olav had not wanted her to travel to the people's Boiling Camp, but when she'd insisted, he'd finally taken her there himself and helped her set up a wigwam in the maple grove.

Once they were married, Olav had been accepted as one of them by the People of her village. Now he joined the other men in tapping wooden spiles into slashes made in the maple trunks and in hanging birchbark baskets onto the spiles. When the baskets were full of sap, he carried them to the kettle Silver Grass stirred over an outdoor fire, boiling the water from the sap

158

until it thickened into syrup.

It was good to see her people again. The village by the river was deserted in winter because the Chippewa, as was their custom, divided into family groups and set up solitary lodges far apart in the woods so the men of each family would be able, when hunting, to kill enough animals to feed their relatives through the cold moons. At the Boiling Camp, the people came together for the first time since Lake Freezing Moon, November, and there was celebrating.

Silver Grass had always enjoyed Boiling Camp—the rising sap promising spring was on its way, the sweet smell of the syrup, the companionship of the other women as they stirred the thickening syrup after the men had tipped the contents of the kettles into wooden troughs. In the troughs, after steady but gentle stirring, fine grains of maple sugar would form.

Some of the hot syrup went directly into *makuks,* where it would harden into cakes and, always, dabs of syrups were dribbled into the snow for the children.

Silver Grass watched the excited camp children pull the cooling syrup into soft, sticky candy, imagining her baby old enough to run about and join them. She could already tell he'd be large and strong like his father. Would he also have his father's pale hair?

Intent on her own thoughts, she started when Laughing Gull, mother of two of the children, spoke to her.

"It is said Lame Wolf visits in the Ontonagon village."

Silver Grass, having heard the gossip, nodded, saying nothing in return. She doubted Lame Wolf would return here. After all, she was now married, and he must know he'd made a formidable enemy when he'd wounded Olav.

After a time Laughing Gull said, "If you want me, I'll

help when your child is ready to come."

Silver Grass smiled at her gratefully. "It will be good to have a woman with me. I'll send for you."

When the moon became a ghost, the sap began to turn bitter, a sign the weather was warming. The fires were extinguished, the kettles emptied, the spiles removed from the trees, and the camp struck. Dogs were harnessed to loaded *nobugidabans,* toboggans, and the people left for their village beside the river. Since he and Silver Grass had no dogs, Olav pulled their toboggan himself. When it began to snow, he tried to induce Silver Grass to ride on it, along with their belongings.

"I don't feel tired," she told him. "Besides, if no dogs are available, women *pull* toboggans."

Olav hugged her to his side. "Not *my* woman."

He had begun teaching her to speak his native tongue. As they neared the cabin, he started singing a Swedish song, making animal noises—geese honking and ducks quacking—between the words. A song, she decided, that might be sung to a child.

"Do you understand the words?" he asked, pausing.

"I recognized the sounds more than the words," she confessed.

"A child's song. Song ends asking which bird has no voice."

She frowned. "All birds sing their own song."

"Swans don't."

"Swans whistle," she insisted.

"Here, yes. In old country, no."

Since he still called her his Swan Maiden, Silver Grass started to tell him that she had no intention of being one of his silent swans when her attention was caught by the scent of woodsmoke. It came, she was sure, from their cabin. Nobody should be in their cabin. She caught Olav's arm, stopping him.

"Smoke comes from a fire in our cabin," she warned.

He sniffed the air, then scowled. "Wait here. Stay hidden. I go look."

"Be careful. I heard Lame Wolf was seen in Ontonagon."

"He won't surprise me twice."

She watched Olav stride away from her, worrying that he walked into danger. Could the intruder be Lame Wolf? But would he build a fire in the cabin, thus warning them of his presence? She shook her head. He was more wily than that. But if it wasn't Lame Wolf, who could it be? Now that Alex was dead, Olav had no enemies that she knew of.

Time passed. Her apprehension grew when Olav neither returned nor called to her. What had happened? No longer willing to wait, she left the toboggan and began a cautious approach to the cabin, flitting from the trunk of one huge pine to the next. Soon she came within view of the cabin, then within earshot. While she hesitated, peering around a pine trunk, the door of the cabin opened. She froze, watching and listening.

To her amazement, a white woman stood in the doorway, her back to Silver Grass. Olav loomed beyond her, inside the cabin. Who was this? Because the woman spoke in Swedish and was also crying, Silver Grass could understand only some of her words.

"Olav . . . promise . . . sailed from Sweden . . . wife . . . turn me away . . . wife . . . promise . . ." The woman's voice broke and she dropped her head into her hands, weeping.

Olav drew the woman into his arms, holding her tenderly. "My dear Freda," he said in the same tongue, "wait . . . wife . . . Sweden . . ." He paused, staring over Freda's head into the pines.

Silver Grass, unmoving, held her breath until he

161

looked away.

". . . not know," Olav went on, stroking Freda's back, "how to tell . . . many years . . . you and I . . . Silver Grass . . . not my wife . . ."

The sight of him holding this woman of his own people, this Freda, was like a knife piercing Silver Grass's heart. His words came like a shower of arrows, sharp and wounding. *Not his wife.* He meant, she knew, herself.

She and Olav had been married in the way of her people, sacred in her eyes. Now she realized her people's way meant nothing to him. Though he'd told her they'd also be married someday by a minister of his people, they never had. He'd claimed the Blackrobe who visited the town once a moon was the wrong kind of holy man. She'd believed him . . . then.

Watching him pull the sobbing Freda inside the cabin and shut the door, it seemed clear to Silver Grass what the real reason had been. In Sweden, before he'd sailed across the Great Salt Sea, he'd married Freda in the way of *his* people. Freda had come after him, come here to find her husband. Freda, not Silver Grass, was his wife.

Swallowing her grief and humiliation, Silver Grass turned away from the cabin and hurried back to the toboggan. When she reached it, she rolled what supplies she could carry into a blanket and tied the blanket onto her shoulders. Eyes burning with unshed tears, she started toward that part of the forest where she and Broken Reed had lodged the winter before she'd met Olav—their abandoned wigwam would still be there, she hoped.

Because of the thickening snowfall and her anguish, she didn't notice the dark figure who slipped from behind a pine trunk and moved to intercept her. Only when he stepped in front of her did she start in alarm.

162

"Lame Wolf!"

"You leave the white man?" He jerked his head in the direction of the cabin.

"He has a white wife." The words were bitter as willow bark on her tongue.

"I saw her go into the cabin. It doesn't matter. I will take care of you."

She stared at him in consternation, realizing he must have been waiting by the cabin for their return from Boiling Camp. Why? she wondered. But all she said was, "You aren't my husband."

He gestured toward her swollen stomach, then in the direction she was heading, away from the village. "You need a man to hunt for you if you live alone in the woods."

"I want no husband!" she cried.

"I give my word I will be like your brother." His dark eyes, gazing into hers, were clear and sober, evidence he hadn't been drinking firewater. "I will be your child's uncle."

This second reminder of the baby she carried made her pause to consider. Lame Wolf was right—alone, she might not survive. If she died, so would her son. Slowly, reluctantly, she nodded. "I accept your offer, my brother."

"I have your *nobugidaban.*"

He'd left it under a pine. Wordlessly, she untied the blanket filled with supplies that she carried and he packed it onto the toboggan. He gripped the thong handle, pulling, and they fell into step.

In a while, as the snow grew deeper, he stopped, lifted her without asking, and sat her on the laden toboggan. "We'll go faster now," he said.

Sad and tired, Silver Grass didn't argue. Looking back, she saw that the snow, falling thick and fast, would soon cover their tracks completely. Olav couldn't follow her trail; she wasn't so sure he'd even try.

Before they reached the winter wigwam, she roused enough to ask, "Why did you wait by the cabin?"

"To see with my own eyes how the white man treated you. If I saw you were happy, I wouldn't harm him. But if he mistreated you . . ." Lame Wolf didn't finish.

The menace in his voice was clear, making her shudder at the thought of Olav lying mortally wounded. Though he'd betrayed her, she didn't want him dead. "Heed what I say," she told Lame Wolf. "You will not hurt Olav. You will not kill him. I have left him, but I don't wish him harm. Stay away."

"I won't go near him," Lame Wolf agreed.

They reached the winter wigwam at dusk, with the snow still falling. As she rose awkwardly from the toboggan, the exhausted Silver Grass realized she might not have made it here without Lame Wolf's help.

"Your heart is good, my brother," she told him.

They cleaned accumulated debris from the inside of the birchbark lodge, then Lame Wolf pulled the toboggan in and went to gather firewood. On his return, she built a fire in the center pit of the wigwam while he unloaded their supplies. Once the kettle was in place on a tripod, she piled snow in to melt so there'd be water to make a stew from the frozen rabbit carcasses Lame Wolf had in his pack.

After spreading mats to sit on, she dozed while the stew cooked . . .

She glided through the air on wide white wings, her long, graceful neck stretched out in flight. Above, the moon glowed, making a silver pathway over the lake below, a pathway meant for a swan. She spiraled down in the peaceful moonlight, drawn by the silvered water. Lower and lower she dipped.

164

"Monahbezee," a man's voice called, soft and low. "Monahbezee, my beautiful swan, come to me. Come to me, for I am your lover."

For a moment she thought she knew the voice, thought she remembered a lover, and was tempted. Then a wolf howled, high and wavering, his call taken up by his brothers until the night was filled with wolf song and the caressing voice could no longer be heard.

Temptation vanished. She flapped her powerful wings, rising, leaving behind the lake's silver pathway and the man who called to her. As she rose higher and higher she realized a man could never be her lover, for she was a swan.

Forever . . .

Silver Grass woke with her heart aching with loss. And also to the smell of meat cooking and something poking her in the stomach. It took a moment to realize what she smelled was the rabbit stew she'd made for Lame Wolf and herself and what she felt was the baby kicking inside her. As she busied herself stirring the kettle, she did her best to ignore the heartache.

I belong in a wigwam, not a cabin, she told herself. My son will be born as one of the People; he will live his life as one of the People.

While Silver Grass waited for her child to grow large enough to be born, *Kabibonokka,* Old Cold Maker, delayed his return to the north, making the snow cling to Mother Earth like a lover reluctant to depart. Finally the ice broke in the streams, but the Moon of Putting Snowshoes Away was on the wane before the earliest leaves began to unfurl from their tight buds. The sweet scent and the tiny pink flowers of trailing arbutus peeking out from under the forest duff persuaded Silver Grass that Old Cold Maker was gone.

Standing outside the wigwam, breathing in the fresh

smell of new growth, she remembered that "spring" was her mother's word for this time of the year. "Spring," "summer," "autumn," and "winter" were white words. Whites called moons "months"—the waxing Flower Moon was "May" to them.

The whites counted time, her mother had told her once, differently than the People. Not only in words, but in the way they thought. She hadn't understood then and she wasn't certain she did now. She couldn't believe that a man of the People would have betrayed her in the way Olav had.

She'd tried to bury her memories of him and their time together, but never could she bury them deep enough—they always resurfaced. She'd taken herself and their unborn child away, but no matter how hard she tried to forget him, her heart remained with Olav.

She was remembering the caress in his words when he'd called her his Swan Maiden when she felt the first warning cramp of birth. As the cramping eased, she retrieved the deerskin bundle she kept just inside the flap of the wigwam, then made her way toward the creek that flowed through the pines behind the lodge. She'd selected her birthing place many suns before, choosing a slight rise under the shielding limbs of a giant pine that grew near the willows lining the creek.

When she reached the spot, she knelt and spread the deerskin blanket over the brown needles covering the ground and placed within easy reach a small piece of thong, her knife, and a tiny porcupine-quill decorated pouch her great-grandmother had given her. She waited until another cramp passed before propping the *tikinagen,* the baby-carrying board, against the trunk of the pine. Last of all she put a reed mat next to the deerskin.

Lame Wolf had made the carrier for her child and she'd sewn the rabbitskin blankets for it and gathered the dried moss to stuff inside to keep it clean.

She couldn't have done without Lame Wolf. True to his word, he'd treated her like a sister, sleeping across the fire from her and never attempting to caress her. He hunted, bringing home meat for the kettle, and not once had he touched firewater. Her son might not have a father, but he'd have a loving uncle who'd teach him how to become a man of the People.

Yes, she owed Lame Wolf more than she could repay. Why, then, couldn't she give him her heart?

Rising, she began to pace back and forth along the stream bank, pausing to wait out each cramp. When walking became too painful, she returned to the deerskin, pulled up her tunic, and crouched over the mat, waiting. She'd gone with Broken Reed to help village women with births. Now that it was her turn, her great-grandmother was no longer alive to help, and it was hard to be alone.

When the cramping pain became almost continuous, she bit her lip to keep from moaning, wishing the village was closer so she could have sent Lame Wolf to bring Laughing Gull to help her.

Fluid gushed onto the mat, followed by a great, grinding pain coupled with a forceful urge to push. She took a deep breath and bore down, grunting with effort. Just when she thought she could stand no more, the baby slid from her onto the mat. Before she could reach down to wipe his face, he wailed, his voice strong and loud. A moment later she saw how wrong she'd been—she'd given birth not to a son but to a daughter.

A girl! Her heart leaped with a sudden joy, surprising her. She raised her hand to touch the gold locket she wore around her neck, wondering if her mother had been as happy to find she was a girl.

Still squatting, she wiped her crying daughter's face with a piece of blue trader's cloth. After a mild cramp or two, the afterbirth slipped out. Then she knelt, tied the thong tightly around the cord attaching it to the baby, and cut the afterbirth free.

She washed her daughter and herself in the cold creek water, quickly wrapping the baby in rabbit fur. Resting on the deerskin, she opened her tunic and put her howling baby to her breast, marveling at the girl's tiny, perfect fingers. Her fluff of light hair was like her father's. Her eyes were blue, but it was too early to tell if they'd remain that color or darken.

After the child quieted, Silver Grass fastened her into the cradleboard. She'd already dug the hole to bury the afterbirth and had stacked a small cairn of rocks to set over the filled-in hole to prevent animals from digging it up.

Once everything had been cleaned up, she thrust the small pouch into a pocket of the cradleboard. When the baby's birth cord dried and fell off, it would go into this pouch that once had belonged to Silver Grass's grandfather.

"When the village warriors returned, saying my son had been taken captive by the Iroquois," Broken Reed had told Silver Grass when she'd given her the pouch, "I knew he would never return. I took his birth cord from this pouch, buried it, blackened my face, and mourned his death."

As she strapped the cradleboard onto her back, Silver Grass thought she couldn't bear to bury her own child—or even the cord. She sent a plea to Kitchi Manitou that her daughter would live long, would far outlive her.

Lame Wolf was fascinated by the baby. Ten suns later, as he watched her lying naked in the sun on a mat, vigorously waving her arms and legs while Silver Grass cleaned the inside of the cradleboard, he found her name. "See," he said, "her eyes are not blue, they're as

168

green as the new leaves on that elm by the wigwam. The elm is a good tree, strong and useful. We will name her Elm Leaf."

"It will be as you say," Silver Grass told him, pleased with the name, pleased he took such an interest in her daughter. The yearning in his eyes when he looked at her was far less pleasing. He'd made no move to touch her, but she feared it wouldn't be long before he did. What then?

Though she didn't want his touch, didn't want any man's touch, she knew it wasn't fair to Lame Wolf to keep insisting they live as brother and sister. Her heart was full of gratitude for all he'd done for both her and Elm Leaf; why did she still feel as if she were Olav's wife, and that it would be wrong to share another man's blanket for any reason whatsoever?

What was she to do?

Chapter 12

Silver Grass woke with a start, her skin prickling. She lay on her left side, facing the coals of the fire. There was no sound from the baby sleeping next to her. What had roused her? As she held her breath, listening, she saw, in the grayness that comes before dawn, that Lame Wolf was not on his mat on the other side of the fire.

Where was he? Behind her?

In one quick, supple movement, she sat up, turning at the same time so she faced away from the fire. Lame Wolf loomed over her, his desire plain to see. She swallowed, feeling helpless. She could fight him, take a knife to him—but should she? She crossed her arms over her breasts, her gaze fixed on him.

He sighed and took a step back. "We need supplies," he said.

"It is true," she agreed cautiously.

"Now that Elm Leaf has been born, it's safe for me to leave you and bring my pack of furs to the trader."

She knew Lame Wolf had spent the winter trapping north of Kitchigami and had cached his bale of furs near Ontonagon. Guilt wracked her. She had nothing to trade. In the lean days before Elm Leaf's birth, they'd eaten all of her maple sugar cakes. Once more Lame Wolf would provide for the three of them. He gave so much, she gave so little.

Making up her mind, she took a deep breath and said, "When you return, I will welcome you." She couldn't bring herself to say more, but she saw by his sudden smile he understood her meaning.

She forced herself not to edge away when he reached down and slipped his hand around her nape, his fingers caressing her neck. "My canoe will fly over the water," he said before releasing her and leaving the lodge.

In the days that followed the baby occupied much of Silver Grass's time, but she missed Lame Wolf's presence in the lodge. They'd been together for more than two moons and it seemed strange to have no one to talk to in the evenings, no man to prepare food for. At the same time, she dreaded his return. No matter how she felt, she would keep her word, but she cringed at the thought of being held in Lame Wolf's arms.

Yet she worried when he didn't come back as soon as she expected. The Moon of Strawberries was almost full before she heard the splash of a paddle one evening in the stream near the lodge. Silver Grass frowned. Lame Fox must be very tired, his strokes were slow and uneven. The paddling stopped, but he didn't appear.

Leaving Elm Leaf sleeping in her cradleboard inside the lodge, she hurried through the dusk to the creek bank. To her consternation, she found the prow of Lame Wolf's canoe jammed into the muddy bank with him slumped over the oar.

When she touched him, his skin felt hot as fire and she knew he was feverish. "I'll help you to the lodge," she said, concealing her alarm.

"White man's spots," he muttered, scarcely able to walk as they stumbled toward the wigwam.

She didn't understand what he meant until after she'd eased him onto his mat inside the lodge and seen him clearly in the firelight. His skin was covered with red spots, as though he'd been dabbed with vermilion for a celebration. She'd heard of the spotted disease from her grandmother but had never seen it.

"There's little to be done for this white man's disease," Broken Reed had told her. "Sweat houses don't help. Willow bark and wintergreen tea cool the fever but nothing cures the spots. Either they vanish after a time and the sick one recovers—or else the spots remain and he dies. White man's sicknesses are dangerous for the People."

She made Lame Wolf as comfortable as she could, then returned to the creek to pull the canoe safely onto the bank and unload it. By the time she'd carried the supplies to the wigwam, the leaves she'd crushed into water to brew wintergreen tea had released their medicine and its pungent fragrance filled the air.

He swallowed it without protest and then fell into an uneasy asleep. She watched him worriedly as she nursed Elm Leaf, but didn't begin to truly fear for him until later. After Mother Night spread her cloak of darkness over the lodge, Silver Grass brought her mat to his side of the fire and lay down next to him with the baby.

His shouts roused her from sleep. Lame Wolf writhed and twisted on his sleep-mat, calling out incoherent words. She moved the baby's cradleboard out of his reach before trying to coax him to swallow more of the wintergreen tea.

Weak as he was, he fought her as though he believed she was an enemy warrior trying to kill him. Even without touching him, she could feel the heat of his skin, now a fiery red from the combined spots. When she stepped back from him, he ceased struggling.

172

"Sweat bath," he muttered.

Even if Broken Reed hadn't told her sweat baths were useless for the spotted disease, Silver Grass knew there was no way she could get him to the tiny sweat lodge he'd built near the creek.

Since he grew agitated every time she came close to him, she pulled her mat to one side and spoke soothing words, telling him she was near and was trying to help him.

He quieted. *"Neengay,"* he whispered. "Mother."

"Yes," she murmured, "Mother is here. Take your medicine, my good boy."

He managed two swallows of the tea before pushing the cup away. By now his eyes were swollen shut. "Mother, mother, hold me," he begged, his words so slurred she barely understood them.

She sat beside him and pulled his head and shoulders into her lap, cuddling him to her, the heat from his fever all but searing her flesh. His breathing was fast, each breath rasping noisily in his chest. He twitched and shivered in her arms. She'd never seen anyone so sick. How could he ever get well? To keep herself from crying, she crooned to him as she would to Elm Leaf:

> Sleep, go to sleep
> The owl with his big eyes
> Keeps watch
> Close your eyes, my little owlet
> Sleep, go to sleep . . .

Her voice grew hoarse; her arms and then her entire body began to ache; but still she held him and sang. When, near dawn, he at last relaxed in her arms, she breathed a sigh of relief. Carefully she eased his head and shoulders from her lap onto his sleeping mat. As she did, his eyelids opened, revealing the blank and

173

silent stare of the dead. He'd fallen into the final sleep.

She found herself too exhausted to weep.

When Father Sun rose, she dug Lame Wolf's grave by the riverbank where the ground was soft. When she was finished, she returned to the wigwam and rolled his body onto a deerskin blanket. She laid his bow and arrows beside him, the best of his clothes, and his favorite knife. Wrapping the deerskin around him, she bound it with thongs and then dragged the laden deerskin to the grave.

When his wrapped body rested at the bottom of the hole, she paused to nurse the fretting Elm Leaf. As she held the baby to her breast, she chanted her farewell song to the man she'd come to love as a brother:

> Listen!
> You, who go before me
> You who take the long journey
> The journey into the Shadow Land
> The land of the hereafter
> You make the journey first
> You go before me
> I must follow when my time comes
> When my time comes, then will I follow
> Then will I join you and the happy ones
> The ones who have gone before us
> I will join you and our forefathers
> Join you in the land of the hereafter . . .

Once the baby slept, she returned her to the cradleboard and set it safely in the crotch of a young maple before she filled the hole with dirt, mounding it over the grave. She'd already cut and notched sapling trunks; now she fitted them together in a rectangle around the mounded earth.

It took her until the sun was halfway down the sky to

find and gather enough heavy stones to cover the raw earth within the rectangle. Her last duty was to stack pine torches beside the grave. She and Elm Leaf would spend the next four nights here, keeping the torches lit so Lame Wolf's spirit could find its way safely to the Shadow Land.

She returned to the lodge and, with ashes, blackened her face in mourning. When she sat back on her mat, she noticed the supplies she'd carried inside from Lame Wolf's canoe were piled untidily where she'd left them.

"He shouldn't have gone to sell his furs to the traders in order to buy supplies for us," she said aloud, though there was no one to hear but Elm Leaf. "The spotted disease comes from white men, not from the People. If he'd stayed with us, he'd still be alive." And then she wept.

The Moon of Strawberries waned, becoming a ghost, and still Silver Grass remained at the lodge. Though sunk in grief and guilt, she took good care of her baby, if not of herself. Finally, one morning, she woke feeling sick. Examining her skin, she noticed a few of the dreaded spots and shivered with fear not for herself, but for Elm Leaf.

What if I grow too sick to nurse her? she thought. What if I die? My daughter will die, too, with no one to care for her. I must bring her to the village before I'm too feverish to travel. *Now.*

Silver Grass brought only the cradleboard with them to the canoe. She made good time paddling at first, but as the sun rose to the top of the sky, she grew feverish. Her paddling slowed and her thinking grew confused. By the time the sun was halfway down the sky, she was too sick to remember her destination. Letting the canoe drift as she nursed the baby, she tried to remember where she was headed.

"I wish your father were here," she told Elm Leaf

more than once. As her shaking hands tucked the baby back into the cradleboard, it came to her that they must be going home to Olav.

She came to a fork in the stream and, struggling to recall which creeks fed into the river that ran by the cabin, she steered the canoe to the east, hoping she was right. Her paddle strokes were so feeble that she could do little more than keep the canoe away from the banks as they drifted downstream. Finally she was too weak to prevent it from nosing into a bank. When the baby began to cry, she tried to reach for the cradleboard but fell helplessly onto the canoe bottom, jarring the prow loose from the bank.

The baby wailed as they drifted down the stream again but, delirious with fever, Silver Grass could no longer understand that what she heard were the cries of her daughter. Nor did she notice the crying gradually grow weaker.

Oblivious to the fine spring day and the fresh scent of the new green leaves on the branches he thrust impatiently aside, Olav tramped along a creek, following a deer trail and searching, always searching for some sign his wife had passed this way. He'd explored the banks of every stream for miles around, both on foot and by canoe, all to no avail.

Months had passed since Silver Grass had disappeared in that April snowstorm. It was now the end of June, and Olav was still desperately hunting for her. He'd pestered the Chippewa villagers until he was finally convinced they told him the truth when they said she'd never returned to the village and they had no idea where she'd gone. Yes, they'd heard Lame Wolf had been seen in Ontonagon, but he hadn't come home. How could they say where he might be?

When he traveled to the Ontonagon Chippewa village, Olav learned there that Lame Wolf had visited them but had left; they knew nothing at all of Silver Grass.

Where could she have gone, his beautiful, beloved Swan Maiden? And why? Certain she wouldn't leave of her own free will, he'd become convinced Lame Wolf had abducted her by force, perhaps by tying her to the missing toboggan. Unfortunately, the snowstorm had concealed any tracks he might have followed.

Freda had done her best to console him, but she could not; no one could. He'd search for Silver Grass until the day he died. She'd have borne their child by now, and he prayed both mother and child were well. The baby, though, concerned him far less than she did. He *must* find her. After he did, then he'd have time to solve the problem of Freda.

She'd traveled to Iron River with the last of her savings, expecting to become Mrs. Johansen. When he'd disappointed her, she'd refused to accept money from him to pay for her return to Sandusky, Ohio, where the minister and other immigrant Swedes had settled. Since she had no money for room and board, she remained with him. He, of course, had immediately moved into Broken Reed's empty wigwam that still stood west of the cabin.

Freda insisted on cooking his meals, an arrangement he might have appreciated under other circumstances. But he didn't want Freda, pleasant as she was. He wanted only Silver Grass. No other woman would suit him.

Olav glanced at the lowering sun and calculated the time it would take him to return home. Even though the days had lengthened so it remained light later, if he didn't turn back now he'd find himself tramping through the woods in the dark. He stopped and wiped his forehead with the red bandana he carried.

"Silver Grass!" he shouted as he always did before turning back. "Silver Grass!" He waited in vain for an answer, then called her name twice more because four was the sacred number of the Chippewa.

Again he waited. Only the squawk of a disturbed jay answered him. Sighing, he turned to go home. Before he took a single step, a faint sound caught his ear, one he couldn't immediately identify. No bird he knew had such a call. An animal? Olav frowned in puzzlement. The sound grew slightly louder, rising and falling in volume. Whatever was making the noise seemed distressed. What the devil was it?

It wasn't a woman's voice—not Silver Grass, then. Since it wasn't, what should it matter to him? But he found himself cocking his head this way and that in an effort to determine where the sound came from. Somehow he couldn't bring himself to leave without locating what might be an injured animal—one caught in a trap, perhaps. At last he nodded and pushed through the brush to the creek bank.

Here the sound came much clearer—a pitiful wailing no man with a heart could ignore. "I'm coming," he muttered, and began walking upstream.

Rounding a bend, he caught sight of a canoe caught between two large rocks near the west bank of the creek. He could see no one in the boat. At the same time he pinpointed the wailing as coming from the canoe, he realized what he heard was a baby crying. He began to run along the bank.

He spotted a cradleboard before he reached the canoe and wondered who would have abandoned a child like this. Chippewa mothers always carried their babies with them. He pounded up even with the boat, waded into the water, and reached for the cradleboard containing the crying baby. And then, in the bottom of

178

the canoe, he saw her lying motionless.

"No!" he shouted. "Not dead! You can't be dead!"

Leaving the cradleboard where it was, he freed the canoe, dragged it to shore, and lifted Silver Grass's body into his arms. Instead of holding the dank chill of death, her skin was hot as flame and as red. He hadn't seen such redness since he was twelve and had the measles. She was deathly sick but, thank God, she lived.

"I bring you home. I take care of you," he whispered in English, settling her carefully into the canoe again. Removing his boots, he climbed in, took up the oar, and pushed away from the bank. As he began to paddle rapidly downstream, he grew conscious of the baby's continued crying.

His child!

"Be still, little one," he said. "Papa has found you and all will be well."

He prayed he was right.

In the blue of the long twilight, he pulled the canoe onto the sand of the stream bank by his cabin. As he laid down the paddle, he shouted for Freda. By the time he'd lifted Silver Grass from the canoe, Freda was running down the path toward him.

"The baby," he ordered. "Bring the baby."

Though Silver Grass had remained unconscious since he'd found her, when he started to enter the cabin with her, she opened her eyes.

"No," she whispered in her own tongue. "Wigwam."

He hesitated, uncertain what to do. Sick as she was, it was likely she didn't know what she was saying. And yet . . . He nodded and reversed his steps, carrying her to Broken Reed's wigwam and laying her carefully on the pallet he slept on. He reached for a blanket and saw that Freda, carrying the cradleboard with the whimpering baby, stood framed in the open flap.

179

"The baby is hungry and we have no milk for it," Freda said. "The mother must nurse her child."

Olav shook his head. "She's too sick. You can see for yourself . . ."

"If she has milk, it won't make her any worse to give that milk to the baby who needs it." Brushing past him, Freda knelt beside Silver Grass, laid the cradleboard on the matted floor, and lifted out the baby, naked from the waist down.

Olav blinked. A girl. He had a daughter.

He didn't interfere as Freda unlaced Silver Grass's tunic to expose her breast. As Freda put the child's mouth to the breast, she said, "See, milk drips from her nipple. It will go to waste unless the baby nurses."

Olav felt as though a fist squeezed his heart as he watched his daughter suck. Was he to lose his wife in order that his daughter might live?

He forced the thought from his mind. Silver Grass would *not* die; he wouldn't let her. Turning away, he began preparing a dose of the willow bark medicine she'd left behind when they'd journeyed to the Sugar Camp.

Silver Grass floated in a space between the upper and lower worlds where there was no sun, no moon, no breeze, no light. Sometimes ghost hands touched her, sometimes ghost voices told her to open her mouth or to nurse a baby. Though moving was difficult, she tried to obey the voices.

Once her mother called to her and she tried to answer, eager to join her. But no words came. White wings sprouted from her shoulders, feathers grew from her skin. If she stretched her wings she could rise up, up, she could fly from this dark place, she would stretch her wings and fly away.

180

"Stay with me, my love," a voice begged.

She hesitated. No ghost spoke those words, this was a man with heartache in his voice. Why did he call her his love?

"Don't leave me, my Swan Maiden," he pleaded.

She could feel his hand holding hers. She knew his voice, knew his touch. She loved him. How could she fly away and leave him behind to grieve?

"Olav?" she whispered, and opened her eyes.

"Thank God," he murmured, wrapping his arms around her, his tears dampening her cheek as he held her close.

Aware she'd left the dark place behind and come home, Silver Grass slipped into a deep, healing sleep. She woke to a woman's soft voice.

A pleasant-faced light-haired woman holding a baby knelt beside her. "Your baby needs milk," the woman said, speaking the English words with the same sound Olav gave them.

A name swam up from the depths, like a water monster surfacing in a dark pond. *Freda.* Silver Grass tensed.

"It is good you wake at last," Freda said and smiled. The baby in her arms whimpered. "She wants her mama," Freda added.

Silver Grass's gaze focused on the baby. Her baby. "Elm Leaf," she whispered, trying to reach for her daughter but finding herself too weak. She felt milk begin to ooze from her breasts.

"I will help you," Freda said, putting the baby to Silver Grass's breast with an ease that suggested she'd done this many times before. Elm Leaf immediately began sucking hungrily.

"I'm happy Olav found you," Freda said. "His wife and daughter. How he missed you."

Wife and daughter. Freda meant her and Elm Leaf.

181

Memories, painful and bleak surfaced. "Freda," she whispered. "Freda is Olav's wife."

Freda's blue eyes grew wide with astonishment. "Me? No, no. I come here, he tell me Silver Grass is his wife." She flushed, red suffusing her pale skin. "I make mistake when I come here."

"Mistake was mine." Olav spoke from the wigwam's open flap. He stepped inside and came to kneel beside Silver Grass. "Minister write letter. I never answer. So Freda not know."

Distracted by the baby's sucking, Silver Grass tried to make sense of this. If it was a mistake, why was Freda still here? The effort to think hurt her head, so she looked at her daughter instead. "Elm Leaf," she murmured.

"You call her Elm Leaf?" Olav asked.

She hadn't named the baby, Lame Wolf had. With that recollection, everything else that had happened flooded into her mind, overwhelming her. Tears filled her eyes.

"Don't cry," he begged, brushing a strand of hair from her forehead. "Elm Leaf is a good name. She is beautiful, our daughter. As beautiful as you."

Soothed by his words and by his touch, Silver Grass drifted into sleep again. When next she woke, it was dark in the wigwam, the only light from the coals of the fire. Olav was stretched out on a pallet next to her but there was no sign of Freda or the baby. After a moment, Silver Grass realized she and Olav must be in Broken Reed's wigwam, next to the cabin.

"Olav," she said softly.

He roused quickly, sitting up.

"Have you taken Freda for a second wife?" she asked.

He seemed astounded. "Second wife? Why do you say such a thing?"

"My people sometimes take second wives. And she is still here with you."

"No, not with me. I live in wigwam. She live in cabin. She have no money, no place to go."

As Silver Grass was thinking this over, Olav reached for her, pulling her into his arms and holding her tenderly. "I need one wife only—you."

By dawn everything had been explained—her misunderstanding and what she'd done because of it, his anguished search. Silver Grass was still too weak to make love, but the desire she felt lying in his arms made her eager to recover her strength quickly.

That didn't happen. She improved, she became able to care for herself and Elm Leaf and also to make love with Olav, but she tired easily, never becoming as strong as before her illness. And so, little as she wished to, she came to depend on Freda's help and friendship.

When the Moon of Falling Leaves began to wax, she told Olav she was carrying another child. Though as happy as she, he was concerned.

"We can't stay in wigwam all winter," he told her. "Too cold for you. I build sleep rooms on cabin—one for us, one for Freda."

Silver Grass wanted to assure him she no longer needed Freda's help, but the truth was, she knew she couldn't do without it. She had no doubt Olav's love was for her alone, for he made his devotion to her very clear. He treated Freda like a sister, and she came to realize his feeling for Freda was the same as hers had been for Lame Wolf.

Over the cold months, with Olav often gone, either hunting or working in his forge in town, Silver Grass came to appreciate Freda's company more and more. When the Swedish woman offered to teach Elm Leaf how to read and write when she grew old enough, Silver Grass smiled and nodded. Her daughter went to

183

Freda for comfort as often as she came to her mother, but since children of the People were raised by everyone living in the wigwam, she wasn't troubled.

It wasn't until Boiling Moon that a shadow fell over Silver Leaf's happiness. Much as she longed to go to the Sugar Camp, she knew she hadn't the strength. Olav found a small grove of maples close to the cabin and tapped them, but she found helping him so exhausting she had to give it up.

As her stomach grew bigger and bigger she grew short of breath at the slightest exertion. Freda constantly urged her to rest and, though Silver Grass tried to help with the work, she discovered she no longer could.

By the time the Flower Moon began to wax, Silver Grass spent much of the time lying on her bed.

"She'll feel better after the baby comes," Freda told the worried Olav.

Silver Grass wasn't so sure.

On the day before the full moon, Father Sun shone brightly and a breeze scented with new growth blew warm. Instead of going to the forge, Olav said to Silver Grass and Freda, "The *Astor* stops at Iron River this morning. Her first trip this year. She brings me new bellows, brings Freda's cow. We can watch her sail by from the beach."

"You two go," Freda said. "I make sure the new shed is ready for my cow. Soon we have fresh milk and butter. Even cheese. You will see."

Silver Grass smiled at her. All winter Freda had been telling Olav how badly they needed a cow and now she was to have one. The *Astor,* she knew, was the boat her people called Walk-in-the-Water because of the large wheels to either side that went round and round as the boat skimmed the waves.

"I'd like to see the boat," she told him, hoping she

184

wouldn't become too breathless on the short walk to the lake shore.

When she stood next to Olav looking out over the glittering water of Kitchigami, with the waves creeping over the sand toward her as though trying to count coup by touching her moccasins, Silver Grass was glad she'd made the effort. How beautiful the lake of the Chippewa was, the lake the whites called "Superior."

No matter how hard she tried, she could no longer picture the big lake of the Seneca, named "Ontario" by white men, even though she'd stood beside it like this with her father. She remembered the great crash of the falls at Niagara and how the white foam splashed high, but when she closed her eyes and tried to see the lake below the falls, what she saw instead was Kitchigami.

As she'd left the Seneca behind to become a Chippewa, so had she exchanged one lake for another. Kitchigami was her lake now. She watched a long-legged sandpiper run along the water's edge, calling plaintively. How Elm Leaf would enjoy toddling after the birds and playing in the sand. She'd bring her here soon, after the baby was born.

Olav put an arm around her, drawing her close to his side and she leaned against him, savoring his strength.

"You are my love," he said.

"And you are mine."

They gazed into each other's eyes and, as he smiled at her, she noticed a feather drifting down over his head, a white feather. Reaching up, she plucked it from the air, then stared into the sky. High above a bird flew, so far away she couldn't tell what it was.

"What is it?" Olav asked.

She handed him the feather, remembering another time she'd stood along another shore of this lake with a different feather in her hand, an eagle feather sent by her mother to guide her.

185

"Not from eagle or gull," Olav said, tucking the feather into her hair as she'd done so long ago with the other one.

Very faint and far away she thought she heard a whistling but the sound wasn't repeated. Before she could ask Olav if he'd heard anything, he pointed east.

"Here she comes, the *Astor,*" he said.

The boat with its white paint gleaming in the sunlight was a wonderful sight churning the water as it passed, giving loud toots as it turned toward the mouth of Iron River. In her enjoyment, Silver Grass forgot about the feather.

But that night as she lay next to Olav in the fine, wide bed he'd made for them, she held the white feather in her fingers. The feather was an omen, she knew. Of what? She fell asleep without finding a meaning.

A far-away whistling drew her from the bed, from the cabin and into the night. High above her the flock flew and its whistling surrounded her, piercing her heart with entreaty.

"Come with us, sister," it seemed to say, "for you are one of us. Come. It is time."

How she yearned to go. She must go. She would go. But when she tried to rise she found she was too heavy. Something inside dragged her earthward, forcing her onto her back, wracked with pain. She cried out in agonized disappointment . . .

When she opened her eyes she couldn't understand why she lay in a bed instead of on the ground. Olav stood over her, a lighted candle in his hand.

"I heard a cry," Freda called from outside their door. "Is the baby coming?"

A grinding cramp made Silver Grass clutch her stomach. "Yes," she groaned.

Though Freda tried to make her stay in bed, Silver Grass would not. She would birth this baby as she'd birthed Elm Grass—in the People's way.

She tried her best and, for a time she thought she could. But after the fourth strong bear-down pain, her heart fluttered wildly inside her like a bird trapped in a hand, and weakness overcame her. Her legs trembled, refusing to hold their crouch, and she tumbled sideways onto the matted floor.

As she felt the baby slide free, the meaning of the feather came to her. "Call Olav," she whispered.

Freda shouted for him and almost immediately he was kneeling beside her.

Finding the feather still clutched in her fingers, Silver Grass handed it to him. She motioned him closer, knowing she hadn't the strength to speak above the wailing of their baby.

He bent and put his cheek to hers. "I can't stay," she whispered, each word an effort. "My sisters call me and I must fly away."

As her eyes drooped shut she heard his anguished cry, heard Freda's voice say, "You have another daughter," and then they came with a great flutter of wings to sweep her into the sky with them, her Swan Sisters . . .

Chapter 13

Rain streaked the windows that looked out onto Sandusky City's Washington Park. Inside the cosy parlor, Elma Johansen sat beside the fire with her embroidery in her lap. On the other side of the hearth her younger sister, Marta, struggled with tangled floss. How poor Marta hated needlework.

Boyish voices rose in the hallway and Elma shook her head. Their seven-year-old twin half-brothers were quarreling again.

A moment later the boys burst into the parlor. "I don't want to be a dirty Reb," Piers cried, scowling at his brother.

"You got to be, 'cause I'm the Yank," Erik said.

"It ain't fair, you always get to pick first."

"That's 'cause I was born first."

"I thought twins were supposed to get along with each other," Marta commented, more to Elma than to the boys, who paid her no attention.

Elma waved her hand at the windows. "It's because they're cooped up inside. I declare, it's rained more in Sandusky this March than any I recall."

Marta flung down her still-tangled floss. "I'm sick and tired of the rain. And of sitting like a dried-up old spinster, sewing by the fire." She ran her hands through the dark, curly hair that hung past her shoulders, making it as tangled as the floss.

"You're hardly a spinster," Elma said dryly.

"Polly Baxter's eighteen and she's married, with a baby on the way. Mother won't even let me put my hair up!"

"You're not eighteen for another two months. Then Mother will relent. But didn't I hear you say just yesterday that under *no circumstances* would you ever marry any of the dull-wits around here?"

"Well, they are, you know."

Piers sat down on the stool by Elma's feet. "I ain't no slave-beating Reb," he muttered.

Elma glanced sympathetically at him. Piers could hardly be blamed for refusing. Even little children knew how despicable the Confederate slave-owning way of life was. An idea struck her and she leaned down to speak into Piers's ear.

"You can pretend to be a Reb," she whispered, "but really you're a Union spy collecting information to defeat the entire Confederate Army."

Piers blinked and then grinned. "All right," he told Erik. "I'll be a Reb. Sort of, anyway."

The two boys raced from the room and pounded up the stairs.

"Do tidy your hair," Elma advised her sister, knowing their mother would chide Marta if she didn't.

Marta swiped ineffectually at her tangled mop with one hand. "I wish I had blond hair like yours that just fell into place with a single brushing." She giggled and said in an affected voice, "'The color of the first buttercup of spring.'"

Elma smiled. "You weren't supposed to be listening to the lieutenant."

"I thought he was rather silly. And maybe colorblind as well. Your hair's not buttercup yellow, it's golden. The major's far more interesting, even if he's a trifle old to be courting you."

Elma frowned and set aside her embroidery. "I'm not so sure he *is* courting me."

"Then why does he persist in seeking your company?"

"I wish I knew. The last time he took me riding, he seemed about to ask me something and then changed his mind."

"Maybe he means to propose."

Elma shook her head. "Is that all you ever think about, getting married?"

Marta bit her lip. "I don't really know if I ever want to get married. I certainly haven't yet met a man I'd consider as a husband. Actually, I've met hardly any men. Only boys. They may be my age, but they act about as grown-up as Piers and Erik."

"I've introduced you to quite a number of Army officers and you must admit they're men."

Marta sighed. "They take one look at my hair down around my shoulders and decide I'm too young to bother with. It's you they come to see, anyway." She leaned forward. "Tell me the truth—which one do you favor?"

Elma thought about it. There was no doubt she enjoyed being escorted by the various officers she'd met, but when it came to having a claim on her heart, none of them did.

"If any, I suppose I prefer the major," she said. "He, at least, keeps me guessing."

The grandfather clock on the stair landing struck the half-hour. At the same time, a carriage rattled to a stop outside the front door. Marta jumped up and peered from the window.

"Speak of the devil," she said, "I do believe that's Major Patton coming to call."

Elma rose to her feet. "Are you sure? He didn't mention he would."

"Even if I hadn't seen that bushy mustache of his, I'd know him by his boots," Marta assured her. "No other officer's are so shiny. How he keeps them that way with all this rain and mud is beyond me."

Hearing the clap of the knocker, Elma began putting her needlework away. Marta managed to stab her finger with a needle while hurriedly cramming hers into a box and was sucking the finger when Toivi, their new maid recently arrived from Finland, appeared at the parlor door.

"Major come," Toivi said in heavily accented English. "Want you." She pointed at Elma.

Freda had worked hard training Toivi, but it was clear she still had a long way to go.

"Thank you," Elma said. "Please show him in."

Moments later, a stocky, balding man in his thirties entered the parlor. He wore the blue of the United States Army with the air of a man accustomed to uniforms. He bowed slightly, first to Elma, then to Marta.

"So good of you to see me," he said.

"You're always welcome," Elma told him. "Do be seated. I'll have the maid bring some—"

He didn't allow her to finish. "Sorry to decline your generous offer, but I'm in rather a hurry." He glanced at Marta as he spoke.

Taking the hint, she rose. "Please take my chair, Major Patton. I have things I must attend to."

He inclined his head and watched her leave the room before turning to Elma. "Miss Johansen, I realize what I ask is out of order, but would you mind if I closed the door?"

Though somewhat taken aback, Elma was not in the least afraid of him, so she said, "As you wish, Major."

He slid the door shut, returned to the chair Marta had abandoned, and pulled it closer to Elma's before seating himself. He leaned toward her. "I've formed a high opinion of you in the several weeks that we've known one another, Miss Johansen. I've come to believe you're not only an attractive young lady but one who has a cool head and can be trusted. I have an unusual request to make of you. Whether you're willing to assist me in the matter I propose to discuss, I want you to promise me you'll not repeat what I'm about to say to anyone, including your immediate family."

I was right, she thought, he does want something from me, and it's not marriage. Nor do I believe it's the other—that tawdry, insulting proposition a man sometimes offers a woman.

"I can promise you I will mention what you say to nobody." She kept her voice even, though inwardly she seethed with excited anticipation. What could be so secret that she must tell no one?

"It's well known in Sandusky City," he said, "that your father is a fervent abolitionist, as well as a solid citizen of the community. I hope you won't be hurt if I tell you that's one of the reasons I cultivated your acquaintance."

Elma was hard put to keep her expression from betraying her confusion. What did her father have to do with this?

"I was pleased to discover you share his views," the major went on. "I was further delighted to find you possess what I consider a rare ability among women. Believe me, I intend it as a compliment when I say you have what's known in gambling circles as a 'poker face.' This means that you're able to keep your emotions—whatever they may be—hidden. Your normal expression gives no clue to what you're thinking or feeling."

192

Elma blinked. She wasn't unaware of this trait in herself, since her father sometimes teased her about it, saying she must have inherited it from her mother's people. But she was amazed to hear Major Patton praising her for having such an ability.

"In any case, I've chosen you to help us," he said.

Us? He must mean the Army! Thrilled to the core, she was tempted to say of course she'd do anything she could, but caution persuaded her to temporize. "I'm honored," she said, "but I can't agree until I know what you expect of me."

"I understand." He sat back in the chair, glancing at the door. He lowered his voice. "Is there a possibility someone—a servant, say—might eavesdrop?"

"There's only Toivi. I doubt if she would, and even if she did, her English is so limited she'd understand very little of what was said. My twin brothers, on the other hand—" Elma paused. She rose, marched to the door, and slid it open.

"Aha!" she cried, grabbing Erik's shirttail as he tried to run. "Caught you!" Despite his struggles to get away, she hauled him into the parlor and stood him in front of the major. As she knew he would, Piers trailed reluctantly behind. She pushed him next to his brother.

Major Patton rose and looked sternly down at the boys. "Listening to private conversations is a very bad habit to get into, very bad indeed."

"Not if you're a spy," Piers mumbled. "Sir."

The major's jaw dropped. "A spy! Wherever did you get such a notion?"

"We were playing war, and he said I had to be a Reb." Piers jerked a thumb at his twin. "I didn't want to. So then Elma says I could pretend to be a Reb but really be a spy for the Union. Only it didn't work 'cause Erik found out what I was doing and then he said he was a spy, too. Sir."

193

"And we saw you come so we snuck downstairs to practice being spies," Erik put in. "Sir."

The major appeared to have recovered his equilibrium. He scowled at the twins. "I fail to see how eavesdropping on a Union major qualifies as spying for the Army."

"We sort of pretended you were a Reb, sir," Erik said in a very small voice. "Anyway, Elma caught us before we got to hear anything."

Clicking his boot heels together and standing very straight, the major snapped, "Attention, troops!"

The startled twins tried to copy his posture."

"You will march up the stairs to your playroom," he ordered, "and you will remain in that room until I leave this house. Is that clear?"

"Yessir," the boys said together, their blue eyes wide.

"Dismissed!"

The boys rushed from the room. The major followed them to the door, listening to the thumps as they climbed the stairs. He then slid the door closed and came back to Elma.

"Would you mind standing by the windows with me?" he asked her. "I don't believe we could be overheard there, providing we speak softly."

She nodded and crossed to the rain-spattered windows overlooking Washington Square. He came to stand next to her.

"I suppose that's what I'm really asking of you," he said practically in her ear. "To be a spy."

A spy! Her heart leaped. A spy for the Union. Could she play the part?

"What would I have to do?" she asked.

"I know you're aware we've imprisoned captured Confederate officers on Johnson's Island in the bay. What you do not know—" he lowered his voice "—is that the Rebel sympathizers, the Copperheads, have infiltrated your fair city and are plotting to release these prisoners."

"No!"

"It's true. Unfortunately, we aren't sure who the guilty parties are, nor who their contacts at the prison might be. That's where you come in. We suspect the contact might be through the prison hospital, so this is my plan. Under the auspices of several local churches, the good ladies of the community have offered, in Christian charity, to provide extra blankets and such basic commodities as bread and milk for Rebel prisoners who are ill. I will arrange for you to be the go-between, delivering such articles as have been collected by the churchwomen to Johnson's Island."

To think of actually setting foot on the island and seeing Rebs face-to-face was a daunting prospect, but a challenge that appealed to her. She tamped down her rising excitement.

"I see no difficulty doing what you ask of me," she told him. "Is there more?"

He nodded. "I hope your frequent visits to the prison hospital will tempt the Reb sympathizer, whoever he is, to view you as an unwitting go-between. If anyone from Sandusky City approaches you with a request to carry out what might seem like an innocent favor, make certain we will be on the alert. The regularity of your visits may also tempt the Confederate officer who is the plotter inside the prison to try to use you in some fashion. Naturally, you'll report anything even slightly suspicious to me."

"Of course," she murmured, eager to embark on such an adventure. Second thoughts prompted her to add, "You would have to speak to my father first. He's inclined to try to protect me overmuch."

"I'm sure I can gain your father's cooperation. Without, you understand, revealing all I've told you."

"I wouldn't expect you to." If he did, she knew, her father, who worried far too much about what might happen to her, would never permit her to set foot on Johnson's Island. He might not, in any case, she thought dispiritedly, since his concern for her seemed far greated than was warranted, greater than any he showed for Marta or the twins. Still, if another woman went with her . . .

"Perhaps," she said, "my father's anxieties might be somewhat allayed if my sister accompanied me."

"I'll keep that in mind," the major said, "though I don't anticipate any danger to you whatsoever, none at all." He took her hand and bowed over it. "I assure you that your country will be grateful for your efforts, Miss Johansen."

On Tuesday of the following week Elma and Marta walked up the gangplank of the *Island Lady*, the sidewheeler ferry that was to take them to Johnson's Island. A corporal and a private followed, carrying boxes of church-donated blankets and food which they stowed belowdecks.

Standing at the rail near the bow, next to Elma, Marta covered her ears to block the warning toots of the steam whistle as the boat prepared to leave the dock. Elma smiled, noticing that already the brisk April breeze had teased strands of her sister's unruly dark hair from under her bonnet.

"I'm so excited I could die," Marta said. "I never, ever thought Mother would agree to let me go."

"It was Papa's decision," Elma reminded her. She had no idea what Major Patton might have said to her father to get him to consent to her going, with or without Marta. Perhaps he'd played on her father's patriotism. Olav Johansen loved his adopted country as fiercely as he hated slavery.

"I do believe Papa thinks I'll take care of you," Marta said, glancing at her sideways.

"And so you would if I needed to be cared for."

"You never do; you never have. You're so strong I don't believe you ever will. But Papa doesn't seem to understand that. I think it has something to do with our real mother."

Elma's hand went up to touch the outline of the gold locket resting underneath the bodice of her gown. "Yet Mother Freda says you're the one who looks the most like Silver Grass."

"Yes, I know. But you're the one who acts like her, who reminds Papa of her. Sometimes he even forgets and calls you 'Elm Leaf,' as she did."

After they'd moved to Sandusky and Papa had married Freda, Freda had changed her name from Elm Leaf to Elma. She'd been too young to care. She had no memory at all of her real mother. Freda, kind and loving, though firm, was the only mother she remembered. Freda had never treated either her or Marta any differently than she did the twins, her own children. But Elma knew in her heart that Papa, much as he loved Marta and the boys, favored her over them, just a little.

How different her life might have been if her real mother had lived. So different she couldn't imagine it.

Marta flung her arms wide, knocking her bonnet askew without seeming to notice. "It's a wonderful day! Spring at last!"

Elma reached over and straightened her sister's bonnet, envying Marta's spontaneity. She often wished she could behave more freely instead of examining things from all sides before acting.

It *was* a lovely day. The sun shone warm on the bay, and beyond the island prison, Lake Erie's waters glittered and gleamed, tempting her. She felt a longing to sail past Johnson's Island into the lake, sail on to Swan Isle, where the Johansens had their summer cottage. In fact, her father owned the entire small island. She pictured the white sand beach with the pines beyond and took a deep breath, imagining she could smell their aromatic scent.

"I can hardly wait until it's warm enough to sail our boat to the cottage," she said.

"Yes, that's always fun," Marta agreed. "But this is fun, too. Just think, we're going to see real, live Rebs up close."

Elma stared at Johnson's Island, very near now—it was but three miles north of Sandusky City and a half-mile south of the Marblehead Peninsula. She could see the prison buildings clustered on the island's south-eastern end. Once it had been heavily wooded, but now few trees remained—they'd been cut down and used to build the prison barracks and stockade, as well as for firewood. Above the palings of the stockade, the Stars and Stripes whipped in the wind.

When the ferry pulled up at the dock and they headed for the gangplank, suddenly nervous, Elma reached for Marta's hand. Her sister glanced at her in surprise, but gave her gloved fingers a squeeze. Marta knew only that they were delivering supplies to sick prisoners, nothing more. Actually, that's all they did have to do. Her assignment was to watch and listen and to wait for anything out of the ordinary, then report it. Simple enough. She should have no difficulty playing her part.

Major Patton was waiting on the dock. He greeted them, supervised the unloading of the supplies, and then escorted Elma and Marta, the private and corporal following, to the prison hospital, located outside the stockade. Dr. Woodbridge, middle-aged and balding, met them at the door.

198

"Delighted to see you, young ladies," he said. "Major Patton tells me he's arranged for you to deliver food and blankets to my patients. Most generous, most generous, indeed."

"The Churches united in taking up collections," Elma said. "We are merely the bearers of their charity."

"I beg to differ," Dr. Woodbridge said, ushering them into his office. "It is charity itself when two lovely ladies take time to visit these poor, unfortunate men."

"I'll leave you with the doctor," Major Patton said. "He'll arrange to have a guard escort you to the dock when you're ready to go." He bowed to them and went out, taking the corporal and private with him.

Elma noticed Marta's nose wrinkling. She'd been doing her best to ignore the ghastly smell inside the hospital—a combination of disinfectants, human waste, and a sweet, sickening odor that reminded her of spoiled meat. She swallowed, gritting her teeth.

"How many patients do you have here, doctor?" she asked.

"Thirty-six at present. The hospital holds forty."

"Who takes care of them?"

"Other prisoners. Volunteers. The Army provides no nurses of any kind. I try to recruit men who had some knowledge of illness. With little success, unfortunately—though I occasionally turn up a prize." He motioned to someone in the hall outside his office and a thin man in a ragged gray uniform appeared in the doorway.

"Jones, find Captain Drury and tell him he's wanted in my office."

A few minutes later, when a tall, auburn-haired man entered the office, Elma stared at him in surprise, her hand involuntarily rising to her locket. She'd never seen hair quite that color—except for the curl of her grandmother's hair inside the locket. His trim mustache

199

was the same unusual color as his hair, a deep, dark red. His hair wasn't all that surprised her. Because the doctor had called him Captain Drury, she'd expected to see a man in a blue uniform. He wore gray. Apparently he was one of the volunteer Rebs.

"You wanted to see me, sir?" he said.

"The Misses Johansen," Dr. Woodbridge told him, "are angels of mercy bringing supplies to the afflicted."

Captain Drury bowed. "I'm honored to meet you, Miss Johansen," he said to Marta. Then he looked at her. "And you, Miss Johansen. A rare privilege, I assure you."

His eyes were gray-blue, like the tobacco smoke that drifted from her father's pipe. A spark sprang to life in those eyes as they met hers, sending a frisson of anticipation along her spine. Something about him stirred her in a way no other man ever had.

"Captain Hunt Drury, at your service, ladies," he said, but his smoky gaze was on her, not Marta. His drawl caressed her ears. Somehow she couldn't bring herself to glance away.

"Captain," Dr. Woodbridge said, "I'll leave it to you to decide how best to distribute what these young ladies have brought to the hospital patients. That will spare them the necessity to enter the wards."

For some reason the doctor didn't want her near the patients, Elma told herself. Why? This would prevent her from carrying out her assignment, so it wouldn't do. She raised her chin. "Oh, but, sir, I assured the good ladies of the church that I'd deliver what they gave me to the patients myself."

The doctor frowned. "There are sights here no well-brought up young lady could be expected to endure."

"If you're worried I may faint," Elma said, "I assure you that I've never fallen into a swoon in my entire life. Nor will I do so here in your hospital."

"She's right, Doctor," Marta put in. "Even when Erik—he's our little brother—cut his leg and the blood kept coming and coming, Elma was the one who carried him into the house and bound the wound. Her gown was soaked through with blood, but she bore up wonderfully well. Better than our mother."

"If I might make a suggestion, sir?" Captain Drury waited for the doctor's curt nod before continuing. "Perhaps it might satisfy Miss Elma if she were to be escorted to the convalescent ward, where the men aren't too critically ill to be disturbed. I could supervise her distribution of supplies there."

Dr. Woodbridge's brow cleared. "Excellent. I knew I could count on you, Captain. We'll take the young ladies there." He turned to Elma. "I'm sure you understand that I can't permit you to disturb the sicker patients."

Though half-believing Captain Drury had served up that excuse to the doctor on a silver platter, Elma wasn't inclined to argue further, since she really didn't want to parade past wretchedly ill men. For that matter, she wasn't very keen on viewing convalescents, but she'd promised the major she'd meet as many of the patients as possible.

"Whatever you say, Dr. Woodbridge," she said sweetly, earning a quick glance from Marta, who knew from past experience that the sweeter Elma sounded, the less her words were to be trusted.

"Why don't I locate Lieutenant Jones and have him bring along the supplies, sir?" The captain asked. "I'll meet you in the ward."

Dr. Woodbridge waved his assent and Captain Drury left the room. The doctor looked from Elma to Marta and back. "Are you carrying smelling salts in your reticules, or shall I bring some with me?"

"Thank you, but we have everything we need," Elma

said firmly. She certainly didn't plan to have an attack of the vapors, and she doubted Marta would either, from sheer stubbornness, if nothing else. If Elma could bear it, then Marta would die rather than admit she couldn't.

"Follow me, ladies," the doctor said.

Though Elma thought she'd grown accustomed to the odors, when they entered a large room filled with cots the stench grew fearful, making it hard not to grimace. Marta swallowed convulsively once, her hand rising toward her face, but she managed neither to gag nor hold her nose.

Elma had no idea what to expect from the patients sitting and lying on the cots and she blinked when, almost in unison, every man smiled.

"My God, boys," a dark-haired man cried, "either angels have come to earth or we've all died and gone to heaven."

His sally produced a few ragged cheers.

"Enough of that," Dr. Woodbridge ordered. "I won't permit you to waste the time of these young ladies with nonsense. They've come to—"

The arrival of Captain Drury, followed by Lieutenant Jones pushing a cart containing the supply boxes, interrupted the doctor.

"I've put Captain Drury in charge of the distribution of the supplies the church ladies of Sandusky City have gathered for you men," Dr. Woodbridge went on. "The Misses Johansen will deliver to each one of you what the captain decides is your lot. You may get on with it, captain."

Captain Drury reached into the open box and lifted out a towel-wrapped batch of hot-cross buns. When he folded back the towel, the clean fragrance of yeast bread mingled with the fetid ward odor. Some of the men sighed.

The captain broke off one bun and handed it to Marta. "First man to your right," he said, "Lieutenant Greenbeau." Every eye followed Marta as she crossed to the cot with the roll in her hand.

Every eye . . . except the captain's and Elma's. Sensing he was watching her, she glanced at him and found herself once again unable to look away. He boldly took her hand in his, smiling at her before laying a roll on her palm. He released her hand before anyone noticed. Elma tried to tell herself her face couldn't possibly reveal to him or to the others how his touch had shaken her, but for once she wasn't sure.

"Thank you, captain," she said, adding a soupçon of tartness to the words. "To whom shall I deliver this?"

"One hot-cross bun to Lieutenant Melchior," he said in his caressing drawl, "first cot to the left."

As she and Marta continued to hand out rolls and other foodstuffs, the gaunt faces and sunken eyes of the patients caught at Elma's heart. Rebs these prisoners might be, but they were also sick men, deserving of care. And to think these were the convalescents! God help the poor wretches she and Marta wouldn't see in person.

"I've told Lieutenant Jones where the blankets and other things need to go, sir," the captain said at last. "I believe he can take care of it now."

The doctor, who'd seemed rather bored after a time, nodded. "Time to be off, then, ladies."

As they left the ward with the doctor leading the way, the men called thanks and blessings after them. "Come back, please come back again," one cried.

Elma turned in the doorway and waved. "We will be back," she said. "This is *au revoir,* not goodbye."

As she faced forward again, Captain Drury, behind her, whispered in her ear, *"Je vous trouve très jolie."*

His warm breath in her ear sent a thrill tingling

through her. Her French was not fluent, but she knew he'd said she was pretty.

She smiled in pleasure, a smile that faded immediately. What was the matter with her? He was a Reb. How dare a Reb prisoner say such a thing to her? She could pity the sick men, even if she couldn't forgive them for their beliefs, but she owed Hunt Drury no pity. She owed him nothing. He was nothing to her and he never would or could be.

Unless, of course, she discovered he was the man she'd been sent to unmask.

Chapter 14

Elma decided not to mention Hunt Drury's behavior to Major Patton. The major had said to watch for anything unusual, but what the Confederate captain had actually said to her had no bearing on a plot to release the prisoners. Unfortunately, no matter how many times she reminded herself he was a Reb, she couldn't forget Captain Drury's words or the way his touch had tingled through her.

The following week, when she next boarded the *Island Lady* for the crossing to Johnson's Island, to her annoyance she found herself hoping the captain would be at the hospital when she arrived. Seeing the Navy gunboat, the USS *Michigan,* anchored in the bay, guarding the island, brought it home to her that the man she was looking forward to meeting again was a prisoner of war, her enemy.

Even Marta—her best friend as well as her sister— would never forgive her if she fell in love with a Reb. Elma shook her head in dismay. Love? Where had that ridiculous notion come from? Why, she didn't even *like* Hunt Drury!

Marta, suffering from a cold and cough, wasn't with her today because their mother had decided she ought to stay in the house until she improved. When Papa came home from work he'd be displeased to find Elma had gone alone, but by then she'd be back and he'd be able to see for himself she was perfectly fine and he had no reason to worry about her.

Her supplies this time weren't heavy—several varieties of home-baked breads and rolls, plus three dozen fresh eggs—so she was carrying the two baskets herself.

A guard, a sergeant, met her at the Johnson's Island dock and escorted her to the hospital, carrying the baskets for her. On her arrival she found that Dr. Woodbridge was busy with a sick patient, so she sat in his office to wait, the sergeant standing by the open door.

After a few minutes, Captain Drury arrived. Though she'd schooled herself to show no emotion whatsoever when she saw him, Elma couldn't control the leap of her heart.

He bowed, saying formally, "It's kind of you to come again, Miss Johansen. Turning to the guard, he said, "Sergeant Maybrook, isn't it?"

"That's my name," the sergenat, a man of about forty, said. "You're Drury, ain't you?"

Unlike Dr. Woodbridge, apparently the enlisted men didn't bother with courtesy ranks for enemy officers.

"I am," the captain said. "Dr. Woodbridge asked me to tell the guard with Miss Johansen that if he'd be so kind as to escort her to the ward and stay with her, she wouldn't have to wait until the doctor finished with his work."

Sergeant Maybrook grimaced. "I don't know nothing about that."

"Would you like me to take you to the doctor so he can repeat his order to you personally?"

The sergeant shook his head. "It ain't that I don't

believe you, it's just, I don't know my way around inside the hospital." And don't want to, his tone indicated.

"I'll be your guide—if Miss Johansen doesn't mind."

"Not at all," she said coolly. "I'd appreciate your help delivering the food to the patients." She rose from her chair. Both men reached for the baskets, each carrying one.

The patients in the convalescent ward greeted her with enthusiasm, and she smiled at them one by one. Though she couldn't say she found the smell in the ward any less offensive, Elma discovered she didn't mind it as much as she had the first time. She was a bit surprised to notice Sergeant Maybrook's weathered complexion turn decidedly pale. Sweat popped out on his forehead when she lifted the basket lid and aroma of fresh baking joined the more noisome smells.

"Either seeing you on your last visit or those hot-cross buns cured Lieutenant Melchior," Captain Drury said. "He's gone back to the barracks." He glanced into her basket. "If you'd break those loaves into thirds," he said, "there'd be a portion for each man. Later I'll distribute the rolls to the sicker patients."

"I've three dozen eggs in the other basket," she said.

"Any of you boys game to take your egg raw?" the captain asked.

Most were.

"I'll dispense the eggs while you give out the bread," he told her.

Sergeant Maybrook followed them to the first bed but backed away hurriedly when the patient dug a hole in his bread, cracked the egg, dumped it into the cavity and stirred it around with his none-too-clean fore-finger. Retreating to the ward door, the sergeant stood his ground there, looking most unhappy and swallowing continuously.

"Some people can't tolerate the hospital atmosphere," the captain said in a low voice. "I'm glad you're not so easily discouraged, Miss Elma."

Hearing her name in his soft drawl caused her pulses to pound and made her forget her own queasy stomach.

They continued apportioning supplies from bed to bed until they arrived at the closed end of the ward. As they were about to begin working their way back along the opposite row of beds, she felt his hand on her arm, keeping her from moving on.

"Poets put words to our feelings," he said quietly. "Walter Landor wrote:

Between us now the mountain and the wood
Seeming darker than last year they stood . . .

"The waters of Lake Erie and the war separate us, Elma, but it won't always be so."

He released her and they went on to the next bed, Elma moving like an automaton, smiling and handing out bread, conscious only of the man beside her, of Hunt Drury. She'd never read Mr. Landor's poems, but the somber words the captain had quoted reverberated in her mind. So many obstacles stood between her and the rebel captain that it seemed impossible to her they could be surmounted, no matter what he thought.

Yet, if she were to be honest with herself, she'd have to admit she wished there was a way to overcome the obstacles. She saw none. Even after the Union won the war, and heaven knew how long that might take, how could the two of them ever reconcile their disparate beliefs? Impossible! She mustn't waste her time on foolish dreams.

You're here to help your country, she reminded

herself sternly, not to be beguiled by the enemy.

The trouble was, Hunt Drury didn't seem like the enemy.

She gave out the last portion of bread to the man in the last cot—a lieutenant who looked no older than she.

"Thank you kindly, Miss Johansen," he said. To the captain, he added, "I do believe I'll wait on my egg, sir. I know I may never see it again but I'll take a chance on getting the egg back the way I like 'em—hard-boiled."

"You can always spot a city lad," the patient next to him said. "They don't fancy anything that ain't had the juices plumb cooked away. Us country boys, now, we take things natural. Lookee here."

Elma watched as he cracked the egg the captain had given him, tipped his head up, and allowed the raw white and yolk to slip from the shell directly into his mouth.

As she swallowed involuntarily, she heard a retching sound and turned just in time to see the sergeant flee from the ward, his hand clapped over his mouth.

"Say goodbye to the men, if you will, Miss Johansen," Captain Drury told her. "We must hurry to catch up to your guard."

Elma smiled and waved, saying, "I'll be back next week."

The captain emptied one basket by placing the rolls in with the eggs. Holding the full one, he handed her the empty basket and, with his hand under her elbow, guided her from the ward.

He rushed her along the corridor to Dr. Woodbridge's office, ushered her inside, and closed the door. They were alone in the room.

"Where's the sergeant?" she asked.

"He'll be along." As he spoke, the captain set down his basket on a chair, then took hers and placed it beside his.

Before she understood what he meant to do, he pulled her into his arms and kissed her.

Shock gave way to bemusement, bemusement to pleasure, pleasure to passion as his lips, warm and ardent, explored hers. It wasn't her first kiss, but never before had she felt such an overwhelming desire to respond, to forget everything but him.

"This is how it will always be between us," he whispered against her lips, and then he released her, stepping back two paces and opening the door.

She stared at him, stunned by her sense of loss when he let her go. The thump of booted feet coming along the hall recalled her to her surroundings, and she hurriedly composed herself before Sergeant Maybrook appeared at the door.

The sergeant frowned, glancing at Hunt Drury, who was now holding the basket with the eggs and the rolls.

"Ah, there you are," the captain said. "I thought it best to bring Miss Johansen here rather than allowing her to remain on the ward." He bowed to Elma. *"Au revoir,"* he said to her before exiting.

She took a deep breath and picked up the empty basket. "I'm ready to leave if you are, Sergeant Maybrook," she said.

"I'm sorry I took sick," he muttered as they left the hospital. "Don't know how anyone can stand the stink in there."

"One grows accustomed to the smell," she said.

He shook his head, obviously disagreeing. "Anyways, I didn't mean to leave you alone with a bunch of dirty Rebs."

"I was perfectly safe."

"Maybe so, they being so sick and all. And Drury did hustle you off the ward real quick. The doc, he swears Drury's to be trusted. But to my way of thinking, you

210

can't trust any Reb."

Without her willing it, her fingers rose to touch her lips as if to feel the captain's kiss.

"The major'll have my hide for deserting you," he said morosely.

Elma thought that over a bit guiltily, though nothing that had happened was her fault. Perhaps her guilt arose because she'd enjoyed Hunt's kiss.

"Why tell Major Patton?" she asked. "I don't plan to. You couldn't help it. What were you to do, be sick in front of us all? I certainly wouldn't have cared to witness that!"

"'Tis right kind of you not to mention it, miss. If ever I escort you to the hospital again I ain't going to let you out of my sight. Take you there on an empty stomach, that's what I'll do.

Elma smiled. "I'm sure that's wise."

As she bade the sergeant farewell and walked up the gangplank, she admitted ruefully to herself that the only one not behaving wisely was Elma Johansen.

A week later, Elma stood before the pier glass in her room, trying to decide which of her hats to wear. The blue looked the best with her gown, but wasn't the deep rose more becoming? As usual for this excursion, she and Marta were not wearing hoops, only crinolines, their mother having decreed hoops inappropriate for riding a ferry.

"I declare," Marta said, "I've never seen you take so much trouble with a hat in my life. We're only going to Johnson's Island, not to the King's Ball."

"We don't have kings in the United States," Elma said.

"All right, then, we're not going to President Lincoln's Ball."

"I don't think the President gives balls in wartime."

Marta rolled her eyes in exasperation. "You've been up in the clouds all week. I know something happened, but you won't tell me what. I can guess, though. Wear the blue, he'll like it the best."

Elma, only half-listening, said, "Do you really think so?" before she realized she'd been tricked. "What I mean is, do *you* prefer the blue hat?" she added hastily.

Marta grinned at her. "Can the man in question be the major?" She shook her head. "No, I don't believe it. So who is he?"

"Not he. Them. I want to look my best for all the sick men, since they seem to look forward to our visits." Which was the truth, she assured herself. Or at least part of it.

When they reached the ferry dock, each carrying a basket of preserves, a nattily dressed man of about forty with a satchel in one hand stepped forward, swept off his hat, and bowed slightly.

"Am I addressing the Misses Johansen?" he asked.

Mindful that Major Patton had explained she might be approached by strangers, Elma was more cordial than she otherwise would have been to a man she didn't know.

"You are," she told him.

"I was informed by a member of the Congregational Church that you two remarkable young ladies carry the church members' donations to the hospital at Johnson's Island Prison from time to time. Is this true?"

"It is," Elma agreed.

"Ah, the good hearts of womankind," he said. "Charitable even to thine enemies. Allow me to introduce myself—Mr. Leonard Tomkins, dealer in toys and novelties. When I heard what the church-women of the community had arranged, it occurred to me that I might also make a contribution. 'Might not the men confined to the hospital be diverted from their misery by some of my wares?' I asked myself. My answer was 'Yes,' and so here I am. How very fortunate it is that I intercepted you on your errand of mercy."

"Just what is it you ask of us?" Elma said.

"I am in hope you might be induced to distribute a few packs of my playing cards and a half-dozen of my finest kaleidoscopes to the hospital inmates who are well enough to be interested in such things."

Elma considered. She would, of course, bring the novelties directly to the major to be examined. If they were as innocent as Mr. Tomkins would have her believe, then the convalescent patients might enjoy receiving them. If not, then at least one Copperhead would be unmasked.

Looking at Mr. Tomkins, it was difficult to imagine such an ordinary-looking man as a devious plotter. Perhaps he was simply good-hearted, as he made himself out to be. In any case, she saw no harm in agreeing to what he'd asked.

"It's kind of you to think of the sick men," she said. "I'll be happy to deliver the cards and kaleidoscopes."

Mr. Tomkins beamed at her, set his satchel on a mooring post, opened it, and removed two packages, one larger than the other.

"I'll make room for those in my basket," Elma told him, quickly transferring some of the preserves from her basket to Marta's. She tucked the packages inside, closed the lid, said, "Good day, Mr. Tomkins," and headed for the ferry gangplank with Marta trailing behind her.

Once they reached the island, at Elma's request, Sergeant Maybrook escorted them to Major Patton's office in the administration building, outside the stockade.

After a thorough examination of the cards and the kaleidoscopes showed nothing that could be construed as a secret message, the major said, "Distribute them to the convalescents with the food. I'll send one of my men in to keep a close watch on the patients who get the cards and the toys."

"Do you want to tell me what that was all about?" Marta asked as they walked from the administration building to the hospital with the sergeant.

"The major is a cautious man," Elma said. "He asked me to bring anything unusual to him first. So I did."

"He must suspect something's afoot," Marta persisted.

"This *is* a prison, after all."

Marta's eyes widened. "An escape plot!"

Noticing the sergeant's curious sidelong glance, Elma poked Marta with her elbow. "Do control your imagination," she said.

After shooting her an indignant look, Marta walked on without saying another word. Elma was grateful, since once her sister got an idea in her head, like a puppy with a toy, she frequently worried it to shreds. This was certainly not the time nor the place to discuss prison escapes.

Once they reached the hospital, to the sergeant's evident relief, Dr. Woodbridge offered to escort them to the ward.

"I'll be waiting outside, sir," he told the doctor.

"I believe the smell bothers him," Elma said after the sergeant left.

"Don't notice it myself," the doctor said, causing Marta to stare at him in amazement as she brought out a handkerchief she'd dampened earlier with cologne, holding it to her nose.

As they walked along the corridor to the ward, the honeysuckle scent on the handkerchief seemed to Elma to intensify the unpleasant odors rather than mask them. When they entered the ward, she didn't immediately see Captain Drury and realized perhaps she wouldn't today. Disappointment made it difficult for her to smile in response to the patients' greeting.

But after she'd opened her basket, she noticed he was present after all, helping a man at the far end of the ward to sit up on his cot. Seeing him brightened her day in the same way the sun did when it unexpectedly broke through gloomy clouds.

"Elma," her sister said, "aren't we going to start handing out the preserves."

Only then did Elma realize how bemusedly she'd been staring at Hunt.

The patients were delighted with the cards and the kaleidoscopes, as well as the preserves. Elma, caught up in the good feeling of giving pleasure to others, didn't notice the blue-uniformed lieutenant standing unobtrusively at the ward entrance until her basket was almost empty. He must be the major's watcher. When, she wondered, had he come in?

When she and Marta finished handing out their gifts, the officer sauntered into the ward, walking slowly between the beds, nodding at each of the men. His gaze, she noticed, took in the names chalked on slates attached to the wall above each cot.

Captain Drury, who had finished tending to the patients and was now talking to Dr. Woodbridge, paid little or no attention to the officer, though the doctor slanted him a sharp look.

"Come for a spoonful of the applesauce they brought me, have ye, lieutenant?" one of the patients asked.

"Not today, thanks," the lieutenant said easily. "I might take a peek into that kaleidoscope, though. Haven't looked into one since I was a boy." He lifted the toy from the man's cot and held it to his eye for a

215

moment before returning it.

He nodded at the doctor and at Elma and Marta before taking up his former position at the door.

As Elma closed her empty basket, a patient called, "Miss Johansen, when will you be back?"

"I'm not sure," she said. "I may surprise you by returning sooner than usual."

"We know your first name, but we don't know your sister's," another said.

The doctor frowned, but before he could speak, Marta said, "It begins with an M and that's all I'm going to tell you."

As they left, some of the men called possible names after them—"Mary? Minnie? Maureen?" Marta paused at the door to turn and shake her head as she waved goodbye.

"It doesn't do to become too friendly with these men," Dr. Woodbridge chided her when they reached his office. "They may deserve your sympathy because they're ill, but you must remember, they are prisoners of war."

"It was just in fun," Marta said, biting her lip.

"In the future I'd prefer you maintain your reserve the way your sister does," he said.

Hunt Drury, standing behind the doctor, winked at Elma and, remembering how he'd kissed her in this very office, she flushed. Why hadn't she struggled free? Or slapped him? What must he think of her?

"I'll do my best," Marta promised.

"I know you're busy, sir," Captain Drury said. "Shall I escort the young ladies to Sergeant Maybrook?"

"If you would, captain."

At the door leading outside, Hunt caught Elma's arm, detaining her so that Marta exited first. As she did, he bent and whispered in Elma's ear, "I'll have a surprise ready for you on your next visit."

216

Then he let her go and she joined Marta and the sergeant. At least in body. In spirit, she was still standing next to Hunt, his breath stirring the strands of hair beside her ear, sending shivers of delight along her spine.

She was thankful that Marta said little on the way to the ferry because she was too distracted to respond. Once aboard, though, her sister drew her to a vacant spot along the rail.

"I know who he is," Marta said in a low tone. "Are you out of your mind?"

Elma gathered her wits. "I haven't the slightest idea what you mean."

"Ha. You gave yourself away, you know. To me, at least. Never before have I seen you light up like a candle when you looked at a man. You did just that when you saw Captain Drury. I have to admit he's handsome enough, but you heard what the doctor said. He's a prisoner, Elma."

"There's absolutely nothing between us!"

"Then why did he hold you back and whisper to you at the door?"

Elma drew in her breath. "You mean you heard him?"

Marta shook her head. "He spoke too low. Luckily the sergeant didn't notice anything, even though you were all dreamy-eyed when you joined us. Where's that famous reserve of yours that Dr. Woodbridge praises?"

Elma glanced around to make certain no one was close enough to overhear. She was so confused by her feelings she had to talk to someone and the only person possible was Marta.

"I can't help myself," she admitted. "I seem to lose what sense I have when Hunt touches me. And I—I find I want him to touch me."

Marta stared at her wide-eyed. "Do you love him?"

Elma frowned. "How do I know? I mean, how can I? It's impossible. And yet—" She broke off and gazed wistfully toward the island the boat was rapidly leaving behind.

After bidding the Johansen sisters farewell, Hunt Drury helped Dr. Woodbridge change the dressing on young Lathrop's leg stump. He didn't need to be a doctor to see the wound had turned gangrenous, a death warrant for poor Lathrop. There was no help for him. No way out but death.

The rest of his fellow prisoners, though, had a chance for freedom. At least those well enough to walk on their own. If everything went well. Unfortunately, Hunt was no longer sure it would.

He could tell that Major Patton, the commandant, knew something was up. He must suspect messages were being sent from Sandusky or he wouldn't have sent his aide to the convalescent ward to spy on the patients. Were the Johansen sisters the innocents they seemed to be, or had they been recruited by the major?

As he disposed of the soiled dressings in the trash barrel, Hunt decided the younger sister was probably exactly what she seemed. Elma was more of an enigma. He smiled wryly. An extremely fascinating enigma. He'd been surprised by how that one relatively chaste kiss in the doctor's office had rocked him back on his heels.

Had the major taken Elma into his confidence? Hunt thought it likely. But the message hadn't been intercepted, because if it had been, there'd have been a general clamp-down by now. At the very least, the guards would have been doubled. Which meant the message was waiting for him in one of the kaleidoscopes or on a playing card.

Hunt shook his head. Wrong. The major would have examined the novelties thoroughly. He'd found nothing. Therefore the message was in a less obvious place. Or invisible. Or both. Assume invisible ink, then, that heat would make legible. But written on what? How could he go about a search without revealing to the major's aide what he was up to?

He'd finished helping the doctor with his rounds before a possibility occurred to Hunt; the playing cards had come in flimsy pasteboard boxes. The insides of those boxes were blank; it would be easy enough to inscribe a message there. He'd noticed one of the patients toss his card box onto the floor. If it remained there, Jones would sweep it out with rest of the trash tonight. Somehow the other two card boxes had to be dropped onto the floor by then. He'd do his best to arrange that they were.

When they reached the office, Dr. Woodbridge invited him in. "Have a seat, Captain," he said, "I'd like your opinion on the advisability of allowing those two young women to return here. I must say I was surprised to begin with when Major Patton informed me they'd be allowed in the hospital."

"The men enjoy the visits, sir."

The doctor sent him a sharp glance. "No doubt you do, too."

"They're very attractive young ladies."

"I'm not too old to notice." The doctor's tone was dry. "But I fear the younger one will cause trouble, innocently, to be sure, but commotion of any sort in a prison is dangerous and to be avoided."

Hunt smiled ruefully. "Even though I'm on the side that might benefit from confusion, sir, I must admit you're quite right."

Dr. Woodbridge nodded. "I find you such a reasonable man I sometimes have difficulty remembering you are a prisoner. Well, then, I shall speak to the major and strongly urge that the next visit of the Johansen sisters be their last."

Final visit for her or not, Hunt knew it would be the last time he'd see Elma, and then only if she returned in the next several days. The escape was set for this coming weekend, the message would provide the exact time to set their plans in motion. He felt a pang of regret over Elma. If he had time enough and if they weren't on opposite sides—but he had no time and they were enemies. "The mountain and the wood" were insurmountable obstacles neither could cross . . .

Chapter 15

Hunt found no way to retrieve the last of the playing card boxes that evening. To his disappointment, the two swept out with the trash bore no trace of invisible ink when he applied heat. The patient who had the third box had slipped his deck of cards back into it, making it all but impossible to acquire "accidentally," especially since the Union lieutenant—Patton's watchdog—showed every indication of spending the night on the ward. Hunt couldn't take the chance of raising suspicions by asking to borrow the cards.

He had no choice but to wait. Eventually the major would call off his watchdog; Hunt could only hope it would be before the weekend.

If only he'd been able to take the patients into his confidence! But Colonel Dodd, who was masterminding the escape plot from the barracks, had sharply limited those in the know.

"The fewer men in on the plans, the less chance of discovery," Dodd had insisted.

Hunt realized the colonel was right, but it was damn frustrating all the same. There was also the possibility no message had been sent yet, that it was still to come. But he couldn't be certain until he got his hands on that last card box.

What the hell was he to do? He'd heard the watchdog questioning the doctor about the normal routine on the convalescent ward. The patients there took care of themselves and each other after dark—it was unusual for any of them to call for help. So if he or Jones showed up unexpectedly this evening, the damned watchdog would be at their heels, watching every move. And by eleven, unless the doctor needed him, he and Jones would be locked into their bedroom by the hospital's night guard.

He'd have to wait until morning, when he and Jones helped serve breakfast. The doctor himself brought used tea leaves from the Union officers' mess to the hospital to be resteeped so his patients could count on a hot drink at breakfast—steaming hot. And he'd begged, borrowed or stolen heavy stoneware mugs to serve the tea in.

"I firmly believe a stimulant of piping hot tea does as much good as many of my medicines," Dr. Woodbridge told everyone.

Hunt tamped down his impatience. Since he had to wait, he'd put the time to use by finishing the carving he was working on. He had the doctor to thank, not only for his gift of a jackknife, but for the doctor's insistence he be permitted to keep it to make carvings in the room where he slept. Fellow prisoners and even some of the guards kept him well supplied with odd bits of wood.

He'd carved boats at first, then animals, giving his work to those who asked for them. This was his first attempt at a bird because he'd seen wings when he'd turned the piece of birchwood over in his hands. At first he'd thought it might be a hawk, but as the carving took shape, a seagull in flight emerged from the wood. Today, when Elma had come into the ward and her green eyes had met his, he'd known who the seagull was

222

meant for.

If circumstances prevented him from giving it to her in person, he'd leave it in the doctor's office with a note asking him to see that she received this gift.

Sitting on his cot with the stub of a candle sputtering on the upended crate between his bed and the cot where Jones was sleeping, Hunt sighed and set aside the knife. Damn, but he hated misusing the doctor's trust in him. Dr. Woodbridge was one of the finest and most selfless men he'd ever met. Unfortunately, war bred deceit, there was no help for it, none at all, and he owed his first loyalty to his comrades.

When the guard unlocked the door soon after dawn, Hunt was already dressed. With the finished seagull in his pocket, he hurried to the kitchen with Jones. Not long after, they wheeled the food trolley to the convalescent ward and began handing round the steaming mugs of tea.

Though the Union lieutenant looked a bit haggard this morning, he was certainly on the alert, his gaze shifting constantly from Hunt to Jones as they served the patients.

When he handed Severin, the patient with the third card box, his tea, Hunt noticed Severin was playing solitaire on his cot with the cards. He saw no sign of the box—where the hell was it? He didn't dare pause to search and call the watchdog's attention to Severin, who was busy concentrating on his game.

"Careful with that mug," Hunt warned as he passed on. He'd reached the far end of the ward when he heard a shout of pain.

"Jesus Christ!" Severin yelled. "I've scalded the hide off me prick, damned if I ain't."

Racing back, Hunt saw that Severin had upset the mug and tea was dripping from his sodden bedcovers. Severin had flung himself off the cot, hopping about

223

precariously on his one good leg while he moaned about his burn.

The Union lieutenant reached Severin at the same time Hunt did. Hunt extended a steadying hand to Severin, his gaze probing the cot, searching for the box. When he finally saw it he nudged a fold of the blanket over it, later slipping the cardboard box into his pocket under cover of stripping the wet covers from the bed.

He didn't think the watchdog had noticed. Nor was he followed when he left the ward. Holing himself up in a storage room, Hunt pried the box apart, lit a candle, and held the flame under the flimsy cardboard, far enough away to prevent a fire but close enough to allow heat to reach the box. His heart leaped as printed letters sprang into view. "All in readiness. Saturday at 11:55 P.M."

He'd no sooner finished reading the message than the storage room door was flung open to reveal the Union lieutenant framed in the doorway, his Colt drawn. Hunt attempted to set fire to the box, but the lieutenant grabbed it from his hand.

"We've suspected you all along, Drury," the lieutenant said. "Now we've caught you red-handed."

On the morning following her most recent visit, Elma stepped off the Johnson Island ferry with three quarts of strawberries packed in her basket, her "surprise" for the sick men at the hospital. The strawberries had been promised to the Congregational Church women by a local farmer who raised them.

"They ain't perfect," he'd warned, "being a tad overripe. My pigs already got all they can eat, so I figure those sick Rebs might's well have these."

The berries had been waiting at the Church for Elma the day before, when she'd returned from the island,

GET
FOUR
FREE
BOOKS

(AN $18.00 VALUE)

and she'd seen they'd have to be delivered by today or they'd rot.

Because Marta's piano lesson was today, Elma was alone. There'd been no time to send a message about her arrival, so she didn't expect to be met, but she glanced up and down the dock, hoping to see Sergeant Maybrook. Since he was nowhere in sight, she approached the private guarding the dock.

"Howdy, Miss Johansen," the private said. "This ain't your regular day, is it?"

"No, I brought something special as a surprise. Do you think it would be all right if I went on to the hospital by myself?"

He hesitated finally saying, "I ain't got no authority to give you permission."

"Then maybe I'd better go to Major Patton for that permission."

The private scratched his head. "Only trouble is, I can't leave here to take you to the major."

She smiled at him. "I can find my own way there."

"I don't know about that, Miss Johansen. Not today, anyhow."

Lifting the lid of the basket, she showed him the strawberries. "You can see I really *must* get these delivered before they spoil."

He stared so wistfully at the berries that she added, "Do try a couple."

"They're sure real ripe," he said after devouring three strawberries. "Even kind of past ripe."

"I'm positive Major Patton will want to see me," she said firmly. "After all, he was the one who asked me to make these visits to the island."

He scratched his head again. "Anyways, *you* ain't no Copperhead," he said at last. "I guess no harm'll come of me letting you past, seeing as how you're going directly to the major."

225

Elma concealed her start of surprise at his mention of Copperheads. Had something unusual happened here? If so, it wasn't obvious from where she stood. Everything looked much the same to her. Of course, she couldn't see inside the stockade.

"Thank you," she told the private, walking past him toward the administration building.

On her way, she saw Sergeant Maybrook hurrying along, obviously on his way to the hospital. Deciding that if she caught up with him she'd have an escort and wouldn't need to bother the major, she hiked up her skirts and ran, thankful she was wearing only crinolines instead of the more fashionable hoop. She could shout and alert him so he'd slow his pace, but ladies didn't shout. Not that they were encouraged to run, either, but it was the lesser evil.

Hindered by her skirts, she didn't reach the sergeant until he had opened the hospital door. Instead of entering, he stood aside. Thinking he'd seen her after all and was holding the door open for her, she swept past him, looking his way to nod her thanks. She ran full tilt into someone, knocking herself momentarily breathless, the basket flying out of her hand.

Hunt didn't waste time thanking the gods of chance. Acting quickly, he grasped Elma around the waist, whirled her to face away from him, and lunged for the Union lieutenant's Colt, yanking it free of the holster.

"I'm sure neither of you gentleman would care to see a lady hurt," he drawled. "Sergeant Maybrook, I'll thank you to hand me your pistol, butt forward."

Scowling, the sergeant did as he was told. With one arm pinning Elma against him and a Colt in each hand, Hunt eased through the door. "I do believe we need two escorts," he said. "One lieutenant and one sergeant will fill the bill nicely. Please walk ahead of us, gentlemen. I'll let you know where we're going."

226

He directed them along a path behind the hospital to where a clump of trees hid the water's edge. They met no one, and he prayed that if anyone spotted them from the rear, it would appear he was a prisoner of the two men.

He breathed a sigh of relief when he saw the boat was moored where he'd been told it would be, hidden in the reeds of the shallows.

Only then did he speak to Elma for the first time. "I'm sorry for the inconvenience, Miss Johansen. I fear it will last a while longer." Keeping one Colt trained on the men, he shoved the other under his belt while he urged her into the boat.

"You blackguard," the lieutenant muttered.

The sergeant continued to scowl fearsomely.

"You were correct all along, Sergeant Maybrook," Hunt said as he climbed into the boat. "Never trust an enemy. But be assured I shan't harm Miss Johansen."

He glanced at Elma. "Though I won't hurt you, I make no promises concerning the lieutenant and sergeant. I should shoot them to delay discovery of my escape, but if you obey my orders, I'll permit them to live. Be so kind as to cast off, please."

Since she had no choice, she obeyed, unhooking the mooring rope and pushing off from the bank with one of the oars.

"Ungentlemanly it may be," he told her, "but circumstances force me to request you to do the rowing until we're well away from shore." He raised his voice to carry. "You two stay where you are. I swear I'll shoot if you try to run."

Papa had taught them all how to handle oars so Elma had had no problem maneuvering the boat into the bay. Following Hunt's instructions, she headed for Marblehead, the nearest mainland, her thoughts in a jumble. He'd frightened her at first, and she was still apprehensive, but somehow she believed he wouldn't harm her. That didn't reconcile her to the fact he'd forced her to assist in his escape. Not in the least. She was furious with him, as well as disillusioned.

"Nicely calculated," Hunt commented after a time. "By the sergeant, I've no doubt. He'd be the one to decide when they were beyond pistol range. I'd only have wounded him, anyway. The lieutenant, now, I might well have killed him."

Glancing toward the island, she saw the two men fleeing from the shore.

"I'll take the oars now," Hunt said. "We need more speed. Thanks for your help."

Relinquishing the oars, she slid back to the next seat. "My help was certainly not freely given," she snapped. "I would never willingly assist any Reb to escape."

"Ah, but you came along so opportunely, my sweet Elma. How could I resist taking you hostage?"

"I'm not your sweet Elma!"

"No, not yet."

"Not ever!"

He grinned at her. "Time will tell."

"The sooner we part, the happier I'll be."

"You disappoint me. I thought the fact that you didn't struggle while we fled to the boat meant you cared enough about me to want me to escape."

She gestured at the Colts, one tucked through his belt on either side. "You were armed!"

"Come, Elma, you must have known I was bluffing when I threatened to harm you if they didn't do my bidding. I'd never hurt you. Luckily the sergeant and lieutenant weren't aware of that."

"How can I know what you might do? You're a Reb—capable of any frightfulness. I detest you!"

"Just the same, you're going to help me get to Canada."

228

"Canada!" Even as she said the word, she realized she should have realized where he was headed. The Canadian shore was no more than seventy miles across Lake Erie from Sandusky. In Canada, he'd be safe from any pursuit by the United States Army.

I won't do it, she told herself. Let him shoot me!

"You'll never reach Canada," she said. "Not in a rowboat."

"I'll get there." His tone was no-nonsense grim. "From talk I've overheard, I know we'll find sailboats moored near that peninsula dead ahead, and you're going to help me steal one."

Elma gritted her teeth to keep back an angry refusal—which would get her nowhere. Obviously, the only way to stop him was to pretend to go along with his plans until she saw a chance to thwart him.

She forced a smile. "If I recall correctly, you did mention you had a surprise for me on my next visit to Johnson's Island. I must admit I've never been so surprised in my life. I do hope you have no further surprises in store. Like my accompanying you to Canada."

He shook his head. "Much as I enjoy your company, I fear you'd prove to be a liability on our arrival there. Once I've acquired the sailboat, we'll simply bid one another a fond farewell."

"Hardly fond," she snapped.

Hunt shrugged and glanced over his shoulder to gauge their nearness to Marblehead. "There, by God," he said, pulling toward a cove where a single sailboat bobbed at its offshore mooring.

In vain, Elma searched both cove and boat for a sign of life. Her heart sank when she saw nothing that might prevent Hunt from appropriating the boat and sailing for Canada. Escaping. No doubt to make his way south until he reached Confederate troops and took up arms

229

against the Union again. Or, even worse, plotted again, this time with southern sympathizers in Canada, to free the Rebel officers on Johnson Island.

I won't let him get away with it, she vowed. I'll stop him somehow.

Her chance came when Hunt pulled the rowboat even with the sailboat, shipped the oars, and rose, reaching for the bow of the other boat. She jumped to her feet and rocked the rowboat violently. Losing his balance, Hunt lunged for the sailboat, missed, and plunged overboard, his head slamming against the sailboat's hull as he fell into the water.

Elma, reseating herself, grasped the oars and began to pull away. Hunt would surface soon, she told herself. He certainly wouldn't drown so close to the sailboat. But it would take him a while to climb aboard, hoist the sails, and be on his way. In the meantime, she'd reach shore, find someone, and tell them a Reb had escaped. They'd send a boat after him, and—"

Why hadn't he surfaced? Surely he'd been under at least a minute. Maybe two. Or three. She bit her lip, remembering the smack he'd given his head before he'd gone under. Was it possible he'd been hurt so badly he couldn't save himself? Was he drowning? Had she killed him?

Heart pounding in dread, she swung around to row back to the sailboat, scanning the water, praying for the sight of Hunt's head bobbing in the waves. She didn't want him dead; she'd never wanted him dead.

"Please don't let him drown," she whispered, a vise gripping around her heart at the thought of those smoke-gray eyes closed forever.

Then suddenly a hand clutched the side of the rowboat, tipping it. "Hunt!" she cried, her voice tremulous with relief. He didn't answer. Nor did he try to pull himself into the boat.

230

Shipping the oars, she dropped to her knees and edged carefully forward to look over the side. She stared down at his dazed face, blood oozing from a cut on his temple. He gagged and coughed, spewing out water.

"Hunt? Are you all right?"

He didn't seem to hear her.

"Can you get aboard?" she asked. "Give me your other hand and I'll help you."

He made no response other than the coughing. He gave no indication he knew she was there. Her alarm grew. Lake Erie didn't warm up until well along in the summer, and then only near shore. She had to get him out of the water. But how? As if in answer, the end of the rowboat swung around and thunked against the sailboat.

She glanced over her shoulder, saw a rope hanging from the edge of the sailboat, and lunged for it, rocking her boat so hard she almost fell. But she had to grip on the rope. Yanking on it, she pulled off about three feet of slack before finding that the other end of the rope was firmly attached somewhere aboard the sailboat.

The length of her boat bumped against the bigger boat's hull with every wave—luckily Hunt's grip was on the far side of the rowboat or he'd have been caught between. As quickly as she could, she looped the end of the rope into a running noose and dropped it over Hunt's head. The boat tipped dangerously as she reached over its side to grab his free arm and pull it up so she could work the rope under one armpit. Then she anchored his hand onto the side of the boat. When she was sure he had a firm grip, she pried the fingers of his other hand loose and worked the rope over that arm until it was underneath each of his arms. She then yanked the noose taut.

"Hunt," she said sharply, "listen to me. If you don't,

you'll die. I've put a rope around you. I'm going to climb aboard the sailboat and pull you out of the water. When I tell you to let go, do it. Or else I won't be able to help you." She could only pray he was able to comprehend her words.

Knowing her skirts would hinder her climb, she ripped them off, tossed them onto the deck above her, grasped the forward rail on the sailboat, and dragged herself aboard. To her great relief, she found the rope attached to a capstan and quickly wound the slack about the wood. Once the rope came taut, though, she was stymied. Hurrying to the side, she stared down at Hunt, still in the water and clinging to the rowboat. Even if she was able to convince him to let go, she wasn't strong enough to pull him up. What now?

An idea struck her. Taking a deep breath she shouted, "Captain Drury! This is your commanding officer. You are hereby ordered to climb into the rowboat." Recalling something she'd heard snapped at soldiers, she added loudly, "On the double, Captain!"

For a long moment nothing happened. Then, when she was about to give up hope, Hunt heaved himself up. She rushed back to the capstan and took up the slack in the rope, hearing his grunt as he dropped into the bottom of the rowboat below. When the rope was taut again, she returned to the rail.

"Captain Drury! Climb aboard the sailboat. That's an order."

The struggle exhausted them both but finally Hunt lay gasping on the deck of the sailboat. Making certain the rope still around him was taut so he couldn't slide off into the water, Elma sat beside him in her bodice and pantalettes, watching him anxiously as she tried to decide what to do now.

She didn't know exactly when she'd made up her mind that Hunt Drury wasn't going back to Johnson

Island or when she'd decided it was up to her to find a way for him to stay free. She dismissed the idea of Canada. Too far. Besides, though she knew her way around a sailboat, she'd never crossed the lake alone.

She had to get him away from Sandusky long enough to give him a chance to recover from his head injury. After all, it was her fault he was hurt. Where was she to go?

A whiff of pine scent brought by the freshening breeze gave her the solution: Swan Isle. The family cottage. No one was there. Her father never set foot on the isle until late June, and this was only the first week of that month. Hunt could be left there safely. With luck, she could sail to Swan Isle and back before her father returned from the foundry this evening. She'd worry about explanations later.

Elma got to her feet, tested the wind, and hoisted the double sails. When she felt the boat tug against the mooring line she unhooked it, noticing the rowboat was drifting ashore. They'd believe Hunt had landed on Marblehead. As she tacked out of the bay into the lake, she hoped the sailboat wouldn't be discovered missing until after she got back.

Swan Isle, east of Sandusky, wasn't far—maybe eight miles from shore. When she returned, she'd sail right into the harbor and tell her story. What would it be? Tacking carefully to avoid an approaching schooner she smiled. Of course. The captain had a prearranged rendezvous with a Canadian-bound ship. He'd boarded the ship, leaving her free to sail home.

As she sailed on, she cast anxious glances at Hunt, sprawled facedown on the deck. Occasionally he twitched or moved his hand, assuring her that he was alive. His clothes were soaking wet, but she thought the warm sun ought to prevent him from getting dangerously chilled. Since she could do nothing for him at the

233

moment, she concentrated on setting the quickest course to Swan Isle.

Hunt drifted into darkness, gradually becoming aware he lay on something hard, something that rose and fell and swayed beneath him. Was he dreaming he was aboard ship? After a time he realized his clothes were wet. Soaked through, making him chilly, even though he could feel the heat of the sun on his face. His head hurt like the devil.

He opened his eyes. A boat, yes, a sailboat. He was facing open water with a blur of shoreline in the distance. Where the hell was he? Slowly, cautiously, he turned his head, wincing with pain. What he saw made him think that if he hadn't already been flat on his face, he might have fallen over.

Elma crouched at the tiller, her fair hair loose and blowing in the wind. From the neck to the waist she was modestly clad, but below that . . . I must be dreaming, he told himself.

Then he saw her skirt and petticoats bunched together amidships. Why would that detail be in a dream? Looking at her again—staring, actually—he smiled despite his throbbing head and his confusion. Damned if he remembered how he got here, but he certainly appreciated the view.

Chapter 16

"You're out of your mind!" Marta cried, staring aghast at her older sister. "You know you promised Papa last evening not to leave the house except to visit friends he knew and approved of. As upset as he was over your abduction by an escaping Reb, it's a wonder he didn't lock you in this room and throw away the key."

Elma glanced apprehensively at her closed bedroom door. "Do keep your voice down, Marta. Of course I don't like going against my word, but I can't simply abandon Captain Drury. I'd never forgive myself if anything happened to him. On the other hand, there's no reason for me to openly defy Papa. He'll be much happier if he doesn't know what I'm doing. That's where *you* come in."

"You're going to get both of us in a peck of trouble," Marta pointed out. "Or, more likely, a bushel."

"If my ruse is discovered, I'll take all the blame, I promise. But it won't be. Papa hardly knows the Emersons, so the chances of him speaking to any of the family is slight. Mother will be told we plan to visit the Emerson girls and we'll leave the house together. Then we'll separate. You'll call on Sally and Zoe, saying I'll be along if I finish my errands in time which isn't actually a lie. Or not quite, anyway. My errands will simply take too long."

Marta made a face. "Spending an entire morning with Sally and Zoe Emerson is no pleasure. They chatter continuously and say nothing of consequence. Sometimes I wonder if they share even one idea between the two of them."

"Exactly why I chose them. No one ever listens to anything they say. I'm sure they'll invite you to take the noon meal with them, they always do. After you eat you can wait a decent interval before excusing yourself and going on the Congregational Church bazaar. I'll meet you there and we'll arrive home together before Papa returns from work."

"But to sail alone to Swan Isle—"

"*Ssh!* You have no idea how your voice carries, Marta. I'll be perfectly safe. It's a wonderful day; there's hardly a cloud in the sky, and the breeze is just right for sailing."

"It's not the sailing that worries me." Marta's tone was low and sober. "It's *him.* You'll be all by yourself on Swan Isle with a Reb. Lord only knows what might happen."

"Captain Drury was in no condition to be a menace to anyone when last I saw him. In any case, he's a gentleman." Elma wasn't as sure as she sounded, remembering how Hunt had swept her into his arms and kissed her in the doctor's office. *That* wasn't the act of a gentleman. On the other hand, she had to admit she'd done nothing to discourage him.

This time it would be different. When she reached the island, she'd make it clear he was to keep his distance. Recalling that he'd actually seen her minus her skirts brought a flush to her cheeks, and she turned her head to hide her telltale blush. No one would ever learn what had happened because she'd never tell a soul

236

about her dreadful lapse of modesty, not even Marta.

She hoped against hope that Hunt had been too dazed to pay attention to what he saw. He'd certainly not get another opportunity!

Hunt sat on the warm island sand, idly flipping stones into the blue waters of the cove. Snuggled into the pines behind him was the log cabin Elma had told him her family used as a summer cottage. They'd docked here yesterday, she'd unearthed a hidden key for him and left. Once inside the cabin, he'd stripped off his wet clothes, rolled himself in a blanket, and fallen onto a bed, sleeping so profoundly he hadn't roused until well after dawn.

Hanging on a hook in the cabin, he'd found an ancient pair of trousers the right length, though wide in the waist. After he'd plunged into the lake to bathe, he'd tied on the trousers with a piece of rope and then draped his still damp clothes over bushes to dry. A thorough search turned up no food and he was getting damned hungry. Except for the hunger and the frustration of being marooned on a Lake Erie island, he was comfortable enough. He'd certainly been in more perilous situations.

Rejoice in the moment, he told himself, savoring his freedom. The sun shone warm on his bare back, and he hadn't enjoyed the squish of damp beach sand under his toes for longer than he could recall. His head still ached but was rapidly improving. From the time they'd been boys, his Cousin Neal had insisted that Hunt Drury had the hardest damn head in creation. It looked as though Neal was right.

The thought of his cousin made him sigh. Once he and Neal Vickers had been as close as brothers but, as it had the country, the war had split them apart. The last he'd heard, Neal was a U. S. Army captain. No matter that Neal fought for the wrong side, God grant that he still lived.

The white sails of a small boat caught Hunt's attention. He'd watched various boats and ships pass the island, none coming close. He shielded his eyes against the sun and stared at the tiny boat on the expanse of water separating him from the mainland. This sailboat was definitely headed his way.

Elma said she'd be back this morning, and he trusted her to keep her word. If she'd meant to turn him in, she'd had her chance yesterday, when they were still in Sandusky Bay and he was too dazed by his fall overboard to put up any resistance.

What a woman she was. He'd never met one quite like her. Every inch a lady, but not too delicate to endure the unpleasant conditions of a prison hospital in order to carry out her duties. He suspected Major Patton had deliberately recruited her, hoping she'd be chosen as an unwitting messenger, a messenger who could be closely watched. It was entirely possible, though, that she was fully aware that what she carried into the hospital might be other than it seemed. He wasn't certain.

He couldn't believe she was an experienced spy—her manner was far too innocent. She didn't even seem to know how to flirt; there wasn't so much as a suggestion of the coquette about her, unlike most of the girls he'd known in Charleston. Yet something about her drew him to her. It was true he'd been without female companionship for a long time, and she *was* attractive, but what he felt for her was more than the mere desire of a man for a woman.

How did she feel about him? Though she called him her enemy and professed to dislike him, she'd helped him escape. Still, it didn't do to be too trusting. Was she coming to him now in the boat, or had she sent someone else, someone who meant to take him prisoner again?

Hunt leaped to his feet, retrieved his remaining Colt—he seemed to have lost one—from the stoop of the cottage, and retreated to the cover of the pines, where he watched the white sails flit closer and closer to the little island.

Even after he was certain it was a woman at the tiller, he stayed hidden, waiting until she had skillfully maneuvered her boat next to the small dock, thrown a line over the mooring post, and clambered over the side onto the wooden boards of the dock, basket in hand.

Catching a tantalizing glimpse of her slender ankles, he smiled as yesterday's vision of Elma at the tiller in her pantalettes came to him. But with a smile came a surge of desire that threatened to overwhelm his judgment.

Steady, Drury, he warned himself. The lady already doesn't trust Rebs; don't prove her right. At least, not without some encouragement.

Damn, but she was a beauty. Not only because of her unusual face, with its high cheekbones and seagreen eyes, nor because of the striking contrast of olive skin with light hair. And it wasn't because he'd had a secret view of the delicious curves now concealed by her voluminous skirts. No, her beauty was more than the sum of these. Perhaps some of it came from her courageous spirit.

Though she was illuminated by the sun, light also seemed to shine from her, enveloping her in a golden haze as she walked up the path to the cabin. He'd never beheld anything so wondrous in his life.

He stepped from concealment and sauntered toward her.

Elma swallowed, her step faltering as she caught sight of Hunt wearing nothing but an old pair of her

239

father's trousers held on by a rope at his waist. Auburn hair curled over his naked chest, disappearing under the cloth at his waist. She willed herself to look away, but could not. Her gaze traveled to his face, noting the glint of amusement in his gray eyes. Because she was staring?

She flushed, aware he couldn't help but see the red staining her cheeks.

As he neared her, she thrust the basket at him. "I brought food," she said. "Fried chicken and biscuits and succotash and bread and a strawberry-rhubarb pie." Why was she babbling on like a witless ninny?

He took the basket from her. "I'm starving; I thank you from the bottom of my heart. I regret my informal dress, but my clothes are still wet."

She bit her lip. "I'm afraid the wet clothes are my fault."

He raised an eyebrow. "Your fault I was clumsy enough to rock the boat and fall overboard?"

"*I* rocked the boat," she admitted. "I was trying to prevent you from escaping. But I didn't mean to drown you, really I didn't."

"If you were trying to prevent me from escaping," he said, grinning, "I'd say you made a poor job of it. Why didn't you turn me over to the authorities when you had the chance?"

"I—I'd rather not discuss it. Please go ahead and eat."

"Won't you join me?"

Elma shook her head. "I'm not hungry, thank you. Would you like to go inside where there's a table and chairs?"

"No, picnics should be eaten in the open air."

His remark pleased her. "I'll show you the place my sister and I named Picnic Rock when we were little," she said impulsively. "It's just up ahead in the pines."

When they reached the spot, he placed the basket on

240

the flat top of the sandstone outcropping but refused to be seated until she was. By the time Elma remembered her vow to be formal and distant with him, they were already sitting side by side on the pine needles.

Never in her life had she been so close to a man who wore so few clothes. She tried to keep her eyes focused straight ahead, but still she noticed the ripple of the muscles under the bare skin of his back. To her shock she found herself tempted to touch his skin and feel the strength of those muscles under her fingers.

She cleared her throat, searching for words to put between them. "I trust your head isn't too painful."

"A tad sore, that's all. I expect Cousin Neal is right about the hardness of my head."

"Cousin Neal?"

As he ate, he told her about Neal Vickers, reminiscing about their shared childhood.

"What a pity you're now fighting on opposite sides," she said when he finished.

"It's even more of a pity you and I are on opposite sides," he told her. "I believe Neal has forgiven me for my beliefs, but I'm not certain you ever will."

His gray eyes gazed into hers, asking a question that unsettled her, a question she was sure had nothing to do with forgiveness. She blinked, glancing away, only to be confronted by the whorls of his auburn chest hair. Long enough, she decided, mesmerized, to curl around her finger.

"It's the exact same color," she murmured without thinking about what she was saying.

"What's the same color?"

Quickly she shifted her gaze to his head, aware she was once again blushing. "Your hair is the same color as my grandmother's," she told him, unable to come up with anything but the truth.

"Grandmothers usually have gray hair. Or white."

"She died young." Elma's hand went up to touch the

heart-shaped locked she wore. "Like my mother. But she left a strand of her hair inside here."

"May I look?"

"I don't mind, but it's difficult for me to open the locket unless I take it off."

"I'll help." Before she had a chance to agree or refuse, he leaned over and gently opened the locket's latch. She caught her breath, feeling the warmth of his hands against the bare skin of her throat.

"There are two snippets of auburn hair inside," he said.

"One is supposed to be that of a distant ancestor; the other is my grandmother's."

"I agree, the color does resemble mine," he said, closing the locket carefully. His hands slid up from her throat to cup her face. "I wonder if they were beauties like you."

Bemused by his touch and his nearness, Elma could hardly breathe, much less talk. If he kissed her, as she desperately hoped he would, she'd be lost. With her last ounce of will, she pulled away from him and jumped to her feet.

"If you're quite through eating," she said, surprised that her voice wasn't trembling, "we must store the leftovers. I'll show you the best place to keep food so it won't spoil—in the stone cooler my father built under the floor of the cabin. I'm not certain how often I can get over to the island with more supplies, so—"

He rose and held up his hand. "How long do you intend to keep me here?"

She stared at him. "Keep you here? What an odd way to put it. I—I—" She paused, suddenly aware she had no ready answer. What *did* she intend to do about Captain Hunt Drury of the Confederate Army, now that he'd recovered from his injury?

"Do you mean to turn me in after all?" he asked.

Did she? In another week or two her father would be

242

moving them to the cabin for the summer, so Hunt would have to be gone by then. The only alternative to turning him in was to help him escape to Canada. Is that what she meant to do? Because she didn't know, Elma stared at him helplessly.

He picked up the basket and took her hand. "For now, let's go and find the stone cooler," he said. "On the way, you can tell me about your childhood—it's your turn. How long have you lived in Sandusky? Were you born here?"

His questions and the feel of his fingers closed around hers distracted her from her dilemma of what to do about getting him off the island. Hesitantly, she began telling him how her mother had died when Marta was born, how her father had then married Freda and moved all of them from the shore of Lake Superior to the shore of Lake Erie.

By the time they reached the cabin she was talking about her twin half-brothers. "I dearly love them both, but Erik and Piers can really be double-trouble," she said.

He nodded in sympathy. "I expect our parents felt the same way about Neal and me when we were boys together."

Realizing they were still hand-in-hand, she sought an excuse to free herself and found one when she noticed his clothes draped on bushes near the cabin. "Your clothes must be dry," she said, pulling away, "I'll bring them inside."

Hunt went in ahead of her. She found him in the main room of the cabin, looking around.

"You mentioned that your father had built this cabin with his own hands," he said. "Do you suppose your parents lived in a similar cabin when they were first married?"

"I know they did, for Papa told me so. A smaller cabin, but much like this. With a wigwam nearby for

243

my mother's great-grandmother." Elma put a hand to her mouth after she spoke, for the words had slipped out without her thinking.

Freda had repeatedly cautioned both her and Marta not to mention their mother's Indian heritage for fear it might reduce their chances for an advantageous marriage.

"In Sweden we'd think nothing of it," Freda had insisted, "but in this country, in the United States, people look upon the Indians as inferior creatures. Your papa, if you ask him, will tell you such is the truth. But it might be wise not to bother him with such questions for these beliefs anger and upset him."

Hunt gazed at her intently. "You have Indian ancestors?"

His knowing could make no real difference to her life and it would be a relief to talk openly about what she and Marta had only whispered to themselves in private. "My mother's mother was a British lady who married a Seneca Indian. After her parents died, my mother journeyed from Lake Ontario to Lake Superior to her grandfather's people, the Chippewa. She found only her great-grandmother still alive. My father, newly arrived from Sweden, was working in a copper mine near the Chippewa village."

Elma sighed. "He says he fell in love with my mother the first time he saw her."

"I know the feeling." Hunt's tone was wry. "There's nothing a man can do about it but accept fate."

She glanced at him and found him smiling at her. "How did your mother feel about your father?" he asked.

"Papa says she took some convincing."

"That trait must run in the female line of your family. I don't find *you* easy to convince."

Elma's heart speeded. He was implying he'd fallen in love with her at first sight. She wanted to believe him,

244

but could she?

Keep your head on straight, she warned herself, edging away from him. "The cooler's just over here, near the corner."

After Hunt had placed the remaining food inside the cooler and set the empty picnic basket on the table, he once again took Elma's hand, urging her toward the door. "Would you show me around the island?" he asked.

Knowing she ought to say goodbye and climb onto her boat, Elma found herself tempted to stay a bit longer with Hunt. Small as the isle was, she had enough time to do as he asked and still sail back and arrive home before Papa got there.

"There's not much to see except the pine grove," she told him.

"Ah, but I love pines. The scent of the trees reminds me of home. Shall we walk through the grove?"

As they strolled underneath the interlaced branches of the pines, he dropped her hand to put his arm around her shoulders, drawing her closer to his side. Aware she should move away, she argued that there was no harm in allowing herself this much closeness.

"I wish we could walk forever like this," he said softly.

Though she didn't admit it aloud, she fervently agreed. Nestled against his side she felt safe and cherished. She felt loved. It wasn't until they came out from under the trees at the far end of the island that she realized clouds had shut away the sun.

Elma pulled free, alarmed as she gazed at the sky.

"It looks as though there might be some weather brewing," Hunt observed.

She bit her lip as she noted how dark the clouds were and how the wind had picked up. Why hadn't she paid attention to the weather?

"I must hurry back!" she said.

245

He caught her arm. "Are you mad? Look at that stormy sky. I've heard that storms here are more dangerous than on any other of the Great Lakes because Erie's so shallow."

Elma couldn't deny the truth of his words. She'd grown up hearing terrifying tales of storm winds lifting water from the lake's shallow bottom to create waves so vast and dangerous that no boat could survive. Erie was the graveyard of many a lake boat. The storm clouds and the already rising wind warned her she'd waited too long to risk even the short trip from Swan Isle to Sandusky.

Yet if she didn't leave, her ruse would be discovered. Marta would surely tell Papa exactly where she was and why, once he began questioning her.

"I must go!" she cried.

"Absolutely not!" Hunt tightened his grasp on her arm.

"But if I don't return before Papa—" She broke off as a jagged streak of lightning split the dark clouds. Thunder rumbled.

"Nothing your father will do or say is worse than drowning," Hunt insisted. "Come, we'll go batten down the boat so she'll ride out the storm safely. But I'm damned if I'll let you try to sail her until the storm's over."

"You don't understand," she wailed.

"You can explain on the way."

The rain began while they were securing the boat, becoming a downpour by the time they finished. When they reached the cabin, they were soaked to the skin. Elma climbed the ladder into the loft bedroom she shared with Marta to search for dry clothes, but all she could find was an old white nightgown with a scoop neck. Luckily the gown was of flannel, making it opaque, but the ribbons that were supposed to thread around the neck and be tied to keep the neckline modest were gone, making the scoop far too low.

She slipped a faded green shawl they'd used as a dresser scarf over her shoulders, crossing it in front so she was decently covered. Still, she felt dreadfully undressed as she climbed barefoot down to the main cabin.

Hunt had exchanged her father's old trousers for his own gray ones, but he wore nothing else. He stood by the window, his back to her, gazing at the storm. When she joined him, he slid his arm around her waist, making her more aware of him than of the lightning and thunder outside.

As the windblown rain whipped across the window, she warned herself that being close to him was more dangerous than any storm, no matter how violent. Yet she didn't move.

He turned to her, tilting her face up with his hand. "I dream every night of you," he murmured, his forefinger tracing the outline of her lips.

She shivered under his feather-touch, a touch she felt to the very marrow of her bones.

"You're cold; I'll warm you," he said, wrapping his arms around her and pulling her against the heat of his body.

She wasn't cold, not at all; she was on fire, aflame with the pervasive need he lit within her. When he kissed her the shawl, tied too loosely, slipped from her shoulders as she raised her arms to hold him closer. It didn't matter. Nothing mattered except Hunt's embrace.

"This seems like a dream to me," he whispered in her ear, then trailed kisses along her throat to where the neck of the gown barely covered her breasts.

He lifted his head to look at her and the glow in his eyes turned her knees to jelly. His hands eased the gown from her shoulders, freeing her breasts.

"Beautiful," he murmured. "Made for love. My love."

Then his mouth closed around her nipple and she thought she'd die of the agonizing pleasure coursing through her, finally centering deep and low inside, making her arch against him.

He eased her onto her back on the bearskin rug in front of the hearth, holding her in his arms. Her bare breasts pressing against his naked chest excited her, the thrust of his tongue into her mouth filled her with an aching need to have more and more of him.

He tasted sweet and tart, of honey and rhubarb, with the same delicious underlying flavor she remembered so well. Time had stopped, this was forever, she would never let him go.

She was hardly aware of him slipping her gown over her head, she didn't notice when he removed his trousers, she only knew the wonderful sensation of warm flesh against warm flesh, his skin against hers.

"We're together," he said hoarsely. "Together, despite all odds. Nothing will ever truly separate us again."

Scarcely able to think, much less talk, she murmured incoherent agreement.

His hands caressed her breasts, then slid over her hip until his fingers touched her between her legs, beginning a throbbing inside that grew stronger, so demanding that all she could was gasp, "Please, please . . ." without knowing what she begged for.

He rose over her, his knee pushing her legs gently apart and she opened to him eagerly. She felt his hardness against her softness, probing, easing inside her slowly. Too slowly. She wanted, she needed. She wrapped herself around him, pulling him onto her, into her. For an instant she thought she felt pain, but then, as he thrust deep inside her, there came the most intense pleasure she'd ever experienced.

She lost herself, she became a part of him, no longer two but one, together, never to be separated again, no

248

barriers between them. No darkness, only light as explosively bright as lightning, light crackling around them, exploding inside her until she was consumed by its bright fire.

Gradually she came back to herself, aware of Hunt's arms holding her and the tickling softness of the bearskin under her. She saw his smile, tender and loving.

"You're mine," he said softly.

"Then you must be mine," she told him, her fingers twining in his chest hair.

He raised an eyebrow. "Must be?"

"Are."

He ran his forefinger gently over her breast, circling her nipple. "I guess I am yours, at that."

She heard the faint surprise in his tone, but, bemused by his renewed caresses, she paid no attention, refusing to remember there was any world beyond the two of them.

"No mountain, no wood between us," he murmured against her lips.

"Nothing between us," she whispered.

Nothing but love, her heart added. She would have repeated the words aloud if, at that moment, he hadn't pulled her on top of him, holding her close and kissing her. As the throbbing began deep inside her once more she realized with amazed delight that the wonder she'd just experienced was going to happen all over again.

Chapter 17

She was alone in a sailboat on dark waters under a gray sky with no land in view. Though she tried with all her might to reach the tiller, she couldn't move and the boat drifted, rudderless. She was lost on an unknown sea with no way to help herself.

A flash of white caught her eye, momentarily lifting her hopes, but it was only a seagull winging its way across the water. She watched it circle the boat four times, then alight on the stern, fixing a beady eye on her.

Opening its beak, it squawked, "Gone, gone, gone."

"No!" she cried. "No, you lie!"

The bird flapped its powerful wings and soared aloft, higher and higher into the sullen sky, its mournful mew drifting faintly to her ears.

"Gone . . ."

Elma opened her eyes to see sun slanting in through the window. Still unsettled by the dream, she stared at the knotty pine ceiling in confusion until it came to her where she was: in the cabin on Swan Isle . . . with Hunt . . . lying on the bearskin in front of the hearth where they'd made love during the storm. While she slept, the storm must have passed over. She turned to

250

look for Hunt, but he was no longer beside her.

When she sat up, the paisley shawl covering her slipped down, reminding her she was naked. She clutched the shawl around her, wondering when he'd gotten up and fetched the shawl from the cedar chest to cover her. She hadn't heard a sound.

Where was he now? As she started to rise she noticed, on the raised hearth beside her, a carving she'd never seen before—a seagull, wings spread in flight. The wooden bird rested on a folded piece of paper. She picked up bird and paper.

"I made the seagull for you," she read. *"It was to have been a surprise. Try not to hate me."* There was no signature.

Elma stared from the note to the exquisite carving momentarily puzzled until the ominous portent of the dream came back to her. She leaped to her feet in alarm, hurriedly wrapped the shawl about her, and ran to the door. Looking down to the dock, she saw no sign of her sailboat. Gone. Gone, like Hunt.

"No!" she cried, clutching the bird and the note in her hand. "No, he wouldn't leave me! Not after—" She cut off her anguished lament. He *had* left her, difficult as it was to accept. She flung the carving and the note away.

Clenching her teeth to hold back tears, she retrieved her still damp clothes and dressed, anger gradually replacing her heartbreak until, by the time she'd tidied her hair, she was fuming. How dare he steal her boat and leave her stranded here? Somehow, someday, she vowed, though she had no idea how, where, or when, she'd get even with Hunt Drury. As she left the cabin to circle the island to see if she could spot the sails of her boat, she imagined him at her mercy, smiling grimly when she pictured herself being as ruthless and cruel to him as he'd been to her.

Once outside, she realized how low the sun was. In Sandusky, Papa would have gotten home by now. He'd be furious. With poor Marta left to suffer the brunt of it before confessing all, but confess she would. Perhaps Papa was already on his way to Swan Isle in the ketch. Giving up any idea of trying to see where Hunt was headed in her boat—it could only be Canada—she ran down to the dock and looked toward Sandusky.

Did those sails belong to the ketch? Quite possibly. Elma bit her lip. She'd be humiliated past bearing if Papa came to suspect what actually had happened, so she'd best have some acceptable story ready. And that meant she must straighten the cabin. Quickly.

She rushed back, stuffed the flannel nightgown and the old pants Hunt had worn into the picnic basket, then removed the leftover food from the cooler and put it on top of the clothes. She slid the paisley shawl into the cedar chest, folded a blanket Hunt must have used, and smoothed the bearskin. By the time she finished, the ketch was sailing into the cove.

Elma started out the door with the basket and paused to retrieve the discarded note and carving, thrusting them hastily into her pocket. On the way to the dock she rehearsed her story, which was actually the simple truth. What she left out was her own affair.

She'd begin by admitting she'd told a lie about the prison escape. The Reb, she'd say, had been injured in the escape and he hadn't been met by a Canadian-bound ship. Instead, she'd left him on Swan Isle because his wounds had made her feel so sorry for him she'd been unable to turn him in as she should have done.

When she brought food for him today, he'd tricked her and sailed off in her boat. Yes, she knew she'd been a silly goose and she'd learned her lesson.

Elma blinked back tears. A more devastating lesson than Papa would ever know . . .

The following week the Sandusky *Register* hailed Elma Johansen as the "brave and beautiful heroine" who'd helped foil an escape plot by "Confederate officers held on Johnson's Island." The article described her "harrowing experiences" when the single successful escapee took her prisoner.

Two weeks later another article appeared after an interview with Dr. Woodbridge, who described Elma as "an angel of mercy."

"Please don't read any more from the newspaper to me," Elma begged Marta. "I don't care to know what they print. It's not the truth, anyway."

"You ought to be glad no one knows the truth except you and me and Papa," Marta said. "He didn't even tell Mother everything."

Just as I haven't told you everything, Elma thought.

"You can't hide in your room refusing to see callers forever," Marta went on.

"I never want to speak to any man again."

"Major Patton blames himself, that's what he told Papa. He said he wouldn't be surprised if neither you nor Papa ever forgave him. Papa said it wasn't the major's fault, but his own. I couldn't help hearing because they talked so loud."

Elma sprang up from her bedroom rocker and began pacing back and forth. "Why do they all insist on assuming blame when I'm the only one at fault? I have nothing to forgive the major for, I simply don't want to see him again because he's a man. I hate men! Except for Papa."

Someone tapped on the door. When Marta opened it, Toivi handed her a card, saying, "Man want give to

Miss Elma. He wait." Marta thanked her and closed the door again before offering the card to her sister.

Elma refused it. "I will see no one."

Glancing at the card, Marta said, "This is from a total stranger. At least *I* never heard of any Captain Neal Vickers."

Elma stared at her. "Who? Give me that." She studied the meticulously hand-printed letters on the card with disbelief. Was Hunt's cousin here in Sandusky?

"You look like you've seen a ghost," Marta said. "Who is he?"

Elma told her.

"Maybe he read about Captain Drury's escape in the paper," Marta pointed out. "Since you say they were close, he might want to ask you about his cousin. You *were* the last one to see him."

She didn't want to talk about Hunt; she didn't even wish to think about him. At night she dreamed of him, dreams where they shared tender caresses, where he made exquisite love to her. Elma clenched her fists, forcing the dream images from her mind. She wanted no reminder of Hunt, and she opened her mouth to say Neal Vickers could go to the devil for all she cared but paused before the words emerged.

Captain Vickers was no Reb. He wasn't an enemy, he was a loyal Union officer. He couldn't help being related to a wrong-headed, deceiving scoundrel, and she must not let her hatred of his cousin make her prejudge him. Besides, to be truthful, she was a bit curious about the captain.

"You've convinced me I shouldn't hide as I've been doing," she said to Marta. "Please go down and tell Captain Vickers I'll be along in a few minutes. And send Toivi up to help me get into my hoop."

Intent on creating a proper impression, she chose a

254

new afternoon gown of pale green, one she'd been saving for an occasion. Since she'd always done her own hair, she swept it expertly into a twist, using a tortoise-shell comb, allowing a few artful strands to escape along her nape.

"Pretty, you," Toivi offered.

Elma smiled at her, nodding in thanks, and squeezed her skirts through the bedroom door. Descending the stairs, she paused, listening to the voices from the parlor where Marta was talking to Captain Vickers. He sounded, she decided, a good deal like his cousin, though with much less of a drawl.

He rose when she entered the room and bowed. She saw a tall man, handsome in his blue uniform, his black hair cut quite short. Though he sported a small mustache, he wore no beard. Otherwise he was quite like Hunt, too much so—especially his eyes. They were gray and, at the moment, admiration gleamed in them.

She raised her chin, determined not to be charmed by him and offered her hand. "How kind of you to call, captain," she said coolly.

"The pleasure is mine, Miss Johansen. I realize it's an imposition for a stranger to arrive on your doorstep; it's exceedingly kind of you to agree to see me."

"Do sit down," she said, seating herself on the lyrebacked chair near the door.

"Your sister has been telling me how the two of you brought food to the Confederate prisoners on Johnson's Island. A noble gesture, indeed."

"I believe you must have had a reason for seeking me out, Captain," she said.

"If you'll excuse me," Marta put in, "I'll have Toivi bring refreshments."

He watched Marta leave the parlor before replying. "I understand you've been through an unhappy experience and I hesitate to ask any questions that

255

might bring back unpleasant recollections."

"In other words, you wish me to tell you about your cousin, Captain Drury, is that not so?"

He sighed. "We were—we are—very close. It's natural I should worry about him."

"He was quite well the last time I saw him." Despite her attempt to speak calmly, the words snapped out.

"Thank you. I'm sure you have no fond recollection of the encounter."

Was it her imagination or did she hear an odd undercurrent in his voice? She glanced at him and found he was regarding her intently.

"I must say I admire your courage, Miss Johansen. I wish we could have met under more auspicious circumstances, for I would like your permission to call on you again—and not to discuss my wayward cousin. But no doubt you don't care to see anyone who might remind you of—"

"Nonsense!" Annoyance colored her cheeks and tinged her words. "I've put the experience behind me once and for all. Why should a United States Army officer remind me of the Rebel prisoner who—" About to say "betrayed me," she caught herself in time. "Who used me to further his escape?" she finished.

"I'm glad to hear you will judge me on my own merits. I'll do my best to prove worthy of your trust. May I then have the pleasure of escorting you to the concert in the park this coming Sunday afternoon?"

"If my father approves, Captain Vickers." Elma was quite certain her father, still upset over her escapade, would do no such thing.

She was wrong.

"I see no harm in you listening to music in public, during the day, with this army captain," her father said that evening. "Fresh air and sunshine will bring the

256

roses back to your cheeks. Besides, Freda and I will be attending ourselves."

No doubt to keep an eye on me, she thought. Not that he needed to; she had no reason to wish to be alone with Captain Vickers. Or with him at all. So it surprised her when she found herself looking forward to Sunday.

She deliberately wore the green taffeta again, telling herself she didn't care that he'd already seen her in the gown. What did it matter? She was never going to permit herself to fall in love again, certainly not with a man whose eyes reminded her of the one who'd betrayed her.

"He's very handsome," Marta told her as she helped her dress. "I tend to prefer dark-haired men, you know." she sighed. "Unfortunately, the captain has eyes for you and you alone. I think he was interested in you even before he saw you—he asked ever so many questions about you while he was waiting for you to come downstairs that day. I think you're attracted to him as well. When you walked into the room I swear I saw lightning flash between the two of you."

Marta's exaggeration caught at Elma, unhappily reminding her of what had happened on Swan Isle during the storm. She pulled her thoughts determinedly back to the present. "Lightning? How you do go on."

"He wanted to know if you had a steady beau. Oh, he didn't come right out with it but I knew what he was asking. I told him you weren't interested in men at the moment, and he seemed to find that amusing."

Elma looked at her sister in despair. "Must you always say the first thing that comes into your head?"

"I only spoke the truth. Didn't you want Captain Vickers to hear it?" Marta looked so stricken that Elma put her arms around her sister.

257

"Never mind. It doesn't matter." As she consoled Marta, she wondered why Neal Vickers would be amused by Marta's comment, since he knew nothing about any of them other than what he might have read lately in the newspapers about her. He'd soon discover she wasn't interested in *him*.

By Sunday noon, the day promised to be extremely warm for the end of June, despite the breeze off the lake. Later, when she left the house to walk the two blocks to the park with Captain Vickers, Elma raised her green and white striped parasol against the sun's hot rays.

The captain offered his arm to her and, as she laid her gloved hand on his sleeve, she felt a strange, unexpected frisson. Touching him, she thought, was like touching Hunt Drury. But that was surely a foolish fancy, and the quicker she rid herself of it, the better.

The music began before they reached the bandstand, the stirring "Battle Cry of Freedom" making her pulse leap with patriotic fervor. "Isn't that a glorious song?" she cried.

"It makes one eager to rally round a cause," he agreed.

"*A* cause? Freedom for the slaves is *the* cause."

"The Confederates might argue that freedom to govern themselves is also a cause."

She looked at him, astonished to hear such words from a Union officer.

"In a war, there are always two sides," he said mildly. "Stirring battle cries send men rushing to fight, but the reverse side of the coin is the losses suffered in war, told in the sad songs of farewell like 'The Soldier's Lament.'"

"That *is* a mournful song. It must be hard to leave one's family and friends behind to go and fight."

"It can be equally painful for those left behind, never

258

knowing when or if they'll see their loved one again."

Again he'd surprised her. She'd often been in the company of officers, and they tended to talk of exploits in battle or to smother her with flattery. None had ever spoken like Captain Vickers. How well she knew the pain of being left. Not that she ever wanted to see Hunt Drury again!

As they neared the park, she met so many people she knew that she grew quite weary of smiling and nodding. It looked as though every inhabitant of the city had turned out to see and hear the band play.

"The park's uncomfortably crowded," he said. "Since the music's loud enough to be heard blocks away, shall we stroll past instead of trying to fight our way through the throng?"

"If you like."

He led her past the park and up Miami, one of the diagonal streets, leading them away from the center of town. By the time he turned off on Poplar, the music had become too faint for her to recognize the tune.

"I believe we're getting rather far from Washington Park," she said.

"I understand there's a small park near here where I thought we might rest," he said.

Since he was correct—West Park was only a few blocks away—she decided not to insist on retracing their steps. It would be equally convenient to return to the concert from West Park.

They found the small triangular park deserted. Not a soul sat on the iron benches in the shade of the spreading elms.

"Shall we take a few moment's respite here?" he asked.

She seated herself on one of the benches and he sat beside her. Since the bench was shaded, she collapsed her parasol. A mockingbird trilled from a nearby tree,

259

a carriage rattled past on the street beyond the park—
familiar, peaceful sounds. But Captain Vickers's nearness kept her from relaxing.

"You are the most beautiful woman I have ever
seen," he told her. "I envy my cousin for meeting you
before I had the chance."

She couldn't help be pleased that he thought her
beautiful, but what he'd said about his cousin riled her.
"You have no cause to envy Hunt Drury," she said
tartly.

"He's such a charmer I feared you might have
conceived a *tendresse* for him despite the fact he so
callously abducted you."

"I was not charmed by Captain Drury!" she
snapped.

"Then there's hope for me?"

"I'm afraid I—" She broke off, startled, when he
tipped her face toward him with his forefinger under
her chin.

"I want to look at you," he said softly, leaning to her,
his gray eyes holding hers.

He was so close his breath stirred a tendril of her
hair, close enough that his male scent filled her nostrils,
a scent that excited her with its familiarity. Hunt! her
senses told her. She closed her eyes and swayed toward
him.

His mouth covered hers, his kiss thrilling her as no
man's could except Hunt's. When her lips parted
involuntarily and she tasted him, her memory told her
it was Hunt she tasted. No matter who this man
claimed to be, her body told her he was actually Hunt
Drury.

But how could he be?

She pulled away, trembling, opening her eyes to
stare at him. Black hair. No beard. Small mustache.
Hunt had auburn hair, a full beard and no mustache.

260

But hair could be dyed, beards could be shaved off, mustaches could be grown. And blue uniforms could be bought or stolen.

Eyes were difficult to disguise. Especially eyes as gray as storm clouds, gray eyes that glowed when he looked at her, as he did now. Indignation fought against the spell those eyes were casting over her. What was he up to, passing himself off as his cousin, a Union captain, and seeking her out?

Her first impulse was to denounce him, but she discarded it. No, she told herself. Play along. He didn't come back here merely to see you, he's up to no good, and it must have something to do with Johnson's Island. You must pretend to believe he's Captain Vickers until you discover his reason for returning to Sandusky.

If she could manage to convince him she believed he was Neal Vickers and he tried to use her in whatever devious plan he had in mind, with luck she'd be able to expose him and his wicked Rebel plot. This was her chance for revenge, and she meant to take it.

Looking away from him, she said, doing her best to sound prim and proper, "I'm not accustomed to being kissed against my will, Captain Vickers. If I were not a lady, I would certainly slap your face."

"I don't believe the kiss *was* against your will."

"I found myself quite paralyzed by your boldness," she said. "Otherwise you may be sure I would have struggled."

"In that case, do forgive me." His voice mocked her.

She glanced at him from under her eyelashes as she'd seen her friends do when flirting with their swains. "I don't know if I should. I never dreamed an officer and gentleman would take such liberties. Why, sir, you've all but made a public spectacle of me."

"There's no one about to see us," he murmured,

capturing her hand.

She allowed him to retain her hand but leaned away from him. "The street is lined with houses. Houses have windows and the people inside do, after all, look through those windows."

Despite her anger at his deception, she had to fight against her inexplicable longing to be in his arms. How could she still desire the caresses of her betrayer, a man callous enough to attempt to use her for his own nefarious purposes not once, but twice? Still, in a way, she was enjoying the situation because she had the upper hand and he didn't know it.

Would Hunt Drury be jealous if she allowed Neal Vickers to make love to her? The thought made her smile. Not that she intended to go further than a kiss or two.

"I can see by your smile you've forgiven me," he said. Holding her gloved hand between his, he brought it to his lips and the warmth of his mouth through the thin cloth made her breath catch.

"I'm sure my father will be looking for me at the concert," she said.

"With the crowd in Washington Park, he won't be certain whether you're there or not."

"Nevertheless, I think we should walk back." Again she cast him what she hoped was a coquettish look.

"Not until you agree to see me again."

"I'm not certain I should. How can I trust you to behave?"

He leaned toward her. "I could promise, but you, Elma Johansen, are temptation incarnate, and I've always had a devil of a time resisting temptation." He brushed his forefinger over her lips.

Without thinking, driven by an inner pulsing need she couldn't quite control, she parted her lips and her tongue touched his finger, lingering in a far more

262

intimate caress than she'd intended.

He drew in his breath. His eyes darkened with passion, his hands gripped her shoulders, and for one suspenseful moment, she thought he meant to pull her into his arms and kiss her as she longed to be kissed.

He regained control of himself with an effort and let her go. Damn her, what was she up to? The Elma he thought he knew was no coquette. She never would have behaved in such an abandoned fashion. Had he been wrong about her?

She'd given no indication she'd penetrated his disguise, so she must believe he was his cousin, Neal Vickers. Yet she'd not only allowed Neal to kiss her, but had flirted outrageously with him. He'd come within an inch of losing his head a moment ago. How could she be so heartlessly wanton?

He knew he'd been the first man to make love to her, but now it appeared he might not be the last. Or rather, Hunt Drury had been the first, but Neal Vickers could be the next. He smiled wryly. Hell of a thing to be jealous of yourself.

"I might consider seeing you again," she said, picking up her parasol and twirling it in her fingers. "And then again, I might not be able to. Have you met Major Patton? A fascinating man. He takes up much of my time, you know."

He came alert. Just as he'd hoped—she knew Patton socially. Her connection with Patton was a key element in his plans. Pushing away the nagging question of what liberties she allowed the major, he said, "I believe there's an organ recital at one of the churches on Tuesday evening," he said. "Will you attend with me?"

I wonder where he plans to take me instead? she asked herself, certain he didn't mean to sit in a church pew listening to the organ.

"I imagine my father will find a church recital an

improving activity," she said demurely.

"Do you mean he's going?"

She smiled inwardly at the alarm in his voice. "I fear Papa doesn't care for recitals. What I meant was that he'd have no objection to you taking me."

Elma took a great deal of care choosing her ensemble for Tuesday evening. She meant to strive for a certain look and she wasn't quite sure how best to achieve it.

"Why not your rose gown?" Marta asked. "It truly becomes you."

"Too missish. I want to seem more sophisticated."

"Sophisticated! You?"

Elma raised her eyebrows. "Why not?"

"To go to church?"

"I have my reasons."

"I'm not sure I like Captain Vickers. Not if he's going to change you."

"Would you please hand me the brown silk?" Elma said.

"You've never liked it," Marta reminded her as she obeyed.

After Elma donned the tobacco-brown dress, she examined herself critically in the pier glass. The bodice was of figured moiré, the material of the skirt plain with multiple tiers.

"It makes you look like someone else," Marta offered.

"Since that's my aim, I'll wear it. With, I think, my new straw hat with the tan ostrich feather."

"But you'll be all in tans and browns. Not in the least colorful."

Elma didn't argue. Her sister had no idea of the impression she wished to create, that of a woman of the world, not a sweet young thing in rose taffeta bedecked

264

with bows and ruffles. She changed her hairdo, creating a low pompadour in the front and sides with combs and allowing the rest of her hair to fall naturally onto her shoulders. After she'd tilted the straw at a daring angle, she anchored it with hatpins and studied her mirror image carefully, finally nodding.

"I'd swear you were twenty-five, at least," Marta said. "I can't think why you'd want to give the impression of being so old."

"Someday I'll tell you," Elma promised.

Marta regarded her with narrowed eyes. "I can tell you're excited but you don't look happy. Are you up to something you'll regret later?"

"Who can see into the future?"

Captain Vickers was waiting for her in the parlor. "Your father and I had an interesting conversation," he told her once they'd left the house and stepped into the blue of evening. "He's very concerned for your safety. After the events of several weeks ago, I can understand why."

You ought to, you caused most of what happened, she thought cynically. What she said was, "I'm sure I'm perfectly safe with you."

She pretended not to see the quick glance he gave her.

"We seem to be going the wrong way," she said after a moment. "Perhaps you're not aware the Congregational Church is in the other direction."

"I thought we'd take the long way around," he murmured.

Once they rounded the corner, she noticed a carriage waiting up ahead and was unsurprised when he led her to it.

"Such extravagance," she commented as he helped her in. "A carriage for a ride of a few blocks."

When he'd seated himself beside her and lifted the

reins, he gave her a long look. "You *are* a minx. I believe you knew from the beginning I had no intention of taking you to the recital."

Elma widened her eyes and laid her palm against her chest. "Such an accusation! And just where *are* you taking me?"

"A place where we can be alone for a hour or so."

"Why, Captain, whatever gave you the idea I'd wish to be alone with you?"

"*You* did. If I'm wrong, you'd best tell me now."

"How can I? I don't yet know whether or not I'll like being alone with you. I declare, I never expected to be abducted even once in my life. I do hope this abduction won't prove to be as unpleasant as the first. But then, how could it be? After all, *you're* not a traitorous Reb."

Chapter 18

As they left Sandusky on a road that ran along the shore of the lake, Elma, to counteract her nervousness, began to hum, not paying attention to what song she'd chosen until she reached the chorus and the words formed in her mind: *Farewell, farewell, my own true love* . . . She stopped abruptly.

"You've been very quiet, Captain Vickers," she said.

"I've been thinking that perhaps we should have attended the organ recital instead."

"But we didn't."

He sighed, almost immediately turning the horse onto a path that led into the darkness of a pine grove. Here he stopped, tethered the animal, and helped her from the carriage.

"I thought we might stroll along the shore," he said, "It's but a short distance through the pines."

She knew they were in a seldom-frequented spot with no houses or even farms nearby. Ordinarily she'd never have agreed to come to such a lonesome place with any man of her acquaintance, and certainly not with one who was a stranger. But he wasn't the stranger he pretended to be. Even so, she wondered if she'd regret her rashness.

"Your cousin told me pine trees reminded him of home," she said as they walked toward the lake with the dry needles crunching under their feet.

"Yes, they would. We have many varieties of pine in Virginia."

"You both grew up in Virginia, and yet you have less of a drawl than your cousin."

"I was sent north to college. To my ruination, Cousin Hunt once told me."

"To my way of thinking, salvation would be more appropriate."

"That's another way of looking at it," he said as they came onto the beach.

It was not yet fully dark. A few salmon-tinged clouds lay low over the lake in the dark blue sky of the long summer twilight. Waves lapped the sand in a gentle caress while the breeze whispered softly through the pine branches. A night for lovers, and she was with her lover. A lover who'd betrayed her once and was planning to betray her again.

"Beautiful," he murmured.

"Yes, the evening is lovely."

"I didn't mean the evening, I meant you." Putting his hands on her shoulders, he turned her to face him.

She'd vowed she wouldn't let his touch affect her, but she had no control over her pounding pulses.

"Did he mean anything to you?" he demanded. "Anything at all?"

She knew very well who he meant. If he thought she was going to admit that she'd never forget that day on Swan Isle with Hunt Drury, he was very much mistaken.

Batting her eyes, he said demurely, "Whoever are you talking about? If you mean Major Patton, why of course I like him, or I wouldn't permit him to call."

"I meant Hunt. My cousin."

268

"It's not easy to forget—or forgive—an enemy."

"An enemy is all he was to you, then."

She contrived to look amazed. "What else *could* he be?"

Was he never going to kiss her? Deciding to confuse him as much as possible by her behavior, she slipped her arms around his neck and drew his head down until their lips met. Almost immediately she knew she'd made what might prove to be a fatal mistake. He pulled her close, his fierce and hungry kiss stirring a passion she'd hoped and prayed would never awaken again.

Her lips parted, inviting him to take all he wanted. She was helpless against the onslaught of desire blazing through her, demanding fulfillment. She was in the arms of the only man in the world who could satisfy that demand—how could she resist?

His hands, warm and urgent, cupped her breasts through the silk of her gown, making her moan with the need to feel his mouth against her bared breasts. She'd thought she could tease him; she hadn't dreamed it would be this way, that his caresses would sweep away her resolve until all she wanted was for him to make love to her, to never stop making love to her . . .

"Lovely Elma," he breathed against her lips.

She came close to betraying herself by murmuring his real name in return. The shock of her near slip enabled her to come to her senses enough to slide her hands between them and push him away.

When he released her she found her knees so weak she very nearly lost her balance. Annoyed at herself for her loss of control, she walked away from him toward the water's edge.

"Did you know my family owns an island in Lake Erie?" she found herself saying. "An isle, really. We usually spend our summers at the cabin there."

"Not this year?" He spoke from close behind her.

269

"Not until after the Fourth of July, my father decided." He claimed the delay was because he'd volunteered to set off the gunpowder on one of the foundry's anvils—a dawn tradition on Independence Day. She suspected, though, that Papa was giving her time to recover from what he thought of as her unpleasant experience on Swan Isle. Dear God, if only Papa knew!

Hunt's arms came around her, drawing her back against him before she had the wit to resist. His warm breath in her ear sent a tingling along her spine.

"I'd like to hold you forever," he whispered.

As Elma repeated to herself that she must remember to call him Neal Vickers, even in her own mind, she eased free of his grasp before she found herself once again caught in an insidious web of desire.

"Forever is a poet's word," she said as coolly as she could. "Since we're mortal, we won't last forever. At least in the flesh."

"I never dreamed I'd find a philosopher in Sandusky, Ohio." His tone was mocking.

"What did you expect to find? A sobbing victim, shattered by your cousin's abduction?"

He laughed. "Ah, Elma, you're a delight. You will let me call you Elma, won't you?"

"Since you already have, I suppose I have no choice. Shouldn't we be getting back?"

"There's time yet to walk along the water's edge." He offered her his arm. "After all, that's why we came."

In a pig's ear, she thought inelegantly. "How true," she simpered.

"I wonder if I might impose upon your goodwill," he said after they'd strolled for awhile. "I believe you mentioned that you and Major Patton are friends?"

"Acquaintances, at least."

"I've never met the major and my leave grows short,

270

so I doubt I'd have the chance under ordinary circumstances. I thought perhaps you might be willing to effect an introduction between us and maybe even put in a good word for me."

So he *was* up to something, exactly as she'd suspected. "I believe I could arrange to introduce you to Major Patton," she said cautiously.

"Before I came here, I was approached by a Mr. Rogers, a wealthy Cincinnati businessman who wished to reward those who prevented the prison break on Johnson's Island. In fact, to show his appreciation for their bravery and acumen, he wants to throw a gigantic party at the West House in Sandusky for the officers and men who guard the prisoners. He begged me to approach Major Patton and present his offer. How could I refuse?"

"I agree it would have been difficult. It seems very kind of this man."

"Then you'll help me?"

"Gladly. I'm a great admirer of Major Patton's. He's honest, upright, and very clever. If anyone deserves a reward, he does." She hoped her praise of the major would stick in his craw.

"You seem quite fond of him. I suppose, like all your admirers, he's completely smitten with you."

She shrugged, not wanting to overdo it. Once again she was to be put in the uncomfortable position of go-between. At least the major had been open with her, which was more than she could say for Hunt—no, Neal Vickers. How surprised he'd be when he discovered how neatly she'd revenged herself on him.

He stopped abruptly and gripped her shoulders so tightly it hurt. "Do you let the major kiss you like this?"

He gathered her close and his mouth came down on hers, hard and ruthless.

I won't dissolve, she told herself. I won't, I won't.

To no avail. How could she resist him when her body betrayed her by ardently responding, by demanding more?

"Well?" he asked hoarsely against her lips.

"No," she whispered, not adding, no one but you. I hate you but there'll never be anyone else who can make me feel as though the world's well lost for one kiss.

"I wish to hell I could believe you," he said harshly, releasing her.

As they rode back to Sandusky, Elma chattered on about her sister and their friends, but he heard scarcely one word out of ten.

Damn the woman. She was a wanton, no doubt about it, letting Neal Vickers all but have his way with her. How could he have been so mistaken about her? Yet he still wanted her with a provoking urgency that had come far too close to making him lose his head there by the shore. He'd never in his life made love to a woman against her will, but he'd come within an inch of flinging her onto the sand and taking her whether she agreed or not.

The more he tried to tell himself her behavior was of no importance as long as she helped him convince the major to agree to the party, the angrier he became. What had happened between them on Swan Isle had been a dream come true. Damn it, she had no right to destroy such a beautiful illusion by giving every indication she'd equally enjoy making love with Neal Vickers.

When the time came to say goodnight, he could hardly force himself to be civil to her.

*   *   *

272

Because she was curious to know if Major Patton would be able to penetrate the disguise of Neal Vickers, Elma arranged the meeting between the two men without giving the major any indication things might be amiss.

The major was courteous and amiable, telling Captain Vickers he was gratified that his men's efforts were appreciated and that he'd be glad to meet with Mr. Rogers, the Cincinnati businessman, to discuss a party for the troops.

The men left the Johansen house at the same time but, beforehand, she'd sent Marta to the ferry landing to hand a sealed note to the soldier who patrolled the dock, a note he was to deliver to the major before he boarded the ferry to sail back to Johnson's Island.

Major Patton called on Elma the following day, as her note had requested. "Something's up, is it, my dear?"

"How did you know?"

"I'd like to believe your request was simply for the pleasure of my company but I'm past the age where I can easily fool myself. You want to talk to me either about Captain Vickers or Mr. Rogers—or both. Am I right?" He marched over to the parlor door and slid it open before she could reply, nodding in satisfaction when he found no one listening.

"You've truly frightened my brothers," she said. "They either run into the backyard or to their room the minute they see you coming."

He guided her away from the open windows facing the side yard and up to the closed ones facing the street. "It's always best to speak softly," he warned.

"You didn't seem to recognize Captain Vickers," she said.

He frowned. "Should I have? I don't recall each and every officer I've met in the past, but—"

273

"He's not a Union officer."

Major Patton narrowed his eyes. "You're certain?"

"Quite certain. Under another name, in another uniform, he once took me prisoner."

"By God, you don't mean he's Hunt Drury!"

"He is."

"So Mr. Rogers must be a Copperhead and the so-called party a plot to free Reb prisoners while my troops are being entertained. What gall the man has!"

"He has, indeed," she said emphatically. "I haven't let on that I've seen through his disguise, and I won't until you've set a trap for the two of them."

"I can't allow you to be placed in any danger."

"I won't be. He suspects nothing."

"Your father won't take kindly to—"

"Never mind my father. I'm no longer a child, whatever he may think. If I refuse to see the captain, he might smell a rat and flee. I don't want that to happen. I mean to see him captured and his nefarious plan defeated. To that end I intend to continue treating him as I would any Union officer of my acquaintance. That is to say, in a courteous and friendly manner. I'm quite able to do so. You said yourself that I have a poker face."

The major, obviously not happy with her stand, stared through the window as he pondered. "I don't like it," he said finally, "but I fear you may be right about Vickers becoming suspicious if you drop him immediately after having introduced him to me. You must, however, promise never to be alone with the man."

"I'm not a goose, Major."

He smiled for the first time. "No one is more aware of your quick wits than I, but I sometimes fear you have more courage than prudence."

"I promise to be very careful." The truth was, she

274

didn't dare be alone with the false Neal Vickers, not because he was a Rebel spy, but because she couldn't trust herself.

Sitting alone in the parlor after the major left, Elma tried to feel happy that Hunt Drury was on the way to getting his just desserts, but instead she had a bad case of the dismals. Even the sweet scent of roses drifting in through the open side windows didn't raise her spirits.

She sat sunk in gloomy thoughts until roused by her brothers' quarreling voices outside the window.

"They don't always shoot 'em," Piers insisted. "Sometimes they hang 'em. Just ask Papa, if you don't believe me."

"Ain't you never heard of firing squads?" Erik demanded. "In wars they shoot spies. So you got to stand against the wall and let me shoot you."

"I don't neither!"

Their bickering went on but Elma, frozen in her chair, heard no more. With some satisfaction, she'd imagined seeing Hunt returned to prison because of her, but now she realized that might not be what would happen, not if he was a spy. Tears filled her eyes and rolled down her cheeks unheeded as the full horror of what she'd done settled leadenly into her heart. She was unaware of Marta walking into the room until her sister knelt beside her.

"Elma, what's the matter?" Marta asked.

"I've sentenced him to death," she whispered brokenly, "and I can't bear it."

He'd stayed away from the Johansen house, knowing he couldn't trust himself near Elma. He wasn't sure what would happen the next time he touched her and he knew he couldn't afford to jeopardize the plan.

"I ought to strangle the damn little flirt," he muttered

the night before Rogers' party as he strode along Columbia Avenue toward Washington Square, walking the streets because he couldn't stand being inside the hotel. Rogers was dining with Major Patton tonight. He'd declined, pleading an upset stomach and promising to join them later for coffee. The truth was he needed to be alone for a while.

He was nervous about tomorrow night, but that wasn't his problem. She was. God, how he yearned to hold her in his arms one last time. No matter how it went tomorrow, he'd never see her again.

Independence Day—a perfect time for a party. He and Rogers couldn't have planned it better. And Patton, he was sure, didn't suspect a thing. Probably. It bothered him a tad that Patton had been so cooperative.

In his musings he didn't notice he'd reached her street. He hadn't meant to come this way. Or so he told himself, knowing he lied. A lamp glowed in an upstairs window and he stopped to stare. Was that her bedroom? He imagined her undressing and had to force himself to cease before his own imagination drove him crazy.

He heard a door close. Not the front door, because he could see it. The back door? He shrugged. Probably her father coming out to sit on the back porch and smoke his pipe. Of course it was her father. Why, then, was he easing noiselessly through the side gate and edging toward the back of the house? Not to see Olav Johansen, certainly. Damned foolishness. But he didn't retreat.

He peered around the corner of the house and looked at the porch. No one was there. Like as not he'd heard Olav going in rather than out. Get out of here, he ordered himself. Yet he crept forward instead, far enough for a complete view of the yard.

Movement caught his eye. He held his breath. A woman dressed in white sat on a swing hung on a branch of a large tree.

Marta, he told himself. She's the younger, the most likely to steal out for a swing before bedtime. He drifted along the fence until he was behind the tree and inched closer until he was in back of the woman on the swing, close enough to see how she dug the toe of her shoe into the dirt, barely moving the swing back and forth, back and forth.

The faint scent of clover came to him—Elma's.

He smiled. Making certain she was gripping both ropes with her hands, he reached out and grabbed the wooden seat of the swing, pulling it far back and then letting it go.

"Oh!" she cried as she rose into the air. "That was sneaky, Marta. I almost fell off."

He caught the ropes on the return swoop and stopped the arc. "I'm not Marta," he said softly.

Elma leaped from the swing so hastily she stumbled. He caught her and, once his arms were around her, he didn't let her go.

"I damn well shouldn't be here," he whispered into her ear.

"No, you shouldn't," she agreed breathlessly, clinging to him as tightly as he held her.

Her scent and the feel of her softness against him were intoxicating. When he kissed her he lost all sense of time and place. He even forgot who he was supposed to be. He'd never wanted a woman as desperately as he wanted her. Swan Isle hadn't been enough, he'd never have enough of making love to her.

Her ardent response to his kiss and his caresses fired his passion until he thought he'd go mad with his need for her. He wanted her naked under him and he cursed the layers of cloth separating them. When he finally

277

unbuttoned, untied, and pushed aside enough garments so he could cup her bare breast in his hand, he groaned with pleasure.

"Hunt," she murmured against his lips. "Oh, Hunt."

All but mindless with desire, he very nearly missed what she'd called him.

Hunt.

He pulled back, holding her by the shoulders. "You know."

As she started to answer, he heard a man shout and froze.

"They've followed you," she said, urgently. "Don't get caught. There's a gate into the alley. Run!"

He spun away from her, sprinting for the fence. "Swan Isle," he called back to her. "After the war."

Elma sent up a prayer as she heard the gate click shut behind him. Gathering her wits, she hastily rearranged her clothing, smoothing her hair as she hurried toward the house. She got as far as the porch before her father slammed open the door, calling her name.

"I'm right here, Papa," she said. "Whatever is all the shouting about?"

Chapter 19

Toivi showed Major Patton into the parlor where Elma sat before the fire with a book in her hands. She laid the slim volume aside and rose to greet him. He crossed to her and took her hands. "Excuse my dampness," he said. "We're having a rather wet May."

As they'd had three years ago, she thought. Just as now, it had been raining on that day when the major had first involved her in the affairs of Johnson's Island.

"Do sit down," she said, seating herself and gesturing to a chair on the opposite side of the fire.

As he did so, he glanced at the book she'd left on the table. "Walter Savage Landor. Don't believe I've heard of him."

"He's a poet."

The major's slight nod dismissed poetry. "I've come to say goodbye, my dear."

She blinked in surprise. "But you once spoke of settling in Sandusky after the war."

"I've changed my mind. General Sherman has asked if I wished to be posted to the western plains and I decided my future and perhaps the future of the country lies to the west. I think I've always known the Army was my career."

Elma searched for something to say, uneasy because she suspected she might have had something to do with Major Patton's change of mind. She'd never refused to see him during these last three years, but she'd only encouraged a limited friendship despite being aware he wanted more.

"It's been him all along, hasn't it?" he said, breaking the growing silence. "You've never forgotten the man."

She knew who he meant. "I don't—" she began, intending to deny her feelings, then paused, her glance flickering to the carved seagull on the table beside the book. "Yes," she admitted, "I'm afraid that's true." She looked directly at the major. "You've never accused me of warning him, but I'm sure you've always known that's why he escaped."

Major Patton's smile was wry. "It was some consolation to net Rogers and his ring of conspirators—thanks to you. I didn't wish to discuss Captain Drury with you before now because I hoped the passage of time would make you forget him. To my regret, I was mistaken." He leaned forward. "The war's been over for a year, Elma. You mustn't waste your life pining for him."

He didn't understand that she wasn't pining. What she was doing was waiting. She smiled at him. "I'll miss you."

He rose abruptly. "And I'll miss you. I'm sorry it has to be this way."

She was sorry, too, for she liked Tom Patton very much, and respected his stalwart integrity. But she'd learned what love was, and she didn't love Tom. She walked with him to the door and kissed him on the cheek in farewell. He held her close to him for a moment, then released her and left the house without another word.

Elma sighed. Why couldn't love be directed where it

ought to go? Instead, love caught one unawares.

What if Hunt never returned? She refused to believe he hadn't survived the war because she couldn't bear to think he might be dead. But did his being alive mean he'd come back to her?

Swan Isle, he'd told her. Since the war ended she'd visited the island on every fair day in the spring and fall as well as spending all of last summer there. He hadn't come.

"Why are you moping about in the entry?" Marta demanded from the staircase.

"This rain is enough to make anyone feel dreary," Elma said.

"Papa told me before he left for work this morning that we'd have clear skies by afternoon. He's usually right. What did the major have to say?"

"Come into the parlor and I'll tell you."

When Elma finished, Marta shook her head. "I know I used to make fun of him, but that was when I was still a child. He's really a fine man."

"I can't marry a man I don't love."

Marta rolled her eyes. "I don't intend to fall in love if I can help it. All love seems to do is make people miserable."

"I thought you were more or less engaged to Silas."

It was Marta's turn to sigh. "He thinks so, too. And so do his parents. And mother. Sometimes I feel that Papa and you are the only two people in Sandusky who aren't trying to shove me into Silas Portland's arms."

"Don't you want to marry him?"

"I don't know."

"Then you don't want to. Hold out for the real thing. Wait until you fall in love."

Marta grimaced. "And be miserable?"

*   *   *

281

Papa had been right. Shortly after noon, the rain stopped and the sun broke through the rapidly dispersing clouds. Elma changed her morning gown for a sturdy forest green twill dress requiring only two petticoats, a dress she favored for sailing. She put on the jacket that matched the dress, added a tan hat with a jaunty green feather, and set off for the dock where she kept her sailboat. Actually, Papa had bought the boat for both her and Marta, but her sister had never shown much interest in sailing.

The tiny wooden dock on Swan Isle was empty of boats until she tied hers there. She hadn't allowed herself to become discouraged last year, but she couldn't deny her disappointment forever. The lines of Landor's "Separation" that Hunt had once quoted to her echoed in her mind:

> Between us now the mountain and the wood
> Seem standing darker than last year they
> stood . . .

She blinked back tears, tempted to cast off the lines and sail back to Sandusky without setting foot on the island. But in the end she climbed from the boat and walked slowly toward the cabin sheltered by the pines. She didn't go inside. Instead, she climbed the hill into the pines, finally perching on top of the picnic rock to avoid the underbrush still wet from the rain.

The sun shone warm on the rock, making her drowsy. She leaned back, supporting herself with her arms. Closing her eyes, she relived that magic day here with Hunt yet one more time. She pictured him clearly in her mind, wearing nothing but her father's ragged trousers cinched around his waist with a rope. Though she'd known little of men, she'd realized he was magnificent. She smiled, remembering how ashamed

282

she'd been of her fascination with his auburn chest hair . . .

A jay squawked loudly from a branch above her, interrupting her reverie and making her open her eyes. She blinked, uncertain at first of what she saw.

A man in buckskins, wearing boots and a wide-brimmed hat, strode up the path toward the pines. She sat straighter, indignant that a stranger dared trespass on Swan Isle. Her movement evidently attracted his attention, because he halted, shading his eyes against the sun to peer at the rock she was on.

"Elma?" he called.

She stared at him incredulously. Was it possible? He swept off his hat and his auburn hair gleamed in the sun. Scrambling down in a flurry of skirts, she ran to him, his name catching in her throat.

And then she was in his arms, held tightly against him while he kissed her breathless.

They didn't talk until after the storm of lovemaking, not until they lay close in each other's arms, temporarily sated.

"I've come from Texas," he said. "The future's in the west, and I've made my stake there. And a damn lonesome time it's been without you. Will you marry me and become a Texan along with me?"

"I'd follow you to the moon and beyond," she murmured in joyous contentment, only vaguely aware of the location of Texas. Wherever it was, she'd be happy there. Nothing in life mattered but being with Hunt. Forever.

Chapter 20

Marta, one hand clutching the heart-shaped locket she wore around her neck, stood at her bedroom window staring out it at the turning leaves of the maple, red and gold among the green.

I won't do it, she told herself. I will not set my wedding date for November. Or any other month. Elma was right—I can't marry Silas.

If only her sister were here to support her. But Elma was Mrs. Hunt Drury now, and lived way off in Texas. The newlyweds had invited her to come with them, and she'd been tempted, but how could she go along and be a third wheel? Besides, mother had thrown a fit at the very idea of losing both her girls at once. Even Papa had pulled a long face.

At the last minute, Elma had given her the locket.

"But Papa gave our birth mother's locket to you because the oldest girl was meant to have it," Marta had protested.

"And now I'm giving it to you. What's wrong with that? I want you to wear this locket to remember me."

"As if I could ever forget my only sister!"

Elma had also been her best friend, Marta thought. Now she had no one else she could be as frank with, no

284

one she dared share secrets with, no one to listen to her private feelings.

"You and Silas have been sweethearts since you were children, of course you'll marry him," had been Mother's response to Marta's stammered doubts. "He's following in his father's footsteps, and one day he'll be president of the bank. You'll have a good life with Silas Portland."

Marta grimaced. Sweethearts! Actually, to her way of thinking, Silas was more like a brother. She was fond of him, but she didn't want to spend the rest of her life with him. In fact, she dreaded marrying anyone. She wasn't ready to settle down to making a home for a man and bearing his children. Why, she'd hardly ever been out of Sandusky in her life, and then only to Cincinnati and Cleveland, and once to Detroit.

Elma was lucky she'd gone to Texas with her new husband. What a strange and wonderfully different place Texas must be. There must be many other wonderful places in this country, but if she married Silas she'd probably never see any of them because he didn't like to travel.

Across the alley she saw Edith Knowles, the Portlands' cook, dumping scraps into the dog's dish. Mrs. Portland was furious because Edith had given notice and was leaving at the end of the week.

"To cook in a Wisconsin logging camp, if you can believe it!" was Mrs. Portland's lament.

Marta had decided the logging camp would be far more interesting than the Portlands and Sandusky. She quite liked Edith, a big, rawboned woman in her forties who looked as though she could handle even the toughest lumberjack with one hand tied behind her.

She watched Edith open the alley gate and, through the open window, heard her calling the dog. Marta shook her head. Brownie, like most of the neighborhood dogs, was hanging around the Emerson house waiting for their spaniel to appear. Though Marta wasn't supposed to know such things, she was well aware the spaniel was in heat.

Leaning down, she called to Edith, telling her where Brownie was.

"Thanks," the older woman shouted up to her. "I just made a batch of molasses cookies—come on over and have a couple."

Edith was asking her to share cookies with her in the kitchen. It wouldn't be the first time Marta had sat at the deal table drinking coffee and eating Edith's cookies. Marta liked kitchens—the Portlands' as well as her own. She'd always enjoyed helping with the cooking. Maybe she wouldn't like it so well on her own, but she'd found working in the kitchen with another woman could be fun. Especially good-natured, no-nonsense Edith.

Aware Silas was not at home but with his father at the bank, she nodded at Edith and left her bedroom.

"Dogs'll be dogs," Edith said once Marta was seated at the kitchen table. "If there's a willing bitch in the neighborhood, off they go. Sorta like men, when you come right down to it."

Marta didn't understand exactly what Edith meant, but she knew the cook's conversation would horrify her mother. She, though, found it fascinating.

"How did them sticky buns turn out?" Edith asked, plunking a cup of coffee down in front of her.

"Not as good as yours. I tried to make them the same as I did here with you, but I must have forgotten something. We ate them all, though."

Edith sat across from her and stirred two lumps of sugar into her coffee. "Like it black and sweet," she said, as usual. Marta added both sugar and cream and took a cookie from the heaping plateful on the

286

table between them.

"I'm going to miss you," Marta said.

"I might miss you, too, come to think of it. Ain't often I get me a good kitchen helper. Let me tell you one thing—your cooking's gonna make young Silas a contented husband."

To Marta's surprise and distress, tears she couldn't control filled her eyes and dribbled down her cheeks. Embarrassed, she searched her pockets in vain for a handkerchief.

Edith handed her a plain white cotton square and Marta tried to wipe away the tears, but they kept coming. Finally she gave up and covered her face with her hands and wept.

She heard the scrape of a chair and then felt Edith's hand patting her shoulder. "Go ahead, girl, get it all out," Edith advised. "Better out than in."

Instead of making her feel worse, Edith's sympathy dried her tears. She sniffled a bit more, then used the handkerchief. "I didn't mean to be such a baby," she said.

"You have a spat with young Silas?"

Marta shook her head. "We never fight."

Edith raised her eyebrows.

"I mean it. What do we have to fight about? He always expects me to agree with him and so I do. It's less trouble."

"Don't sound right to me. You got opinions, ain't you?"

Marta bristled. "Of course I have opinions! It's hard to explain, but I just don't care enough to argue about anything with Silas."

"And you're gonna marry that boy?"

Marta found herself shaking her head violently.

"Well, well. There's gonna be some mighty surprised people around this house if you don't."

"Around my house, too," Marta said ruefully. "Everyone will be upset. Even angry." Her voice rose. "I can't marry Silas, I just can't."

"Then don't."

Marta stared at Edith. "It's not so easy as that."

"Most things you want real bad ain't easy," Edith told her. "If you ain't gonna be happy with him, then don't play dog in the manger. Let some other girl make him happy, 'cause you sure won't."

Never once, Marta realized, had she thought it unfair to Silas to marry him feeling the way she did. But it was. He deserved someone who truly loved him, someone like Zoe Emerson, who'd never had eyes for any man but Silas.

"I've been selfish," she admitted, "looking only at my side."

Edith, refilling her own coffee cup, didn't argue.

Marta, foreseeing the hurt feelings and the arguments ahead once she made her decision clear to everyone, shook her head. "I wish I was going to Wisconsin with you," she said.

After a long moment of appraisal, Edith said, "You want to come, come along."

Marta gaped at her, taken aback. "But—but they wouldn't want me at the camp," she managed to stammer.

"They want *me* real bad on account of the owner knows me and my cooking and he likes both. If I show up with a kitchen helper—cookees, they call 'em—and say I won't work without the one I brought, he'll take you on."

"You mean you're acquainted with the man who owns the logging camp?"

Edith nodded. "Worked in one of his camps before, in Michigan."

"I don't really want to be a kitchen helper in a logging camp, do I? Marta asked herself, still shaken by being taken up on her wish.

"Let me think about it," she temporized.

"You got three days."

As soon as she returned home, Marta gathered her courage and informed her mother she intended to tell Silas that she couldn't marry him. Once Freda found she couldn't budge Marta from her decision, she went into a tizzy. Papa hardly got inside the door from work before Marta heard her pleading with him to "talk some sense" into his daughter, adding that Marta was "as stubborn a Swede as you, Olav."

Papa put off the talk until after the evening meal, when he invited Marta to join him on the back porch, the September weather being mild.

"Let's see," Papa began as he lit his pipe, "you're twenty this year, aren't you?" He seemed surprised at his own words, muttering in Swedish about the swift passage of time. "Twenty is surely not too young for a woman to marry."

"You've no need to point out that I'm practically an old maid," Marta said.

"That wasn't my intention." He took her hand, smoothing it between his. "You have small hands, like Silver Grass," he said. "And you have her beautiful dark hair as well."

Marta bit her lip, aware Papa must be remembering that her birth mother had died at the age of twenty. She didn't want memories of the past to hurt him, so she blurted, "Papa, I don't love Silas in the way a woman should love the man she marries. He's like my brother."

"Many marriages based on mutual fondness work out very well."

"Please believe me—it wouldn't work for me. I watched Elma and Hunt, and I know there can be more than fondness. If I marry, I want what they have. Do you know what I mean?"

He sighed. "My sweet little girl, I know all too well what you mean—you want to give your heart away and have his in return."

She blinked in surprise at his understanding.

"There's pain in love such as that." Sadness tinged his voice.

"I learned about the pain from Elma. But in the end she was so very happy. I may not find what she and Hunt have—actually I'm not sure I want to—but I refuse to marry a man I don't love."

"If you don't marry, what will you do?"

Marta didn't realize she'd made up her mind until the words poured out. "Right now I want to go to Wisconsin with Edith Knowles and be her kitchen helper at the logging camp." She watched her father apprehensively, positive he'd be against it.

There was a long silence before he spoke. "This is a rather sudden decision, isn't it?"

She thought a moment. "Maybe. But I've always wished to see more of the country than just Sandusky. And I like Edith—and cooking."

"I fear a logging camp is not the exciting place you might believe it to be. As a kitchen helper you'll work hard, Marta. Much harder than you can imagine."

"I want to try."

"I hear the stubborness in your voice. Even as a baby you had an obstinate streak, and you've never lost it." He shook his head. "Lumberjacks are rough and tough. To place an innocent young girl among such men—" He broke off and rose. "Before I go any further, I'll have to talk with Edith Knowles."

She watched him descend the back steps and cross the yard. By the time he reached the alley gate the gathering darkness hid him from view. Should she wait here? Since the alternative was to go inside and face

Freda, she remained where she was. It seemed a very long time before he returned.

She sprang to her feet when she heard the alley gate close. When he reached the back porch he stood at the bottom of the steps looking up at her.

"Edith's a good woman," he said. "An unusually strong woman. I don't like where you're going, but everyone, man or woman, should be allowed to choose. Edith has promised she'll watch out for you and keep you safe. I believe her." He climbed the stairs slowly and rested his hand on Marta's head. "You're certain going to Wisconsin *is* your choice?"

She raised her chin, "I am, Papa."

He sighed. "I won't stand in your way. But you must promise me you won't let pride stop you from coming home if you don't like it there."

"I promise." She'd never felt such a confused muddle of emotions in her life. Elation and excitement mingled uneasily with apprehension and doubt—she'd never really expected to be allowed to go.

Papa put his arm around her shoulders and drew her with him toward the back door, saying, "I fear your mother won't be happy with my decision."

There was no doubt of that, she told herself, wondering if she herself was entirely happy about Papa's decision . . .

The steamer *Maybelle,* out of Chicago, docked at Marinette, Wisconsin, just before sunset on the second day of October. Marta was given little chance to see much of the bustling town because Edith hurried her toward a row of waiting wagons so fast she caught no more than a glimpse of plain wooden buildings and men in brightly colored shirts stomping along the wooden sidewalks in their heavy boots. She did notice how gouged the sidewalk was, and mentioned it to Edith.

"That's on account of jacks wear hobnailed boots," Edith said. "Calks, they call 'em—steel points on the soles. Got to have something sharp to get a good grip with their feet when they drive the logs down the river. Plays heck with wooden sidewalks and floors, though."

"Oh." Marta didn't understand entirely, but she supposed she would in time. So far, the trip had been disappointing, mostly because she was not a good sailor. She hadn't disgraced herself by getting really seasick, but she'd felt queasy for almost the entire voyage up Lake Michigan.

"Pendelton-Terwilliger, Camp 1," was lettered on the red banner flying above the wagon Edith steered her to.

"Howdy, Miz Edith," the grizzled driver said as they approached. "Good to see ya. Signed on here only 'cause I heard you was gonna be the cook. A man can eat just so much berled slop afore he dies." All the while, his small, dark eyes gazed curiously at Marta.

"Hello, Joe," Edith said. "This here's my cookee, Miss Johansen. You can call her Miss Marta. And let me warn you right off, best watch your language around her or you'll have me to reckon with."

"What I got to say is pure enough for a parson's ears, danged if it ain't. Howdy, Miz Marta. You be a sight for sore eyes. I swear I ain't never seen a cookee as purty as you."

"Hello, Joe," Marta said, understanding she wasn't going to be told his last name.

"Only you two passengers. The rest is supplies for the camp van—B.&L. chawin' baccy, calks, pacs, pants and shirts, and a case o' Scandihoovian dynamite to keep the Skandies happy."

Marta settled herself beside Edith, who sat next to Joe. He clicked to the team and the horses started off.

292

"You got many Skandies this year?" Edith asked.

"Some. Canucks and Paddies, too. All the boys ain't in yet. You remember MacDougal? He was set to be bull-o'-the-woods, only he came roaring into camp drunk's a skunk. Old Beau wasn't there, Mr. Terwilliger was. Well, he up and fired Mac on the spot. Said Mac insulted him." Joe spit off to one side of the wagon.

"I didn't understand much of that," Marta ventured to Edith. "What on earth is Scandi—whatever dynamite?"

"Snuff. The Skandies—that's the Swedes and Danes and like that—they like their snuff strong. Canucks are French-Canadians, and the Paddies are the Irish. Bull-of-the-woods is the camp foreman, that's an important job."

"Yeah," Joe put in. "Mac's one of the best."

"Sober." Edith's voice was tart.

Joe shot her a sly look. "Seems like I recollect Mac was sort of sweet on you at that camp over on the Saginaw."

Marta was amazed to see Edith flush. "You'd best mind your own business," Edith said tartly.

They left the town behind and very shortly the woods closed around the narrow track, shutting out the twilight and plunging them into gloom. Soon Joe lit the kerosene lanterns hanging on either side of the wagon. As they went on, Marta began to believe the forest of lofty straight-trunked white pines must be endless. Accustomed to the small pine groves near Sandusky, she found the dense growth daunting.

"Yessir, it's high time we got up to this neck o' the woods and let some daylight into the swamp," Joe said. "I heard tell Wisconsin's got enough pine to last a hundred years or more."

As they drove on and on, Marta began to believe it

might be true. An owl hooted four times somewhere among the trees, its mournful cry making her shiver. She'd known logging camps were in the woods, but she hadn't imagined a wilderness as vast as the one they traveled through.

"When do we arrive?" she asked, huddling into her hooded cape and keeping a tremor from her voice with an effort.

"Camp's just down the road a piece," Joe said. "Hey, Edith, I think your cookee needs cheering up. How about one of them Canuck songs like 'Alouette'?" Without waiting for an answer, he began singing a rollicking tune.

Edith promptly joined him. Marta listened with fascination. She and Elma had taken French lessons for a year, but she could barely make out the words because Edith pronounced them one way and Joe another, neither quite the way she'd been taught. Because the words were repeated so often, she soon understood enough to join in, and as she sang, her spirits rose.

Eventually she saw lights up ahead in the gloom. When they pulled into camp they were singing another French song, "En Roulant Ma Boule."

"Hello the wagon," a man's voice called, stopping them in mid-song. "I recognize Joe's bellow and Edith's alto, but I confess, the soprano has me puzzled."

"Evening, Mr. Pendleton," Joe said, reining in the horses by one of the wooden buildings. "Edith's gone and brought a cookee with her."

Marta tensed. Beauford Pendleton, one of the camp owners, was the man who'd hired Edith.

"Either I keep her or Joe takes us back to town now," Edith said without making any move to climb down from the wagon.

"As you well know, my dear Edith, the camp cook's

word is law." Mr. Pendleton sounded amused. "By all means, keep your cookee."

Encouraged, Marta pulled back her hood far enough to peer at the stocky middle-aged man standing beside the wagon. He reached up his hand to help her climb down, then assisted Edith.

"This here's Miss Marta Johansen," Edith said. "Marta, this is the boss, Mr. Pendleton."

"How do you do?" Mr. Pendleton inclined his head slightly, his shrewd dark eyes taking in her appearance.

After traveling on the boat and then the wagon, Marta felt not only sadly bedraggled but near exhaustion. Grateful that she didn't have to contemplate turning around to travel back to Marinette, she smiled, saying, "I'm pleased to be working for you, sir."

"Why, you're a pretty little thing, aren't you?" He seemed unhappy about it and frowned at Edith.

"You oughta know I wouldn't bring some flighty flibbertigibbet to camp," Edith said, scowling back at him. "The girl can't help her looks."

Her words caused Mr. Pendleton to chuckle. "I trust your judgment, Edith. The cook shack is all set up and waiting for you. The boys and I are looking forward to a good breakfast."

Marta was so glad to be able to crawl into the waiting bunk—the upper, above Edith's—that she paid little attention to the cabin. Not until morning did she take an interest in her surroundings.

Edith roused her at five the next morning, calling, "Daylight in the swamp, rise and shine."

Her mattress, Marta realized as she sat up, was stuffed with straw. And so was the pillow. The gray blankets reminded her of the army blankets she'd seen in the hospital on Johnson's Island. Well, she hadn't expected luxurious accommodations. She hurried into her new working clothes, rather drab and certainly unfashionable, chosen by Edith for their warmth and utility. Edith had an apron waiting for her in the kitchen.

The kitchen stove was an enormous black monster that took up a quarter of the kitchen. The walls were lined with cupboards, complete with mixing board counters. Off the kitchen was a large dining room with a long crudely fashioned table in the center, the top covered with oilcloth. Benchlike seats ran along both sides.

The small bedroom she and Edith slept in was off to one side of the kitchen, near the stove. The necessary was, of course, outside.

"Snug little shack," Edith said approvingly as she cut slabs of bacon into an iron spider. "Even got its own pump for water. I been in worse. You can stir up some pancake batter—I'll tell you how much of everything as you go along. We only got half a camp of men to feed this morning, so you're getting an easy start."

Hurrying back and forth at Edith's bidding, setting the table with tin plates, pumping water, carrying wood in from the outside woodpile to stack near the stove, Marta began to wonder how it would be when the camp was full.

"Give the old gut-hammer a crack or two," Edith ordered at last. Noticing Marta's blank look, she grinned. "That's the iron triangle outside the door. Bang it good and hard with the iron rod you'll find hung beside the triangle. You got to figure to make enough noise to wake the dead."

The gut-hammer made such a loud jangle when she hit it that Marta wondered if they could hear the clang way off in Marinette. Before the echoes died, men began pouring out of a large building she realized must be the bunkhouse.

To Marta's surprise, breakfast was a completely silent meal except for the clink of forks against the tin plates as the men shoveled food into their mouths. Not one of them spoke except to ask for the pitcher of molasses to drizzle over their pancakes.

"No talking in the dining room's the rule at all the camps," Edith told her. "Seeing as how lumberjacks are loud enough to be heard from one end of camp to the other, with every other word a cussword, I figure the rule got made to keep the cook from going crazy." She smiled at Marta. "Cooks are important people. If a camp ain't got a cook, a pretty good cook, it can't keep workers."

The men noticed Marta, but not one of them leered or tried to touch so much as her hand.

"You're perfectly safe," Edith said. "Any funny business and they know they're liable to get my iron spider slammed across the side of their heads. Plus whatever Old Beau'd do to them."

As time went by, Marta came to understand "Old Beau" was the camp's nickname for Mr. Pendleton, though those who used it would never dream of calling him that to his face. An affectionate nickname, she presumed, since he seemed well liked. The other owner, whether present or not, was always referred to as Mr. Terwilliger—with emphasis on the mister.

Marta had been there almost a week when she woke smelling smoke. "Is there a fire in the woods?" she asked Edith.

"Not our woods, thank God," Edith said, "but somewheres around, all right."

That evening, with a smoky pall hiding the sunset, Mr. Pendleton came by with news. "There's a bad fire in Peshtigo—started in the slashings around the camps. We're some fifty miles from there, so we ought to be safe enough, but God help those caught in the flames."

"Slashings fires are always bad," Edith told Marta after he left. "Terrible. They start on cut-over land where there's lots of dry branches and bark left by the jacks once the area's logged-out, and they sweep through the woods, burning everything that can't run fast enough to get out of the way. I saw a fire like that when I cooked in one of Old Beau's camps over by the Saginaw. Thought we'd all be ashes by morning. I sure don't ever want to be that close to another."

Shorty afterward, they heard that on the same day the town of Peshtigo had burned to the ground, Chicago had also gone up in flames, the fire all but destroying the city.

"Fires like that make you wonder if hell's not sneaking up on us," Edith commented.

The next day Mr. Pendleton stopped by the cook shack to see Marta. "I'm sorry you've had an introduction into one of the hazards of logging camps—fire—before learning much else about them," he said. "I've decided to give you a tour of ours so I can show you what goes on in a camp from day to day."

Boss or not, Marta glanced at Edith for permission because they were in the midst of baking bread. "I'll manage—you go ahead," Edith said.

"I suspect you're not going to make a life-long career of cooking in a logging camp," Mr. Pendleton said as they walked around the clearing where the buildings were.

"No, sir, I'm not," she said honestly. "Though I do like to cook."

"Frankly, I'm surprised you've stuck it out this long."

"It's hard work," she admitted. "I was ready to quit by the second day. My father told me not to let pride stand in my way if I didn't like it here, but pride's hard to overcome. I found I couldn't give up. And I'm glad I didn't, because I'm settling in all right now."

Goodness, how she was chattering to Mr. Pendleton.

298

Elma was right, she'd never learn not to blurt out every thought that came into her head.

"That's the kind of spirit I like to see," Mr. Pendleton said. "Edith knew what she was doing when she brought you along. Are you interested in what we do here?"

"Edith explained that logging is like harvesting a crop but instead of wheat or corn, you harvest trees."

Mr. Pendleton smiled. "I've never thought of it that way, but she's right. Instead of planting, we buy our standing crop, chop down the trees, cut the logs, skid them to the river, stack them in piles until the ice breaks, then slide the logs into the water and rush them down on the swift spring current to the sawmills. We cut only the white pine; spruce and cedar aren't worth the taking.

"Joe said there was enough pine in Wisconsin to last for a hundred years." She gestured at the tall trees surrounding the camp. "After that wagon ride from Marinette, I can believe it."

"Not that long, Marta. I give it ten years at the most. Long enough to get my son involved." He gazed into the distance, but she had a feeling he was seeing some inner vision instead of the pines. "Larch belongs here in the woods," he muttered as though to himself. "Not behind a damned Boston desk."

"Is Larch your son?" she asked when he didn't say anything more.

He blinked at her as though surprised to see her standing beside him. "Larch? Yes. Yes, he is. I think you two'd get along just fine—he's only a few years older than you and interested in everything, like you are."

Marta didn't know about Larch, but after their conversation as they toured the camp, she decided she quite liked Mr. Pendleton. Since he dropped in often to talk to Edith and to her, her liking for him grew.

She was totally unprepared when, on the first of November, Will, the head chopper, suddenly threw open the door to the cook shack. She watched uncomprehendingly as two of the jacks carried a man inside and laid him on the floor.

Mr. Pendleton!

"Tree fell on him," Will said. "Can you fix him up, Miz Edith?"

Standing beside Edith, Marta stared down at Mr. Pendleton's bloodsoaked clothes, shocked and horrified at the way one leg was bent at an impossible angle. His face was such a strange grayish color that Marta feared he was dead.

"Fetch a wagon," Edith ordered, "on the double! You got to haul him into town to the doc. I'll do what I can, but it won't be enough—he's hurt too damn bad."

With Edith ordering her around, Marta had no time to feel faint or even light-headed. She helped the older woman straighten the broken leg and tie it to a flat board with strips of heavy cotton from a cut up apron. Edith used the rest of the apron to bind the worst of the bleeding wounds. As they were finishing, he opened his eyes and looked at Marta, who was kneeling beside him.

"Larch," he mumbled.

"Yes, your son," Marta said.

"Telegraph Larch. Tell him to come."

"I'll see to it," Marta promised.

"You're Marta."

"Yes, sir, I am."

"Take care of my boy, Marta." She had to lean close to hear the words. "He—needs—you."

Even though she supposed he'd begun to ramble, not aware of his words, she said, "I promise I will. I promise."

Chapter 21

Beau Pendleton didn't die. Two weeks after the accident, Duncan MacDougal, the fired foreman, showed up at camp with Larch Pendleton and stopped by the cook shanty.

Edith introduced them to Marta, then asked, "How's Old—I mean, Mr. Pendleton?"

"He's improving," Larch said.

Marta watched Old Beau's son as he talked to Edith. Evidently he took after his mother, since he didn't resemble his stocky, dark-haired father. Over six foot, she decided, as ruggedly built as any lumberjack, with hair as blond as Olav Johansen's before he'd begun to turn gray.

Larch glanced at her, meeting her gaze with eyes as bright a blue as an October sky. She looked away, trying not to blush at being caught staring, telling herself she'd never seen a man who looked less like he needed to be taken care of than Larch Pendleton.

"We knew the doc in Marinette patched up your pa as best he could," Edith was saying. "But we all thought he was in a mighty big hurry to load a man in such poor shape onto the first Chicago-bound boat that came by. Your pa's a tough old codger or he wouldn't've made it to Chicago alive."

"Blame my father, not the Marinette doctor," Larch said. "Dad kept insisting they get him to Boston, and you know how stubborn he can be. This time his stubbornness almost did kill him—he was more dead than alive when the train from Chicago pulled into Boston."

"But he's better now?" Marta asked.

Larch frowned. "He'll live, but none of the doctors can predict if he'll ever walk again."

"He'll hate it if he can't," she blurted, then flushed a bright red. Why couldn't she learn to keep her mouth shut?

"You're right," Larch said. "Dad's not one to stay put. In any case, he sent me to fill in for him for the time being. I'm not and never will be Old Beau, but I'll do my best, starting at the bottom." Larch put a hand on MacDougal's shoulder. "Dad hired Mac to teach me the ropes from swamper on up."

"What's a swamper?" Marta asked.

Mac, around forty, and nearly as tall as Larch, with sandy hair and beard, grinned at her. "He's the jack who clears the brush to make skid roads to get the logs to the river. I ain't swamped in twenty years or so, but I guess a man never forgets how." He glanced at Edith. "There's more than one thing a man don't forget real easy."

Edith eyed him levelly. "Lots of water under the bridge since then, Mac."

Larch touched Marta's arm and, when she looked at him, gestured toward the door. It took her a moment to realize he was warning her they ought to give Mac and Edith some privacy by stepping outside. She immediately lifted her hooded cloak off a peg, slipped it on, and let Larch escort her from the cook shack.

The day was mild for November—sunny, with only a

302

chill wind to hint winter was on the way. Her time here had barely begun; winter was the season for logging.

"Dad mentioned the camp had a young lady as cookee," Larch said, "but I never expected to find a girl as pretty as you stuck away in this wilderness."

Pleased with his compliment, though slightly put off by his smoothness, Marta smiled. "To tell you the truth, I didn't have the slightest idea how isolated a logging camp was before I arrived here with Edith." Seeing a chance to switch the subject from herself, she added, "I'd quite forgotten hearing that she and Mr. MacDougal were old acquaintances."

"More than that, so the story goes. I met them both at my dad's camp in Michigan, on the Saginaw River. Mac's a good sort, and so is Edith. I rather hope they—"

At that moment, Edith's voice, raised to a shout, came clearly through the door. "If ever I catch you with a bottle of rotgut, Duncan MacDougal, I swear I'll break it over your thick Scot's head."

Larch raised his eyebrows. "I'm afraid Mac does like his drink."

"I'm aware Mr. Terwilliger fired him as foreman for that reason. Yet your father must trust Mac, or he wouldn't have hired him to help you."

"Dad usually knows what he's doing. But enough of Mac. You must have Sunday off, like the rest of the camp—am I right?"

"In a way. We serve only a cold supper on Sunday."

"You certainly must get tired of this place. Perhaps I might show you the sights of Marinette one of these Sundays."

Marta bit her lip, uncertain of how to word her refusal. Much as she'd like to spend time with Larch, Edith's word was law. "I don't believe there's much for me to see in the town," she said, knowing she'd die

303

before repeating Edith's words.

"You stay out of Marinette," Edith had advised. "There may be decent people in the town, but they'll have nothing to do with lumberjacks or anyone associated with the logging camps. It's hard to blame them. When the jacks get paid, they roll into town to get drunk and to—" She'd paused and eyed Marta for long moments. "Well, girl," she said finally, "considering you're better off knowing, I guess I have to spell it right out. Men got appetites you don't know nothing about, and I ain't talking about food.

"I ain't going into it any more than to say the jacks pay women to go to bed with them. Harlots, the Bible calls such women. Scarlet women. All logging towns are full of the breed. Full of whorehouses and saloons, 'cause the jacks want to spend their money on whores and rotgut. And that's why you'd best keep out of Marinette."

Conscious of Larch's intent gaze, Marta blushed as she recalled Edith's speech, then chided herself. As if he could see into her mind! What a goose he must think her, turning red every time he spoke.

"I—I would like to talk to you again sometime," she said. "Your father used to tell me fascinating things about Boston. I'd like to hear more about the city."

Larch's finger brushed gently against her cheek in a touch as light as a snowflake. "By all means." Something in his voice suggested he wasn't thinking of Boston.

Neither was she. His fleeting caress had set her heart to pounding—something Silas's touch had never done. Feeling strangely unsettled, she searched his blue eyes, uncertain what she sought there.

He smiled down at her, assured and handsome, and she was suddenly conscious of the gap between them— he, the boss's son and she, a lowly cookee. Marta raised her chin, reminding herself she was Olav Johansen's daughter, every bit as good as Beau Pendleton's son.

"You really are quite extraordinarily lovely," he said, a bit hoarsely. The door to the cook shack opened and he added hastily, "I'll come to call on Sunday."

"What did you think of young Pendleton?" Edith asked that evening as they got ready for bed.

"He doesn't look much like his father," Marta replied evasively.

"I don't think he's a bad sort." Marta smiled at hearing Edith's words echo what Larch had said about her. "Boston ain't Sandusky, though."

Marta frowned as she tried to decipher exactly what the older woman meant. Was Edith pointing out the gap between them?

"He's a rich man's son," Edith went on.

"I realize that." Tartness crept into her voice.

Edith, who never missed anything, raised her eyebrows. "Too late already, is it? I was afraid of that. The lad's a real charmer, and there's no gainsaying you're pretty enough to attract his attention. Still, there's always the hope Mac will keep him too busy for much fooling around."

Marta drew herself up indignantly. "I should think you'd know by now I'm not one of those featherbrains who casts herself at the feet of the first man who flatters her."

"Never said you were. But it's plain to see he's going after you, and your head's bound to be turned. Young Larch ain't no dull Silas Portland. I figure not many girls ever refuse Larch's attentions, and that tends to go to a young man's head. He gets to thinking of women as notches on his gun instead of people with feelings. You watch yourself if you don't want to end up hurt and betrayed. Or worse."

Marta stared at her, too shocked to be angry. Was

305

Edith actually suggesting she might not only lose her head over Larch but her scruples as well?

"It's happened to nice girls before," Edith said, as though reading her mind. "And don't you forget it. A bit of flirting never hurt a girl but you just remember that, no matter how sweet he talks, Larch Pendleton of Boston ain't never going to marry a nobody from Sandusky."

"I'm not a nobody!"

"To the Pendletons and their ilk you are, and don't you forget it." Edith blew out the lamp, plunging them into darkness and ending the conversation.

Disturbed and furious, Marta climbed into her bunk. She'd show Edith! Yes, and Larch, too, if he tried any more of his practiced wiles on her.

Though Marta tried to deny how impatiently she waited, Sunday was a long time coming. She'd seen Larch with the other men at mealtimes, but those were such hectic occasions for her and Edith that she'd been too busy to so much as exchange a glance with him.

When she rose on Sunday morning, instead of donning one of her drab work dresses, she put on a striped silk walking dress in a dark red and, since it was cut for a bustle, she wore one. To her amazement, she found Edith in an equally stylish gown of a lively chestnut brown.

"My, ain't you the fine lady," Edith said, shaking her head. "We're a pair, we are. And neither of them worth the bother. Not that many men are."

Which must mean Edith expected Mac to come calling.

"I swore I'd never again give the man so much as the time of day," Edith went on, "and here I am, dressing up like a fool."

"You look very nice," Marta assured her. It was the truth. When she took the trouble to fix herself up,

306

Edith Knowles was still a handsome woman.

"Duncan MacDougal's not a bad sort," Edith said, "but he's weak when it comes to the booze." She sighed. "I swear he'd rather be swigging away at a bottle of forty-rod than doing anything else in life. At least I got enough sense this time not to count on him changing."

By the time Larch appeared, asking Marta if she cared to come view the skid road he'd personally swamped out, the first snow of the season had begun to fall in a flurry of lazy white flakes. She fastened a heavy wool shawl around her shoulders and donned her hooded cape. As soon as they were outside, she thrust her gloved hands into her beaver muff, making it unnecessary for him to offer his arm.

As they passed the bunkhouse, she heard a fiddle playing and the stomp of boots.

"That's probably some of the Canucks dancing," Larch said. "They like singing and dancing almost as much as they enjoy fighting."

Marta, who'd witnessed very few fights before she came to the camp, where they were almost a daily occurrence, shook her head. "I can't get over how two lumberjacks can pound away at each other one minute and a few minutes later be the best of friends."

"I hope we'll be friends without the fighting," he said, smiling at her.

He had a beguiling smile, one that made the corners of her own lips curl up in response. There was certainly no harm in a friendship with Larch, yet she replied cautiously, "Perhaps we will be in time, Mr. Pendleton."

As they left the camp clearing to enter the woods, he said, "You make me feel like my father with your 'mister.' As a first step toward our friendship, why not call me Larch?"

His words were the same as anyone else's and yet unlike his father, he gave them a different intonation, one she thought she'd never tire of hearing. "You don't talk like the people back home in Sandusky," she said. "Or even like your father."

"I'm afraid that's what Harvard does to a man." His tone poked fun at himself.

She knew, of course, that Harvard was a fancy eastern university, but until now she'd never met anyone who'd gone there. "Then your father didn't attend Harvard?"

"Dad came from Vermont. He likes to call himself a self-educated man. As, I suppose, he is."

Under the trees, the branches of the pines, high above, shut away much of the snow and the soft flakes floated down sparingly. She caught one on her tongue and laughed happily, stimulated by the cold and by the handsome man beside her. "My sister and I used to make a game out of seeing who could taste the first snowflake," she said, her face upturned.

"I'd much rather taste the flake that's just now landed on your lips."

Without giving her time to think, he bent and touched her upper lip with the tip of his tongue. stepping back before she could pull away. She drew her hand from her muff, bringing it to her mouth as if the feel of her glove could stop the tingling delight coursing through her from the unexpected caress.

"I don't—that wasn't fair," she stammered.

He captured her hand in his. "Haven't you heard that all's fair in love and war?"

She stared at him wide-eyed. "But this is neither."

"You're wrong. Love at first sight, that's what it was, striking like lightning. Has it never happened to you before?"

Bemused by the warmth in his eyes, she forgot that she'd meant to pull her hand away. Unsure she was being altogether truthful, she said, "Never. And that includes now."

He placed his free hand over his heart. "You wound me, Marta. How can you be so heartless?"

Hearing the teasing tone in his voice, she smiled in relief. Not only didn't he mean a word he was saying but she didn't have to take him seriously either.

"Where is this wonderful road of yours?" she asked, deciding it was past time to put an end to his nonsense. She tugged at her hand and he released her.

"Do you realize there's no end to the wonderful roads we could travel together?" he said as they walked on.

"I've been at the camp long enough to learn that skid roads are fit for nothing but logs," she said firmly. "What is Mr. MacDougal teaching you next?"

"Scaling. Not much more of a challenge than swamping, I suspect. What can there be to scaling the bark off a log?"

"Your father once told me you were interested in everything. Apparently that doesn't include scaling."

"He seems to have discussed a variety of subjects with you."

"I thoroughly enjoyed our conversations. I liked him very much."

"Better than you like me?"

She glanced sideways at him and found him watching her. "I don't know you well enough to say."

"We have all winter to become better acquainted." He spoke softly, almost caressingly, making her breath catch. Somehow he'd turned the most innocent of words into what seemed almost like a declaration of love.

A charmer, Edith had called Larch. Oh, how right she'd been!

"Are you quite certain we're headed in the right direction?" she asked.

"We would be if you'd follow my lead. Apparently your last name isn't Johansen for nothing."

"Swedes are no more stubborn than anyone else. Why do you deliberately keep misunderstanding what I'm saying? I'll put it as plainly as I can—are you or are you not taking me to look at the road you swamped out?"

He stopped and grinned at her. "Would you believe me if I told you I think we're lost?"

"I would not." She gestured toward a tree. "One of the first things your father pointed out to me is how blazes notched into the pine trunks show the way back to camp."

He threw back his head and laughed. "Undermined by my own father, what a setdown. You're a real prize, Marta. I do believe I'm going to enjoy this winter."

"I'm not so sure *I* am," she said tartly.

"I assure you that you will."

He rested his hands on her shoulders, his gaze holding hers. How very blue his eyes were. Looking into them made her feel like she was a child again, lying on the grass and staring up at the summer sky until she grew dizzy with the sensation that nothing existed except the sky and she was helplessly falling up into the blue.

"I think it's time we returned to camp," she said breathlessly, trying to break free of the spell he was casting over her.

He didn't answer, didn't speak at all, just bent his head toward her, coming closer and closer until his lips, warm despite the chill around them, covered hers, infusing a languorous heat that seeped deep within her, stirring her far past anything she'd ever experienced.

She thought in confusion that no matter how many times Silas may have pressed his lips against hers, she'd never really been kissed before.

Chapter 22

The snow fell all that Sunday, not ceasing until the following evening, when over two feet covered the frozen ground. Marta's determination not to allow herself to be alone with Larch again eroded day by day, until by the following Sunday, when a jingling of harness bells announced his arrival at the cook shack with a horse and sleigh, she couldn't deny her eagerness to see him again. Still, she tried to be cautious.

"Do come with us, Edith," she begged, after Larch invited her for a ride.

Edith shook her head. "You run along. I'm getting too old to enjoy going out in the cold and that's the truth."

Maybe it was, Marta thought, and then again, maybe Edith wanted to stay in because she either hoped or knew Mac intended to drop by.

Marta bundled up warmly and allowed Larch to help her into the sleigh, pulling the red wool blanket with its varicolored Hudson Bay stripes over her lap. He climbed in beside her and tucked the blanket around them both. The horse tossed its head, haloed with the white vapor of its breath, eyeing them with what seemed to be surprise.

"He's one of the camp horses," Larch said. "I imagine he's wondering why the sleigh isn't loaded with logs."

"I love sleigh rides," she confessed as he urged the horse onto the track leading from the camp. "Otherwise I might not have come with you today."

"Oh? Why not?"

"I don't know Boston customs, but in Sandusky, a girl doesn't allow young men to kiss her."

"Ever? Come, now, I can't believe that."

"I mean casually."

"But I didn't kiss you casually. I was desperately in earnest."

Her glance confirmed her impression that he was teasing her. She raised her chin. "We're barely acquainted, Mr. Pendleton, and it's not proper."

"My name's Larch, and the devil with propriety. Don't you realize you have the most tempting pair of lips in all of Wisconsin? On second thought, the entire United States. Or even the world."

Despite her resolve to make her point, his extravagant banter amused her. "Were you never taught to put temptation behind you?"

"If you were behind me, how could I kiss you?"

She laughed, sending a white cloud of breath into the cold air. "Prevention's the idea, isn't it?"

"Not *my* idea. I have a better one."

"I won't ask what it is."

"I'm perfectly willing to tell you without being asked. But the telling requires you to use your imagination. First, you must imagine the months have rolled by and May is here and this is a delightfully warm spring afternoon. Are you trying?"

She nodded. "The wildflowers are blooming in grassy glades, the birds are singing, and not just the pines but all the trees are green."

312

"You're doing extremely well. Now, ask yourself why the flowers are blooming. The answer is to attract the bees. As for the birds—they're singing sweet courting songs. The sun's warmth is not merely to make the grass grow, but to encourage everyone in the world to hold out their arms and be embraced by spring."

"You should be a writer," she said admiringly. "I could never put it half so well."

"Life tends to intrude on dreams," he said, and she heard a tinge of both anger and sadness in his words. He gestured as though to wipe away what he'd said. "Close your eyes and picture yourself sitting in the glade. White butterflies flit among the bright blossoms. You turn your face up, welcoming the sun's gentle caress."

Eyes shut, Marta raised her face to the sky.

"And then," he said softly, "a butterfly brushes against your lips, seeking the honeyed nectar that lies within. You smile and wave the innocent creature harmlessly away, but at the same time you understand you've been touched by the magic essence of spring itself."

Her eyes fluttered open to meet his blue gaze. "We're in that dream glade, you and I," he said. "Like the butterfly, I know where the sweetest honey is to be found, and so I kiss you and, like a flower, you open to me and the two of us hold each other forever in a lover's springtime."

Enthralled by the shimmering image he'd created, she couldn't move or speak, searching his eyes as if seeking his magic glade within them. *A lover's springtime. Forever.* If only it could be like that!

The wind shifted a snow-covered branch overhanging the road, causing it to lose its burden. Snow showered the sleigh, the chill caress reminding Marta that spring was a long way off. As she brushed off the snow, she told herself not only was it winter but, if she had any sense, she'd never kiss Larch again.

"Do you write?" she asked, hoping plain words instead of poetic ones would help dissipate the lingering shards of the daydream they'd shared.

"Not any more." His clipped tone told her he didn't care to pursue the subject. "Haven't you heard? I've been promoted to chopper."

"I trust you find that more to your liking than scaling."

"I'll admit there's an art to learning the intricacies of using an ax. Although what I've learned revealed something I find disturbing. Mac doesn't want to say I'm right, but I sense he fears I am and hopes it isn't true."

"I don't follow your meaning."

Their sleigh was quite alone on the narrow track leading to Marinette, but Larch glanced all around as though worrying about eavesdroppers.

"The tree that fell on my father had been undercut in such a way that a single ax blow would send it crashing."

"Is that so unusual?"

"It is when the path of fall is directly across the main trail used by the jacks. You see, an expert chopper can and does direct a fall exactly where it ought to go—and that would never be across a well-used trail."

She stared at him. "You're implying someone *meant* that tree to fall on your father. Whoever would commit such a horrible deed?"

He shook his head. "I wish I knew."

"Everyone at the camp likes him. They wish he was still there instead of Mr. Terwilliger."

"And instead of me, probably. Like you, Mac assures me my father had no enemies, but I now have

314

doubts that Dad's injuries were caused by an accident."

He drew back on the reins, slowing the horse, and turned into a narrow, unmarked track leading into the woods. After the sleigh had traveled several hundred yards, he halted the horse in a clearing rimmed by pines except for where an ice-covered stream meandered. Near the stream, leafless saplings thrust their bare boughs toward the sky.

After he'd helped her from the sleigh, Marta glanced around the snowy clearing, wondering why he'd brought her here. She glanced at him questioningly.

He smiled. "Don't you recognize our glade?"

"How can you expect me to," she asked, "when you failed to mention the stream?"

"Guilty as charged. How could I have possibly forgotten?" He slapped his hand dramatically against his chest, then winced in pain.

She was instantly solicitous. "What's the matter?"

"An accident. When I was chopping yesterday, my ax blade flew off the handle and gave me a rather hard whack. My own fault—a good chopper checks his ax helve daily."

Marta caught back a gasp, knowing that if the ax head had struck him blade on he might have been killed. She bit her lip, recalling what he'd said about his father.

"Two accidents to Pendletons?" As usual the words came out her mouth as soon as they entered her mind.

Larch blinked. "That didn't occur to me," he said slowly, fingering the new beard he'd begun to grow since he'd arrived at the camp. "Or to Mac."

"I could be wrong."

"Yes. Or you could be right."

Suddenly afraid for him, Marta caught his arm. "Please be extra careful."

He smiled at her. "Would you care if I were hurt?"

She let go and stepped back. "Of course. I hate to see anyone injured."

He put his hands on her shoulders. "Why are you so reluctant to admit you like me? Your eyes give you away, you know."

She did her best to ignore her racing heart while keeping her voice steady. "I like most people I meet."

"But you don't want most people to kiss you—or do you?"

She pulled free of him. "We weren't talking about kissing."

"We are now. And no matter how you try to deny it, you want me to kiss you. Since I can't imagine anything I'd rather do, your wish is my command." He took a step toward her.

Marta backed away until she found herself up against the sleigh.

"Aha, trapped!"

She glared at him, holding her muff defensively in front of her. "Don't you dare touch me!"

He sighed. "Under the circumstances, I suppose I'll have to settle for your hand."

Before she understood his intent, he'd eased her right hand from the muff and pulled off her glove. Bringing her hand to his mouth, he kissed her palm, then caressed it with his moist, warm tongue. She felt a matching liquid warmth deep inside and her knees threatened to give way, as though her bones were ice melting in the spring sun.

He slipped her glove on and eased her hand back inside the muff.

"I—I've never in my life met anyone like you," she blurted.

His smile suggested he knew she really meant that she'd never met any man who could make her feel the way he did. God knew it was the truth. Never in her wildest dreams did she imagine a man could turn her to mush merely by kissing her hand.

"And I'm beginning to believe I've never met a girl quite like you." He tipped her chin up with his forefinger.

Her breath faltered at the glow she saw in his eyes, the warmth within her growing and spreading.

"I'm only doing what we both want," he said softly.

She forced words out. "I—I don't believe it's a good idea."

"Maybe not," he whispered against her lips.

He pulled her into his arms. For an instant or two she was conscious of tiny details—the tickle of his beard against her skin, his male scent—and then his mouth covered hers and she dissolved with pleasure.

It was November, not May, and snow covered the ground, but she wished the kiss would go on forever and ever. Her muff dropped into the snow unheeded as her arms encircled his neck, drawing him closer. When he finally released her, she couldn't keep back a tiny moan of disappointment.

"If I kiss you any longer, you'll have me forgetting how cold it is," he said with a strange hoarseness in his voice. "This may be the place but, my sweet Marta, it's not the time. Though I'm beginning to wonder how I can last until May."

Back in the sleigh, returning to camp, Larch pulled her close to him, keeping an arm around her, aware he wasn't ready to let her go. It had begun as a game, because there was no other amusement at the camp and she was the prettiest girl he'd seen in a long time. He didn't mean to let things get out of hand. He knew better. If he made love to Marta, as he urgently wanted to, not only would Edith tear into him like the dragon

317

she could be, but his dad would have his hide once he found out Larch had gone back on his word.

"Marta's a nice girl," Old Beau had warned him the day before he'd left Boston. "See that you treat her that way." He'd assured his still weak father, propped on pillows in bed, that he'd behave as though the girl was his sister.

That was before he saw her.

Damn it, Marta Johansen had been made for lovemaking. Her innocent, intensely provocative responses to his so-far-circumspect caresses hinted at a hidden unlit fire she didn't even know she possessed. He wanted to be the one to light that fire and to fuel it until they both were consumed.

He gritted his teeth at the bolt of desire ramming through him at the mere thought of her naked in his arms.

"Why are you making faces?" she asked.

"Because I can't kiss you again until next Sunday," he told her.

He'd have to keep it a game. Or else stop seeing her altogether. A pang went through him at the thought. No, he could and would stay in control of himself. At least through the winter. A man would have to be damned inventive to figure out how to comfortably but secretly make love to a woman in a logging camp in the midst of winter. There was no privacy unless they walked in the woods, and the woods were as cold as hell, too cold for what he had in mind. Or rather, what he shouldn't have in mind.

"You shouldn't be kissing me at all," she said, easing from under his arm and edging away from him. "And I shouldn't be letting you."

"It's too late for regrets." He smiled at her.

"I don't have regrets. But—" She broke off, her attention apparently caught by something she saw in

318

the woods. "Stop!" she cried.

Marta leaped from the sleigh even before he'd brought the horse to a standstill. She waded through the snow into the pines that crowded close to the narrow track and was kneeling beside something by the time he caught up with her. An animal? He caught his breath. Damned if it wasn't an Indian boy, lying sprawled unconscious in the blood-spattered snow.

"He's hurt," Marta said. "You'll have to carry him to the wagon."

The boy, who looked to be about ten, gave no sign of rousing until Larch was laying him gently on the floor of the cook shack. Then his eyes opened and he stared into Larch's face with incomprehension that rapidly changed to alarm.

"Take it easy," Larch advised him. "You're hurt and we're trying to help you."

The boy's hand rose to touch the bloody gash running across his temple. He winced. "Where?" he mumbled.

"If you mean where are you," Larch said, "you're at the Pendleton-Terwilliger logging camp. If you mean where did you get hurt, we found you in the woods beside the road into town."

The boy glanced around, stopping to stare at Marta, who knelt at his other side. "I see you feeding birds," he said.

She blinked. "Why, yes, I do scatter breadcrumbs in the woods for the bluejays and chickadees."

"Let me have a look at that gash," Edith said, kneeling beside Larch and setting down the basin of water she carried. She leaned over the boy. "What'd you do, young man, fall out of a tree?"

"Yes."

"I'm going to wash the cut with soap and water," Edith told him. "It might sting a bit."

If the cleansing did hurt, you'd never know it from the boy's stoic expression, Larch thought admiringly as he helped the boy sit up after Edith had finished. "I'm Larch," he said.

For a moment he didn't believe the boy meant to give him his name, but then he muttered reluctantly, "Little Fox."

"My name is Marta," Marta said, smiling at the boy. "If you see me feeding the birds again, you'll know what to call me."

"Where do you live?" Larch asked.

"On the Menominee Indian Reservation," Edith answered for the boy. She gestured vaguely westward. "Couple of miles off in the woods, over that way."

"Is that right?" Larch asked Little Fox.

"Yes."

"I'll help you home."

"No!" The boy broke free of his grasp and jumped to his feet, staggering against one of the cupboards. Larch rose and steadied him.

"Look, you're not strong enough to go off by yourself," Larch told him.

The boy stared at him with frightened eyes until Marta came and put a hand on Little Fox's shoulder. "You must be hungry," she said. "Will you stay and eat? Maybe then you'll feel stronger."

Little Fox let out his breath in a ragged sigh. "I eat with you," he said.

Larch was amazed at the amount of food the boy consumed. The poor kid must have been starving.

As if reading his thoughts, Edith said, "Them on the reservation ain't got much. Old Beau used to send a few supplies over once a month, but Mr. Terwilliger's stopped that. Says he don't aim to use up his profits feeding Indians."

Anger simmered in Larch. It might be true he was

learning logging from the bottom up, but his father was an equal partner in the business and he was here as his father's representative. The least Terwilliger could have done was to discuss the matter with him. It made him wonder what else Terwilliger hadn't bothered to mention.

"We'll see about that," he said tersely.

"Then I take it I have your permission to send bread and cold beans and ham home with Little Fox," Edith said.

Larch nodded. Turning to the boy, he said, "Why don't you want me to help you get home?"

Little Fox hung his head. "My father say no go near camp."

Larch considered for a moment, then said, "What if I tell your father I asked you to guide me to the reservation because I had food to give your people? It's the truth."

Little Fox looked from Larch to Marta.

"I think you should accept Larch's offer to help," she told him. "He's Old Beau's son."

Little Fox glanced at Larch in surprise. After a moment he smiled shyly. "Your father have good heart. I take you to my people."

The next day, Larch lingered in the cook shack after the men filed out following the evening meal. He was bone tired, as he was every day after working with Mac, but he had a few questions to ask Marta.

He intercepted her as she carried a tray of dirty dishes from the dining room.

"I've been wondering why that Indian boy trusted your word instead of mine," he said. "He was afraid of me until you told him I was Old Beau's son."

"I have twin half-brothers about his age," she said,

brushing past him.

He shook his head. "No, I don't think that's the explanation. It was as though, in the midst of strangers, Little Fox sensed you were a friend."

"He *had* seen me before."

Larch shook his head, unsatisfied. "There was something more."

She set the tray onto the counter with a bang. "My mother was a Chippewa," she said. "Is that what you want to hear?"

He stared at her, dumbfounded.

"Please don't bother me anymore tonight," she said crossly. "Can't you see I'm too busy for idle conversation?"

Edith cleared her throat loudly. His glance at her showed she stood with arms akimbo, glaring at him. He was intruding in her domain and, as camp cook, she had every right to throw him out the door. Not wanting a confrontation with Edith, Larch retreated.

The snow crunched under his boots as he strode toward the small sleeping room attached to the camp office, where he and Mac bedded down. Terwilliger never slept at the camp; he rented a suite in a Marinette hotel.

Mac took one look at his face as he stomped inside and shook his head. "Never annoy the cook," he advised.

Larch didn't answer, preoccupied with the word echoing in his mind. He didn't use it, but everyone else at camp did, usually with a sneer accompanying the word; *half-breed*. Even the Canucks looked down their noses at half-breeds, though some of the jacks suspected, rightly or wrongly, that many or all French Canadians carried Indian blood.

He slammed his fist into his palm, once, twice, three times. "It doesn't make a damn bit of difference," he snarled at Mac. "None. Do you hear me? None!"

Mac shrugged. "I don't know what the hell's bitten you, but I ain't going to argue. If you're spoiling for a fight, you picked the wrong man."

Larch paid no attention to Mac's words. "It's not as though I plan to marry her," he muttered.

Mac's eyes narrowed. "Then you ought to keep in mind she's a nice girl."

Larch scowled at him.

"I said my piece, that's it," Mac told him. "Time to turn in." He sighed. "Sure do miss my goodnight nip, always made me sleep like a babe."

By the time Larch climbed into his bunk, Mac was snoring. Since he'd been at camp, sleep usually poleaxed him as quickly as it did Mac, but not tonight. Tired as he was, he lay awake.

He still wanted her as much as ever, there was no doubt about that. Merely thinking about kissing her aroused him. And he'd had enough experience with women to know she wanted him, too, nice girl or not. Her eager response yesterday had driven him wild with need. The way he saw it, she couldn't possibly expect him to offer marriage, and so what it amounted to was that she was offering herself to him without demanding the promise of a ring and a minister in return.

Why shouldn't he take advantage of such a generous offer?

Take advantage of a nice girl?

He grimaced.

No doubt her Indian heritage made her more hot-blooded than the girls he'd known. Now that he'd given her a taste of what passion could be like, if he didn't make love to her, some other man would come along and . . . He clenched his fists. Damn it, the girl was his, and he meant to be the first to have her.

Chapter 23

Christmas Day dawned fair, with several feet of snow on the ground and the temperature hovering around zero. The jacks had the day off, so many had drawn their stakes and gone into Marinette.

"They'll blow every cent they've earned," Edith said as she and Marta rolled out the crusts for pumpkin and mincemeat pies. "Spend it on rotgut and scarlet women. We'll be feeding a lot of dead-broke and hungover jacks, come tomorrow."

"This will be the strangest Christmas I've ever had." Despite her best intentions, Marta's voice quavered. Though she hadn't missed her family so very much after the first week or so, this was her first Christmas away from home.

Before Edith could reply, the door opened and Larch entered the cook shack. "I come bringing gifts," he announced with a smile, flourishing two boxes.

As far as Marta was concerned, the day brightened with his appearance. "I have a surprise for you, too," she said shyly.

Edith had taught her how to knit, and Marta had found that, in contrast to her struggles with embroidery, she had a real knack for knitting. With Edith's help, she'd made a bright blue stocking cap trimmed with white for Larch.

With a flourish, Larch handed the larger box to Edith and the smaller to her.

Edith lifted the lid. "A shelf clock! How could you know I've always wanted one?" Setting the steepled clock with its frosted door carefully on a counter, she flung her arms around Larch and hugged him.

Marta found a small velvet case within her box. Opening it, she gasped in pleased surprise. A gold butterfly pin with enameled white wings lay on a blue satin lining. She met Larch's intent gaze.

"I couldn't bring you a real butterfly, so this one will have to do until May," he said.

"It's beautiful," she told him, warmed by his words as much as by the gift. Nothing could have pleased her more than what he'd given her—a butterfly that promised a lover's eternal springtime.

"Edith gave me a hug," he pointed out expectantly.

Blushing, Marta put her arms around him, intending to make her hug as brief as possible, but she was thrilled when his arms held her tightly for a long, blissful moment before he released her.

When Edith handed the three linen handkerchiefs she'd made and embroidered with an L to Larch, he kissed her cheek as he thanked her.

Hesitantly, Marta brought out the knitted stocking cap. Larch immediately put the cap on, reached for her, and kissed her quickly on the lips, embarrassing her and making her ache for more at the same time.

"Your thoughtful gift will keep me warm until May," he told her. "After that . . ." He smiled at her.

He doesn't think the less of me, she told herself happily. Mother Freda had always warned her and Elma never to reveal their Chippewa ancestry lest they be shunned. Yet she'd told Larch and he hadn't acted a bit differently toward her.

"Where's Mac?" Edith asked.

"I think he said he'll be over later," Larch said.

"That means he's in Marinette, right?" Edith's tone was bitter.

Larch nodded reluctantly. "I almost forgot," he said, reaching into a pocket of his blue plaid mackinaw. "Little Fox's family sent over gifts for us." He drew out a pair of exquisitely beaded deerskin moccasins and handed them to Marta.

While she exclaimed over them, he added, "Mine fit perfectly."

She would, she told herself, knit a red scarf for Little Fox.

Larch peeled off his mackinaw and sat on a kitchen stool talking to them while she and Edith returned to their pie-making. They'd just slid the last pie in the oven when the door opened again.

"Merry Christmas!" Mac exclaimed, stomping the snow off his boots as he came inside. He began to unfasten his red plaid mackinaw as he walked toward Edith. "Brought you a little something from town," he said to her, reaching inside his coat and pulling out a furry ball that squirmed in his grasp.

"Whatever—? Why, it's a kitten!" Edith clasped the little black and white cat to her bosom.

"You're always going on about mice in the pantry," Mac said, "so when I heard Big Blondie's tiger cat had kittens, I made up my mind to get one of them for you."

Edith cuddled the kitten, stroking its head. "So you're a bordello cat, are you?" she crooned. "Ah, well, I don't hold your origins against you."

"Then I guess you like her," Mac said.

Edith smiled at him in a way Marta had never seen her smile at anyone. "Nobody ever gave me a nicer gift." She reached inside one of the cupboards, brought out a glass jar decorated with a red yarn bow, and handed it to Mac. "Merry Christmas to you, too."

Mac grinned as he held up the preserve jar. "Be

326

damned if you ain't gone and made me my favorite—sweet pickles. Aw, Edith, fancy you remembering all this time."

"Why don't we take a little walk around the camp?" Larch said to Marta, sliding off the stool and reaching for his mackinaw.

Since it was obvious to her that Edith and Mac wanted to be alone, she hurried to get her outdoor clothes on.

Despite the sunshine, the day was so cold the snow squeaked under their boots as they walked away from the cook shack. The north wind pierced through all the layers of her clothes to chill her very bones. When Larch paused outside the small building that housed the camp office and invited her in "just for a moment," she nodded, eager to be out of the frigid air.

The bookkeeper was not at work on the holiday, so they were alone. The blanket separating the bedroom from the office was pulled aside, and she glanced curiously through the opening.

"Your bedroom is as small as the one Edith and I share," she said without thinking, then blushed. Ladies didn't comment on their own or anyone else's sleeping arrangements. In fact, she shouldn't be alone here with Larch, even though they weren't actually inside his bedroom.

Stepping quickly away from the opening, she brushed against a small table, dislodging papers that fell to the floor. Flustered, she bent to retrieve them. Among the papers was a photograph of an attractive young woman; written in a looping hand at the bottom was: *To my darling Larch, all my love, Susan.*

She stared at the words for a long moment. To her, the *darling* implied more than a casual acquaintance. Why had she assumed she was the only girl who interested Larch?

Larch took the photograph and papers from her

hand and replaced them on the table. "A girl I know in Boston," he said offhandedly.

Trying to mask her upset, Martha asked, "She's very pretty."

"But I only have eyes for you."

Even as she warmed to his words, she wondered if he'd have said the same thing if he'd been in Boston with Susan and Susan had seen a picture of her.

Jealousy is an ignoble emotion, she reminded herself. Besides, you've no cause to be jealous. Since Larch has made you no promises, he hasn't broken any.

Putting his forefinger under her chin, he forced her to meet his gaze. "Has anyone ever told you that you have a most expressive face?"

"I'll admit my sister claims I can be read as easily as an open book," she said ruefully.

"Believe me, when I'm with you, I never think of any other girl." He watched her carefully, then sighed. "I see that's not good enough."

"I have no claim on your affections," she said primly, stepping back so he was no longer touching her.

He caught her shoulders. "If that's true, why do I dream of you every night? Why does my heart lift when I come into the dining room to eat and happen to catch your eye and earn a smile? Why can't I ever get enough of kissing you?"

He leaned to her. His mouth captured hers and she was lost, as always, in the wonder of his kiss. When he held her in his arms, nothing else existed except Larch.

"Do you have any idea what you do to me?" he whispered against her lips. "I want you, Marta. You and no one else."

No one else. There was no one else for her, either. And there never would be. She was, she realized, hopelessly in love with Larch Pendleton.

He released her to fling off his mackinaw. Then he

unfastened her cloak and drew her close once more, trailing kisses over her face and throat. Bemused by his caresses, she was hardly aware of his fingers undoing the buttons of her bodice and untying the ribbons of her chemise until the warmth of his lips on her breast sent such fire pulsing through her that she felt she might swoon in his arms.

"Larch?" she murmured wonderingly.

His only answer was to push aside her chemise and take her nipple into his mouth, making her moan in agitated pleasure as she arched against him, her fingers tangling in his hair.

He lifted her off her feet and the next she knew he was easing her onto his bunk. "It's all right, I won't hurt you," he said hoarsely. "I'd never hurt you, darling."

Darling. The word echoed in her mind, shattering the spell he'd cast over her. He called her darling, yet for all she knew, he was Susan's darling. She pushed at him as he started to lie beside her.

"No," she said breathlessly. "No, I must leave. Now."

Rather than letting her go, he kissed her, sweetly, persuasively, sapping her will. How could she bear to leave his arms when all the delights in the world lay within them? She struggled against her own inclination to remain, fought against the pleasant languor over-taking her.

Dinner, she told herself. Edith needs my help with Christmas dinner. The ham, the stuffed goose . . .

Like a cold wind, Edith's warning words swept through her mind. "A goose, that's what I was at your age," she'd said early this morning when Marta was mixing the stuffing. "A goose with no more sense than this plucked one here. A few sweet words, a few kisses, and he got what he wanted. Never saw him again. True, there was pleasure in it for me as well as him, but there ain't no pleasure birthing a baby alone and unwed.

"I got saved from total disgrace by my childless older

sister. She and her husband took me in before the baby came, and she claimed my little girl as hers when it was born. People may have suspected the truth, but they never knew for sure. I made some mistakes after that, but I ain't never been such a goose again."

She'd turned and fixed narrowed eyes on Marta. "My daughter, the one what thinks she's my niece, is about your age. I can't be around to warn her, but you're right handy here, and danged if I ain't grown fond of you. Take a long look at this plucked goose, Marta girl, and mind my words. Don't you be one."

But Larch wouldn't be like the unknown man who'd used and then deserted Edith, Marta assured herself, still clinging to him. At the same time, she found it impossible to dismiss her mental image of the plucked goose lying naked and forlorn on the kitchen counter.

Larch wouldn't—wouldn't what? Lie with her? She didn't understand everything meant by those words, but lying with her surely must be what he was attempting to do right now.

But he wouldn't desert her afterward.

Not even for Susan in Boston?

"Larch!" she cried.

He pulled back, startled, staring at her.

"I refuse to be a goose!" She slid away from him, eased from the bunk and turned her back, shivering as she did up her disarrayed clothes.

By the time she pulled on her cloak in the office, he was standing beside her. "Don't come back with me," she said without looking at him.

Hands gripping her shoulders, he turned her roughly to face him. "I lost my head. I'm sorry if I frightened you. I didn't mean to."

"I wasn't frightened. But—" She bit her lip, her words trailing off.

His smile was one-sided. "But you're a nice girl. God knows, everyone's told me that time and again."

Face flaming, she stammered, "I—I don't think I'm so nice as they say. If I really was, I wouldn't like—" Again she found herself unable to go on.

Larch leaned to her and brushed his lips over her forehead. "You're trying to say you like kissing me and you like me to hold you—am I right?"

She nodded.

"Is there an unwritten law that says nice girls can't enjoy being kissed just as much as naughty ones do?" he demanded.

"I—I suppose not."

"Then what's this goose business?"

She pulled away from him. "We're having stuffed goose along with ham for Christmas dinner. I must get back and help Edith."

He grasped her arm as she reached for her muff. "Wait I'll come with you."

"There's no need. I—"

"Have you considered that Edith may not be quite ready for your return?"

She gaped at him. "Whyever not? We still have to—" She broke off, her hand flying to her mouth. "Oh!" Then she shook her head. "I don't believe it! Not Edith."

Larch grinned at her. "Yes, Edith. And certainly Mac. Surely you've grasped how fond they are of one another. Humor me. I'll come with you and we'll walk slowly to the cook shack. When we arrive, I'll knock and wait to be invited in. To save everyone's feelings, I'll say I was afraid the kitten might escape if I entered without warning. That way, whether I'm right or wrong, no one is embarrassed . . . except you, it seems. We haven't even left here and already you look mortally embarrassed."

"But they're not married," she blurted. "And they're old."

Larch burst into delighted laughter. "Why did you

331

think we were allowing them some privacy? Just so they could talk?"

Marta felt if her face turned any redder she'd be the color of a beet.

"As a matter of fact," Larch said, "Mac told me he *did* ask Edith to marry him a couple of years ago, in Michigan, but she turned him down because of his weakness for the bottle. And this may shock you, but I once had a man of seventy tell me, 'Sonny, you're never too old.'"

The notion she was learning too much too quickly gave Marta a queasy feeling. First Edith and now Larch had told her more than she wished to know about what went on between men and women. How far removed the plain facts were from butterflies and promises of a romantic tryst in the spring.

"I see I've succeeded in upsetting you all over again," Larch said. "I'm sorry."

"It's my fault as much as yours."

"No. I was far too blunt. You had to know about Edith and Mac, but I should have found a better way to—"

"Perhaps it's as well you were blunt." She kept her face averted as she pulled on her gloves and picked up her muff. "I might not have understood otherwise. 'Nice' girls tend to be far too naive." She took a deep breath and forced herself to look straight at him. "I won't be so easily fooled now. Isn't that all to the good?"

December ended without Marta exchanging more than a hurried greeting with Larch, and she told herself she didn't care, that the fewer chances she had to be alone with him, the better. But when he came by the cook shack on the first Sunday in January with an extra pair of snowshoes and invited her for a walk in the winter woods, she accepted with alacrity.

Though she'd never before had on a pair of

snowshoes, she soon caught the knack of shuffling along so that their framed web kept her on top of the snow.

"Listen," she said as the pines closed around them, "I hear a chickadee."

"The woods are full of them; they live in the pines."

"Where will they go when the trees have all been cut down?" she asked.

"You sound like Little Fox's grandfather. He doesn't speak English, but Little Fox translated his words for me.

"'White men cut the trees as we harvest wild rice, but rice grows quickly, rice can be harvested each fall. Pines grow so slowly that even if seeds were planted to replace those cut, my grandson's grandson would not see them tall and strong around us as they now are. When the trees are gone the animals will vanish. Our hunters will bring home no meat, our women will have no hides to make our clothes. We will die.'"

Though she'd never before questioned the whys of logging, the old Menominee's words of protest struck a chord in Marta.

"Why must you cut down all the trees?" she asked. "I realize the country needs lumber for building, but couldn't you save some of the pines?"

"If we did, another logger would move in behind us and finish them off. Not only is lumber necessary, but once the trees are gone, the land can be used for farming."

"I don't think the Menominee people want to be farmers," she said.

Larch shook his head. "They won't have much choice."

"It's not really fair."

"Life is seldom fair. We all have to adjust to its vagaries. Me. You. The Menominee."

"Did you learn that at Harvard?" Her voice carried

a slight edge.

"No. It's a lesson I learned on my own." His tone suggested he didn't care to pursue the subject.

She remembered the day of the sleigh ride, and how he'd turned aside her comments about his writing. He'd been as terse then. Did the lesson he'd learned have something to do with writing? His writing? She didn't dare ask for fear of being rebuffed.

They were now skirting a cut-over area. With no trees to block the wind or the snowfall, huge drifts covered many of the raw stumps, leaving only a few poking desolately through the glittering whiteness. A spot of red caught Marta's eye.

"Look," she cried, pointing. "Isn't that a jack's knit cap on that stump? Shall we bring the cap to the cook shack where whoever lost it can claim it?"

Larch nodded and together they showshoed into the clearing.

"No!" The cry halted them both, and they peered around.

Marta was the first to spot Little Fox, perched in a pine, wearing the red scarf she'd knitted for him.

"Trap," Little Fox warned, easing down to a lower branch, then leaping onto the snow-covered ground.

"Trap?" Larch echoed.

Little Fox, busy digging his snowshoes from where he'd hidden them under the snow, said, "For *mukwah*. Bear."

"A bear trap? Where?" Larch demanded.

The boy pointed toward the stump with the cap on it. "I see man come, set trap, cover up so we no see trap. He put hat there, then go away. I think trap was not for bear, but for man. I wait. You come. I know trap was for you." He pointed at Larch.

Marta stared at Little Fox, hardly believing her ears. A bear trap set for Larch?

Larch reached down and picked up a long and hefty

branch half-buried in the snow. "Show me where," he told Little Fox.

Her heart in her mouth, Marta watched them advance slowly toward the stump, Larch pushing the branch ahead of his snowshoes. Just before they reached the stump, a loud, sickening clank, accompanied by the crunch of wood being crushed, told her that he'd sprung the trap with the stick.

Little Fox eased to the left side of the stump, reached out, lifted the cap, and pulled it over his bare head. He turned and grinned at her. "Red," he said. "Like scarf."

Larch slogged back to her, his expression grim. "The cap was bait. If I'd tried to retrieve that cap, I'd have stepped into the bear trap."

"Get hurt bad," Little Fox agreed, joining them.

"Who was the man you saw setting the trap?"

The boy turned his hands palm upward, clearly signifying he didn't know him.

"Was he one of the lumberjacks?" Larch persisted.

"Wear the same coat."

"Had you ever seen him before?"

"No."

Larch put a hand on the boy's shoulder. "You said the trap was set for me. Why do you think so?"

"On day when no one chopping trees, choppers no come into woods. But you come, sometimes with her, sometime alone. She come alone sometime to feed birds at edge of woods. She no come here." He gestured toward the cut-over clearing.

"That's the second accident you've had," Marta said to Larch. "Or in this case, almost had."

"More probably the third."

"The third? You didn't tell me!"

"At the time, I thought it was a widow-maker—you know, a branch heavy with snow and ice that breaks off and falls with no warning. One of the jacks shouted a warning and I flung myself aside—the branch missed

335

me. At the time, it never occurred to me it could be anything but a case of me being in the wrong place at the wrong time, but now I wonder. There'd be little difficulty in sawing almost through a branch, looping a rope around it, and then, at the right time, giving the rope a hard yank. If the rope was placed right, it would slip off the end of the branch as the branch fell, leaving no evidence. Except for the sawn end, if anyone thought to look. I certainly didn't."

Little Fox listened with interest. "Bad heart try to hurt you one time, two times, three times," he said to Larch. "You got enemy?"

"Evidently I have. I wish I knew who he was."

Who would want to harm Larch? Marta wondered. Any one of the three so-called accidents could have not only maimed him seriously, but might have killed him. Had the same enemy crippled Old Beau?

"So many accidents happen at a logging camp," she said unhappily, thinking of the numerous cuts Edith had patched up. Several of the jacks had been seriously enough injured to be taken into Marinette to the doctor. "It's the perfect location to get away with murder."

When she realized what she'd said, she gasped, but it was too late, the word was out.

Murder.

She and Larch stared at one another until finally he cupped her face in his mittened hands. "Don't look so stricken," he murmured. "I've already proven it's not that easy to kill me."

She flung her arms around his neck. "I couldn't bear it if anything happened to you," she cried.

He kissed her, his lips gentle and reassuring at first, the kiss deepening as she responded with all her heart.

"If she your wife," Little Fox asked, "why you no live in her lodge?"

Marta and Larch sprang apart, having forgotten the

336

boy entirely.

"Let's return to camp," Larch said after a moment, speaking to Little Fox while ignoring the boy's question. "I'm sure Edith can find some food for you to take back to the Menominee village."

"Boss man no want me in camp," Little Fox said.

"What boss man?"

"Hear men say 'Raff-tee.'"

Rafferty, Marta knew, was bull-of-the-woods, hired by Mr. Terwilliger after he'd fired Mac.

"Rafferty bosses the men," Larch said, "but he isn't the chief boss. I'm Rafferty's boss. So if you're with me, it's all right."

Still the boy hung back. "Raff-tee say he shoot me if he catch me."

Noticing Larch's jaw setting in a grim line, and understanding he was close to making this an issue between himself and Rafferty with poor Little Fox caught in the middle, Marta said hastily, "I'll go into camp alone and bring the food to the edge of the woods, all right?"

She could see Larch meant to refuse, but before he could say a word, she touched his sleeve and added, "That way we can have a few more minutes alone."

Larch nodded curtly and Little Fox's eyes flashed her a message of relief. She didn't care much for Rafferty, a coarse, hulking man with a touch of the bully about him. Didn't Larch understand that if he forced Rafferty to back down, like as not, the wood's boss would search for ways to take his humiliation out on the boy, making it unsafe for Little Fox to come anywhere near the camp?

Larch had meant to lock horns with Rafferty, the two of them like belligerent bucks fighting for supremacy of the deer herd. She shook her head. Why men chose to meet head-on in the center of the bridge when there were alternate ways to cross the stream was beyond her understanding. Why was it, she wondered as she hurried toward the camp, that men sought confrontation, whereas women realized compromise was usually better in the long run?

Edith bundled up leftover bread and meat, and Marta returned with it to the woods. Little Fox took the bundle from her with a smile and immediately set off through the pines.

"I notice it seems to be a custom among the Menominees not to say goodbye when they leave," she said, hoping to distract Larch, who was still glowering.

"He's just a kid," Larch muttered. "A harmless kid."

She had the wit to realize he wasn't responding to what she'd said, but was still annoyed with Rafferty. "If you're not interested in my company—" she began.

"Did you know his old grandfather claims we're desecrating sacred ground of their ancestors?" Larch asked. "There's supposed to have been a burial ground where the camp is."

Marta grimaced, not liking the notion of living over ancient graves.

"I told him when the pines had all been cut the camp would be abandoned, but the old man seemed to feel we've already disturbed the spirits of his ancestors past any redemption."

The thought made her shiver. She might not believe in spirits taking revenge on the living but it was true Old Beau had been crippled and Larch had narrowly missed serious injury three times . . .

Chapter 24

Shortly after the New Year, Joe brought a sleighload of supplies that Edith had ordered from Marinette. With the supplies were several Chicago and Boston newspapers. They were far from current—the latest Boston paper was dated November 15.

The October fire that had devastated the city was still being featured in the Chicago papers.

"Loss estimated to be upward of $200,000," Edith read. "They go on and on about Chicago, and never a word about how Peshtigo burned to the ground that very same day, October eighth."

Marta shivered. Though some fifty miles away, Peshtigo was close enough to their camp that the frightful forest fire had caused a pall of smoke so thick it had turned the sun into a red ball. She remembered ashes drifting on the wind, and the fear of everyone in camp that the wind might shift and place them in grave danger.

"Upward of a thousand moose birds got born on the eighth," Joe had said to her after the fire.

Moose birds were what the jacks called bluejays, and some of them, like Joe, seemed to believe dead lumberjacks were reincarnated into jays. She was never sure whether they truly believed this or were teasing her. In any case, the Peshtigo fire had been a terrible tragedy. Not wishing to dwell on it, Marta turned her attention to the Boston paper.

"It says here the Tweed Ring was overthrown in New York City," she told Edith. "What on earth is a Tweed Ring?"

"Tweed is some kind of politician, that's all I know. You can't trust a one of them. Good God, it says here fifteen Chinese got lynched in Los Angeles, California—they call it a race riot. Sure don't like the sound of that, nosiree. Oh, yes, and they arrested that Mormon leader out in Utah for polygamy."

"What's polygamy?" Marta asked.

"That's when a man keeps marrying without divorcing any of his wives or them dying off. I heard tell polygamy was a part of the Mormon religion, even though it's plainly against U.S. law."

Marta frowned. "Mormon men have more than one wife? Never mind the law—how do they get the women to agree to such a thing?"

Edith shrugged. "Wouldn't suit me, but I ain't a Mormon, so I can't say."

Coming to a page that announced Boston weddings and engagements, Marta was about to turn it over when a familiar name caught her eye. She stared at the newsprint, not wanting to believe what she saw.

Mr. and Mrs. Lawrence Yates III announce the engagement of their daughter, Susan Haviland Yates, to Larch Henry Pendleton, son of Mr. and Mrs. Beaumont St. Cyr Pendleton . . .

She stopped, stunned, unable to read on, the newspaper sliding from her nerveless fingers.

"Whatever's the matter?" Edith asked in alarm.

Despite taking a deep, quivering breath, Marta found she couldn't answer. Edith picked up and scanned the paper.

Engaged. The word reverberated in Marta's head. He'd been engaged since November. To the pretty girl in the picture who called him darling. Engaged to Susan, and yet pretending he had no ties.

"How could he be such a hypocrite?" she cried.

Edith folded the paper and set it aside. "The fact is, Marta girl, you can't trust most men. Look at it this way—you learned what he was like before it was too late."

Anguished, her heart aching, Marta struggled not to burst into tears. "I—I fell in love with him," she whispered.

"Hard not to, with a good-looking young man like Larch paying you all the attention in the world. Let me tell you, I worried plenty over what was going to happen to you when the bubble burst. I tried to warn you, but you weren't listening. Not that I knew he was engaged but—" She broke off.

"But you *knew* Larch Pendleton would never marry me," Marta said bitterly. "I suppose I knew it, too. Still, when he kissed me it didn't seem to matter." Nothing had mattered except being in his arms.

He won't touch me again, she vowed. Not ever.

"Old Beau never gave up on nothing," Edith said, "and Larch is a Pendleton, like his pa. You got to figure he might not be willing to call it quits with you."

Marta set her jaw. "After I congratulate him on his engagement, I plan to treat him the same as I would any jack in camp; I'll be polite but distant."

Edith sighed. "I don't condone the way he's treated you, but with all them accidents, I can't help hoping he lives long enough to get married."

The accidents. Marta hugged herself. No matter how

angry she was at Larch, the thought of him being killed tore at her heart.

"That no-good son-of-a-he-goat Rafferty had the nerve to blame Mac for setting that bear trap." Edith's voice rose indignantly. "Why, Mac's the last person in the world would be that sneaky. He likes a good fight, 'specially when he's drinking; he might knock a jack down in a brawl and stomp on him, but he's no back-stabber. Besides, he and Old Beau's been through a lot together. Mac would never harm a hair of Larch's head, drunk or sober. What it is, I think Rafferty's afraid Mac's going to get his job once young Larch takes over."

"I thought Mr. Terwilliger and Beau Pendleton were equal partners."

"Yeah, that's true, but Old Beau ran the camp his own way till the tree fell on him. Mark my words, Larch will step into his shoes one of these days even if he doesn't want to."

"Doesn't want to?" No matter that Larch had betrayed her, everything about him still interested Marta.

"The boy never wanted to run logging camps. Or sit behind a desk in Boston, looking after his pa's other businesses. Likely never would've come to Wisconsin, neither, if Old Beau hadn't been crippled like he was."

Remembering the clues she'd picked up from things Larch had said, Marta nodded to herself. "He wants to write, doesn't he?"

"Told you, did he?" Edith sounded surprised.

"Not exactly."

"Well, anyway, Old Beau don't think much of writers or artists and such, and so he was dead set against it. He's got only one son, and he expects Larch to take over Pendleton Enterprises one day."

"Poor Larch." Marta spoke without thinking.

"Shouldn't think you'd feel sorry for him."

"It's difficult for anyone to give up a dream."

Edith laid her hand on Marta's shoulder. "Girl, you hit the nail on the head. Some of us never quite get the knack of setting aside our dreams, no matter how foolish."

May. A dream of butterflies and love. Marta swallowed, blinking back tears.

That same evening, Larch lingered in the kitchen after the meal.

"I thought you might like to snowshoe over to the Indian camp this Sunday," he said. "What do you think?"

Unhappily conscious of her food-stained apron and the untidy wisps of hair straggling onto her forehead, Marta raised her chin. "I'm afraid I'll be too busy to go anywhere with you—not only this coming Sunday, but every Sunday from now on. Or any other day."

He frowned and lowered his voice. "What's the matter, Marta?"

She ignored the question. "Before I forget, I'd like to congratulate you on your engagement to Susan Yates. I'm sure you two will be very happy. Now, if you'll excuse me, I've work to do." She started to turn away, but he gripped her arm.

"Marta, you must listen. I—"

"I don't care to hear anything you have to say." She wrenched free and retreated to the stove, where Edith was dipping heated water from the copper boiler to wash the dishes.

"Get out," Edith advised Larch, her voice grim. "You know I don't allow men in my kitchen when I'm working."

He opened his mouth, but Edith didn't give him a chance to protest. "You may be a Pendleton, but I'm the camp cook and I rule my kitchen. If you don't like

343

it, go find yourself a new cook, because I'm telling you now, you ain't coming in here no more except for meals with the other men."

Fists clenched, he whirled and slammed out the door. Marta managed to help Edith clean up the kitchen, but after the last plate was put away, she could no longer hold back the tears. Hurrying into the bedroom, she flung herself onto her bunk and wept until she fell into an exhausted sleep.

Marta couldn't bear to stay inside all the time but was determined to avoid Larch. Since she knew he slept late on Sundays, like most of the jacks, she took to rising early that day and going into the woods to feed the birds the crumbs she'd saved all week for them. This ploy worked until the last Sunday in February.

Though the thermometer registered below zero, the sun shone, turning the snow to glittering diamonds. Since there was no wind, the cold was bearable and Marta hurried to where a small stand of maples intermingled with the pines. The snow, though deep, was crusted hard enough to support the weight of the birds, so she sprinkled the crumbs directly onto the snow instead of scattering them along a branch.

Retreating a few feet, she leaned against the bare trunk of a maple and waited for the birds to arrive. The last time she'd counted six chickadees, two bluejays, and four pine tits.

The jays came first, a pair, the male's feathers much bluer than the female's. But almost as soon as they settled onto the snow to peck at the crumbs, they flew up again and perched high in a nearby pine, squawking loudly.

Warning of an intruder? A deer? A fox? She'd caught sight of a fox slipping through the trees once. Marta turned to look and put her mittened hand to her mouth in dismay.

Larch loomed over her. "It's taken me two months to run you down," he said irritably. "Now that I finally have, you're damn well going to listen to what I have to say."

Recovering her wits, Marta snapped, "I don't care to hear—"

"Care or not, you *will* listen."

He stood between her and the camp. When she tried to dodge around him, he stopped her by clamping his mittened hands onto her shoulders.

"I mean to break the engagement," he said.

"That's none of my affair. Please let me—"

He shook her. "It has everything to do with you, damn it. Susan and I have been friends for years, but I never should have let my mother push me into asking Susan to marry me. That was my original mistake. Then I met you. Now I can't possibly marry Susan."

Marta swallowed, fighting her treacherous urge to believe him. "I see no reason your having met me should change anything."

"You must know I'm in love with you."

Her breath caught, leaving her speechless. Larch Pendleton was in love with her?

"And you love me," he said fiercely. "I see it in your eyes, but I need to hear you tell me you do."

Marta shook her head. "No! No, I—"

"Tell me!"

She struggled to free herself, determined not to give in and have her heart broken all over again. Caught off balance, Larch fell sideways, dragging her down with him.

As they landed in the snow, she heard a loud crack and something hit the branch of the maple above them.

"Some bastard's shooting at us," Larch muttered

into her ear, and she belatedly realized what she'd heard was the crack of a rifle and the bullet slamming into the maple.

"Larch!" Mac's shout came from the woods beyond them. "You all right?"

"So far," Larch called back, not raising his head. His arms tightened protectively around Marta.

Afraid to move, she stayed where she was. "Another accident?" she whispered fearfully.

"Where the devil are you?" Mac demanded, his voice coming from nearby.

"Did you see a man with a rifle?" Larch asked.

"Earlier. Not now."

"Someone took a shot at us." As Mac cursed, Larch cautiously raised his head, then rose, pulling her up with him. She stared at Mac, who was wearing snowshoes and cradling a rifle across his chest.

"*You've* got a gun!" she blurted, remembering that Rafferty had told Edith he suspected Mac.

"Mac's the only man in camp I'm positive wouldn't take a potshot at me," Larch said, brushing snow from her cloak.

"Been deer hunting," Mac said. "Edith got a hankering for venison. I may be getting on, but my eyesight's still good enough so I sure as hell wouldn't mistake Larch for a deer."

"Who was the man you saw earlier?" Larch asked.

"Couldn't tell, too far away. He wore a red plaid mackinaw, like most of the jacks." Mac glanced around and then looked up into the trees. Lowering his voice, he said, "Some of the boys claim the Injuns are laying for us on account of we're violating their ancestors' bones."

"Could it have been an Indian you saw?" Larch asked.

Mac shrugged. "Hard to say. But that Injun kid's

346

always snooping around. What for, that's what I'd like to know. For once I agree with Rafferty—the camp's off limits to all Injuns."

"Oh, please, no!" Marta cried. "Little Fox is harmless, I'm sure of it."

"Maybe so," Mac said, "but why's he spying on us?"

"Take a look through the woods and see if you can spot the man you saw earlier," Larch said to Mac. "Though I doubt he's hanging around waiting to be caught. I'll see Marta back to camp."

"Consider it done."

Still shaken from their brush with death, Marta made no objection, even when Larch put an arm around her waist to guide her through the snow.

"If anything happened to you—" Larch's voice faltered, his grip tightening. He halted, pulling her into his embrace. "Ah, God, Marta, I couldn't bear it."

She knew she should pull away, yet she did not. For the moment, no place on earth seemed safer than the circle of his arms.

"This might happen again," he said. "I don't dare take the chance. I can't put you in danger, and I fear you *are* in danger when we're together outside. I don't believe whoever is stalking me intends you to be the victim—I'm his target. Yet he made it obvious that if you're in the way, you're doomed, too. He's a man with no conscience and no scruples and therefore more dangerous than a ferocious beast." He held her away and gazed into her eyes. "Do you understand what I'm saying?"

"I—I didn't mean to see you again—" she began.

He put his mittened hand over her mouth. "Never mind that. I meant what I told you before we were shot at. You're the one I want, and you're the one I'll have. But for your sake we mustn't be together until I run down the devil who's after me. Which means I can't see

347

you alone." He smiled wryly. "Even if Edith agrees to my presence in the cook shack of a Sunday, I doubt she'll consent to giving us any privacy."

Unsure what to believe, unsettled by the near accident and his closeness, wanting to trust him but afraid to, Marta felt her mind roil in confusion. "I think I prefer not being alone with you," she said finally.

He grinned. "Is that because you don't trust me, or because you don't trust yourself?"

"A little of both."

He bent and brushed his lips over hers in a brief, teasing kiss, then let her go. "I could kiss you for hours and I damn well would if I could be sure the bastard with the rifle had given me up for today. But I can't take any risk—I must get you safely inside."

"You'll be in constant danger working with the men," she protested. "You don't know which one of them—"

"I'm safer in a crowd." He took her hand and resumed walking toward the camp clearing. "I mean to stay alive, Marta. I'm damned if I'll be cheated out of May."

Edith reluctantly agreed that Larch could come visiting with Mac on Sundays. So each Sunday in March, and the first Sunday in April, Marta, Edith, Mac, and Larch played High, Low, Jack and the Game in the dining room with Mac's battered deck of cards. Other than those Sundays, Marta and Larch had no chance to talk, and even then, anything they said to one another was overheard by Edith and Mac.

During the second week in April, the ice in the Peshtigo River broke with a crack heard all through the camp, and in a few days the river was clear of ice and running at full spate, fueled by melting snow upstream. Excitement spread through the camp. Time for the drive!

Marta helped Edith pack the cook wagon, since they were to feed the men helping with the drive. The jacks who weren't needed had already drawn their stakes and left camp.

"Cooking out of a wagon's kind of tricky, but you get used to it," Edith told Marta. "Got to feed them jacks good to keep them frisky enough to stay on top."

"Stay on top?"

Edith stared at her, then shook her head. "Guess you've never seen a log drive. Some of the jacks, the catty ones, ride the logs downriver to the lake where the sawmill is. 'White water men,' they are. Pretty dang exciting. If there's a jam, it gets downright perilous."

"Catty," Marta knew, meant "sure-footed."

"I don't doubt Larch'll be one of them," Edith went on. "Mac says the boy's a natural white-water man."

Riding logs down a rushing river seemed dangerous in itself to Marta. "Are log-jams common?" she asked.

"Sure to happen. Never seen a spring go by they didn't jam up at least once. That's a sight you'll never forget—them big old pine logs crossed like straws, some upended, not a one of them going anywhere, damming the river and a-creaking and a-grinding and a-groaning in complaint."

"How do they get the logs moving again?"

"A couple of them catty jacks dance out on the pile-up—least, to us on shore it looks like dancing on account of it's hard to keep their footing on them shifting logs. They got to find the king log, the key one that's holding back all the rest, and move it to break up the jam. Takes a heap of hooking peaveys first in one log, then another and another until they locate the key jammer.

"Finally, one of them gets ahold of the king log,

twists it free, and rolls it down. The logs shift and start moving, and the jacks race for shore before it's too late. Once the jam gives way, all that backed-up water and them pent-up logs haul on down the river hell-bent for election. Them that don't make shore got to try to ride it out, and death rides right along with them. You're lucky if you don't lose more than one white-water man a spring."

Marta swallowed. "Larch has never done it before, has he?"

"He's bound to try it, Mac says."

"But if it's so dangerous, why would he want to?"

"Men are always thinking they got to prove themselves by doing something risky. Women got more sense."

Marta's heart contracted with fear to think of Larch catty-footing on a bobbing log in a rushing river with only his calked boots giving him purchase. True, he'd be carrying the long pole with the curved iron hook on one end that they called a peavey, but how much use would calked boots or iron hooks be when a log-jam gave way?

That evening, with the cook wagon parked near the riverbank, she and Edith ladled dinner onto plates and passed them out to the river crew, Larch and Mac among them. Both cooking and cleaning up were less convenient than at the camp, but Marta enjoyed the novelty. They slept inside a tent set up beside the wagon.

Before dawn the next morning, Marta woke abruptly, thinking she'd heard someone call her name. But Edith, she saw in the dim gray light, was still sleeping. The call, if there'd been one, wasn't repeated. Shivering in the chill morning, she told herself she might as well dress, since she'd soon have to rise anyway to help Edith hitch up the horses to pull the wagon downstream. Marta pulled on her clothes quickly and left the tent.

She hadn't quite reached the wagon when Little Fox appeared, startling her. Before she could ask if he was the one who'd called her, he put his fingers to his lips.

He leaned close, whispering, "Before sun go down, I hear bad words."

"Who spoke them?" she asked, keeping her voice low.

"Raff-tee and man he call Ter-will. They set trap for Larch downriver." He pointed. "If he ride logs this sun, he die."

Marta stared at the boy. He must mean Rafferty and Mr. Terwilliger. But why would Mr. Terwilliger want to harm Larch? Could his motive have something to do with the Terwilliger/Pendleton partnership? Whatever the reason, Larch was in danger.

"Where is Larch?" she demanded.

"He go downriver to log piles."

"How about Mac?"

"He tell Larch he forget something. He go back to camp."

So neither Larch nor Mac was near enough to be warned. What was she to do? Quickly she made up her mind. Camp was some distance away, and Little Fox was faster than she was.

"You go tell Mac," she ordered. "I'll hurry downstream to find Larch."

Little Fox took off at a run. Marta hitched up her skirts and hurried along the muddy track through the morning mist with the river on her left and the stumps of pines to her right. Fear edged her thoughts; she prayed she'd reach Larch in time to warn him. But even if she did, she had no idea what kind of trap might be waiting for him. Would he believe her? He had to! But could she convince him to stay off the river?

The sun had not yet risen when she neared the rollways of logs. Hearing men's voices, she eased into the scrub growth along the bank, not wishing to encounter Rafferty unexpectedly. The spindly willows no sooner hid her from sight of the road when an arm snaked around her throat from behind, cutting off her cry of alarm.

Rafferty's gruff voice spoke in her ear. "I tried to catch that damn Injun brat yesterday, but the slick little bugger vanished right before my eyes. Figured he'd go to you and you'd high-tail it down here—so I been waiting."

She struggled to free herself; he tightened his grip, choking her until she couldn't breathe. Her vision dimmed and darkened and she fell into nothingness.

When she came to, she found herself gagged and tied to a trunk of a dead tree in the midst of cut-over forest. She was alone—neither Rafferty nor anyone else was in sight. Nor could she hear any voices, or even the rush of the river. Where was she? A familiar scent filled her nostrils, reminding her of Edith and the cooking wagon. Why, oh, why hadn't she roused Edith and told her where she was going?

But was it smoke from Edith's cooking fire she smelled? She strained her neck to look around her. A whimper rose in her throat as she spotted a tendril of smoke curling around the trunk of the tree where she was tied. When she listened she heard with dismay the crackle of burning pine needles.

Oh, dear God, a slashings fire—the fear of every logger. And here she was in the midst of it, helpless to save herself.

Chapter 25

"Larch!" Mac's shout carried over the rush of the river and the splash of logs rolling into the water.

Larch, riding a log downstream, glanced briefly at the bank, his attention focused on keeping his balance, and saw Mac gesturing frantically as he yelled, "Ashore! Hurry!"

Easier said than done on tumbling logs in fast water. Larch was two hundred yards downstream by the time he managed to work his way from one log to another and reach the bank. Mac rushed up to him.

"Where's Marta?" Mac asked.

Larch stared at him. "Isn't she with Edith?"

"You mean you haven't seen her?"

"No. What the hell's wrong?"

"The Injun boy come after me. You know I was headed back to camp. Never got there. Changed my mind and turned around. Figured I'd gotten along for six months without that pint of forty-rod hid under my bunk so I might as well try for seven. Anyways, Little Fox meets me with some cockamamie story about Rafferty laying a trap for you. I wouldn't've believed him except he said he'd told Marta and she was off to warn you.

"So we come hightailing along the track and find Edith harnessing up the horses, worried as hell 'cause Marta was missing. Little Fox repeats his tale and she figures out from what he says that Terwilliger's somehow mixed up in it, along with Rafferty. Edith orders the boy to go find Marta."

Larch grabbed Mac's shirtfront. "Get to the point—where is she?"

"Take it easy, lad. My tongue's going as fast as it can. I leave Edith and hike lickety-split down the track to look for you and about halfway along the boy sticks his head out of the brush and stops me. Claims he found a sign that told him Marta ran into the brush right there and then a man grabbed her and carried her off. He says for me to get you; he'd follow the trail the man left and notch stumps so we'd know the way. It's all cut-over and slashings along—" Mac broke off abruptly, raising his head to sniff the air. "Jesus H. Christ, I smell smoke!"

Alarm arrowed through Larch as he caught the same sinister scent. "What the devil are we waiting for? Which way did Little Fox go?"

"If we angle east—" Mac pointed—"we'll pick up his notches without taking the long way round."

They plunged through the skim of growth along the bank and into the wilderness of stumps left from their winter's logging. Before they found the first of Little Fox's trail signs, smoke drifted above the stumps, carried on the spring breeze.

She's safe, Larch told himself, fighting the curl of fear rising within him. Marta's safe, she has to be!

The smoke thickened, making it harder to find the notches, and up ahead Larch could hear the ominous crackle of flames as the fire fed on the slashings—piles of branches lopped off the felled trees and left to rot.

354

"The kid's trail leads smack-dab into the damn fire," Mac said hoarsely, then began to cough.

Larch gritted his teeth, holding back his impulse to shout that he knew the danger, so for God's sake don't talk about it.

"Never liked that Rafferty," Mac muttered. "Nor Terwilliger, neither."

Intent on his own anguish, Larch barely noticed Mac had dropped the "Mr." All he could think of was Marta. A world without her would be a world without life. A winter world where spring never came. He couldn't bear it if anything happened to her.

A thick gray pall hung over the stumps, cutting the visibility to a few feet. Breathing grew difficult. The crackle of the fire became louder.

As they stumbled on, eyes watering from the increasingly dense smoke, Larch tried not to remember his father's account, written in the aftermath of last October's Peshtigo fire, but one line from the letter continued to dance like an evil flame in his mind.

They found strapping lumberjacks reduced to no more than thimblefuls of ashes . . .

Not Marta. Please God, not Marta.

"I'll kill the bastards if they've hurt her," he cried, choking on the last words as he breathed in a lungful of smoke.

As he tried to catch his breath, Larch thought he heard a faint call to his right. He gripped Mac's sleeve. "Listen!"

The call wasn't repeated but he plunged to the left, shouting, "Marta!" Mac stumbled behind him.

The answer, when it came, was more of a croak than a word. And it came from Little Fox, sprawled on the ground beside a motionless Marta.

Larch reached down and lifted her into his arms. "Help the boy," he said to Mac.

The journey back to the river was a nightmare of smoke and heat, lit by flames and fueled by the fear of losing the way. Neither he nor Mac realized until the smoke began to thin that rain had begun to pour down. Eventually they staggered, exhausted and dripping wet onto the track beside the river, and found Edith and the cook wagon.

"Should be safe here," Mac said. "Rain's not letting up so the fire won't spread."

Edith opened the back of the wagon and, as Larch laid Marta within its shelter, he was able for the first time, to take stock of her injuries. He swallowed, shocked.

Little Fox, laid beside her by Mac, rose onto his elbow. "She's not dead?" Anguish threaded through the words.

"She's alive," Edith assured them all.

"Larch," Little Fox said. "Listen, Larch."

Larch tore his attention from Marta's singed hair and the ugly red burns on her face and arms. Little Fox, though also burned, was not as badly injured.

"I hear Raff-tee and Ter-will make plan," the boy said. "Logjam where river go round Big Rock. Raff-tee push you in river there, you die."

So Terwilliger was behind the other so-called accidents. Had he also been responsible for Beau's injuries? I'll beat the truth out of him if I have to, Larch told himself grimly.

"You're a good and brave friend," he said to Little Fox. "I can never repay you."

"My people's way," the boy said. "You help me; I help you."

Marta moaned and her eyes opened. Larch bent over her. She focused on him and sighed.

"I knew you'd come to save me," she whispered.

Afraid to touch her, Larch could only nod and try to

smile reassuringly while tears ran down his cheeks unheeded.

"We'd best get her tended to," Edith said, touching his arm. "My old grandma always swore by cold water compresses for burns. You and Mac go down to the river and dip me up a pail or two for a start."

Three months later, Marta sat before her dressing table in her Sandusky bedroom, staring at her reflection. She sighed. After the fire, Edith had clipped what remained of Marta's hair close to her scalp in order to better treat her burns. Though her hair had grown since then and dark curls now capped her head, to her mind she still looked shorn.

"If I wasn't wearing a skirt they'd take me for a boy," she muttered.

Toivi, standing near the door, giggled. "Too pretty for boy."

Marta fingered the silver scar at her temple and shook her head. "I might have been once," she said sadly, "but not now, not with these scars."

"You got little tiny scar there, you got teeny-tiny scar here—" Toivi touched her own chin—"nobody hardly see."

"Look at my arms!" Marta thrust them toward Toivi. "They'll never look right."

Toivi shrugged. "You got scars on arms but they work right. My sister, she break arm, hers never work right."

Marta bit her lip. "I'm sorry about your sister. I don't mean to be such a terrible complainer. What worries me is that I'm afraid Mr. Pendleton might come to Sandusky despite my warning that he must stay away. If he does, I'll refuse to see him. I simply can't face him. He'll remember how I looked before and pity me. I don't want his pity!"

"You tell me he write many love letters."

With no one in the house her age except Toivi, Marta had confided in her to a limited extent. "I believe he was writing to a memory," she said. "The one time I answered him I tried to explain that I was no longer the same girl he once knew, but he didn't seem to understand."

"You same to me," Toivi said.

Marta jumped up and hugged her. "I don't know what I'd have done without you these last months. You're so good for me; you never let me get away with feeling sorry for myself."

Later, after Toivi left the bedroom, Marta chose a blue ribbon the color of her gown and tied it around her head much as she'd worn ribbons as a young girl. Childish, maybe, but feminine rather than boyish.

She was searching the drawers of her wardrobe for a misplaced pair of blue gloves when she heard the bang of the front door knocker. Her windows didn't face the street, so she had no way to tell who might be at the door. Since it was before noon, it was likely to be a member of her mother's Ladies' Aid Society, coming by to collect the shawls Freda had crocheted for the old people at the Poor Farm.

Certainly it wouldn't be Larch. Not after she'd told him so plainly in her letter that she didn't want to see him again.

Toivi had improved her English, but the complexities of announcing a visitor still eluded her. Through her closed bedroom door Marta heard Toivi shout up the stairs.

"Someone come to see you, Miss Marta."

Since she could hardly bellow back, "What's the person's name?" Marta hurried to the top of the stairs and gestured frantically at Toivi to climb up to where she was.

"Who is it?" she asked in a low tone when Toivi obeyed.

"He say he Mr. Pendleton."

Marta clutched her chest where her heart felt as though it was about to hammer its way free. "No!"

"He say he is."

"I mean, no, I can't see him. I can't possibly."

"Marta!" Freda exclaimed.

Unnoticed, Freda had come up the back stairs and, standing in the hall, had undoubtedly overheard the entire conversation.

Marta turned. "Yes, Mother?"

"If you don't care to see your visitor, you will be courteous enough to go down to the parlor and tell him so. You will not leave it up to poor Toivi."

"But I—"

"You will do as I say. Toivi, you're needed in the kitchen, come with me." Freda walked briskly toward the rear staircase, Toivi trailing after her.

With no choice left to her, Marta took a deep breath and started down the stairs. I must be firm, she told herself. I'll simply repeat what I said in the letter and try not to see the pity in his eyes. She hesitated at the parlor door but finally pushed it open and stepped inside. She stopped dead, staring.

The man standing by the window smiled at her. "You forgot I'm also Mr. Pendleton, didn't you?" With the aid of a gold-handled cane, he limped slowly toward her.

Never had she imagined Larch's father would visit her!

Gathering her wits she said, "I—that is, please do sit down, sir. I'm so glad to see you've recovered."

He gestured toward the settee and, when she seated herself, he eased alongside her. Clasping her hands in

359

his, he gazed at her.

"It's good to see you, Marta. I thought of you often in Boston when I was confined to my bed, wondering how you liked the camp and hoping you were all right. I'm sorry you had to undergo such a terrible experience at the hands of my erstwhile partner and his henchman Rafferty. You'll be glad to know they're both confined to jail, awaiting trial.

"I'm ashamed to admit I never suspected Matthew Terwilliger would be capable of concocting such a nefarious plot, much less carrying it out. But then, I had no idea he was a high-stakes gambler in such desperate need of money that he was willing to murder both me and my son to gain full control of our lumber company finances. As for Rafferty—there's always men like him willing to sell their soul for money."

She nodded, saying nothing, still not easily able to discuss what had happened to her at Rafferty's hands.

"And while I lay in my bed in Boston," Beau continued, "I also wondered how you liked my son. Larch wrote his mother and me so rarely, and then mostly about the logging, that I wasn't sure how you two were getting along until he came home last month."

She drew her hands gently away and clasped them in her lap. "Your son and I did become friends."

Old Beau chuckled. "Larch was a good deal more honest about what happened between you than you're being, my dear. He told me he's in love with you and wants to marry you."

"He's engaged to another woman."

"Marta, look at me."

She met his dark gaze reluctantly. It was difficult enough for her to skirt the truth without looking him in the eyes while she did so.

"The truth is," Beau said, "his mother and Susan's

360

mother engineered that engagement and furthermore, you're already aware of this. You also know Larch broke the engagement."

"I believe he did mention something like that in a letter," she admitted, reddening.

He leaned toward her. "What the devil is the matter with you, girl? Don't you love him?"

She tried to say no, she didn't love Larch, but the lie stuck in her throat, forcing her to nod in agreement.

"I knew it!" he crowed. "The very first time I set eyes on you, I said to myself that at last I'd met the right girl for Larch. Thank the Lord the boy had the sense to realize you were."

"I—I can't marry your son, sir." Misery coated her words.

"Why not?"

Marta bit her lip. "I should think you could tell from looking at me."

"That devil Terwilliger may have crippled me, but my eyesight's as good as ever. You don't look quite as peppy as you used to, but otherwise I don't see any difference."

Marta searched his face for telltale signs of pity, but saw only honest confusion. Finally she pointed to her temple and her chin, then extended her arms for him to look at.

He ran a gentle finger over the still red scars on her left arm. "How lucky you were, my dear, to escape without being disfigured."

She blinked. "But—but I *am* disfigured."

"Where?"

"The skin of my arms will never look normal. And my face—" her voice faltered but she went on—"my face is also scarred. When he sees me, Larch won't want the girl I am now, but I suspect he may insist on marrying me out of pity. I won't—I can't—"

361

Beau's scowl stopped her. "Do you mean to say you think my son is so puerile that he'd choose a woman to be his wife on the basis of her appearance alone?"

"Not exactly, but—"

"Then just what *do* you mean?"

"Larch has a romantic dream," she blurted, "an impossible dream of a lover's springtime, and I just don't fit into such a perfect dream anymore."

Beau closed his eyes and leaned back on the settee. "My boy's a dreamer, true enough. You ought to see the flowery poetry he used to write. Foolish stuff."

"Why don't you want him to be a writer?" she demanded.

He opened one eye. "Larch has talent, but no man—or woman, either—has anything to write about until he knows something of the real world. After he's experienced a few of the difficulties of living, I've no doubt he'll be able to write something worth reading."

Marta thought this over. "Are you really on his side?"

"Always have been. Why else would I be here? Larch needs you. He needs the woman you are, the one he fell in love with. Do you truly believe two barely visible scars on your face and those on your arms change you into another person?"

She wrung her hands. "I don't know."

"When I look at you I see the same attractive, eager, and resilient girl I met at the camp. Pretty as you are, Susan Yates is prettier. Yet Larch prefers you. Think about it."

The front door knocker banged loudly three times.

"Damn, I knew I was cutting it fine." Beau struggled to his feet and reached for his cane. "Lead me through to the back before that maid of yours opens the door. If Larch finds me here, he'll skin me alive for interfering."

362

Marta rose, staring at him incredulously. Larch, here?

"Don't just stand there, girl. Hurry!"

Opening the parlor door, Marta caught Toivi before she reached the door. "Wait until I take Mr. Pendleton into the kitchen before you answer."

After leaving Beau with her mother in the kitchen, Marta returned to the entryway, forcing herself not to run, trying to decide what to say when she entered the parlor, only to find she had no need for words.

Larch stood framed in the open parlor door and the moment she came into view he strode to her, wrapped his arms around her, and held her tightly.

"I'm never letting you go again," he said before he kissed her with a fierce and fiery passion that held no trace of pity, the kiss more convincing than ten thousand words.

Marta's September wedding to Larch was held in the same church where Elma had been married. Elma and Hunt came all the way from Texas to attend, bringing their six-month-old son, Neal, with them.

"Larch Pendleton's a lucky man to be getting you for his wife," Elma told her.

"Oh, Elma, I love him so much. I'm really the lucky one."

Elma was her sister's matron-of-honor and the Emerson girls were her attendants. Zoe, now Mrs. Silas Portland, admitted before the ceremony that she was in the family way.

"I only hope you'll be as happy as Silas and me," Zoe told Marta.

At the reception Edith informed Marta that she wasn't the only new bride. "Me and Mac tied the knot up in Marinette two months back," she confided. "I

363

figured I was being three kinds of a fool, but I was wrong. I ain't never been so happy."

"I wish you'd told me you were getting married," Marta said. "I would have liked to have been there."

"We didn't invite nobody 'cause we weren't too sure it'd take. Only thing Mac complains about so far is that I let the cat sleep in our bed. I tell him he was the one gave me that cat in the first place and she was sleeping with me before he was."

Marta learned later that Old Beau had installed Edith and Mac as caretakers of his hunting and fishing lodge in Michigan's Upper Peninsula near Escanaba, and that they'd be taking Little Fox to live at the hunting camp with them.

"He's gonna be the guide for Old Beau's friends," Mac confided. "Ain't no better guide than an Injun."

Marta's parents and Old Beau easily became friends; Larch's mother, Grace, remained polite but distant to all the Johansens, including Marta. Her coolness lasted until December, when Larch announced to his folks at Christmas that they were on the way to becoming grandparents. Grace slowly began to thaw.

In June, when Henrietta Grace Pendleton was born, Larch's mother at last granted Marta full acceptance in the family.

From the beginning, though, it was Grandpa Beau who won Henrietta's heart.

Chapter 26

In the long northern twilight, twelve-year-old Henrietta Pendleton edged cautiously along the side of her family's summer cottage on Mackinac Island. She could hear her father's deep voice punctuated by the tenor voices of the other men, all of them sitting on the front porch enjoying the evening as they smoked their pipes and cigars. All except Grandpa Beau, that is. He was down at the dock. If she didn't get caught on the way, she planned to join him.

The women were still inside but would soon be going out to sit with the men. She meant to be well away by then. Grandmother would scold her later. Mama would pretend to be cross but wouldn't be really angry because she knew how Henrietta hated dressing up and attending adult parties.

Last year it hadn't been so bad because Aunt Elma and Uncle Hunt had been visiting here from Texas with Cousin Neal. He was only a couple of years older and they'd had fun exploring the island together. But this year Neil wasn't here and Mama expected her to be more ladylike.

"I've taken your side for years," Mama had warned just yesterday, "but you can't be a tomboy forever. You mustn't forget you're a girl and girls eventually become young ladies. In fact, whether you choose to accept it or not, you're a young lady already."

Henrietta grimaced. Though she didn't like the recent changes in her body, she realized she couldn't stop what was happening to her. Mama was right—girls were doomed to be women. Ladies. It was enough to take all the fun out of life.

Reaching the rear of the house, she hiked up her skirts, dashed across the lawn, and ducked under the grape arbor, followed by the faint scent of tobacco smoke drifting on the breeze. Hidden from view by the tangled vines, she hurried to the end of the arbor, where she turned to the left and half-slid down the steep path to the water. In a few moments she'd be with her grandfather and he wouldn't care that she'd run away from the party; he had, too.

Small stones dislodged by her feet tumbled downhill ahead of her, some of them clattering onto the wooden planks below. She was disappointed to see that Grandpa Beau's sailboat was gone—he must have sailed it to the repair yard already. Why hadn't he waited for her?

"Hey!" A boy climbed from a moored rowboat onto the small pier. "Watch what you're doing with those rocks."

Henrietta tried and failed to slow her precipitous descent, arriving at the pier in a small shower of dirt and gravel. There was still enough light in the July sky to show the ferocious scowl on the boy's face.

She met his belligerence with her own. "What do you mean by tying your boat to our pier?" she demanded.

"It's not my boat," he said. "I borrowed it."

"Well, it *is* my dock."

"Who says so?"

"I'm Henrietta Pendleton, we live up there"—she

gestured toward the hill with her head—"and my grandfather owns this pier."

"He told me I could tie up here," the boy said, giving her a superior smile.

She thrust out her lower lip. "Why should I believe you?"

"'Cause I'm Garth Laidlaw, and Laidlaws don't tell lies."

Arms akimbo, she assessed him. About the age of her Cousin Neal, so maybe fourteen, she decided. She wasn't short but he was half a head taller, with dark eyes and darker hair. It annoyed her to notice he was examining her just as thoroughly. "I never heard of the Laidlaws," she said tartly, determined not to back down.

He grinned at her. "I never heard of the Pendletons till I met your grandpa."

His grin made it hard for her to stay angry. She offered Garth a tentative smile and her right hand.

When he didn't hesitate to shake her hand, her opinion of him inched higher. Most boys acted as though there was something wrong with a girl who wanted to shake hands. Maybe she and Garth Laidlaw could be friends.

"Are you here for the summer?" she asked.

He shook his head. "I live on the island."

"Even in the winter?"

"Sure."

"That sounds like fun. Mackinac Island's about my favorite place in the whole world. I've never been anywhere more beautiful."

"You can get tired of living here. Someday, when I'm captain of my own boat, I'll see if you're right about the island."

"They're only called boats on the Great Lakes," she said. "Ships sail out of Boston, not boats."

"I said boat and I meant boat. I'm a lakesman; I don't plan on captaining a ship."

Henrietta bit her lip. She'd gotten his back up by showing off her knowledge, something she was overly inclined to do. Not that she meant to apologize, but she'd try to be more careful.

"I guess you must be from Boston," he said.

"My grandparents are. My parents live in Detroit. Two years ago Grandpa Beau and my father had our summer cottage built on the island, so now we all spend summers here."

He looked up the hill at her house. "You mean you call that big place a cottage?"

"We just use it in the summer," she said, wondering why he sounded sort of angry.

"You could put two houses the size of the one where I live in your 'cottage' and still have room left over."

Henrietta wasn't stupid. She knew Grandpa Beau was a wealthy man and that her father was well off, too. So was her Texas uncle. Others, she realized, had far less money. Like the Laidlaws, evidently. In her family, money was never discussed. Not knowing what else to do, she changed the subject.

"Let's walk to the end of the dock and sit there," she said.

He came along without arguing, making her hope that he wanted to be friends. She didn't know anyone her age on the island except a couple of older girls who took care to do nothing that might soil their gowns and therefore looked down their noses at her usually grubby dresses. In any case, she almost always got along better with boys than girls.

"Living on an island, you must know a lot about boats," she said when they were sitting side by side, their legs dangling over the edge of the dock.

"Not as much as I'd like to," he said.

368

"I'm a pretty fair sailor," she told him, not boasting, merely stating a fact.

He smiled challengingly. "Yeah? I'll bet you can't handle your grandpa's sailboat alone."

"Just you wait and see." Actually, she hadn't yet, not if he meant being alone in the boat, but her grandfather did let her sail the boat by herself when he took her with him.

Garth leaned back against a post, watching Henrietta Pendleton as she tried to convince him she was an experienced sailor. She didn't giggle and flirt like the island girls he knew, but she didn't behave like a rich summer visitor, either. For one thing, she was easy to talk to, and for another, she didn't seem to care or even to notice that her fancy gown was torn and dirty. He remembered seeing her around last summer, with a boy; he'd figured them both for summer visitors and hadn't paid much attention.

In the fading light he couldn't tell exactly what color her eyes were—green, he thought, like deep lake water—but no one could miss that curly red hair. She wasn't exactly pretty, but he didn't seem to be able to stop looking at her.

"I'll believe it when I see you sail the boat alone," he told her. Island girls didn't pilot boats, and he doubted any girl would be much good at it.

"I don't know everything there is to know," she admitted. "But you don't either—you already said so."

"I would know, except—" He paused, not certain he wanted to reveal any more of himself to Henrietta.

"Except for what?"

He scowled. "My ma doesn't want me to be a sailor."

"What does she want you to be?"

"A teacher, like her." His words were reluctant. When she didn't respond, he added, "Would you want to be a teacher if you were a man and could ship out on

369

the lake boats?"

"I never thought about it before."

"Being a sailor on a lake boat is hard work, work for men," he said. "Anyone can teach, even women."

Henrietta's eyes narrowed. "*I* could work on a lake boat if I wanted to."

"Yeah—as a cook, maybe."

"Cook? I'd be a captain!"

He laughed so hard tears came to his eyes.

Henrietta jumped to her feet and glared down at him. "I could, I tell you!"

"A lady captain? What would the sailors say—'Aye, aye, ma'am?'" He burst into renewed laughter.

Her hard shove caught him unawares. Arms flailing wildly, he toppled off the dock into the cold water.

Henrietta stared down at Garth splashing and sputtering, her satisfaction over having given him his just deserts waning as she began to worry that he couldn't swim.

"Give me a hand up," he called, reaching toward her.

It was the least she could do. She crouched down at the dock's edge, extending her arm. Garth grasped her hand and gave an unexpected yank, making her overbalance and plunge into the water next to him. Buoyed up by her skirts but made clumsy by layers of clothes, she swam awkwardly toward shore. Garth beat her there.

"You're no gentleman," she sputtered as she waded onto the tiny pebble-strewn beach.

"Never claimed to be," he retorted. "The way I see it, one bad turn deserves another. Now we're even." He leaped onto the dock and climbed into his boat.

"Goodbye and good riddance," she snapped, turning her back to him as he pushed away.

Muttering, she started up the path to the top of the hill. So much for Garth Laidlaw. How could she ever have imagined she wanted to be friends with such a lout?

"*Au revoir, ma belle capitaine,*" he called to her, the amusement in his voice making her grind her teeth.

"I'll show him," she muttered. "He'll laugh out of the other side of his mouth when I'm a captain and he's a lowly sailor who has to take orders from me."

By the time she reached the top of the hill, Henrietta's mind was made up. One way or another, she was determined to captain a lake boat. "And they won't call me ma'am, they'll call me sir," she whispered fiercely to herself as, dripping wet, she made her way to the back door and the scolding she knew was waiting.

She lay in wait for her grandfather the next morning, intercepting him as he left the house so that she could walk into town with him to retrieve his sailboat from the boatyard.

"Can you teach me how to become a boat captain?" she asked without preamble.

His glance was unruffled. "Depends on what size boat we're talking about."

"A big one, maybe even a lake steamer."

He was silent a moment. "That's a pretty tall order. As far as I know there's never been a female steamer captain. While that doesn't mean you can't be the first, in order to get there you'd have to set the precedent of being the first woman sailor on a lake steamer. Captains don't start at the top, you know, they work their way up from common seaman through third, second, then first mate before making captain. There's a lot to learn on the way, Rietta."

"You've always told me I'm smart enough to learn anything I set my mind to."

Grandpa Beau nodded. "And so you are. But are you tough enough to bear up under the slurs and barbs you'd face as a woman invading a man's territory? You'll have to ask yourself how badly you want to become a lake captain. Is it a mere whim or a deep-seated urge?"

"It's what I want to do," she said stubbornly.

He stopped walking and hooked his cane over his arm. Putting both his hands on her shoulders, he turned her to face him, his brown eyes intent. "There'll be no one in the family taking your side except me," he warned.

She smiled. "Hasn't it always been that way?"

He dropped his hands and retrieved his cane and they retreated to the edge of the road as a horse and buggy rattled past, then continued walking. Henrietta took a deep breath of the cool morning air. To her right, down the hill, the sun sparkled on the blue water. The island lay in the Straits of Mackinac, where Lake Michigan met Lake Huron, but was officially in Lake Huron, as grandpa had showed her on the map. A lumber schooner, sails billowing, headed toward Lake Michigan, and farther off she could see the dark smear of a steamer's smoke.

While she appreciated the grace and beauty of sailing vessels, steamers appealed to her practical side. With wood or coal to fuel them, steamers had no need to depend on the wind, which made them more reliable. And, she supposed, also more complicated. But since she'd never failed at anything, how could she fail at learning to captain a steamer?

"I met a boy named Garth Laidlaw yesterday," she told her grandfather. "He said you let him use our pier."

"What did you think of him?"

Henrietta grimaced. "He's a smart-aleck."

Grandpa Beau grinned. "So he proved to be a match for you, did he?"

About to deny it indignantly, she held back the words. Actually, she and Garth *had* ended up about even.

"He lives with his widowed mother," her grandfather went on. "She won't let him have a boat, so he borrows his uncle's rowboat whenever he can. I promised him a sail with us—you don't mind, do you?"

"I guess not." She spoke with ill grace. Sailing with Grandpa Beau was a private thing she didn't care to share with anyone—especially Garth Laidlaw.

He shot her a shrewd glance. "I think the boy needs a friend or two, Rietta. For her own reasons, his mother keeps him too close to home. It's not good for a lad to be tied to apron strings."

"He wants to be a lakesman," she blurted.

Her grandfather sighed. "I know. Like his father was. His mother's dead set against it."

She was about to ask him why when old Captain Parker hailed them from the porch of his bungalow snuggled into the hillside.

"Come and set a spell," the old man invited.

Henrietta followed her grandfather eagerly. Captain Parker had been on the boats most all his life and told hair-raising tales of his days on the lakes.

"We're heading for the boatyard to see how Seth is getting on with the repairs to my boat," Grandpa Beau said as he eased gratefully into the chair next to the captain.

Though her grandfather didn't always use a cane, Henrietta knew he couldn't walk very far without his legs "giving out," as he called it, the result of a long-ago accident.

"Seth's not a man you can rush," the captain observed.

"Wasn't planning to. Just left the boat there last evening, so what I'm making is a friendly call. He'll know that."

As she leaned against the porch rail, Henrietta noticed the captain's bright blue gaze focusing on her.

"I see your girl here's growing up," he said. "Favors her pa, 'cept for that red hair."

Grandfather smiled. "I understand that color hair comes from an English ancestory, a lady, by all accounts, and a determined woman. Rietta takes after her in more ways than one. She's decided she wants to be a lake captain."

"Does she, now?" Captain Parker shook his head. "Pretty tough haul for a woman." He leaned forward in his rocker and spoke to her directly. "Gal, us sailors got many a fool notion, superstitions, some calls 'em. One of 'em is that a woman aboard a boat brings bad luck. I ain't saying I believe she does, but there's plenty that swear it's true."

"Then I'll prove to them they're wrong," she said.

The old man cackled, his prominent adam's apple bobbing up and down. He lifted his billed cap and ran a hand over his nearly bald head. "Feisty, ain't she?" he said to her grandfather.

"That and more," Grandpa Beau admitted.

Captain Parker settled back and began rocking slowly, his chair creaking with every move. "The lakes were always good to me," he said. "'Lucky Lem,' my mates called me. Had plenty a close call, but never did a boat sink under me." He closed his eyes. "Been in some tricky weather, yessir, that I have. I remember the worst—in November '69, it was. You ever heard that song about 'Lost Off Lake Huron's Shore'?" His eyes opened and he looked from her to her grandfather.

Henrietta shook her head. To her surprise, Grandpa Beau cleared his throat and began to sing:

Around the beach the sea gulls scream;
Their dismal notes prolong—

"Yes, yes, that's it," the captain said. "'Twas sung

374

about the schooner *Persia*, lost with all hands in Lake Huron, not far from the straits here. A bad blow, that was, lasting four days, nine boats sunk and a passel of men drownded."

Henrietta wondered if he was trying to scare her. If so, she wouldn't let him. Everyone knew that boats sometimes sank, but she'd be as lucky as Captain Parker when she took to the lakes. Lucky and careful too.

"Why don't captains stay in port when the weather's bad?" she asked.

"They do if they can. Storms come up awful sudden on the lakes, though. There's some fifteen hundred rolling miles of water from the top of Superior to the toe of Ontario, and every mile is perilous in its own way. Erie's so dang shallow that even a line squall scoops water from the lake bottom, making the fiercest waves I ever come across.

"Michigan's so long the wind sweeps along her length and you're up against backbreaking seas. Besides, she gets waterspouts—tornadoes, they calls 'em on land. Ontario gets her share of waterspouts, too. Come up out of nowhere, they do, and if they're on a collision course with your boat, she's a goner and you with her.

"Superior, now, she wouldn't be so bad, 'cept for the early blizzards. She's a big lake and a captain's got room to maneuver—most of the time, anyways, though it gets tricky along the Keweenaw Peninsula. Huron's my favorite lake, despite the traffic being so heavy, always a chance of collision. Been a lot of them."

"I hear they're working on figuring out a standard method for signaling to pass on the lakes," Grandpa Beau said. "And all the boats are supposed to carry foghorns now."

375

"'Bout time. But there's always bound to be some fool captain what says, 'I know my way up and down the lakes blindfolded and if I got steam up, I can whistle if I have to—what the hell do I need to use a foghorn for?'" He glanced at Henrietta. "Excuse the language, gal. Not that you won't hear a dang sight worse on the boats."

"On a clear day I should think the big boats would be able to see one another a long way off," Henrietta said. "So if they run into one another, it must be in fog, at night, or in a storm."

"Wish I could say you're right, but it ain't always bad weather, nor darkness, neither. There's a pile of boats sailing these waters and a heap of captains wanting to beat each other into port—too many boats going too fast. I come close to getting sideswiped more times than I like to think about. I always figured I was a pretty good sailor, but I got to admit I almost rammed a schooner amidships once.

"Head-on's the worst, 'cause the two boats can be so badly damaged that even if they don't both sink, the boat still afloat ain't got time to rescue the crew of the other. Like in '82, when the schooners *Clayton Belle* and *Thomas Parsons* collided on the open lake, ten miles from Port Huron. The *Belle* went to the bottom in seven minutes, only three men escaped. That's where young Laidlow was lost. Left a wife and son, he did. They still live on the island."

Henrietta blinked. So Garth's father had been lost at sea. "Was Mr. Laidlaw a captain?" she asked.

The old man shook his head. "Working his way up, though, he might have made captain someday."

"His son wants to work on the boats," Grandpa Beau said.

"His ma's against it. She lost her man to the lakes; she don't want to lose her son as well."

"You can't stop a boy from following his dream," her grandfather said. "My own son's a case in point. He always wanted to be a writer, and nothing changed his mind."

Captain Parker nodded. "He's doing right well with it. I read his last book, and I'd say he knows the logging business through and through—the bad with the good. Seems to me the Laidlaw lad's got the same kind of perseverance your son showed. Sooner or later young Garth'll hit the decks—but not with his ma's blessings."

I mean to hit the decks, too, Henrietta thought but didn't say. No matter who tries to stop me.

"We'd best be getting on," Grandpa Beau said, rising from the chair.

"Always glad to see you," the captain said. "As for you, little gal, stop by sometimes. You don't have to wait for your grandpop to bring you."

"Thank you, Captain Parker, I'd like to," Henrietta told him.

At the boatyard, where he was helping Seth Newcomb scrape the bottom of a mackinaw boat before repairing it, Garth Laidlaw noticed Henrietta approaching with her grandfather and wished he could go and hide. No matter what she'd done, he never should have yanked Henrietta into the water. Boys weren't supposed to treat girls that way.

He lowered his head, focusing on the scraper in his hands, hoping against hope that he might not be noticed. After a few moments he couldn't resist a quick sidelong glance. To his dismay, Henrietta was staring at him with her lake-green eyes.

"Hello, Garth," she said.

He mumbled a greeting both to her and her grandfather, waiting for the ax to fall, unable to imagine that she hadn't told her entire family what he'd done to her the night before. Her grandfather must be

377

boiling mad—he'd ruined his chances of ever sailing on the Pendleton boat. The only thing he could pray for was that his mother didn't find out; she'd give him both sides of her tongue and then some.

"Rietta tells me the two of you have met," Mr. Pendleton said to him.

Garth cleared his throat. "Uh, yeah. I mean, yes, sir." It didn't make sense that Mr. Pendleton seemed to be smiling at him. He risked a quick look at Henrietta, who gazed back at him without any expression whatsoever.

"As soon as Mr. Newcomb gets my boat into shape, I'll take you and Rietta for a sail," Mr. Pendleton went on.

As Garth searched for words, he realized she hadn't tattled on him. Not to her grandfather, and so probably not to anyone. "Thank you, sir," he managed to say.

Mr. Pendleton nodded and limped off to talk to Seth.

Garth fixed his attention on Henrietta. "How come you didn't tell?"

She raised her eyebrows. "Tell what?"

"You know—about getting pulled into the lake."

"Oh, that."

"Your folks must have noticed your clothes were wet. What'd you say?"

She shrugged. "That I fell off the pier."

Garth frowned. "When you stomped off up the hill you were mad as h—as heck. I figured sure you'd tattle on me."

"You deserved it! The only reason I kept quiet was because I shoved you in the water first—so how could I complain about what you did to me?"

Damned if she didn't reason like a boy. He had no idea girls could be so sensible. Garth smiled. "If you promise not to do it to me again, I won't to you."

378

"I promise. If you annoy me, I'll think of something else the next time. Something worse."

His smile broadened into a grin. "I guess I'd better watch out."

"Do you work for Mr. Newcomb?"

"When he needs me. I do most of the painting."

"It sounds like fun." Her tone was wistful.

He looked at her askance. "Well it ain't—isn't, I mean." It was hard to talk one way with the guys and another with people like Mr. Pendleton and Henrietta. His mother insisted he ought to use proper English no matter who he spoke to, but he couldn't do that—his pals would think he was stuck up.

She was silent a moment, then said, *"Votre île est très intéressante."*

Though she didn't say the words in the same way as the Canuck islanders he knew, he understood her. *"C'est mon avis,"* he answered. "At least, sometimes I think the island's interesting. But why talk in French?"

To his surprise, she blushed. "I thought maybe you just knew a few words and were showing off. Last night, I mean."

As it came back to him what he'd said to her in farewell the evening before, he smiled to himself. His beautiful captain, he'd called her. She might not always act like one, but Henrietta *was* a girl, after all—what she really wanted to know was if he'd meant what he said. He wouldn't have said so in any language if he hadn't thought she was pretty, but he wasn't about to tell her that.

"Some of my friends speak better French than they do English," he said.

"Oh." She didn't meet his gaze.

He relented a little. "If they saw you, they'd say the same as I did."

The delight in her eyes was worth the trifling embarrassment he felt in paying the compliment.

"Except they wouldn't know I mean to be a lakes captain," she said after a moment.

He laughed, feeling more drawn to Henrietta all the time. "They wouldn't believe it."

"I know. You don't, either. But I mean what I say."

He made a mock bow. "The day I come across you at the tiller of a steamer, I'll be the first to admit I was wrong."

"See that you remember." She turned away from him, looking across and up at the old fort on the hill above town. "Grandpa keeps saying he'll take me to visit Fort Mackinac, but he hasn't yet. My cousin and I meant to go up there last summer, but we never did. You must have been there—what's it like?"

"I'll show you if you want." His words astounded him. Was he actually offering to escort a girl, and a summer visitor at that? His friends would never let him live it down. He half-hoped she'd either put him off or refuse outright.

"When?" she asked.

Might as well get it over with. "Uh—tomorrow?"

"All right. Shall we meet here?"

He nodded, relieved he wouldn't have to call for her and run the gauntlet of meeting her parents. Now that he was stuck with going with her, he was glad. She wasn't like anyone he'd ever met, boy or girl. She was different. And her red hair fascinated him.

The visit to the fort was the first of their rambles around the island. They also sailed frequently with Grandpa Beau. By the time September neared and the day drew close for the Pendletons to leave the island, Henrietta and Garth were good friends.

Or at least, that's what she told herself, even though she knew she found him far more interesting than any other boy she'd ever called her friend.

They decided to have a farewell picnic in the pines near Mission Point, but they'd gotten no farther than Captain Parker's cottage when the rain began. They took shelter on his porch and Henrietta suggested they share the contents of their picnic basket with the old captain, a favorite of them both.

"I ain't been on a picnic since Lord knows when," he declared, welcoming them into his small, neat-as-a-ship's-cabin bungalow.

"Been looking through my old things," he went on. "Got quite a collection, more'n I realized. Lookee here." He lifted a small bottle from a table, holding it on the palm of his hand before handing it to Henrietta.

"Why, there's a teeny-tiny boat inside!" she exclaimed. "It's perfect; I love it. I never could figure out how they get ship models inside the bottles."

"This one's a model of my first boat, the *Compromise*."

"That's a funny name for a boat," Garth commented, taking the bottle from her to examine. "She's a schooner, isn't she?"

"Right enough. Don't know where the name came from, but she was a right fair boat to captain, that she was."

"Someday maybe I'll get to have a model of my first boat inside a bottle," Garth said.

"Me, too," Henrietta chimed in.

"Shouldn't be surprised." Captain Parker took the bottle from Garth and set it back on the table before unearthing an old quilt for them to spread on the floor so they could have what he called a "real" picnic.

Henrietta and Garth sat on the quilt to eat, but the captain chose what he called his "easy chair."

"Old bones, you know," he said. "Come to think of it, you wouldn't know. Young'uns never figure to get old. Far as I'm concerned, it's a dang miracle I'm still here at eighty-three. It's the lake air—healthiest in the country."

As they ate, he spun yarns of his days on the lakes, then dozed off in his chair. Henrietta and Garth eased from the room onto the porch where they stood watching the rain. It wasn't one of the spectacular summer storms, complete with thunder and lightning, just a steady, soaking rain, the kind that sometimes went on for days.

"It's hard to believe that I'm leaving tomorrow," she said. "I don't want to. I wish I could live here forever."

"You wouldn't say that if you had to stay here, like me."

She glanced sideways at him. "Of course I wouldn't, because I'd *be* here then, wouldn't I?"

Henrietta had never been able to decide if his eyes were a deep, dark brown or actually black. Sometimes, like now, when she looked at him, she couldn't seem to look away. It made her feel strange—her heart pounded and she couldn't breathe right.

Uncomfortable, she tried to think of something amusing to say, but instead, to her dismay, blurted out, "Will you kiss me goodbye?"

Garth was obviously taken aback. "Now?"

She forced a smile to hide her nervousness. "Well, if you want to wait till I'm getting on the ferry tomorrow with all those people around—"

He rolled his eyes. Taking a deep breath, he bent his head and she tilted her face up toward him. Not sure if she was supposed to close her eyes or not, she decided to leave them open so she wouldn't miss anything. His expression was so solemn she almost giggled, but when his lips, soft and warm, brushed over hers, the impulse to laugh fled.

The kiss, her first, lasted only a moment, but Henrietta knew she'd never forget it.

Chapter 27

Henrietta paused at the rail of the *Lake Flyer* to glance eastward, nodding in approval at the gray morning sky. The sunset the evening before had been a spectacular fiery red and, as everyone on the lakes knew, "Evening red and morning gray sets the sailor on his way." With fair weather assured, by noon they'd be winding their way along the St. Clair River; even with heavy river traffic, they'd dock at Detroit before dusk.

"Looks like I'll get to have supper with the folks tonight," she heard one sailor say to another.

"The captain made damn good downbound time," the second sailor agreed.

"What the hell did you think he'd do—hasn't he got Sir Henry aboard? Every sailor on the lakes knows *Flyer*'s the luckiest boat afloat on account of her."

Henrietta smiled to herself. She'd been Henry from the moment she set foot aboard the *Flyer* four years ago—four long, hard years as a seaman. When she finally made third mate three months ago, the crew took to calling her Sir Henry—though not to her face.

She had no illusions about why, at eighteen, she'd gotten a berth on the boat; by then Grandpa Beau owned the steamer company. But, damn it, she'd earned her way up to third mate, working as well or better than any sailor aboard and she'd earned their respect on the way. The crew might brag about the good luck of the *Flyer* now, but at first they'd been convinced one misfortune after another would dog the boat—because she'd signed on.

"Too bad old Jellyroll's retiring," the second sailor said. "He wasn't one to ride herd on us. I hope to hell we don't get some spit and polish first mate replacing him."

Listening to the other sailors agree, Henrietta thought the *Flyer* could do with bit more polish. But, since she and Jellers worked well enough together despite his tendency toward laxness, she couldn't help sharing the crew's uneasiness about the new first mate. A boat's crew became a family; it was hard to lose a member and have a stranger take his place.

As a downbound boat on Lake Huron, the *Flyer* wasn't hugging the Michigan coastline as the upbound vessels did, keeping her course far enough from shore that land wasn't visible at the moment. It would be, though, before they reached the river because Huron narrowed at the bottom.

Henrietta spotted a lumber schooner off to their port side, making good time with her sails filled with wind, a fair sight to see, scudding along this fair June morning. Schooners and other sailing vessels were far more graceful than the bulky steamers, but Henrietta wouldn't trade places, not for anything. Steamers were the future, sailing ships the past. If she wanted to play with sails, she'd do so in her time off the *Flyer*.

She thought of what she'd overheard the sailor saying—that he'd be there in time to have supper with his folks. As she would. Being home would be enjoyable—providing her mother hadn't planned a party during her three-day layover. The party itself wouldn't be so difficult to get through, but knowing her mother, there'd be a new young and eligible man invited in the hopes he and Henrietta would hit it off.

"Yes, I know you love your work," mama had said more than once lately. "To some extent I understand, though I can't think why you'd want to wear trousers and tunic, it's such unbecoming garb for a woman. Still, you can't be planning to sail the lakes for the rest of your life. Whether you admit it or not, I know you must be thinking of settling down, getting married, and raising a family. After all, you're almost twenty-two."

Mama really *didn't* understand. The thought of being tied to a home, a husband, and children made Henrietta grit her teeth. She'd tried to explain how she felt, but without success.

"You'll feel differently when you fall in love," her mother had said with a dreamy smile. "The first time I met your father, I knew he was the only man I could ever love. Whether you believe me or not, one day the same thing will happen to you, and once you've met *the* man, nothing else will seem important."

Constantly surrounded by men, Henrietta had not yet felt more than a friendly interest in any of them. Even if she had, she'd never have dared to show it. The lone female aboard a boat couldn't afford to have a romance with a shipmate. She'd had a difficult enough time earning her right to be treated as a sailor instead of as a woman to compromise her position.

Maybe I'm immune to love, she told herself, just as some people seem immune to certain diseases. Love couldn't be classed as a disease, and yet she'd observed that love often made those afflicted by it as miserable as any illness.

In any case, nothing—not even love, should it crop up unexpectedly and overwhelm her—could possibly make her swerve from her goal. One day she'd be a lake captain, come hell or high water. Or love.

Henrietta had predicted correctly. Her parents took her to a party the second night she spent at home. One of Papa's old college friends, Jack Ventry, a Cleveland banker, had his yacht moored in Lake St. Clair and invited friends and acquaintances to celebrate his son's graduation from Harvard aboard the craft. Certain that her mother had already chosen the recent graduate as her future son-in-law, Henrietta greeted him warily when he was introduced to her by the banker as "my son Amory."

Amory proved pleasant enough; since he was interested in sailing, they spent much of the evening discussing boats. By the time she was ready to leave, it was clear to her that Amory was also quite interested in her—and disappointed to discover how little time she had free.

"I can understand your fascination with steamers," he said, "but surely four years aboard them has taught you more than you need to know."

"Did your father learn all he needed to know about banking in four years?" she countered, keeping her tone light, since she tended to like Amory. "Lake boats are my career."

He smiled. "Not forever, one hopes. After all, you're a woman—and most attractive, too. I don't believe I've ever seen quite such a gorgeous shade of red hair."

Ignoring the compliment, she said, "Many women have careers these days."

"That may be true, but not aboard lake boats. You can hardly combine that with marriage."

"I'm not planning to."

"I'm delighted to hear it."

She saw that he'd misunderstood, that he took her words to mean she was merely waiting for a man to propose marriage before she gave up the boats. "What

I mean is—"

"Ah, there you are, Rietta," her father said, coming up to them. "If you're ready, we'll go."

"We'll speak of this another time," Amory said, giving her a meaningful look. "I hope I may call on you tomorrow."

"Yes, of course," her father told him. "Good to see you again, Amory."

"Nice young chap," he said to Henrietta as they joined her mother.

"Amory Ventry?" her mother said. "Yes, indeed. And good looking as well."

Amory succeeded in monopolizing Henrietta's remaining time at home. Reluctantly she admitted that he improved on acquaintance rather than the opposite and that she rather enjoyed his company. She was not happy, though, when he took Papa's place as her escort to the Detroit waterfront the evening she was to rejoin her boat.

"I seem to have displeased you," Amory said as he handed her down from the buggy onto the wooden planks.

She had no intention of telling him that any crew member who observed that her escort was a young man rather than her father would lose no time spreading the news. For the entire trip up the lake and beyond, she could expect to be teased unmercifully.

"Perhaps I'll see you at Mackinac Island later this summer," Amory said. "My father plans to set anchor there in late August and spend two weeks at the Grand Hotel."

"I'm not certain I'll have a chance to get to the island this year," she said.

He leaned closer. "Will you try?"

Out of the corner of her eye she could see a man standing at the foot of the gangplank, though she couldn't be sure which of her shipmates he was. The last thing in the world she wanted was for Amory to kiss her, thus giving the *Flyer*'s crew more ammunition. Hastily stepping back, she said, "I can't promise."

She bent to lift and then shoulder her seabag—an action she'd trained her father not to interfere with—only to find Amory reaching for it, too. Good God, she'd never live it down if her mates saw him carrying her seabag to the boat for her.

"I'll take that," a man's voice said. At the same time, he plucked the canvas bag from not only her fingers but Amory's too. Then he slung it over his shoulder.

Henrietta, her annoyance growing, found herself staring at a black-bearded stranger. Or was he? There was something familiar about him, something that made the breath catch in her throat.

"See here—" Amory began.

The bearded man cut him off. "I'm Garth Laidlaw, the *Flyer*'s first mate. I'll see Sir Henry—that is, Third Mate Pendleton—aboard safely."

Garth Laidlaw! "Goodbye, Amory," Henrietta said hastily, thoroughly shaken and wanting an end to the confrontation, needing to be alone in her miniscule cabin, where she could regain her equilibrium.

She hardly heard Amory's farewell as she hurried toward the gangplank with Garth matching her step for step.

"I didn't know you were the new first mate," she managed to say as they reached the deck.

"That's because I'm not as famous as you." His voice was deep, like her father's, no longer the boyish tenor she remembered.

His eyes, though, were the same. She'd recognized those penetrating dark eyes even before Garth had given his name. "Famous?" she countered. "I'm certainly not!"

388

"The luck of Sir Henry, the only female sailor on the steamers, and a redhead at that, is known to every lakesman, including me. You could at least say you're glad to see me after ten long years."

"I don't yet know if I am," she snapped.

He chuckled. "You're just as touchy at twenty-one as you were at twelve. I imagine as stubborn, too. So I doubt you'll take kindly to being told I'd rather you were ashore with your fiancé than part of my crew on the *Flyer.*"

"Amory isn't my fiancé—not that it's any of your business. And the feeling's mutual. I'd prefer any other first mate on the lakes to you."

"I can see this berth is going to be interesting," he said, amusement threading through his words.

How dare he be amused when she felt so horribly confused and angry? "You're lucky I'm not still twelve," she muttered, "Or I might shove you overboard."

"I'm sure you remember what happened the time you did."

Recalling very well, she made no rejoinder. "I'll take my bag," she said, tugging at it. "I'm quite capable of handing my own belongings."

He relinquished the seabag. Shouldering it, she turned away, tossing him a "Good evening, Mr. Laidlaw."

"You've got it wrong—it's *Au revoir.*"

His voice echoed in her mind all the way to her tiny cubicle in the crew's quarters, the privacy necessary because she was a woman. As she stowed her belongings, she told herself what had jolted her was the unexpectedness of his appearance. If she'd only known the name of the new first mate—unfortunately she hadn't bothered to ask.

She'd expected to see Garth when she'd returned to

Mackinac Island the summer she was thirteen, but he'd aleady "gone decking," sailor cant for signing aboard a lake boat.

"The lad needed a clean break from his mother," Captain Parker had told her. "If he didn't go off-island young, he'd've been hanging onto her apron strings for the rest of his life. I don't say I'm not sorry for the poor woman, but you can't deny a boy his dream."

Captain Parker had died the next year; much as she loved the island, it was never the same with both Garth and the old captain gone. As time passed she'd gradually forgotten Garth—or so she'd told herself.

If it was true, why was she so shaken over meeting him again? On the wharf, when she'd gazed into his dark eyes something had flared between them, dazzling her, making her momentarily unaware that anything else besides Garth existed. The sensation hadn't lasted more than an instant, but there was no denying it had happened. She couldn't help but wonder if he'd felt it as well.

Nonsense, she told herself firmly: anything you felt was from the shock of seeing Garth again so unexpectedly after ten years. And he certainly isn't charmed with you—he said right out he didn't want you aboard. No doubt because you're a woman.

Yet she *was* aboard and meant to stay here; she knew more about the *Flyer* than he did. Her grandfather might own the line, but by God, she'd earned her right to be third mate—as Garth would soon discover. No, not Garth, Mr. Laidlaw, since the first mate was always addressed as "mister."

"I'll show *you*, Mr. Laidlaw," she muttered.

Soon after their upbound freighter cleared the St. Clair River and steamed into the lake a fire started on the main deck, fueled by undisposed-of paint rags. Though the flames were quickly extinguished, the incident upset the crew. Fire was always dangerous on a boat, and since their cargo was mostly coal, doubly so on this trip.

As third mate, Henrietta was asked by the first mate for an explanation he could take to Captain Riggs. She might have blamed herself for being careless, but she knew very well she hadn't been.

"When I made my inspection before the *Flyer* set sail, Mr. Laidlaw," she said stiffly, "there were no rags stuffed between the forward smokestack and the pilothouse. I don't know when or why they were placed there."

"Are you telling me you believe the rags were placed there some time after the *Flyer* left the dock?" Garth's voice held doubt.

She looked him in the eye. "I am. I also believe it unlikely that any of the crew could have left them there accidentally, since no painting was being done at the time."

Garth was silent for a long moment, finally asking, "Are you suggesting the fire was set deliberately?"

Henrietta took a deep breath. "I think the paint rags were put where they were found by someone who made sure to wait until after I'd made my rounds. I don't know why. Nor do I know how the fire started."

"Is it possible the incident was intended to get you into trouble?"

Henrietta couldn't believe that any of the crew wished her harm. "No, Mr. Laidlaw. While the intent may have been to cause trouble, I don't think it was aimed at me."

Garth stared at her, wondering if she told the truth about the feelings of the crew. His own feelings for her were damned confused. He'd known when he'd signed on the *Flyer* that she was third mate and he'd assured himself he'd treat her exactly the same as any other sailor. What he hadn't allowed for was the unexpected jolt of attraction when he'd first set eyes on her again after ten years. Never mind that she persisted in playing at being a lakesman and knotted her glorious hair up under her cap, Henrietta was now a lovely young woman, a woman any man would want.

Unfortunately, as long as they worked on the same boat, she was untouchable, as far as he was concerned.

"Do you know of any particular troublemaker in the crew?" he asked her.

"We haven't had any such problems before," she told him.

He raised an incredulous eyebrow. "Never?"

She shrugged. "Naturally the men sometimes have disagreements with one another."

"But not with you?"

Her chin went up. "Not for the past two years."

He could well imagine she must have found her first year as a common seaman difficult, even if her grandfather did own the line. Evidently Henrietta hadn't lost either her stubborn determination to have her way or her ability to hold her own. In his opinion, women didn't belong on the boats, and though he had to admire her gumption, she was no exception.

Considering the wealth behind her, how could she be serious about a career on the lakes? She was only playing at being a sailor.

"Someone put those rags there and set them afire," he said, careful not to let his expression reveal anything of what he felt. "One of the crew members must be responsible. You've worked with them longer than I have—who could it have been?"

"We did take on three new hands at Duluth a few months ago," she said slowly. "I can't believe any of them would have pulled such a dangerous stunt, but I don't really know any of them well."

"Name them."

She bit her lip, hesitating.

"Without proof, I can't accuse any of the three," he said. "Give me their names and I'll keep an eye out."

She rattled off three names, then added, "I honestly don't think—"

"I'll do the thinking, Third Mate Pendleton, while we both watch and wait."

"Aye, sir," she said stiffly.

He watched her walk away. Never had he expected to see a woman in men's garb, much less enjoy the sight, but he couldn't help admiring the trim fit of her dark trousers and tunic, both concealing and revealing at the same time. It was a wonder any sailor aboard could keep his mind on his work.

But the time the *Flyer* reached the Straits of Mackinac, there'd been two more fires aboard, both discovered in time to prevent major damage.

"Up till now the *Flyer*'s been the luckiest boat I ever shipped on," Second Mate Larson told Garth.

Garth slanted the older, weatherbeaten and grizzled lakesman a look. "You calling me a Jonah?"

"No, mister, that I ain't. What I think is, we got one of them firebugs aboard. It ain't you, 'cause you was with me when the second fire started. It sure as hell ain't Captain Riggs, nor Sir Henry, neither. Nor one of the *Flyer*'s longtime sailors, else he'd've done it before this trip. That leaves the three Minnesota boys."

Garth nodded. Pauling, Grayson, and Jones, the sailors who signed on at Duluth. "I'll talk to the captain," he said. "Meanwhile, you dog Pauling and I'll watch Grayson and Jones."

"You can't watch two men at once. Best you let the third mate keep an eye on Jones. Sir Henry don't miss much and that's a fact."

Realizing he'd seem to be doubting both Larson's

393

word and Henrietta's ability if he disagreed, Garth nodded. It was true she'd proved as capable a sailor as a man, but he could't help thinking of her as a woman and thus someone who needed to be protected.

"Aye, mister," Larson said. "I'll let Sir Henry know."

Henrietta, standing watch the night after the *Flyer* cleared the Soo Locks and steamed into Lake Superior, paused at the rail to button her pea jacket against the chill north breeze and gaze at the sickle moon. You could certainly hang your oilskins on its up-pointing ends, she thought. In sailor lore that meant you wouldn't need them—in other words, no rain in sight.

As usual, when she wasn't busy, an image of Garth slipped into her mind. There was no doubt he'd grown into one of the best looking men she'd ever met. She wondered if he remembered their rained-out Mackinac Island picnic that they'd wound up having at Captain Parker's. More precisely, she was curious to know if he recalled that she'd asked him to kiss her. How shameless she'd been at twelve!

Even at anchor a boat was never quiet, and under steam she was downright noisy. The *Flyer* creaked and rattled and groaned—all familiar noises that Henrietta heard without noticing—but the clink of metal against metal drew her attention. She straightened, turning from the rail to scan the darkness. The sound came again, from near the stern, she decided.

Quickly, leaving her lantern hooked in its protective niche on a bulkhead, she made her way toward the rear of the boat. Whatever she heard might be completely harmless, but it was her duty to check on anything she found unusual whether the boat had a firebug aboard or not. Jones wasn't supposed to be on duty tonight but that didn't mean he wasn't awake and on deck anyway. Of course, the guilty sailor might not be Jones; the only way to identify the culprit was to catch him in the act.

When she reached the end of the aft cabin, she paused, reluctant to leave cover for the open deck lest she be seen. Peering into the darkness she saw the stern lantern had been snuffed. Though it was her duty to relight the lantern immediately, she waited, listening.

At the stern, a match flared, briefly illuminating a man's face. Jones? She couldn't be certain. Nor could she be sure whether the sailor was simply trying to light the lantern or had a more sinister reason for striking the match. What she did know was that she smelled the betraying stench of kerosene.

Throwing caution to the winds, she dashed toward the stern. Before she got there a great flare of light erupted in front of her and flames leaped upward. In their light she saw a dark figure rushing at her. Shouting, "Fire!" she jumped to one side, reaching for the belaying pin tucked into the waistband of her trousers.

Despite her evasive maneuver, the sailor crashed into her. As he tried to wrestle her to the deck, she jerked her arm free, raising the belaying pin. She swung it with all her strength. The solid thunk as wood hit skull made her wince. He dragged her down as he fell and they both hit the deck hard. Stunned by her blow, he struggled to rise. As she rolled free of him and staggered to her feet, she heard shouts. Feet pounded along the deck.

She stared down at the sailor, now on his knees, retching. In yellow glow of the flames, she identified him.

"Stay put, Jones," she ordered. "It's too late to run."

Garth reached them first. Taking in the scene at a glance, he ordered two of the men coming up behind him to take Jones prisoner and the others to fight the blaze.

"Are you all right?" he asked, reaching as though to put an arm around her.

She side-stepped, regretting having to forgo the comfort of being held close to him for a moment but aware she didn't dare show weakness, either to him or to the crew. "I'm fine," she said firmly. "Luckily I remembered Captain Parker telling us that belaying pins were good for other things besides holding ropes in place."

Chapter 28

The *Lake Flyer*, not seriously damaged by the fire, delivered her cargo of coal to Duluth, where the sailor, Jones, was remanded to the authorities. After loading iron ore, she pulled anchor for the downbound trip to Cleveland. With the firebug off the boat, all went well until after Captain Riggs cleared the Soo Locks and threaded through St. Mary's River, negotiated the De Tour passage, and steamed into Lake Huron.

Garth, standing in the pilothouse, peered dubiously at the gray clouds hiding the sunset. While evening gray and morning red didn't always mean "rain upon the sailor's head," the old warning rhyme held more than a grain of truth. Captain Riggs's barometer held steady, so a storm wasn't likely, but there was more to bad lake weather than storms. Fog, for example.

Knowing their foghorn had been destroyed in the second fire and wouldn't be replaced until they reached their home port of Detroit, Garth said to the captain, "Looks like we might run into a bit of mist before morning, sir."

Captain Riggs nodded. "Shouldn't be a problem; we'll make do with our steam whistle. You can't lose that like you can the damn horn. If we've got steam up, we can always whistle. And if we haven't got steam up, hell, it means we're safe in port so we don't have to worry."

Garth, who'd heard similar comments from other captains, smiled. Some of the lake skippers, after years of seat-of-the-pants navigation, were chary of new-fangled devices—including foghorns for their boats. As for the recent government navigation charts, veteran skippers scorned them as being the work of "desk pilots".

"Hell, them fancy mapmakers ain't never sailed these waters," one of Garth's earlier skippers had insisted. "They ain't got no idee how to check position off Grand Traverse Bay by how strong the smell of cherry blossoms in the wind is or how to reckon position by how long it takes for a boat whistle to echo back from Pictured Rocks."

Yet, since the government gave away a set of charts to each vessel, almost all carried them whether they used them or not. Garth studied them every chance he got and he'd noticed Henrietta did, too.

Unfortunately, neither charts nor experience were of much use in fog. No sailor liked fog at any time, but darkness made fog doubly dangerous. While Garth wasn't bothered by the *Flyer* using her steam whistle in place of a horn if they ran into fog tonight, he hoped to hell that any sailing vessel they came near was abiding by the rules and carrying a horn—you couldn't make sails whistle.

Though downbound and thus too far off shore to see the lights of what few towns there were in this neck of the woods, by his reckoning the *Flyer* had passed St. Ignace and was about due west of Mackinaw City when the fog and the night both closed in around the boat. Captain Riggs immediately ordered the engine room to throttle down and the boat slowed, feeling her way

398

through the shrouded night and blowing her whistle at intervals.

As he stood near the bow staring into the darkness, Garth fought the closed-in feeling that fog always gave him, the suffocating sensation he was being wound into a cocoon the way a spider bound a fly caught in its web. He took a deep breath and sought to distract himself by thinking of something besides the weather.

What came to him was the La Salle's *Griffin*, the first sailing vessel ever built on the lakes, was last seen about here in September of 1679, sailing along in fair weather. No one had ever discovered exactly what had happened to her. According to old Captain Parker, lake skippers still argued about where in Lake Huron the *Griffin* had been lost; Parker himself had figured she went down somewhere around Manitoulin Island. At the moment the *Flyer* wasn't far off that same island.

Manitoulin was the largest of a multitude of isles that ran a third of the way down the eastern side of Huron, separating the lake proper from North Channel, an island-dotted passageway leading into Georgian Bay, a bay larger than Lake Ontario and almost as large as Erie. Garth was trying to decide if Huron's Saginaw Bay or Michigan's Green Bay was the next largest in the lakes when he heard Henrietta's hail.

"Mr. Laidlaw, are you there?"

"Aye," he answered, turning from the rail.

He saw the muted glow of her lantern before she emerged from the mist clotting the decks. "Sir," she said, "one of the men swears he saw the masts of an upbound schooner off to starboard just before the fog closed in."

"The lookout didn't report her."

"I'm aware of that. So is Hanks, the sailor who reported his own sighting to me. Hanks claims a doctor

399

once told him that he was unusually farsighted. I don't know about that but I've always found him to be honest."

"If a schooner's out there, she can hear our whistle," Garth said, "so she should be able to judge where we are."

Henrietta nodded, then tipped her head toward starboard and he understood that she was listening, just as he was, for some answering signal from the schooner. Fog did distort and muffle sound, but if the other boat blew a horn they ought to hear it. They heard nothing but the familiar noises of the *Flyer* and her intermittent whistle.

"Maybe Hanks was mistaken," Garth said at last.

"Perhaps." She sounded doubtful—and uneasy.

Without warning, an eerie feeling of dread swept over Garth, raising the hair on his nape. "Damn," he muttered, suddenly certain with absolutely no proof that Hank's schooner was not only out there but on a collision course with the *Flyer*.

"Captain!" he shouted, running toward the pilot-house. "Order the whistle sounded continuously!"

Henrietta, alarmed by Garth's sudden action, certain he must have seen or heard something she'd missed, stared into the darkness beyond the starboard rail, her eyes and ears straining to pick up any inkling of danger.

What was that creaking? Merely the *Flyer*? No, the pitch was different. Oh, God, it couldn't be the schooner, not so close, not with the *Flyer's* whistle now continuously hooting, giving their position loud and clear.

Suddenly something loomed out of the fog to starboard near midship. Sails. "No!" she screamed, her protest lost in a grinding, rending, jolting crash.

To Henrietta, flung sprawling onto the deck, the sight of the schooner's bow thrust deep into the

400

bowels of the *Flyer* was beyond belief. For a few frozen moments she lay where she'd been tossed, staring blankly at the impossible. The *Flyer* had been rammed!

Finally realizing what her duty was, she forced herself to her feet and stumbled toward her lifeboat station. The *Flyer* was taking on water. Sinking. Lifebelts. Get the crew in the boats. Get the boats in the water. Push off and row.

The decks were a nightmare of confusion. Men shouted hoarsely, some running aimlessly about. Henrietta grabbed one of them and hauled him with her, calling repeatedly to others, "Let's get the boats in the water, sailors."

Eventually she discovered that only the boats on the port side had survived the collision and, with the ship listing to starboard, it proved to be damn near impossible to lower the remaining two boats off the port side. The first tipped when the stern rope broke, flinging those inside into the water and then dropping on top of them.

While the survivors struggled to climb in again, the second boat splashed down so close to the first that some of the swimmers were injured. Then men who hadn't reached the boats while they were still on deck began leaping overboard and, once in the water, fighting for a place aboard one of the lifeboats.

Though she tried desperately, Henrietta couldn't enforce order. By the light of the distress flares rocketed into the sky, she watched in horror from the deck as those already aboard the overloaded boats kicked away swimmers trying to climb in.

Strong hands spun her away from the rail, gripping her arm. "Why the hell aren't you in one of those lifeboats?" Garth said angrily.

"Who's left on board?" she asked instead of answering.

"Captain Riggs won't leave the bridge. When I went back to report to him, he ordered me to hurry up and get the hell off the boat any way I could." Garth stared down at the melee in and around the lifeboats. "No hope there."

Pulling her with him, he struggled to the stern and around to the steeply slanted starboard deck, shipping water badly now that two boats had jarred loose from one another, exposing the jagged hole rammed in the *Flyer*. There was no sign of the schooner in the foggy night. Had she sunk already?

Knowing there were no undamaged lifeboats on this side, Henrietta wondered why they'd come here until Garth raised his lantern. In its dim glow Henrietta saw men in the water clutching long slabs of wood.

The *Merribell* was a lumber schooner," Garth said. "We stand a chance."

Henrietta nodded, not saying she realized how slim a chance it was. True, the schooner's cargo, logs and planks, would float and support weight but Huron's water, even in June, was cold. How long could they survive in chill seas?

He balanced the lantern on the slanting roof to the rear cabin. "Take off your shoes," he ordered and she obeyed.

Easing into the water was no problem—by now the deck was awash. Garth quickly found a good-sized log, and side by side they clung to the middle, kicking frantically with their feet in a effort to get far enough away from the *Flyer* so they wouldn't be dragged under when she finally sank.

For some time her desperate exertion kept Henrietta from thinking or even feeling chilled. The lake that had seemed fairly smooth from the vantage point of the deck now proved choppy, slapping waves into her face. At first she heard yells and splashing around them, but

402

as they drifted into the fog the sounds faded and disappeared. Soon it was as though the stricken boats and their crews had never been. She and Garth were alone in a dark, never-ending wilderness of fog and water.

"Are we lost?" she gasped at last, near exhaustion.

"If you mean doomed," he muttered, "hell, no. We're still afloat and still breathing."

That wasn't what she meant and he knew it. "But where's land?" she asked.

He leaned toward her until his cold, wet cheek touched hers. "We'll find it."

As time went on, eventually she slipped into a state of numbness. Only Garth's repeated insistence that she hang on kept her gripping the log.

When she finally felt something solid beneath her feet, she was too far gone to understand what it was. Even Garth's cry of, "Land! We've come ashore!" didn't register. He removed her hands from the log and led her from the water; she stumbled after him with no comprehension of what she was doing.

Weaving between pine trees, Garth knew he had to find some way to get the two of them warm before his strength gave out. Since he had no way of knowing if anyone lived within miles of where they'd washed ashore, he decided the best he could do for now was to locate a likely place to try to build a fire. When he staggered against the wigwam, at first he didn't understand what it was he'd run into.

The abandoned lodge had seen better days, but it was shelter. He dragged Henrietta inside and set about gathering dried pine needles and dead branches to kindle a fire in a pit under the center smokehole of the wigwam. He breathed a sigh of relief when he discovered, by lighting one, that his oilskin wrapped matches had survived the water. Its flame ignited the dry pine needles he'd piled together and he carefully fed dead twigs to the tiny fire until it grew large enough to burn small branches. In time, he had a decent blaze heating the wigwam and could turn his attention to Henrietta.

She lay sprawled on the ground near the fire, her clothes as sodden as his. She was past helping herself to undress, but with coaxing he managed to get her to move and turn enough so he could pull off her trousers and tunic. He laid them across a broken wooden rack, along with his own trousers and jacket. Their underclothes he left on, thinking they ought to dry fairly soon in the fire's heat.

He eased her onto old reed mats he'd found in the lodge, putting her feet toward the fire, then settled himself so he was lying next to her, pulled her shivering body into his arms, and covered them both with the piece of canvas that had been the wigwam's door flap. His eyes drooped shut.

Garth roused from time to time, coming awake just enough to replenish the fire from the stock of wood he'd hauled into the wigwam, then sinking back into exhausted sleep next to Henrietta. He had no idea where they were and at the moment didn't care. They'd survived; nothing else mattered.

As Henrietta gradually swam up from the deep depths of sleep, she thought she heard the chirping of birds. Opening her eyes to dim light, she stared at Garth, realizing in confusion that he was holding her in his arms. For a long moment she couldn't imagine where she was, nor how she'd come to be cuddled next to him.

Snippets of thoughts slipped in and out of her mind. The *Flyer*. Night. Fog. The schooner. A collision. In the water. Lost. Though she had no memory of it, somehow they must have drifted to land, Garth must have carried her to this cabin and built a fire.

Belatedly she realized he also must have removed her outer clothing, because she wore nothing but her drawers, her cotton undervest, and her chemisette. He was also in his underwear.

"Awake?" Garth asked drowsily, making no attempt to release her.

Despite the impropriety of it all, Henrietta had to admit she relished being held close to his warmth. She felt safe in his arms . . . .protected.

"I don't remember coming ashore," she said, delaying the move away from him she knew she ought to make. "Where are we?"

"In an abandoned wigwam—quite possibly on one of the string of islands separating the lake from Georgian Bay."

"Alone?"

"As far as I know."

"None of the others—?" She paused, biting her lip.

"The lifeboats weren't near us last night. I don't know what happened to the men in them."

She remembered him telling her that Captain Riggs, remaining with the *Flyer*, had ordered Garth to save himself. She knew without asking that the captain had intended to go down with his ship and tears filled her eyes.

"Don't cry," Garth pleaded, freeing his hand to brush her hair off her forehead. He leaned closer and touched his lips to hers.

He might have meant the kiss to be comforting, but instead of being soothed, she felt excitement zing through her. Without considering what she did, only aware of what she wanted, Henrietta wrapped her arms around his neck, kissing him in return.

Garth groaned, gathering her closer, intensifying the kiss until her lips parted under his. His tongue invaded her mouth, tasting, exploring, making her melt against him. Other men had kissed her, but never like this. Not like Garth. Certainly no man had ever made her long for his kiss to go on forever.

She'd never felt so alive. Was it because she'd survived a near brush with death or because she was in Garth's arms? Whatever the reason, a wild exhilaration pounded through her. Nothing mattered but the moment, nothing was important except Garth and the thrilling wonder of his caresses.

By the time he unbuttoned her undervest, she was feverish with need, and when at last his hand cupped her bare breast, she moaned in pleasure, a pleasure that rose to a throbbing urgency when he put his mouth to her breast.

"Garth," she whispered, "I want . . ." Unable to describe exactly what it was she wanted, her words trailed off.

"Tell me," he whispered against her mouth.

She arched against him in answer, instinctively seeking all that he could give her without clearly knowing what it was.

"I've always wanted you," he said hoarsely. "Even when we were both too young."

"Yes," she whispered. "Yes, I wanted you, too. I want you now."

He flung off his clothes before easing down her drawers, the last garment separating them. When his fingers gently probed the warmth between her legs, she opened to him, calling his name, and then he raised over her and filled her with himself. For a moment she felt a pressure that came close to pain; then it disappeared and she thought she'd die of pleasure.

But that was only the beginning of the strange and wonderful journey they traveled together, riding a gigantic wave that rose and rose until it crested in an explosion of delight on a magic shore belonging only to the two of them.

Sometime later she smiled at him and said, "Now I know what I want."

He laughed, hugging her to him. "I knew all along."

"Yes, but you're a man and before that you were a boy. Boys learn things early. No one ever tells girls anything about this—even when they become women. At least, not until they get married."

His smile faded. "That'll have to wait until I make captain."

She blinked in surprise. "What will have to wait?"

"Getting married." He raised himself on one elbow to look down at her. "I want to be able to support you in style."

"But I wasn't talking about us getting married!" she cried.

He scowled at her. "Don't you want to marry me?"

"I—I don't know. What I mean is, I'm not ready to get married. When I decide to, I can't imagine marrying any man except you, but in case you've forgotten, I plan to make captain myself. And, like you, before I marry."

He sat up, crossed his arms over his chest, and glared at her. Henrietta sat up, too, grabbed her discarded chemisette, and yanked it over her head, all the while staring at him defiantly.

"You can't mean you want to stay on the boats," he said.

"Why on earth not?"

"Jesus, woman, you damn near drowned last night. Why would you want to risk your neck again?"

"You almost drowned as well, and yet you plan to

continue risking yours," she pointed out. "What's so different?"

"I'm a man!"

"I wasn't aware God gave neck-risking rights only to men."

He shook his head. "I keep forgetting how exasperating you can be. I'll try to explain this simply: you're mine. We're going to get married. I don't want my future wife pursuing a career on the boats."

She clenched her fists. "How would you like it if I said to you, 'You're mine. I don't want my future husband pursuing a career on the boats'?"

He flung up his hands. "It's not the same. Anyway, you wouldn't say it because you understand my life is on the lakes."

"How about my life?"

"You'll be my wife, damn it. You'll stay on shore and raise our family."

"I'm not your wife yet, and I damn well may never be. I'm my own master; you can't tell me what to do!" She sprang to her feet and began to gather her clothes.

He leaped up and caught her wrists, pulling her close to him. "After what happened between us, Henrietta, we can't go back. Or stay apart."

She struggled against him, but he yanked her closer and kissed her with a fierce, demanding passion that burned away every emotion except an answering desire, turning her resistance to ashes. She clung to him, the hot spiral of wanting coiling demandingly within her.

Whether she agreed with all he'd said or not, he was right about one thing—she'd never again be able to stay apart from him.

Chapter 29

"You can't mean you're going back on a boat again!" Henrietta's mother cried, leaning forward in her chair as she stared at her daughter in alarm.

Sitting on the back verandah of their Detroit house, shaded from the hot July sun by graceful elms, Henrietta took a deep breath, warning herself to remain calm. Almost a month had passed since that ill-fated foggy night on Lake Huron. Did her mother think she meant to stay at home in Detroit forever?

"I'm sorry if I'm upsetting you, Mama," she said.

Why couldn't anyone but Grandpa Beau seem to realize she had no intention of giving up her goal of one day captaining her own boat? A sailor certainly didn't get to become a captain by staying ashore.

Her mother didn't understand her.

Neither had Garth. Their hours together marooned on the island had been a wildly passionate mixture of lovemaking and quarreling, leaving her hopelessly confused about how she felt about him. A search boat had spotted the smoke from their fire and rescued them before they'd had to spend a second night on the island; once aboard the search vessel they'd been separated and had no chance to speak privately. Even their stiff and brief farewell at the Cheboygan waterfront had been in public. She hadn't seen Garth since.

Though *Lake Flyer* and the schooner *Merribell* rested on the bottom of Lake Huron, about half the *Flyer*'s crew and four of the schooner's, including their captain, had made it to shore one way or another. Captain Riggs had gone down with his ship and she mourned his loss.

Henrietta sighed. No doubt that was why she felt so miserable.

"I do wish you'd talk to me, dear," her mother said, touching her hand. "It's not knowing what you think and feel that upsets me more than anything else. I can sense you're not happy, and I'm sure you haven't completely recovered from that terrible accident. If you must persist in this fancy of yours to be a lake captain, don't you think it would be wise to take another month to recuperate?"

"I've already signed on another boat, Mama. In any case, I don't need to rest; I'm perfectly healthy."

"I so hoped you meant to sail to Mackinac Island with us and spend August there. Amory's going to be terribly disappointed."

"I'm sure he'll recover," Henrietta said dryly.

"He's a fine young man and very interested in you."

"Mama, I know that. It happens that I'm more interested in becoming a captain than I am in Amory. Or any other young man."

"By the time you can call yourself Captain, I fear you'll be a set-in-your-ways old maid."

Henrietta smiled at her mother, shaking her head, refusing to let herself be irritated. She hadn't told her mother about Garth. How could she when she didn't know her own feelings? All she was sure of was that he was the only man she could ever imagine herself making love with.

410

Her mother blinked back tears. "There's more to this than the boats," she said. "I don't know how we've managed to drift so far apart that you can't bring yourself to confide in me. I wish—" She broke off as Beau Pendleton limped onto the verandah.

"I don't mean to intrude," he began.

Her mother rose. "It's your turn to try to talk to your granddaughter," she said. "Maybe she'll listen to you."

Left alone with Grandpa Beau, Henrietta watched him ease carefully into a chair and lift his bad leg onto a footstool.

He gave her a wry grin. "Old bones, girl. And not improved by having a tree fall on them. I learned too late to watch out for enemies posing as friends."

"That's one problem I don't think I have to worry about," she said.

"Then what problems *are* you mulling over?"

Henrietta eyed him, wondering if she could get away with denying that anything was bothering her. One look at his shrewd dark eyes, eyes that had always seen through her subterfuges, dissuaded her. She'd have to tell him part of the problem, anyway.

"You know Garth Laidlaw and I were together when we were rescued," she said carefully. "What I didn't mention is that he saved my life."

Her grandfather's eyes narrowed. "Why not say so right off?"

"I meant to, but somehow I couldn't bring myself to talk about him. You see, he—he wants to marry me."

Even as she said the words she wondered if they were true. Garth could well have changed his mind after all their quarreling. He hadn't tried to contact her in almost a month. If he still wanted to marry her, wouldn't he at least have written her by now?

Grandfather Beau nodded encouragingly, unsurprised by what she'd said. "And?"

She glared at him. "Obviously I can't marry anyone until after I make captain—if then. I'm not so sure I care to marry."

"Most people do marry, sooner or later. It's the way of things. Nothing wrong with later, if that's your choice. And you don't need to marry the first man who asks you."

"Garth isn't the first man who's asked me!"

Her grandfather smiled. "It's clear he's the first man who matters, though. Are you in love with him?"

"I don't know. We—" She broke off abruptly. It was impossible to tell her grandfather—or anyone—what had happened between them on the island. Or to admit how often she dreamed that they lay together in the same way and woke yearning to be in his arms again.

"We quarreled," she went on. "He wants me to sit ashore and twiddle my thumbs while I wait for him to make captain and then we'd be married. He won't even try to understand why I prefer to stay on the boats. If he loved me—"

"Oh, I think you can be sure he loves you, Rietta. He probably has ever since you pushed him in the lake when you were twelve. But men are possessive critters. We want the woman we choose for a wife to be all ours, heart and soul. Body and mind."

She frowned. "A wife with no ambition of her own? Is that how you feel, Grandpa?"

He sighed. "I used to. Takes time to outgrow that notion, and some men never get beyond it. Of course, some women's sole interest is invested in their marriage and family. Nothing wrong with that. Just as there's nothing wrong with a woman wanting more."

"My mother never seems to want more."

"No? What about her crusade to help American Indians? It seems to me that working for a cause you believe in counts as more."

412

Henrietta thought over what he'd said before speaking. "But Mama doesn't want something for herself alone. I do. Does that mean I'm selfish?"

He shook his head. "Hold on to your dreams, Rietta."

"And love?"

"If it *is* love, you'll find a way to weave love and your dream together; you won't have to give up one for the other. Unfortunately, I can't tell you how. No one can."

The day she left Detroit, her grandfather rode with her to the riverfront.

"I'm proud of you, Second Mate Pendleton," he told her after they stepped down from the buggy and stood gazing at *James K. Paul,* the grain freighter she'd signed on.

"Me, too," she said, grinning. "My first berth as a second mate—and on a boat that you don't own."

Her grandfather, leaning on his cane, waved a deprecating hand. "All the lake skippers know you for a capable sailor, one with expertise, intelligence, and the ability to manage a crew. Now they also realize you don't panic in emergencies."

She shrugged. "I thought the *Flyer*'s fate might wreck Sir Henry's reputation for luck, but Captain Ekholm, the *Paul*'s skipper, tells me the opposite's true. He was a close friend of Captain Riggs, you know. I suspect that's part of the reason he took me on."

"Riggs was a good man and he had a high opinion of you. He forgave me early on for foisting what he called a 'damned lady sailor' off on him."

Henrietta bit her lip. "I miss him."

"You'd better not entertain any idea of going down with your ship once you make captain."

"I fear I'm not anywhere near as noble as Captain Riggs."

"Good!" He hugged her briefly. "Farewell, sailor. I'll wave to the *Paul* when she passes Mackinac Island."

"I'll be sure to wave back." She hoisted her seabag onto her shoulder. "Goodbye, Grandpa."

As she walked away, their parting words echoed in her mind, part of a sailing song she'd learned her first year on the boats:

Oh, down the long lakes we'll sail, boys,
Goodbye, farewell, goodbye, farewell . . .

But it was a homeward-bound song and she was leaving home; she was upbound. For the first time it occurred to her that she might never return. There was always such a possibility when you worked on the boats, but before the sinking of the *Flyer* she hadn't believed it could happen to her. Henrietta Pendleton would never be lost at sea.

Yet she almost had been. She and Garth as well. Garth, she'd heard, was first mate on the *Jupiter*, a freight-passenger vessel for another line. She'd seen the *Jupiter* once, a sleek modern steamer, and she tried to picture him standing on the bridge with the white-haired captain, old Pickens, seventy if he was a day. But the image that came to her was of the smoky interior of the wigwam, with Garth's dark eyes gazing into hers . . .

Henrietta shook her head impatiently and strode on. This was no time for dreamy visions; she had work to do.

The rest of the summer passed quickly. The mild and often rainy September slipped into an October Indian

414

summer when the clear blue weather over the lakes seemed to last forever. The day before Halloween the *Paul* tied up at Detroit overnight and Henrietta made a quick trip home, discovering that her grandparents had returned to Boston.

On the wharf early the next morning, ready to board, she overheard a sailor from another boat mention the *Jupiter* and she paused to eavesdrop.

"He clears the locks, it's fair weather, good sailing, lake as calm as a mirror 'n over he drops, stone cold dead in De Tour Passage," a red-bearded lakesman was telling his mate.

"Old Pick weren't no spring chicken."

"Heard tell he was eighty-one. Anyways, what the first mate does is have the old man carried into his cabin 'n tells the crew the skipper's took sick. What next? He takes over, sails the damn boat all the way down to Port Huron, 'n lets the passengers off afore he gives out old Pick's kicked the bucket. Some get all the luck. If'n I'd done it, I'd've been up to my ears in shit."

"So?"

"So he gets a reward, what else? He gets *Jupiter*."

Unable to stand the suspense any longer, Henrietta broke in. "You mean Laidlaw?" she asked.

Surprised at the interruption, Red-beard turned to stare at her. "Hey, Sir Henry," he said. "I ain't never had a chance t' meet you. My boat—she's the *Four Winds*—could stand a bit 'o your luck, that's for sure."

"I hope she gets it. About the *Jupiter*—you say Captain Pickens is dead. Who's the new captain?"

Red-beard shrugged. "You got the name right—Laidlaw. I swear the man's even luckier 'n you."

Henrietta boarded the *Paul*, excited and thrilled for Garth. It was too bad about Captain Pickens but he was an old man whose time had run out and surely he'd died as he would have wanted to—at the helm of his

415

boat. Garth had taken a chance keeping his death a secret and not pulling into the nearest port, but obviously those running the steamer line had approved of his actions.

"Captain Laidlaw," she whispered, enjoying the sound of the words and not at all jealous he'd reached his goal before she'd reached hers. He'd gone decking years before she had; he'd worked hard and earned his right to his own boat.

She wondered if she'd see him before the shipping season ended and the three-month winter layover began. November, the storm month, was close to hand. The *Paul* would get in at least one more trip, maybe two, before blizzards and the ice in the upper lakes made navigation impossible.

Three weeks later, the *Paul,* outrunning an early blizzard while downbound on Lake Superior, anchored above the locks at Sault Ste. Marie to wait out the storm. Captain Ekholm allowed one boatload of crew members to go ashore, but then the worsening weather made the trip too dangerous for the boat to return to the mother ship.

The temporarily stranded sailors, Henrietta among them, had to find beds for the night. She was standing in the blowing snow, trying to decide which hotel looked the most respectable when she heard someone hail her.

"Henrietta!"

When she turned and saw Garth, her heart began to lurch so crazily she clutched at the breast of her heavy wool peacoat with her gloved hand. Somehow finding her voice, she said, "Captain Laidlaw! I had no idea the *Jupiter* was in port."

He grasped her hand. "It's been a long time."

She nodded, staring at him. "You've shaved off your beard!"

"I don't have to prove I'm old enough to be a captain anymore. Where's your ship?"

She gestured toward the water they were unable to see through the thickening snow. "The *Paul's* out there somewhere but I'm stranded ashore."

"Like me," he said, still holding her hand. "We'd best get in out of this. Where are you staying?"

She hesitated. "I was trying to decide on a hotel."

He shook his head. "We're not the only ones caught short by the blizzard. All the good places are full. To get anything I had to take a two-room suite at the Ojibway—their last available accommodation. Come on, let's go."

As he began to pull her with him, she dug her heels in. "Go where?"

"To the Ojibway, where else? You obviously can't bed down in some dubious marine roominghouse; you'll have to share my suite."

"I don't think—" she began.

"Didn't you hear me say there are no rooms available? Or don't you believe me?"

"You told me once Laidlaws never lie."

"Right." He tugged at her hand.

Two rooms, he'd said. That didn't make it any more proper, but at least it would allow for some privacy. As it was, she could hardly sleep in a snowbank.

"Thank you, Captain," she said formally, falling into step with him.

"I can't think of anyone I'd rather share quarters with than the *Paul's* second mate," he said.

It was the cold wind robbing her of her breath, she told herself, not anticipation of being alone with Garth.

"To think I damned this storm for tying up *Jupiter* at the Soo," he said as he steered her through the hotel lobby. "I even cursed the errand that brought me ashore. Fate moves in wondrous ways."

He might believe that fate had brought them together, but she didn't have to accept his belief. He'd had almost four months to get in touch with her and he'd never sent so much as a brief note. Did he seriously think she intended to throw herself into his arms like some moonstruck maiden?

She quite liked the looks of the suite, comfortable if not luxurious, the two rooms arranged as bedroom and a sitting room. She'd have preferred two bedrooms, but at least the sitting room did have a sofa adequate for sleeping.

Hanging up her wet outer clothing, she listened to the radiators sizzle and clank as steam rattled through them and, above their reassuring noise, heard the threatening howl of the wind as it swept around their corner windows, flinging snow against the dark panes.

"Cozy," Garth said, grasping her hands and swinging her around to face him. "I wondered if I'd ever be alone with you again."

She freed her hands. "I'm starving," she said, fighting her urge to move closer instead of farther from him. "They must have a dining room in the hotel."

He gestured toward a row of covered dishes sitting on a long table. "The desk clerk warned me they anticipated a shortage of food, so I ordered when I registered. I think there's enough for two." He held up a bottle. "And here's the wine I went out to buy and was bringing back when I met you. We'll have a picnic— just like the old days."

She's as skittish as an unmanned sailboat in a brisk breeze, Garth told himself. He'd been so delighted at their unexpected meeting and so eager to hold her again that he hadn't thought back to how angrily they'd parted after their rescue from the island.

He'd told himself then that it was just as well—why in hell would a man want to marry a woman de-

418

termined to be a lake captain? A wife ought to make a home for her man, she ought to be waiting when he was free to come to her. Henrietta was stubborn and talented enough to eventually make captain—and what kind of marriage would that be? She on one boat, he on another, with no home at all to go to.

So he'd done his best to forget her. And succeeded—when he was busy. But she invaded his dreams and his thoughts during every odd moment when he wasn't intent on his duties. How the hell was a man supposed to forget a woman like Henrietta? How could he not remember the sweet fire of the passion he and he alone had roused in her?

And now she was here with him, the lure of her presence setting his blood aflame. God, how he wanted her. Now. Tonight. And tomorrow. For always.

Always was as unlikely as it had ever been, but they did have tonight. Tomorrow. Hours until the storm blew itself out. Providing he could convince her to make love with him. Words wouldn't work and she shied from his touch. He'd have to take it slow, play it by ear, but damn it, they were together, and one way or another he meant to entice her into his arms and keep her there for as long as the storm lasted.

"A picnic would be fun," she agreed. "We always seem to have them in odd places, don't we?"

"Some day we'll have a real, honest-to-goodness outdoor picnic," he promised.

"Will we?" Her voice was wistful.

"Laidlaws keep their promises."

"You make your family sound terribly noble. I hope you don't have any intention of emulating Captain Riggs."

"And go down with the *Jupiter?*" He shook his head. "In the first place, I'm not going to lose my boat to the lakes."

"No captain can be sure of that."

"We'll see. Meanwhile—what's your pleasure as to where we dine?"

"Oh, the floor, by all means. Otherwise it won't be a picnic. We can use the extra blanket for a picnic cloth."

For someone who'd taken no more than one quick, nervous glance into the bedroom, she'd noticed more than he had. "Your wish is my command," he assured her.

He brought two pillows back with the blanket. "In case the food makes me drowsy," he said lightly.

Watching Henrietta set the dishes on the spread-out blanket as he struggled to uncork the wine, Garth thought he'd never tire of looking at her. She moved with such efficient grace that she accomplished tasks in half the time it took most others. And she was easy on the eyes. He couldn't wait to pull the pins from her beautiful hair so it tumbled over her shoulders.

"Picnics call for going barefoot, so I think we should at least take off our shoes," he said.

She nodded. "You're absolutely right. And perhaps jackets as well." With that she peeled off her tunic, making him catch his breath in anticipation, remembering the island and the skimpy undergarments he'd removed from her one by one.

But this was winter, not summer, and to his disappointment, she wore a long-sleeved man-style flannel shirt underneath the tunic. She undid her shoes and pulled them off, flexing her stockinged toes.

The cork came free from the bottle with a muted pop. He poured the red wine into two glasses he'd found in the suite and handed her one. "Not stemmed crystal, I'm afraid."

"Who wants crystal on a picnic?"

He smiled at her, set down his glass, and took off his shoes, then his jacket, joining her on the blanket in his

420

shirtsleeves. Lifting his glass, he clinked it lightly against hers. "To a never-ending storm," he said.

She raised her eyebrows. "What a strange toast for a lake captain!" But she sipped her wine.

He tasted his, happy to find it wasn't as bad as he'd feared—he'd taken the first bottle anyone would sell him. Since he'd also accepted whatever the hotel had to offer from their dwindling supplies of food, the covered dishes held an odd assortment—bread, cheese, jam, sweet pickles, smoked Soo Whitefish, and baked apples.

"This has to be the most interesting meal I've ever sat down to," Henrietta said, cutting a slice of the smoked fish. "Ah, delicious." She continued to eat with enthusiasm and without any of the put-on mannerisms he'd noticed ladies often seemed to think they must use.

How had she managed to grow into such a lovely woman and yet remain as unaffected as she'd been at twelve?

"You're not eating," she accused him.

He decided it wasn't wise to tell her the truth—that he'd rather watch her—so he cut a wedge of cheese off the half-wheel on the plate and ate it.

When he refilled her glass with wine, she shook her head. "Too much wine makes me sleepy."

"That shouldn't prove to be a problem here."

She hesitated, finally smiling. "Then don't be insulted if I fall asleep while you're talking to me."

"I promise."

She lifted her glass and drank. "And Laidlaws always keep their promises," she said as she set it down.

By the time the food was finished, the wine bottle was empty and lying on its side. Henrietta spun it idly.

"When Grandpa Beau saw me aboard the *Paul* for the first time," she said, "and we said our *adieus,* for some strange reason I thought of that song—you know, the homeward-bound one."

Garth cleared his throat and sang in a clear baritone:

Oh, down the long lakes to the straits we'll sail,
Goodbye, farewell, goodbye, farewell
Down through old Huron where a tug we'll hail
Hooray, my boys, we're homeward bound . . .

She joined in on the second verse and by the time they'd finished the tenth she was leaning against him with his arms around her. He looked down and saw tears in her eyes.

"Don't cry," he said.

"Parting is sad."

"But not homecoming."

"To go home you have to leave those you've worked with, you have to leave one family behind for another, you can't have them both. So it's a sad song." She sniffed.

"We're together," he pointed out as he offered his handkerchief to her. "You've no need to be sad."

She wiped away the tears, snuggling closer to him. "I'm glad you found me in the storm," she murmured, closing her eyes.

Just as she'd warned, she fell asleep. Garth eased her head onto one of the pillows, then stood and removed all dishes from the blanket. Returning, he stretched out next to her, using the other pillow, and pulled her gently into his arms. When she didn't rouse, he sighed and closed his eyes, still holding her close. Since he couldn't take advantage of a sleeping woman, he might as well get some rest himself.

Sleep proved impossible. When he did start to drift off, Henrietta would change position, shifting her soft curves against him and fanning the flames he was trying to quell. At last he gave up and kissed her. At least he could allow himself that much.

To his surprise and delight, she wound her arms around his neck, kissing him ardently in return. He groaned and parted her lips with his tongue, tasting her sweetness, relishing her scent and the feel of her under his hands.

They were both half-undressed before he made up his mind he was damned if he meant to make love with her on the hard floor when there was a bed in the next room. Scooping her into his arms, he carried her into the bedroom.

"Garth?" she whispered, her eyes opening as he eased her onto the bed.

"It's all right, love," he told her. "You're with me."

"Yes," she murmured, reaching for him. "I'm where I want to be."

And oh, God, so was he.

Chapter 30

The storm lasted two days, not nearly long enough for Henrietta. How could two days be long enough when she wanted to make love with Garth forever? Wonder of wonders, they hadn't quarreled even once. When she woke early on the third day, saw the sun rising, and realized they'd be able to return to their separate boats, she sighed, already feeling the pain of parting.

She turned to Garth and kissed him awake. He glanced at the brightness shining in the windows, then pulled her into his arms and made love to her with a desperate urgency that matched her own.

"Until next time," he murmured with one final kiss when they could no longer put off facing the day.

She rose reluctantly and gathered her clothes, fearing to talk lest she betray how close she was to crying. She didn't want him to remember her drenched in tears.

While he was dressing, Garth mentioned that the *Jupiter*'s first mate, having his fill of the vagaries of passengers, had signed on a freighter for the next season.

"So you'll be needing a first mate," Henrietta said,

excitement replacing her sadness as she imagined being on the same boat with Garth again, working with him and seeing him every day.

He nodded. "Know of any good ones ready to shift berths?"

"I'm ready to move up to first mate. How about me?"

He stood holding his shirt, staring at her. "You!"

Fully dressed already, she crossed her arms over her chest. "Why not me? I'm certainly qualified."

He shook his head. "Not on my boat. Not you. No."

Anger overrode her excitement. "Are you saying you don't think I'm good enough to be your first mate?"

He flung the shirt on the rumpled bed and glared at her. "Qualifications have nothing to do with it. I don't want you aboard my boat. Can't you understand?"

"No!"

"In the first place, as you damn well know, I want you for my wife, not my first mate. In the second place, if you were a member of my crew you'd distract the hell out of me, and I can't have that. If you need a third reason, I don't think women belong on the boats, and you're a woman. To put it plainly, I want you off the boats and on land, married to me and living in our house."

"Rocking in my chair and knitting while I wait for your winter layover, I suppose," she fumed. "Never! If you loved me you'd realize the boats are as much my life as they are yours and you'd sign me on as your first mate."

"I do love you, damn your stubborn hide!" he shouted. "God only knows why, because you sure as hell try a man's patience past all reason. I love you but you'll never be a part of any crew of mine. Is that clear?" He grabbed his shirt but paused before pulling it over his head. "Come to think of it—if you love me why won't you settle for being my wife?"

425

"There's no use talking to a man who won't understand!" Henrietta flung on her storm coat, yanked open the door, and fled down the hall.

"If you change your mind, let me know," he called after her. "Otherwise all bets are off."

She took his parting words to mean he didn't intend to see her again unless she agreed to give up the boats. And he called *her* stubborn! Her fury at his refusal even to try to look at her side of it dried the tears streaming down her face. By the time she reached the wharf where the small boats were moored, she had herself under enough control so none of the sailors who rowed with her back to the *Paul* had any glimpse of her roiling emotions.

During the three-month winter layover, she refused to languish in Detroit waiting for a letter or a visit she knew wouldn't come. Instead, she accepted Amory's invitation and, with her parents, spent December and January cruising the Caribbean on the Ventry yacht.

Near the end of January, Amory proposed to her.

"Not that I think I have a chance," he added ruefully. "I believe you like me well enough, but I swear our yacht captain has seen more of you on this trip than I have."

"You know how interested I am in boats," she said apologetically, trying to delay an outright refusal. "It has nothing to do with Captain Lowrey himself."

"Since he's sixty-five and bald as an egg, that's obvious. Still, it would be easier to be jealous of a man than a boat."

She sighed. "Amory, I do like you, but I've tried more than once to explain to you that I'm not willing to consider marriage until after I earn the right to captain my own boat. Even then, I'm not sure I'll want to marry. Please don't take it personally."

"But darling, if that's what's holding you back, I

426

have a capital solution. Once we're married I'll buy a yacht and you can be captain to your heart's content."

Play at being captain! Henrietta took a deep breath as she fought to conceal her irritation, reminding herself that Amory didn't mean to insult her, he simply had no conception of what she wanted.

"I'm sorry, but the answer is no," she told him.

Her mother surprised her by calmly accepting her rejection of Amory's offer of marriage.

"Last fall Beau and I had quite a long talk," her mother said. "He believes you're in love with a young man from Mackinac Island, one you met there when you were children. If you don't love Amory, it wouldn't be right to marry him." She smiled at Henrietta. "I almost made the mistake of marrying the wrong man when I was a girl but I backed out at the last minute. It was the wisest decision I ever made. If I hadn't decided as I did, I never would have met your father and fallen in love with him. I would never have been really happy—as happy as I hope you'll be someday."

Amazed at her mother's understanding, Henrietta remained silent.

"We're strong women, we descendents of Octavia Livingstone," her mother continued. "We know what we want and we go after it. I should have recognized the trait in you sooner and given you support, as your Grandpa Beau has always done." She reached out and hugged Henrietta. "Whatever you decide, dear, I'll be behind you from now on."

Henrietta hugged her mother back, tears in her eyes. But though she was thrilled that they were closer than they'd ever been, she couldn't help feeling irked because her grandfather had betrayed a confidence.

When the yacht moored off the elder Pendleton's Jamaican estate and everyone went ashore for a visit,

Henrietta took her grandfather to task.

"You told Mama about Garth," she accused.

"High time someone did," Grandpa Beau countered. "Girls are supposed to confide in their mothers, and you're lucky enough to have the kind of mother who'll understand if given half a chance. She's a wonderful woman. Didn't I know the first time I saw Marta Johansen that she was the perfect wife for my boy?" He grinned. "They hadn't met one another at the time, but I'm always right when it comes to suitability."

Henrietta glared at him. "I suppose you'll tell me next that you chose Garth Laidlaw for me."

"As a matter of fact—"

She covered her ears with her hands. "No! I don't want to hear."

He pulled one of her hands free. "I've got other news you *will* want to hear, Captain Pendleton."

"What news?" Belatedly she realized what he'd called her and dropped her hands to stare at him.

"You heard me right. Your old grandpa has acquired a Great Lakes passenger line, and it just happens that one of my boats needs a captain. What do you say to that?"

For one wonderful moment a wild elation bubbled through her only to frizzle and die when Amory's words echoed in her head: *I'll buy a yacht and you can play at being captain.*

On a larger scale, isn't that exactly what her grandfather had done?

"I haven't earned a boat," she said when she could trust herself to speak calmly.

"Come on, girl, don't be modest," her grandfather urged. "You and I both know you've had enough experience to handle being captain."

"Everyone would know, myself included, that I wouldn't be captaining the boat if my grandfather didn't own the line." She did her best not to sound bitter.

"So what? You'd soon prove your worth to the world. Good God, girl, do you take me for a doting fool? I may love my only granddaughter more than I should, but I'm clear-eyed enough when it comes to judging your ability. What makes you think I'd offer you a boat if I didn't know you'd be a damn good captain?"

"I don't think—" she began.

"Think?" he roared. "What is there to think about? Unless you don't trust your own ability. Is that it? Now that the chance has come are you afraid to try your hand at captaining a boat?"

"No!" she cried. "I'm not afraid!"

"Then prove it to me, Captain Pendleton."

Garth, spending the winter layover with his mother on Mackinac Island, held out until Christmas before finally admitting to himself that however angry Henrietta had made him, he missed her more with every passing day. She was the only woman in the world he wanted; he needed her in a deep, distressing way that made him feel he'd never be completely whole without her.

Early in January he pocketed his pride, crossed the ice from the island to Mackinaw City, and took the train to Detroit.

Discovering the Pendleton estate was situated on Lake St. Clair, he rented a hack and drove through the dirty slush of the city into the country where the sun glinted off banks of clean white snow. Though the sun shone, the thermometer hovered near zero, the chill air turning his breath as well as the horse's into clouds as he turned into the road leading to the estates along the lake.

Garth found the gates of the estate open, passed through them and drew up before a white columned house that reminded him of pictures of old mansions on Southern plantations.

He delayed a moment before climbing down. He'd known from the beginning that Henrietta's family was wealthy—only the rich built so-called summer cottages on Mackinac Island—but she'd never behaved like someone with money behind her and so her family's status had gradually slid into the back of his mind. The imposing house on the extensively landscaped grounds brought it back to him with a wallop.

What the hell would a girl from the Pendleton family want with a nobody from Mackinac Island? he asked himself. He might be Captain Laidlaw now, earning enough to live decently, but he was far from being a rich man. He never *would* be a rich man.

Still, she'd said she loved him and he meant to find out once and for all if that was true. He clenched his jaw and jumped to the ground. No fancy mansion was going to intimidate him. He'd come here to see Henrietta, and by damn, see her he would.

The young maid that answered his knock was pretty despite her sober black uniform. She let him into a huge and elaborate entrance foyer, saying, "If you'll excuse me, sir, I'll go and find Mr. Hastings—he's the butler."

"I don't want Mr. Hastings," Garth said. "It's Miss Pendleton I've come to see."

"I know, sir, but she isn't here, and Mr. Hastings said I was suppose to notify him of any callers for the family and he'd deal with them. So—"

"Wait," he said and smiled. "I'd rather deal with you."

She tried and failed to suppress a giggle. "I'm not supposed to—"

430

"Who'll know the difference? I'll never tell. Where is Miss Pendleton?"

She hesitated, then said, "Off to the Caribbean Islands with the family, sir. On the Ventry yacht. Ever so fancy a boat."

"Ventry?"

"Yes, sir. Mr. and Mrs. J. C. Ventry and their son, Mr. Amory Ventry."

"When will Miss Pendleton be back?"

"Not till the first week in February, sir."

"Thank you." He nodded and turned to leave.

"Don't you want to leave your card, sir?" she asked, gesturing toward the silver salver on a marble-topped table in the entry.

"No card." Garth tried not to scowl at her, but he couldn't force another smile. "In fact, I'd prefer it if you forgot I was here. No need to mention my call to any of the family. Or to Mr. Hastings, either. If he asks, just tell him I came here by mistake."

She blinked uncertainly, biting her lip. "If you say so, sir."

Garth climbed into the buggy, realizing he was lucky that he'd encountered the maid instead of some supercilious butler who wouldn't have told him a damn thing. As he drove away he found himself cursing under his breath and shook his head. What had he expected?

Henrietta had warned him she wasn't the type to sit and wait for any man. Why, then, did it hurt so much that she'd gone off on a yacht with this Amory Ventry? He wondered if Ventry was the man he'd seen escorting Henrietta to the *Flyer* last June. How long had she known him? His grip tightened on the reins. Did she let Ventry kiss her? Hold her?

"Damn it, Henrietta Pendleton," he muttered, "you belong to me!"

431

On a windy mid-March day, Henrietta stood on the wharf admiring the *Athena*, hardly able to believe the boat was hers to captain. While the *Athena* wasn't the newest or the largest passenger vessel in the line, she was trim and seaworthy, with her paint gleaming clean and white in the sun. Henrietta had fallen in love with her at first sight and, once aboard, her affection for the boat had grown.

While the boat was still at her winter mooring, she'd prowled from stem to stern, examining every inch of the *Athena* until she felt she knew the boat by heart.

Though she had some doubts about having accepted the captaincy, her grandfather's challenge to prove to him and to herself that she wasn't afraid had convinced her she had to try. Right or wrong, she'd take charge of the *Athena*.

"I can do it," she told herself firmly, her fingers caressing the family locket her mother had given her in honor of making captain.

She knew the heart-shaped heirloom held a lock of her great-grandmother's hair, hair as red as her own, and she wondered what this redheaded ancestor would have thought of her captaining her own boat. Her mother had described Octavia Livingstone as a strong woman, so perhaps Great-Grandmother Octavia would have approved. She liked to think so.

Henrietta fixed her gaze lovingly on the *Athena*, hardly able to wait for the beginning of the season, when she'd take the helm for the first time.

Never mind how many would be judging her, and no doubt hoping she'd fail. She 'd show them all, Garth Laidlaw included.

In April, the first passenger run to Duluth went slick as a whistle. The *Athena* was not only fast but handled like a dream.

"You know, sir," her first mate, Mr. Kent, told her on the downbound trip, "I'll bet the *Athena* can beat most anything on the lakes, should you want to take up a challenge sometime."

"Has she ever raced any of the boats?" Henrietta asked, aware that there was great rivalry between the lines, and that the passenger and passenger-freight boats often raced one another when bound for the same ports.

"The *Athena*'s former captain didn't believe in racing, sir. Frivolous, was his word for it."

"I have nothing against racing. If the opportunity comes along and I feel there's no risk to the boat, we'll see."

Mr. Kent grinned, obviously pleased. As she watched him walk away, Henrietta thought that if he hadn't been aboard a boat he'd have been cheerfully whistling. But no crew member ever did whistle while afloat because, as everyone knew, you might whistle up storm winds.

She'd learned many strange superstitions during her first year on the boats. No matter how odd they seemed to her, she was careful not to defy any of them because she knew that as far as old beliefs were concerned, tradition had the edge over reason.

One belief she'd managed to overcome was the notion that women on boats brought bad luck. She'd been fortunate to have had the crew of the *Flyer* turn that superstition around and dub her "lucky Henry." Since nicknames spread quickly from boat to boat, it had eased her acceptance by this new crew. Just yesterday she'd heard one of her sailors tell another that now nothing bad would ever happen to the *Athena* because "Captain Henry" was the "luckiest skipper" on the lakes.

She planned to do everything in her power to make it come true.

Though Henrietta had no feelings against the impromptu races between the rival lines, she was wary of taking any chance of upsetting passengers or damaging the boat by forcing the boilers past their capabilities. But when, one a fair day near the end of June, upbound on Lake Huron, the *Athena*'s lookout reported that the steamer off to port, also upbound and slightly ahead of them, was the *Jupiter*, it seemed a heaven-sent opportunity. Nothing would suit her better than to outdo Garth.

"Mr. Kent, in your opinion, can we outrun the *Jupiter*?" she asked.

Her first mate's blue eyes gleamed. "She's fast. It'll be a close one, sir, but I'll lay odds we've got the edge."

"Good! The race is on. Pass the word to the crew, mister."

Garth, aware the upbound passenger steamer off to starboard was the *Athena*, noticed a sudden increase in the amount of dark smoke pouring from her two smokestacks even before, with a derisive toot to her steam whistle, she pulled ahead of the *Jupiter*.

Picturing Henrietta in the pilothouse, her flaming hair bound up beneath her skipper's cap, he smiled wolfishly. So she thought she could beat him, did she?

"Full steam ahead!" he ordered.

Word of the race spread quickly throughout the boat. Before long, passengers lined the rail watching the *Athena* steam ahead while urging the *Jupiter* on.

The smoke from both boats' stacks curled, thick and black, into the cool June air, streaming behind as the *Jupiter* edged up on the *Athena*. But, though he closed the gap, Garth couldn't quite pull his boat ahead and they steamed on up the lake, neither taking the lead.

"Even-steven, sir," Mr. Kent told Henrietta.

"The stokers are shoveling as fast as they can, sir," the chief engineer reported when she asked for more speed.

She'd soon be nearing the busy Straits of Mackinac, where only a fool would risk maximum speed. Either she gained a clean lead on the *Jupiter* here and now, or she'd have to settle for a tie, and she was damned if she meant to do that.

"Tell the stokers I'll guarantee them a bonus if we win," she said.

Henrietta didn't know if it was a result of her offer or not, but shortly thereafter the *Athena* slowly but surely began inching ahead of the *Jupiter*. When she was leading by a ship's length, Henrietta decided she'd proved her point. Traffic was increasing and she didn't care to risk a collision through excessive speed. After giving three hoots to signal the race was over as far as she was concerned, she called for throttle down.

Garth understood what she meant by the three whistles; he knew as well as she did that both boats had too much steam up for traffic safety this close to the Straits. Much as he hated to acknowledge defeat, he returned the *Athena*'s signal and ordered the *Jupiter* slowed.

Waiting in line to go through the Soo locks, Henrietta noticed the *Jupiter* pulling up behind the *Athena* and couldn't resist walking aft. She stood at the stern rail staring across the few feet of water between her and the *Jupiter's* bow, scanning the deck for Garth.

Her breath caught when she saw him at last, his back to her, in conversation with someone blocked from her view by his body. She hadn't set eyes on him for six months, trying all that time to deny how much she missed him. Now, with him so near and yet not close enough to touch, she had all she could do not to hold out her arms to him and call his name.

She compromised by saying, "Captain Laidlaw!"

As Garth turned, she saw the person he'd been talking to. A young woman, obviously a passenger, wearing a deep red traveling costume trimmed with sable that accentuated a wasp waist between svelte hips and a generous bosom. Henrietta's gaze shifted to Garth, whose dark eyes held no discernible emotion.

He bowed slightly. "Congratulations, Captain Pendleton."

The tone of his voice told her nothing. Before she could think of what to say, the lady in red laid a gloved hand on Garth's arm, reclaiming his attention. With a flick of his fingers to his cap, he saluted Henrietta before turning to his companion.

"My heavens, she wears trousers!" she heard the young woman say. "How dreadfully unbecoming to a woman. And quite beyond the pale. I had no idea there were such odd creatures as female captains."

Furious, Henrietta spun around and marched away, hearing Garth's amused chuckle echoing in her ears all the way to the pilothouse, turning the taste of victory bitter in her mouth.

Chapter 31

Though Henrietta spent what free time she had picturing meetings between herself and Garth and how she'd treat him with icy politeness, not until early one morning in mid-September did she encounter the *Jupiter* again, once more at the Soo locks, both boats downbound. They weren't close enough for her to catch so much as a glimpse of Garth, and she tried to convince herself it was just as well.

After the *Athena* cleared the De Tour Passage into Lake Huron, the wind, which had been from the north, shifted to the south, making her recall the Lake's saying: *If you don't like the weather, wait five minutes and it'll change.*

The problem was, it seldom changed for the better. Still, the sky remained clear and the water was no more than choppy. When the *Athena* was off Cheboygan on the Michigan shore, Henrietta noticed a low line of gray clouds to the northeast and frowned. Most lake storms were nor'westers, and they could be terrifying blows. But she'd heard more than one skipper echo old Captain Parker's insistence that nothing could equal the fury of a rare nor'easter.

The thermometer registered a pleasant sixty-five,

but the barometer had begun to drop, increasing Henrietta's unease. When the wind changed once more, this time blowing from the northeast, she really began to worry. She'd taken the *Athena* through one nasty blow and didn't doubt her ability to do it again, but there was a hell of a lot of difference between a blow and Captain Parker's chilling description of a nor'-easter.

"The wind hits you one way and the waves hit you t' other, battering the life from your boat, and you can't keep her nose to the seas on account of that ornery wind blowing the wrong way. You got to keep fighting the wheel or your boat'll drop into the trough, out of control, 'n you've lost her. Worst of all, no matter how hard you fight there's times it ain't no damn use."

Henrietta watched the dark line of clouds and debated whether she ought to make for Michigan's Thunder Bay—the nearest harbor—or steam on down the lake toward Detroit in hopes the storm wouldn't be what the old captain used to call "one of them all-hands-lost boat-breakers."

If she ran for shelter in the nearest bay and the blow turned out to be minor, she'd be labeled lily-livered. On the other hand, if she chanced it and lost her boat and her crew, she'd be blamed—posthumously, no doubt—for not having seat-of-the-pants lake sense.

She stepped from the pilothouse and looked back, spotting the *Jupiter* to her rear starboard. Garth had heard the same stories about nor'easters from Captain Parker that she had. How, she wondered, did he feel about the coming blow? What did he intend to do? There was no way to ask him.

"Mr. Kent," she asked, "did you ever ride out a nor'easter?"

Her first mate cocked an eye at the line of dark clouds rising up the sky. "Looks like we might get one,

438

all right enough, sir. Can't say I ever was unlucky enough to get caught in a nor'easter. But the *Athena's* sturdy and sound, and we got ourselves a good skipper."

She was pleased at his faith in her, but feared it took more than ability and a sturdy boat to survive the unpredictably vicious kind of storm a nor'easter could be. If only she had some way to predict how bad the storm would be! Checking the barometer again, she blinked in alarm. Never had she seen it drop so fast.

What in God's name should she do? If she waited much longer to make up her mind, she'd be past Thunder Bay and a good many miles from the next well-sheltered harbor at Saginaw Bay. If she sailed on and the storm proved to be a boat-breaker, she wouldn't dare turn the *Athena* around to try to get back to Thunder Bay because of the danger of being caught in the troughs of the waves as she turned. Under storm conditions you either headed into the wind or into the seas, you didn't get caught broadside if you wanted your boat to survive.

She had to make a decision now. Shelter in the bay or take her chances? Another glance at the barometer and she took a deep breath, letting it out slowly. Right or wrong, she'd decided.

"We're changing course," she told the helmsmen. "We're pulling into Thunder Bay."

She suffered in silence when the *Jupiter* sailed past with a mocking toot, holding her course down the lake. Let Garth think that because she was a woman she was afraid to take a chance; she was damned if she'd change her mind now.

By the time the *Athena* reached the entrance to the bay, the waves and the wind had begun to kick up, buffeting the boat, and dark clouds covered the sun.

"Mr. Kent," she said, "would you explain to the

passengers that we're riding out the storm in Thunder Bay? Since even at anchor we're going to get a certain amount of pitching and rolling, tell them they'll have time to debark if they prefer trying the hotel accommodations in Alpena to remaining aboard."

Every passenger, some already seasick, opted for land. No sooner had the small boat ferrying the last of them reached shore than a great bolt of lightning split the sky, thunder roared, and the deluge began. Even in the relatively sheltered waters of the bay, whitecaps foamed and crested atop giant waves. Though she knew the *Athena* and her crew were safe enough, Henrietta paced back and forth in the limited confines of the pilothouse, unable to rest easy.

How could she relax when Garth was out on the open lake with the *Jupiter*, fighting the storm? Maybe fighting for the life of his boat and crew. And his own life.

A sailor in oilskins who'd been on deck battening down banged at the pilothouse door and the first mate opened it a crack.

"I seen a distress flair, sir," the sailor said. "Way high up, she was. Must've come from outside the bay."

"Which direction, Perkins?" Mr. Kent asked.

"I'd say to the south, sir."

"Watch for another," the first mate ordered.

"Aye, sir."

Mr. Kent shut the door and glanced at Henrietta. "If Perkins was able to see the flare," he said, "the boat in trouble can't be far off. Could be the *Jupiter*."

"Or an upbound boat." Henrietta spoke the words without really believing them, for she knew in her heart the flare had come from the *Jupiter*.

Garth was in danger. Her hands clenched into fists as she pictured the *Jupiter* helpless, caught in this boat-breaker of a nor'easter. She couldn't bear to lose Garth to the storm. Never mind that they couldn't agree—she loved him. If he drowned, life wouldn't be worth living. Yet what could she do to save him?

Another of Captain Parker's storm tales swept into her mind, a story about how, when he'd captained a freighter, he'd once gone to the rescue of a battered, rudderless schooner.

"We hove to close by, but with them high seas running, wasn't no way we could pick the crew off that doomed schooner. Only thing left to do was try to take her under tow . . ."

The old captain had been fighting the storm himself when he'd made the attempt; his boat hadn't been anchored safe in harbor. Did she have any right to put her boat and her men in danger? If there'd been passengers aboard, she couldn't even consider it—but they'd all gone ashore. Henrietta turned to her first mate.

"Mr. Kent," she asked, "how do you think the crew would feel about the *Athena* risking the storm to answer that distress signal?"

He blinked once before answering. "We're lakesmen. We all know it could be us out there needing help."

She nodded. "If I could, I'd let any man off who didn't want to take the risk, but—" She shrugged, aware she didn't need to mention that the storm prevented anyone from getting ashore.

"Not a one would want off," he said. "I trust you, Captain, and so does your crew. Shall I pass the word we're pulling anchor?"

"If you would, mister."

Since the boilers hadn't had a chance to cool down, it didn't take long for the *Athena* to get steam up. As she fought across the bay, pounded relentlessly by wind and waves, Henrietta thanked God the storm had struck during the day. The storm darkness was bad

441

enough; night would have made any rescue attempt all but impossible.

Once in the open lake, they felt the full force of the storm with seas heavier than Henrietta had ever been in, so heavy the steamer seemed to make no progress at all. Sweat beaded the helmsman's face as he struggled to hold the boat on course. Time, as well as the boat, seemed to stand still.

Once Henrietta thought she heard the faint hoot of a steam whistle over the howl of the wind, and so she began sounding the *Athena*'s whistle at spaced intervals, straining her ears to hear any response.

"Listen!" Mr. Kent cried at last. "She's answering."

The *Athena* immediately ceased whistling so they could home in on the distressed boat.

Until they finally fought their way alongside the other steamer, Henrietta couldn't be sure it was the *Jupiter*. When she saw that it was, both joy and fear gripped her. The *Jupiter* was wallowing in the trough of the waves, shipping water, out of control.

"My guess is her propeller snapped," Mr. Kent said. "She's helpless. A wonder she hasn't foundered."

"The only thing we can do is try to toss her a towline," Henrietta said.

The first mate gave her a quick nod. She was grateful that he didn't point out how difficult that would be, nor voice any doubts about the *Athena*'s ability to take a larger boat under tow.

After three heartbreaking failures, with men on both boats risking their lives on the rain- and wind-lashed decks, a *Jupiter* sailor managed to hook and fish aboard a lifebelt floated from the *Athena* with a three-quarter-inch line tied to it. With a connection between the boats, a heavy ten-inch towline was finally fastened to both vessels.

After maneuvering the *Jupiter* from the wave

troughs, Henrietta made the decision to turn back to Thunder Bay rather than trying to struggle with a tow for miles through the storm to reach the next safe harbor. Turning in heavy seas was perilous because of the danger of both boats becoming trapped in the troughs, but she'd made up her mind it was the lesser risk.

With the first mate's help, both of them struggled with the wheel, the helmsman fought his way through the turn. Ordinarily this would have been the captain's job, but Henrietta had discovered early that though she was strong for a woman she didn't have the muscle-power of most men. When a task called for brawn, she'd learned to delegate, and no one seemed to think the less of her for it.

Fighting the storm and burdened by the tow, the *Athena* took twice as long to retrace her way into the bay than it had to reach the *Jupiter*. True darkness had settled in around both boats by the time they had set their anchors in the safe harbor off Alpena.

Henrietta, though frustrated that the storm still kept her from Garth, fell into an exhausted sleep, waking the next morning to clouds and rain. Essentially, though, the storm was over.

What she wanted to do was be rowed over to the *Jupiter* and Garth, but she knew she must first fulfill her responsibilities as Captain Pendleton.

Gathering the crew on deck, she told them how proud she was of every man on board.

"You showed skill and discipline as lakesmen, but more important was your courage and nerve. You are truly brave men, one and all."

Though she didn't say so, she also meant to see that her grandfather gave a bonus to the entire crew.

"We trusted you to bring us through, sir," Mr. Kent told her later, making her blink back tears.

As the *Athena*'s passengers were being retrieved from shore to continue their interrupted journey down the lake, a boat from the *Jupiter* came alongside and Garth sprang up the rope ladder to the deck.

He faced her, hat in hand. "Captain Pendleton, my boat and all aboard her owe you our lives," he said stiffly. "My crew has asked me to offer you our heartfelt gratitude."

"I'm fortunate to have a courageous crew and a sturdy boat. Captain Laidlaw," she said, taken aback by his extreme formality.

"Your crew and your boat also have a brave captain." He bowed slightly and turned toward the rail.

She started to ask him to wait, then bit off the word before it emerged. Too many people were watching and listening. Best to keep this captain-to-captain—in which case there was no more to be said. In silence, she watched him climb back down into his boat.

Is that all, Garth? her heart asked. Is there never to be any more between us?

An early freeze in the upper lakes ended the season soon after the first of November. Henrietta, feeling out of sorts and unable to contemplate facing the social season she knew would await her in Detroit, accepted her grandparents' invitation to visit them in Boston.

"Your grandmother's inveigled me into renting a villa in the south of France until after the first of the year," Grandpa Beau told her on the second day of her visit. "That means we won't be using our place in the Caribbean or the sailboat for the next two months. If, as you claim, you need some time to yourself, why don't you take the sailboat down to Jamaica and hole up there? On the trip down, Captain Robinson might be able to teach you a few things you don't know about sailing."

Her grandfather's three-masted schooner, *Little Fox*, was his pride and joy. Between him and Frank Robinson, the man he'd hired to captain it, they took care of the boat as though she were a baby. Since she knew more about steamers than schooners, she was sure there was much she could learn from Captain Robinson. While the idea of sailing to the Caribbean didn't ease her heartache, it did bring her out of the doldrums.

"How is it you always know what I need?" she asked her grandfather.

He smiled. "Your grandmother claims I'm a devious man. I haven't a notion why she thinks such a thing."

Neither did Henrietta. At least not until after *Little Fox* was moored off the Pendleton estate near Ochos Rios, she'd been rowed to shore and was welcomed into the sprawling house by Cosie, her grandparents' Jamaican housekeeper.

"Is real good you come, Miss. Jamaica soon cure what ail you."

Henrietta smiled at Cosie. She liked being here—who wouldn't? But Jamaica, with its tropical weather, warm turquoise waters, and always-blooming, always-green plants and trees, seemed not quite real to her, a dream land. She was the child of a harsher clime where the water was never soft and warm, the land where trees lost their leaves in the fall and in the winter nothing bloomed.

In any case, neither Jamaica nor any other spot on earth could cure what ailed her.

"You come with me," Cosie said.

Henrietta followed the housekeeper, somewhat surprised to be led toward the sweeping veranda—actually a deck built halfway around the house—rather than to her bedroom.

Cosie stopped by open glass doors and gestured for Henrietta to go on through. "Cure, he be waiting."

Thinking Cosie was referring to the warm sunshine and scented breeze awaiting her on the deck, Henrietta stepped past her and onto the wooden planks. She stopped short.

To her left, a man stood in the sea breeze. His intent gaze held her motionless. Speechless. Grandfather's doing! She couldn't think how he'd managed it; he was sly as a fox, all right.

"Henrietta?" Garth said, taking a step toward her, opening his arms to her.

She flung herself at him, not caring whether she was doing right or wrong, knowing only that she had never needed anyone more desperately.

His kiss was passionate and demanding, heating her blood until she moaned with need. When he finally lifted his mouth from hers, she breathed his name.

"It's been so long," she whispered.

"Too damned long. And I don't intend to wait any longer."

Agreeing without words, she took his hand, leading him to her bedroom. Once inside, they flung off clothes, coming together flesh-to-flesh with urgent desire, joining together for the magic journey neither could take alone.

Later, as they lay tangled in each other's arms, temporarily sated, Garth fingered the heart-shaped locket that hung from a gold chain around her neck.

"This is new."

"No, old. A family heirloom."

"Five gemstones," he said, touching them one by one. "Yours was a Great Lakes family, I take it."

"Come to think of it, yes. A woman of my family has

lived beside each one of the lakes, from Ontario to Huron."

"And you? Where will you live?" His dark eyes gazed into hers and she saw the uncertainty in them as well as the love.

"With you," she said softly.

"Even though you're a captain now?"

"Yes, I'm a captain. It was a goal I set for myself, something I had to prove I could do."

"I'd say you'd proved yourself beyond any shadow of a doubt. Otherwise I wouldn't be alive and here making love with you."

She kissed him lingeringly. "In proving I could captain a boat, I learned something else—I learned that loving you is more important than anything else in the world. I learned I can live without continuing to be a captain but I can't live without you."

He crushed her to him, whispering in her ear. "You're welcome aboard my boat any time, Captain Pendleton, in any capacity. But as my wife, I do hope you'll take some time out ashore to raise our children."

She pulled away to look at him. "What's wrong with raising them on the boat?"

He rolled his eyes. "Life with you will never be dull. My life, my love, one way or another, we'll always be together—but let's leave the details until later."

She clung to him, wanting never to leave his arms. "Much, much later," she murmured.

After a reprise of their lovemaking, more leisurely this time, as befitted the sultry Jamaican air, Garth rolled to the edge of the bed, where he reached down to fumble with his discarded clothes, finally saying, "Ah!"

Coming back to her, he slipped something into her hand.

She stared in surprise at what he'd given her, recognizing it instantly—Captain Parker's tiny bottle

447

...e exquisite miniature ship inside.

...fore Captain Parker died he left a note saying he ...ted us to have it," Garth said. "Since neither of us was on the island when he did die, the bottle came to my mother. She gave it to me last year after finally becoming reconciled to my being a lakesman. I wanted you to have the bottle, but the time never seemed right."

She cradled the fragile gift in her hand. "He meant this to be ours, not yours or mine. And now it *will* be ours." She gazed at the ship inside the bottle and smiled. "I'd forgotten its name—the *Compromise*. Most appropriate. Do you think he realized the problems we'd have to overcome before we understood what we wanted?"

"If a lake captain lives long enough, I should think he'd come to know just about everything there was. Don't you agree?"

She smiled at him. "Considering how much I've learned already, yes, I'm sure she would."